THE
LAST GREAT
AUSTRALIAN
ADVENTURER

THE
LAST GREAT
AUSTRALIAN
ADVENTURER

GORDON BASS

EBURY
PRESS

An Ebury Press book
Published by Penguin Random House Australia Pty Ltd
Level 3, 100 Pacific Highway, North Sydney NSW 2060
www.penguin.com.au

Penguin
Random House
Australia

First published by Ebury Press in 2017

Addresses for the Penguin Random House group of companies can be found at global.penguinrandomhouse.com/offices.

National Library of Australia
Cataloguing-in-Publication entry (pbk)

Bass, Gordon, author
The last great Australian adventurer: Ben Carlin's epic journey around the world by amphibious jeep/Gordon Bass

ISBN 978 1 92532 4 990 (paperback)

Carlin, Ben – Travel
Half-Safe (Amphibious jeep)
Automobile travel
Ocean travel
Seafaring life
Voyages around the world
Adventure and adventurers – Australia
Atlantic Ocean – Navigation

Cover design by Adam Yazxhi/Maxco
Front cover photograph courtesy Deirdre Carlin
Back cover photograph courtesy Guildford Grammar School
Maps by Alicia Freile/Tango Media
Internal design and typesetting in Adobe Garamond Pro by Midland Typesetters, Australia
Printed in Australia by Griffin Press, an accredited ISO AS/NZS 14001:2004 Environmental Management System printer

Penguin Random House Australia uses papers that are natural, renewable and recyclable products and made from wood grown in sustainable forests. The logging and manufacturing processes are expected to conform to the environmental regulations of the country of origin.

Contents

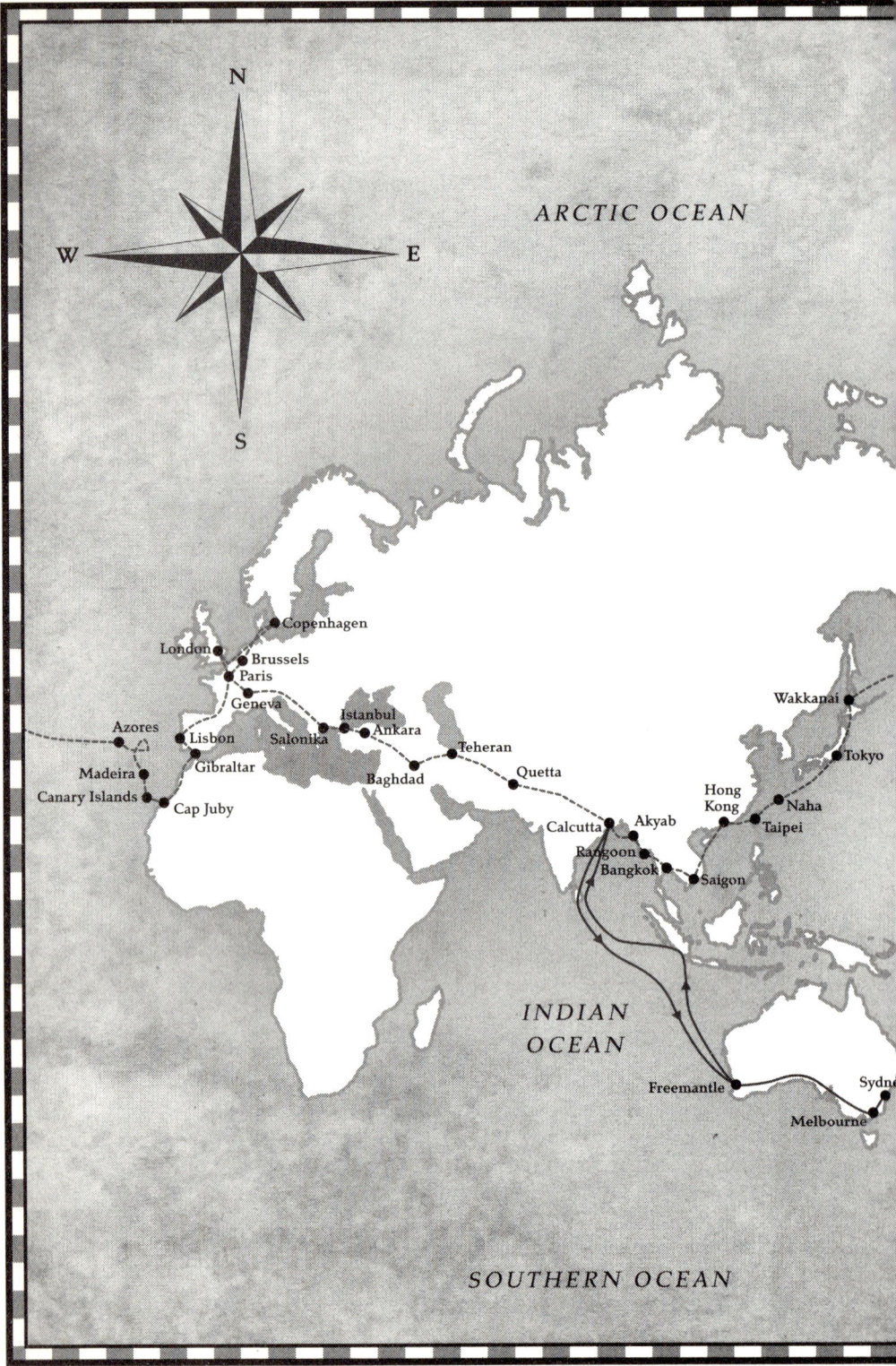

PACIFIC OCEAN

ATLANTIC OCEAN

Shemya

Anchorage

Vancouver

San Francisco

Reno

Los Angeles

Dearborn

Montreal

New York

Halifax

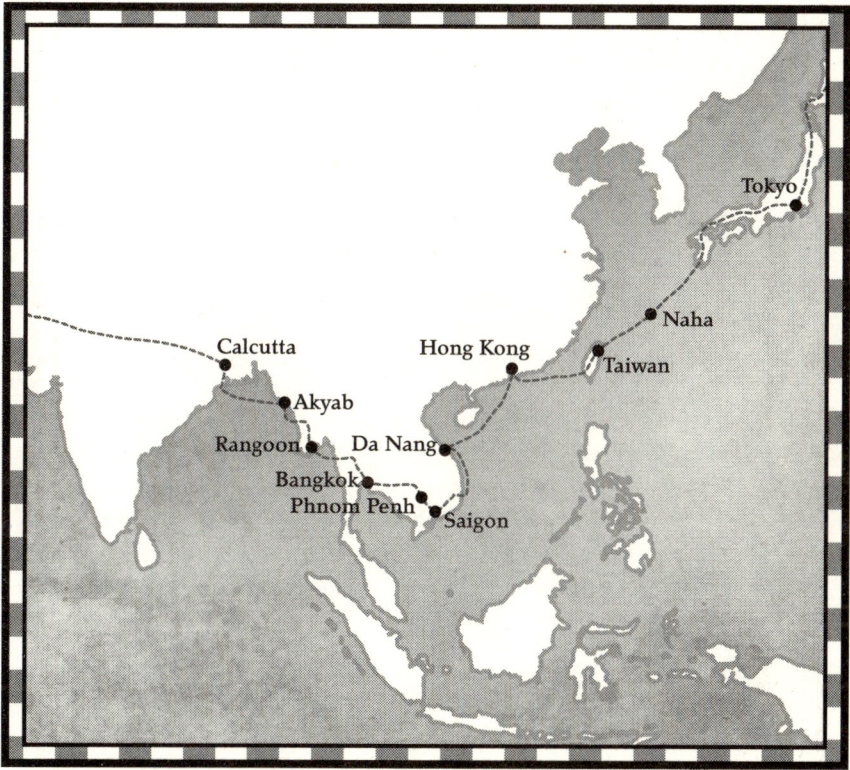

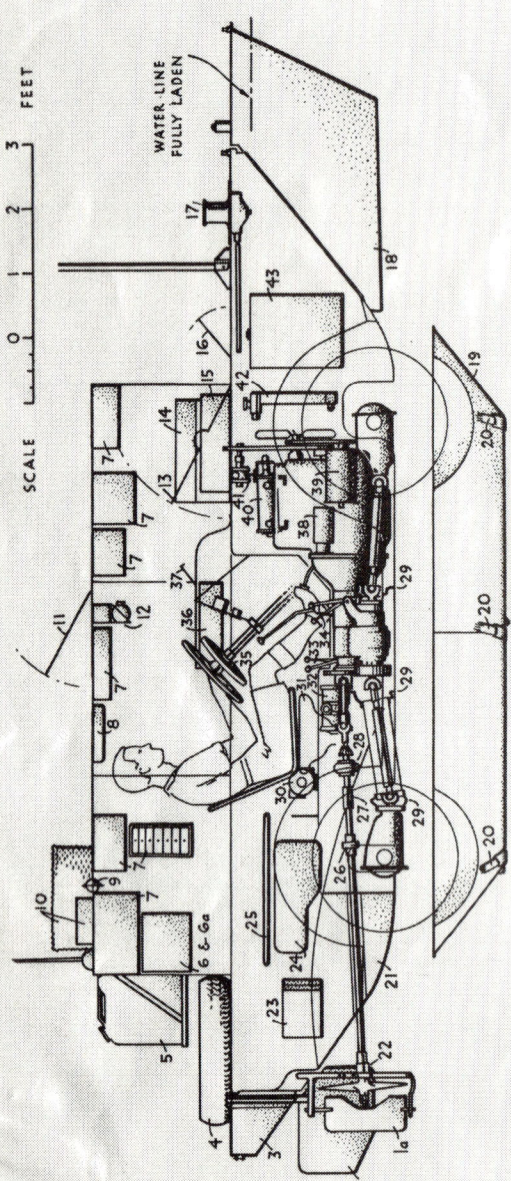

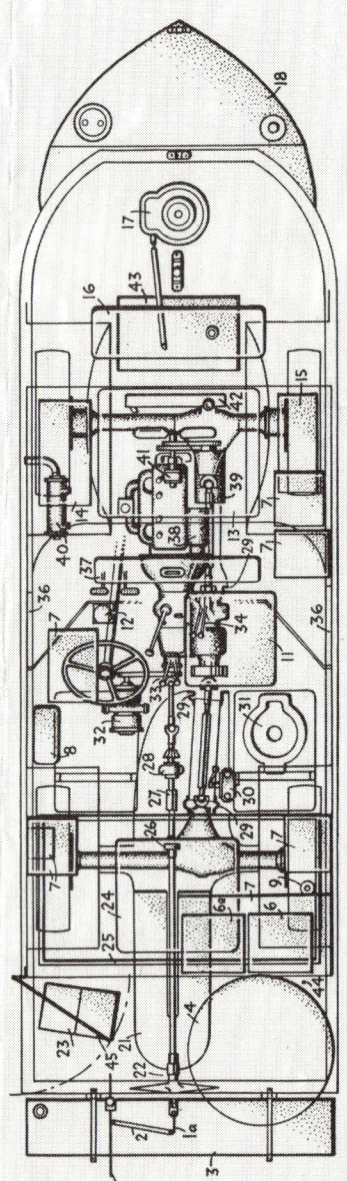

SCALE

WATER LINE
FULLY LADEN

FEET

Half-Safe in original 1947 configuration

1. Primary and 1a auxiliary rudders
2. Rudder link rod
3. Fresh water tank
4. Spare tyre
5. Rack of five jerry cans
6. Radio transmitter and 6a receiver
7. Shelves for stores and equipment
8. Kleenex dispenser
9. Antenna-lead insulator
10. Rubber raft and flares
11. Upper hatch
12. Compass
13. Engine hatch
14. Spares
15. Tool box
16. Radiator air intake (closed at sea)
17. Capstan winch
18. Nose tank (fuel)
19. Belly tank (fuel)
20. Nylon straps
21. Lubricating oil tank
22. Cutless bearing
23. Two 6-volt batteries in series
24. Main fuel tank
25. Bunk frame
26. Propeller shaft joint
27. Propeller shaft gland
28. Propeller shaft thrust bearing
29. Transmission seal
30. Manual bilge pump
31. Toilet
32. Engine driven bilge pump
33. Propeller and bilge pump clutch levers
34. High-low ratio & 2 – four-wheel drive levers
35. Rudder steering wheel
36. Radiator air vents (closed at sea)
37. Hatch
38. Starter
39. Generator
40. Heat exchanger
41. Rain-water pump
42. Radiator

And if a god will wreck me yet again on the wine-dark sea
I can bear that too, with a spirit tempered to endure.
Much have I suffered, labored long and hard by now
in the waves and war . . .

– Homer, The Odyssey

Prologue

26 June 1957. A small Japanese fishing trawler from the port of Hakodate rolls over dark swells on the North Pacific, treading Russian waters to the south-east of the Kamchatka Peninsula. A cold wind slices in from the north-east, whipping salt spray across the deck. Under the slate predawn sky, oilskin-clad fishermen winch a driftnet up from the sea, its nylon web taut with the weight of salmon.

A bright flash of yellow a hundred yards away catches the eye of a leathered fisherman. He turns to squint into the distance. He sees it again. It's an improbable speck riding low in the water, a tiny boat of some sort, no bigger than a car, looking almost like a drifting shipping crate. A stumpy mast juts from its boxy cabin, flying a traditional Japanese carp flag that's torn and blackened by exhaust.

As the vessel crests each wave, the fisherman sees something even stranger: it has wheels.

Now a hatch flips open on the boat's roof and, as the fisherman watches, a man pulls himself out. He appears solid and powerful. He has a full grey beard and a large knife clenched in his teeth.

He is naked.

It's as if Ernest Hemingway himself has materialised in the vastness of the North Pacific, barrel-chested and strong, a strange sight indeed.

The fisherman motions for the rest of the crew to join him. Together they watch as across the waves the bearded man stands on top of his small boat in the sharp wind, pauses and dives into the 4-degree Celsius water.

The two vessels drift closer, until they are just 50 yards apart. Now the crew sees the madman break the surface to fill his lungs. In the icy water his body is the colour of pale marble; in survival mode, it has shunted its warm blood inward to vital organs.

The fishermen see a second man, thinner and much younger, a wool cap pulled low against the cold, emerge from the hatch of the odd vessel. He doesn't try to help the bearded man, but instead aims a camera at him and starts taking pictures, as if it's all he can do.

The bearded man clings to the side of the strange yellow boat for a moment, gasping for breath. Then he inhales deeply and plunges back below the surface.

On the trawler, Captain Amiya Daiichi joins his crew, watching in vain for the man to reappear. He knows now what has happened: the strange boat has snared itself on the submerged skein of his trawler's huge driftnet, which is suspended from a series of floats and stretches for more than a mile across the Pacific. And instead of asking for help, the boat's pilot is in the water, trying to hack through the netting to free his odd vessel.

It's madness. Suicidal.

Two minutes pass, then five. Captain Daiichi knows from experience that the man's core body temperature is plummetting. Once it reaches 32 degrees he will lapse into semi-consciousness, and at 26 degrees he will experience cardiac arrest and respiratory failure. Without protective gear, death will come in minutes. Perhaps he's already dead.

The boat bobs alone in the ocean.

And then –

Sliding over the trawler's gunwale, tangled up in netting with tons of salmon, the bearded man reappears. He's been caught in the trawler's driftnet, hauled up with the teeming catch, and now he collapses onto the gore-slick deck and gasps for air. Stunned, the fishermen pull him free of the net and hustle him into their smoky galley, where they prop him in front of a coal-burning stove, wrap him in a fur coat and force hot sake down his throat to speed his sluggish heartbeat.

As his body warms up, the man turns lucid, then belligerent. In fragments of Japanese he asks for a knife to cut their lines from his propeller. He insists on returning to his vessel. He tears off the coat and storms out of the galley into the cold grey morning, pausing at the gunwale before diving back into the ocean.

He tells the fishermen that he is driving around the world.

Back in the driver's seat of his small yellow vessel, the bearded man pressed a starter button with his foot, glanced at the compass and pushed in the throttle.

His copilot knew better than to say anything.

Ben Carlin, 44 years old, son of Western Australia, veteran of the goldfields, former major in the Indian Army, was two weeks out of northern Japan, rumbling across the North Pacific towards Alaska on his way to Montreal, where he'd begun his journey in 1950. He was seven years into one of the great adventures of the twentieth century. Nine if you counted the two years of false starts.

He was circling the world in a surplus World War II Ford GPA amphibious army jeep called *Half-Safe*.

It was an audacious, death-defying adventure, unlike anything attempted before. And it had once brought the rugged Australian adventurer a measure of fame and notoriety. In the early 1950s he had appeared on radio and TV after an astonishing, near-fatal Atlantic crossing. He had mingled with royalty and celebrities. He had written a highly anticipated book about the gruelling first stage of the journey. He had been praised by *Life* magazine, profiled by the BBC, splashed across the front pages of newspapers in Australia and around the world.

But then things had taken a puzzling turn. Before he was even halfway around the world friends and lovers began abandoning him, the media turned their attention elsewhere, his book failed to sell, and his fame began to ebb. By 1957 the journey was mostly regarded as a pointless stunt, to the extent that anyone thought about it at all. And by the time I found an inscribed copy of Ben's book on my parents' bookshelf, twenty-five years after his death, he was little more than an occasional, obscure footnote in the annals of adventuring.

Prologue

I was fascinated. Why had Ben Carlin's circumnavigation taken so long, and what made him press on year after year, long after the world lost interest? What had he done next? Why had he been forgotten? Who *was* he? The answers, I would eventually find, were evasive and complex. They had to be teased out of the arc of his life.

There was one early clue.

Norman Lindsay, the great Australian writer and artist, spent the better part of his career obsessed with issues of spirit and adventure. He followed Ben's voyage through the years with keen interest, and he saw an extraordinary quality in the man and his quest.

In 1956, Lindsay wrote to Ben from his home in the Blue Mountains to voice admiration and to explain why he believed the amphibious journey had a profound meaning.

As far as collective action goes, Australians have done that splendidly in two world wars, but unless the individual can express the spirit that drives the mass, its moral value is more or less lost. I'm really not making any sort of overstatement when I say that I prize your *Half-Safe* voyage as I prize a fine poem or a picture produced by an Australian. Blood and spirit are inseparable, and I've damned my own destiny sufficiently for anchoring me by the backside in a studio all my life to define as best I can what spirit means to me, while those who have its blood also can go recklessly around the Earth's crust and do all sorts of admirable things and, if they have the wit, make a book out of them, so that poor devils incarcerated in shadows can share them secondhand.

Lindsay understood Ben. He believed he was pursuing some-thing that would elevate him to the pantheon of Australian adventurers like Charles Kingsford Smith and Douglas Mawson, men who could be seen as the last of their generation, the last to press into the unknown with simple machines and minimal safety nets, men who ventured forth without satellite navigation and corporate sponsorships and civilisation just a phone call away.

He saw in Ben Carlin the embodiment of blood and spirit, the manifestation of drive and half-understood obsession. He saw free will.

Lindsay knew that most of us live with dreams unfulfilled and desires out of reach. We remain poor devils in shadows.

But Ben Carlin refused to live in the shadows. Even now, nothing would stop him.

He gripped the tiller of his battered amphibious jeep and steered eastward across the icy, rolling expanse of the North Pacific.

CHAPTER ONE

Beginning

As usual, he was hung over.

It was still early but already the heat shimmered off the concrete and tarmac of Kalaikunda Airfield in West Bengal, in the middle of a flat desolation 80 miles east of Calcutta. Major Frederick Benjamin Carlin of the Royal Indian Engineers had arrived to inspect the airfield's runways and installations, to make a field report he knew no one would read, and to move on, preferably to end the day somewhere cool with a glass of gin in his hand.

The major stood almost 6 feet tall and had a solid build, forged from hard work, coiled with power, suited to violence. With his thick sandy hair and square jaw, people said he looked like a Hollywood star, despite the deep scar on his left cheek and the cruel scowl that so often shadowed his face. He spoke with an Australian accent that betrayed an incongruous upper-class education, and he carried himself with an arrogant confidence.

And this was the last place he wanted to be.

During the final months of World War II, Kalaikunda had thrummed with action as the launching point for American B-29 Superfortress bombing runs against Japanese positions throughout South-East Asia. But now, in March 1946, the fighting was over and Kalaikunda was quiet. The Americans were gone but for a shadow regiment of their dead – hundreds of soldiers buried in rows of temporary graves near a runway, awaiting eventual exhumation and a final return home.

The Americans had left something else behind: thousands of surplus military vehicles parked in drab-green lines, baking in the heat, abandoned to the Indian government.

Major Carlin had no official business with the vehicles, but he was bored. As he drove past he gave them an idle glance. He noticed that one was completely unlike the others. It was, in fact, unlike anything he'd ever seen.

He stopped his jeep and stepped out onto the hot asphalt for a closer look.

The inside of the vehicle's open cockpit looked surprisingly like that of his own army jeep: two seats in front, a bench seat in back, a windscreen that could fold down, all the usual features. And it rode on four knobby tyres. But the otherwise jeep-like vehicle was wrapped in what appeared to be a simple boat hull, and there was a propeller in back. He crouched down for a closer look and saw how its propeller shaft and axles passed through the hull, how its flat bow gave it the profile of a small barge, how in theory it would be equally capable on land and water.

And in that moment the seed of a strange idea emerged from nowhere.

Beginning

Major Carlin turned to his counterpart on the inspection assignment, Group Captain Malcolm 'Mac' Bunting, RAF airfield specialist. 'You know,' he said, 'with a little titivation you could go around the world in one of these things.'

Bunting had served on submarines and flown bombers and knew a few things about military vehicles. 'Impossible,' he spat out dismissively.

But Major Carlin wasn't listening.

His adult life had unfolded as a series of disappointments; things had started to go wrong shortly after his graduation from a prestigious Perth boarding school. He'd lasted just one year at the University of Western Australia, fallen into years of hard labour, run into the law a little too often, and in 1939 quietly fled the country. The outbreak of World War II had promised heroic redemption, and he enlisted in the Indian Army, in which most of the officers were British. But he'd been relegated to an undistinguished support role as a field engineer. He'd spent six years far from combat, digging latrines and pouring concrete for runways from India to Iraq.

His nerves were shot, his health was bad, and his head throbbed from too much cheap gin. A turbulent affair with an American Red Cross secretary was falling apart. He was 33 years old and had nothing to lose. 'I had no idea of going anywhere except perhaps home to Australia to die,' he'd later say.

And so he let the obsession take hold.

'You know, Mac, it *could* be done,' he said, a bit more emphatically. And he didn't just say it; he felt it, he believed it. In that moment Ben Carlin knew he was going to do something extraordinary. And he was going to do it on his own terms.

He was going to drive an amphibious jeep around the world.

As he explained a decade later,

> The more I thought about the idea the more I liked it. Quite
> reasonably possible, it would be difficult enough to be interest-
> ing: a nice exercise in technology, masochism and chance – a
> form of sport – and it might even earn me a few bob. The trip
> would take only 12 months, I thought, a last flutter before the
> inevitable relapse into domesticity.

The Indian Army released Major Carlin from duty on 16 August
1946. Instead of returning home to Western Australia, he opted
for passage to the United States, which seemed like the likeliest
place to find his own amphibious jeep. A week later he boarded
the US transport ship *General W. H. Gordon*, bound from
Bombay for San Francisco. The ship sailed under the soaring
4,200-foot span of the Golden Gate Bridge on 18 September,
and the hunt was on.

Ben Carlin headed east. In Toledo, Ohio, he announced
his intentions to the public relations team at Willys-Overland
Motors, an automotive manufacturer that had built more than
350,000 military jeeps during the war. He pointed out his
intended route on a map, explained how he'd sail from New
York across the Atlantic to North Africa, drive up to the Strait
of Gibraltar and turn right in Europe, then head towards the
Middle East and down into South-East Asia. Then he'd sail up
to Japan, cross the Pacific to Alaska and return to New York.
It would take a year, he said, and he promised their generous
sponsorship and financial support would result in extraordinary
publicity for the company's postwar consumer version of the
army jeep.

At which point Willys told the Australian major, who was getting a bit agitated at their cool reception, that while they had indeed produced hundreds of thousands of army jeeps during the war, they hadn't actually built the rare *amphibious* jeep Ben had seen in India. That was a product of *Ford* Motor Company. Maybe he should try them instead?

Ben retreated to a public library and wrote to Ford, but they weren't interested in his proposal. Then he wrote to every other American automobile manufacturer, even those that had nothing to do with jeeps.

Most never responded.

He bought a used Plymouth, wandered across the States and Canada for a few months, looked up old wartime drinking buddies and felt briefly sorry for himself. Eventually he drove through the first winter blizzard of 1946 to Washington, DC, where he'd heard the War Assets Administration was disposing of surplus equipment.

He spent days poring over catalogues until his eyes ached, scanning pages of fine print and lists of everything the military had ever needed or owned, from propeller manufacturing plants to sewer pipes to linseed oil. He almost missed the critical listing: *Truck, amphibian, ¼-ton, 4x4, standard commodity classification 90 1001.* The US government was auctioning off two Ford GPA amphibious jeeps at the Aberdeen Proving Ground, a sprawling army facility between Washington and Philadelphia.

On 29 January 1947, Ben bid $901 for one rusting, well-used 1942 GPA, drove it off a frozen lot and turned left on Route 40 towards Annapolis, Maryland, a small city on the shore of Chesapeake Bay. Within minutes flakes of rust shook loose inside the petrol tank and clogged the fuel line, and the jeep stuttered to a stop. Ben detached the fuel line, took a breath and blew it clear. At dusk he discovered the headlights were missing, and the next day the bottom of the rusted fuel tank disintegrated completely. He rolled to the side of the road, set a half-gallon can on the dashboard, ran a fuel line to the carburettor, filled the can with petrol every few miles and let gravity do the rest.

He tried not to think about what else might be wrong.

Sleet was falling when Ben arrived at the Annapolis Yacht Yard, which had agreed to give Ben a small corner to work on the jeep, free of charge. The yard's chief welder, Paul Shaw, was a tough, hardworking, third-generation metalworker and offered to help with the jeep; he also had a spare bedroom for rent, 35 dollars a month, meals not included. So on 3 February 1947, Ben moved into Shaw's house on Giddings Avenue, in the kind of middle-class American neighbourhood where a yacht-yard welder could still live on the same tree-lined street as a professor from the neighbouring United States Naval Academy. They were a few blocks from Weems Creek, which flowed into the Severn River, which flowed into the Chesapeake Bay, which opened into the Atlantic Ocean that Ben said he was going to cross.

The idea was moving towards reality.

The way Ben saw it, the GPA, basically a World War II army jeep in a boat hull, needed two essential modifications. The first was a cabin over the open cockpit. It had to be strong enough and watertight enough to withstand the force of the open ocean, even complete submersion in the storms he'd encounter. The second was a drastically increased fuel capacity. According to the War Department, the jeep's 15-gallon fuel tank, under the rear seat, was good for just 37 miles on water at a cruising speed of 4.5 miles per hour in third gear. Ben did the maths – he needed more than *500* gallons of petrol to cross the Atlantic, even with a stop to refuel in the Azores, the Portuguese archipelago halfway across the ocean.

How do you fit 500 gallons of petrol in a jeep?

He poked around and found a pocket of empty space in front of the radiator, enough for a 25-gallon auxiliary petrol tank. Hardly enough. Then inspiration hit: why not carry additional fuel *outside* the existing jeep body? Ben sketched out the idea for a sort of false bow that concealed a 100-gallon tank. Paul Shaw fabricated it from beefy 14-gauge steel, and they bolted it to the flat front of the jeep.

That wasn't enough. Ben designed a rectangular 322-gallon belly tank – 10.5 feet long, 5 feet wide and 14 inches deep – that he could lash to the jeep's flat bottom at sea; when travelling overland he'd carry it on the roof. He ran plastic hoses from the three new tanks to a series of valves in the cockpit where he could switch fuel sources on the go, the way a pilot does in a small aircraft. It was almost enough; he could strap some jerry cans on the back of the jeep to bring the total to 500 gallons.

Next came the cabin. He constructed a rectangular steel frame, 10 feet long, 5 feet wide and 28 inches high, bolted it onto the jeep and boxed it in with panels of quarter-inch masonite, adding some clear perspex panels to the sides to let in light. He installed three panes of quarter-inch safety glass for the windshield.

Inside the jeep he turned the rear bench seat into a bunk, installed a chamber pot under the passenger seat, screwed a toilet paper dispenser onto the dash and created a warren of storage spaces and shelves inside the claustrophobic cabin.

The jeep's welded seams troubled Ben. He'd spent enough time working in the jeep to sense its fragility, and he knew it had been quickly designed and manufactured during the war. So as a safeguard he coated its hull in neoprene – basically, raw wetsuit material – brushing on layer after layer like thick paint, hoping the skin of synthetic rubber would keep the jeep watertight, even if its hull began to fail somewhere in the great expanse of ocean.

He laboured ten to 12 hours a day through the spring and summer, always a Lucky Strike hanging from his lip, often falling asleep in the jeep after working late into the night unless there was a poker game going back at Shaw's house, and by late summer most of the structural work was done. Ben drove the half-finished jeep across town and pulled into the dirt driveway at Paul Shaw's house to make final preparations under the shade of an oak tree.

Around then, a 14-year-old boy named George Bass, who lived around the corner at 11 Ridgely Avenue, stopped by to visit his friend Ron Shaw. George was a skinny kid who played violin and buried himself in the pages of superhero comic books and pulp novels about adventurers. And he couldn't believe that right around the corner a *real* adventurer was working on a crazy contraption that he was going to drive and sail around the world.

Meeting Ben Carlin helped shape my father's life.

'Ben could have been a movie idol,' he recalled nearly

70 years later. 'He was a true adventurer with a perfect scar on his handsome face, and a shock of blond hair that fell across his brow.' We sat in the air-conditioned coolness of his home office in College Station, Texas, in the ranch-style house my parents moved into a few years after I left for college. The four walls of floor-to-ceiling bookshelves that had once sagged with the weight of his archaeological career were now half empty. He was 82 years old and in the midst of distributing his books, letters and journals to libraries and archives, winding down more than a half-century of work that had taken him around the world, discovering and excavating the world's oldest shipwrecks, pioneering the science of nautical archaeology, rewriting history.

'I used to stop by on my way home from school and hold nuts with pliers while he screwed on more pieces of his canopy,' my dad told me. And as they worked, he peppered Ben with questions about his jeep and his proposed venture. 'I asked him if he was afraid of hurricanes. He pointed out the jeep would do better than a large ship, and he drew me a little diagram of how it would just float up and down over the largest waves, like a cork. And I asked what would happen if he had appendicitis in the middle of the Atlantic. He said with annoyance that no one would ever do anything if they just worried about everything.'

My dad paused.

'When I was only 14, I had no idea of the true enormity of what Ben planned to do. Now I've crossed the Atlantic by passenger ship 27 times and sailed through two hurricanes. I know how awesome it can be in a storm. I can't possibly imagine setting out across the Atlantic Ocean in that jeep.'

Ben had messed around in boats in the Swan River during his youth, nothing more. He bought a copy of *Marine Navigation*, a dense textbook by Philip Van Horn Weems and Clarence V. Lee, and late at night when he was done working on the jeep he read about how to steer by the sun and stars, and how to pinpoint his location using just a sextant, wristwatch and nautical almanac. Most sailors come by their knowledge of navigation gradually, through a combination of study and practice. They hone their skills over years. Ben spent a week poring over relevant chapters, later recalling, 'After about ten hours on this book there was just nothing more to learn.'

'He spent a lot of time in our basement memorising tide tables and studying the Weems navigation system, codes, marine engineering, just about everything else he felt he needed to know,' remembered Paul Shaw's son, Ron, who was 16 years old when Ben moved into his family's house in 1947. 'I often wondered how he could retain as much as he did, considering he consumed booze at an immoderate rate. He rarely bought the stuff himself. I remember my mother wondering where my dad's spending money went.

'Ben didn't like to be challenged. He and my dad did a lot of drinking together, and they were very close friends, but they'd fight when they drank.

'In Dad's younger days he would easily have taken Ben down. But Ben was no slouch. He was tough, strong-willed and determined. He didn't shave frequently and he didn't have a lot of formal polish, but he was so self-confident that he radiated a certain amount of sophistication. He had green eyes and a shock of sandy red hair. He had a fairly deep slash on the left side of his face. Maybe it was a wartime injury. We never asked him about it, and he never spoke about it.'

Beginning

The original amphibious jeep had been 15 feet long. Now with its new bow it measured an ungainly 18 feet 3 inches, and a boxy structure, painted sandy beige, turned its open cockpit into an enclosed cabin. In early August it was time for the moment of truth.

'Ben asked me if I wanted to go with him for one of the first sea trials a few blocks away on Weems Creek,' Dad said. My grandfather said no.

Ben drove from the Shaws' driveway down Wardour Street, through a patch of scrub and down to the riverbank, where neighbourhood kids used to swim and catch soft-shell crabs. He stopped on the Wardour Beach, less a beach than a mud bank near a plank pier where a cluster of weekend rowboats was tied up. Half a dozen friends passed around a bottle of champagne and smiled with the excitement and absurdity of it, and Ben, wearing tight swim trunks and a sweatshirt that showed his powerful build, beamed proudly for his gathered court.

Among them was Elinore Arone, a 30-year-old American Red Cross worker Ben had met in India in September 1945. They'd immediately fallen into a stormy relationship that had ended abruptly six months later when Elinore took a job in China. But they'd written to each other while apart, and now Elinore was back in the States, bouncing between friends and relatives, trying to figure out what was next for her. She knew Ben was in Annapolis, but she didn't know why.

So she called him at two o'clock one morning, alone and needing to hear his voice. He told her about a jeep he'd been working on, and about his plan to circle the world, and the idea gripped Elinore just as completely and immediately as it had Ben. She insisted on coming to Annapolis for the jeep's maiden voyage.

Ben helped her into the passenger seat, and Ron and a friend climbed aboard. 'As we approached the water,' Ron recalled, 'a fat lady in a tight bathing suit yelled, "What is that thing?" Ben shouted back proudly, "Madam, it flies!"'

The jeep inched down the muddy bank into the flat water of Weems Creek, near its entrance into the Severn River, where today multimillion-dollar houses crowd the shore and block public access.

There's a series of black-and-white photos from that day. In the first one the jeep is parked at the water's edge with two boys clambering on the back, and in another it's in the water, tipping at an odd angle. You can just make out Elinore's profile in the passenger seat. In the last photo the shadows are longer and the jeep is maybe a hundred yards from shore, floating noticeably lower at the stern. Three of Ben's friends are standing at the end of the plank pier, but two of them are looking back at the photographer instead of the jeep, as if asking, *Hey, are you getting this?*

It was an omen of things to come. A few days later Ben took the jeep farther out for another test run, with Ron and his friend once again on board. This time water gushed in past the propeller shaft seal just as the engine, which powered the bilge pump, died. And the standard-issue hand pump, intended for emergencies just like this, was missing.

Ben scooped furiously with an old tobacco can and screamed for his young crew to help. 'Bail, you bastards!' he shouted. 'Bail!'

The boys scooped desperately with their shoes as the jeep settled in shallow water, then they waded ashore and went home. Ben slept on top of the jeep's boxy cabin, mosquitoes biting him through the night.

'My dad encouraged us to have fun with Ben,' said Ron, 'until he called us bastards.'

Though she'd now seen the jeep's shortcomings, Elinore wasn't deterred. While in Annapolis she made up her mind that she was going around the world with Ben. She had no job or home or attachments, and she'd always sought adventure and experience. In those ways she and Ben were incredibly alike. But Ben shook his head. This round-the-world adventuring business, he explained, was strictly for a man.

Then he repaired the seals, dried out the jeep and, as a concession to safety, had a two-way radio installed on a shelf above the bunk, a big No. 19 Mark II made for a Sherman tank. He didn't know how to use it, so my grandfather, Robert Bass, an English professor at the Naval Academy and a ham radio operator who ran station WCQG from a glassed-in porch at the back of the house, offered to show him.

'Ben couldn't reach my father's radio with his own from only a block away,' remembered my dad. 'That didn't bode well for a distress call from the middle of the Atlantic.'

On 28 October 1947, caught up in the excitement, my grandfather wrote to his mother to tell her *about the Australian who has been up at the Shaws' readying a duck, an amphibious jeep, for a round the world cruise and who is supposed to set out for the Azores alone this week.*

Ben didn't leave that week, or the next. But by mid-October his beer-and-rent money was almost gone, and his visa was about to expire. He decided to sail for New York, try to get some attention, and hurl himself into the winter Atlantic to begin his journey.

The idea was to sail up to the head of Chesapeake Bay, cross over into the Delaware River by way of the heavily trafficked

14-mile-long Chesapeake & Delaware Canal, sail down the Delaware River into the Atlantic, and then hug the coast northward to New York City. It would be a 275-mile test cruise.

The first day a cold snap rimed the windshield with opaque frost, and Ben found himself chugging in blind circles in a rising gale. He made the canal two days later only to be stopped dead for two more days by worse conditions in the Delaware River, where he rammed the jeep into a breakwater, ripped a gash in the new bow, and then drove deep into the oozing mud of the isolated tidal flats along the lower river's western shore. He clambered out of the muck, losing his prized Rolex in the process, and trudged to the tiny fishing town of Leipsic, Delaware, a literal backwater of barely 100 people, where the owner of a schooner with a half-ton derrick said he could haul the jeep out of the muck but for six days kept finding other things to do. In the meantime Ben lived on oysters and clams – all they served in the town's only eating house – and heard endless talk of how locals had been finding muskrats in the flats dead of either disease or pollution, no one knew which. He grew increasingly desperate to move on until finally he spurred the schooner owner into action by promising all but a few gallons of the jeep's petrol as payment.

Back in Annapolis, Paul Shaw welded a plate over the gash and loaned Ben $50, and Ben pointed the jeep straight back to Times Square in New York, this time by land.

He arrived in mid-December and checked into a cheap room at the fleabag Grand Union Hotel on East 32nd Street in Manhattan, in the shadow of the Empire State Building. Twelve dollars a week. He forced himself onto an ascetic 40-cents-a-day diet of raisins, whole-wheat crackers, baked beans and canned spaghetti. The can-opener cost an extravagant 20 cents. He ate with his toothbrush to avoid buying a fork.

The day after Christmas a record two feet of snow brought the city to a standstill. When the city thawed, Ben spent a few precious dollars to fill up with fuel and take a trial run around the tip of Manhattan. He drove down a wooden seaplane-base ramp at the foot of 23rd Street, splashed into the frigid East River, dodged icefloes against the backdrop of the skyline and puttered past towering ocean liners as skeptical seamen and dockworkers looked on.

It created a small buzz, so Ben pitched his story to the New York bureau of the Australian Associated Press, which distributed foreign news to media outlets in Australia. The first reports of his intended venture appeared in Perth's *Sunday Times* on 11 January 1948:

Round World by Amphibious Jeep
New York, Sat: Thirty-five-year-old Australian is to embark from New York on an unique round world trip in a Ford amphibian jeep. He is Major Frederick Benjamin Carlin who served with the Royal Indian Engineers in India, Irak, Persia, Palestine, Syria and Italy. He hopes to complete his trip in 5 months.

But Ben couldn't afford to refuel the jeep. He spent the rest of the winter huddled in his room, occasionally walking 20 blocks to Central Park to toss breadcrumbs to pigeons.

Elinore was now in Florida, where she'd found a job in the West Palm Beach office of Dr Joseph Eller, a polo-playing New York dermatologist who'd once treated a young John F.

Kennedy for acne. It was a good job but Elinore was restless, still thinking about the jeep. She wrote to Ben and said again she was coming with him.

'Strictly a man's venture,' he replied in a fountain pen that kept running dry.

Besides, he'd always planned to go alone. 'I like travelling on my own,' he'd told the *Adelaide News* in January, and if there was one thing Ben didn't do it was back down from a position.

But in truth he'd begun to realise the madness of travelling by himself. Already there had been a few potential volunteer copilots, men who'd heard about Ben and his plan and knew the sea and engines and navigation. But they had all changed their minds once they saw the jeep.

So now, despite his tenuous relationship with Elinore, Ben felt a slight uneasiness at the idea of her jaunting between New York and West Palm Beach with a celebrity doctor while he was sneaking past the Grand Union reception desk to avoid making excuses for overdue rent. And so in February 1948 Ben relented and told her that she could join him on the journey.

Years later, the press would often assume that Elinore had been a reluctant copilot. But during one interview, Elinore stressed that from the beginning she'd wanted to go around the world just as badly as Ben. 'I had to do the persuading,' she said, and left it at that.

Elinore's first assignment was to sweep up as many drugs as she could while she still had access to Dr Eller's West Palm Beach office. *Any sulfur drugs you can snaffle will be useful,* directed Ben. *Sulfanilamide, sulfathiozol, sulfapyridine. Also Benzedrine compounds.* The first three drugs Ben requested were early antibiotics; the fourth was the amphetamine favoured by Beat writers from Jack Kerouac to William Burroughs.

Elinore quit her job in the spring, flew to New York and joined Ben in his tiny hotel room. Together they tried to figure out how to draw attention to the proposed circumnavigation. Ben had once sat in the audience during a broadcast of *Arthur Godfrey's Talent Scouts*, a hugely popular radio show where hopeful entertainers competed for the loudest applause. 'Disgusting,' he'd said, never admitting he might want a taste of fame. But he knew media attention was essential to success.

He studied the examples of adventurers who'd recently been in the news. George W. Truman and Clifford Vassar Evans had just circled the world in a pair of single-engine Piper Super Cruisers. Ben didn't know if they'd made much money, but they were still making public appearances two months after their landing. And, he told Elinore, *Aeroplanes fly around the world almost every day. To the public today a plane flying around the world is in no way extraordinary.* And Thor Heyerdahl had just sailed from Peru to French Polynesia on a reed raft, resulting in sensational publicity and a soon-to-be-published book. *That* was the kind of venture Ben was thinking about. Something exceptional. Something dangerous. Something no one else had even thought of.

Like circling the world in an amphibious jeep.

But he still wasn't sure how he could profit from the adventure. He thought he'd make some money by exhibiting the jeep at stops along the way, but he knew that wouldn't pay his way around the world. He approached ad agencies and suggested sponsorships, and failed to get anywhere.

At the urging of Elinore's brother Domenic, a World War II fighter pilot who was launching a career in publishing, Ben hired publicist Ware Lynch, general manager of a New York PR agency that specialised mainly in entertainment. Lynch happened to represent Save A Friend in Europe (SAFE), a start-up organisation created to help Europeans struggling after the end of World War II by sending shipments of packaged food. So with a bit of creative licence, Ben became an 'inspector general' for SAFE, and the trip had a fresh PR hook: Ben and Elinore would put SAFE's food packages to the test, surviving on them during their Atlantic crossing.

Soon after that Ben received an overdue $1,800, part of his final pay from the Indian Army. Now there was nothing holding them back.

Except public perception.

'Are you married?' asked Lynch. 'Otherwise I can't deal with you.'

A decade earlier aviator Amelia Earhart had set off to fly around the world with navigator Fred Noonan, but Earhart and Noonan were both married, and Earhart's husband had helped select Noonan for the flight. It was all business. But Ben and Elinore had a curious relationship somewhere between friend-ship and romance and partnership. They were planning to set off on an adventure together in very confined quarters. The public would have *questions*. Lynch insisted they get married to make the proceedings 'respectable'.

It made sense for practical reasons. But Elinore, who'd pushed so hard to join Ben in the jeep, suddenly felt she had to protect herself. Before the wedding she typed up a short contract:

> It is agreed that from now until six months after our return to New York City or until six months after premature termina-tion of our project, whichever is earlier, all income, whether in cash or in kind, stemming from our project, whether earned

by one or both of us, will be pooled and disposed of in the following manner:

1. Payment of the cost of and expenses incidental to the trip – running and living expenses, repairs, fees, etc. will be the first charge.

2. The balance will be divided – one third to E. T. Carlin, two thirds to F. B. Carlin.

Ben signed it on 28 May 1948.

With this understanding in place, they were married by City Clerk Murray W. Stand on 8 June at New York City Hall in the presence of Elinore's friend Peter DeAnna, a struggling 27-year-old artist who'd come to New York to study on the GI Bill and later created murals for the National Air and Space Museum in Washington, DC.

With his clients now made respectable, Lynch started pitching the story of the Australian major, his American wife and their odd jeep. Danton Walker, a syndicated columnist who dished celebrity gossip, was interested enough to give them a few lines next to an item about Abbott & Costello, and on 15 June 1948 the first substantial US mention of the proposed journey appeared in the *New York Daily News*:

Major Ben Carlin and his wife will take off from New York Harbor this week in an amphibious jeep 18 ft. long in an attempt to circumvent the globe. An Australian, he is investigator general for SAFE (Save A Friend in Europe), a Swiss food parcel concern.

Walker worked fast and frequently got things wrong, like the difference between *circumnavigate* and *circumvent* and *inspector* and *investigator*. But it was press, and newspapers across the country picked up the story.

And a day after the story appeared, Ben and Elinore were off to circle the world. They had been married eight days.

~

A hundred dockworkers watched as the couple climbed into the boxy cabin of the amphibious jeep with Virginia licence plates at the Downtown Skyport, a facility for seaplanes near Wall Street at the lower end of Manhattan. Ben wore a smirk on his face as he steered into the East River under a clear sky. He glanced back at the bloody masses with their small minds and limited imaginations and doubt. He'd show them. Then he turned towards the Atlantic and his destiny.

But he had overlooked one critical point. The East River, a short waterway that runs along the eastern edge of Manhattan, is connected to Long Island Sound, the Harlem River and New York Bay, and its tides are complicated. When the tide rises, the current can flow *upriver* at nearly 4 knots. As soon as the jeep hit the water the tidal flood sent it scudding slowly upriver, and Ben's smirk faded as the jeep's 54-horsepower engine struggled in vain against the current.

He tried again at 6.15 pm, on the turn of the tide, in the long shadow of skyscrapers, this time riding the ebb current, the jeep threading its way around ferries, cargo ships and tankers, past the Statue of Liberty and onward towards the Narrows, the strait that separates Brooklyn and Staten Island and opens into the Atlantic Ocean. The last light of day faded and the jeep rumbled south towards the grey-blue water, carrying 80,000 calories of packaged SAFE food.

Beginning

Elinore sat cross-legged on the roof, breathing in the salt air.

They stopped at 7.30 to eat, and shortly after they got back underway they smashed into a submerged mass of driftwood. Ben dove in and examined the hull but found no damage, so he got back behind the wheel and ploughed into the night, the jeep's engine spinning at a steady 1,600 revolutions per minute. At midnight the jeep passed the Scotland Lightship, and Ben set a course for 135 degrees, pointing the jeep towards the Azores, a chain of volcanic islands conveniently positioned halfway to the West African coast, 2,250 miles away across the open ocean. New York City glowed amber in the rear-view mirror as Ben drove across the darkening sea, fuelled by cigarettes and adrenaline.

At 4.5 miles per hour, or a little less than 4 knots, this longest, most dangerous part of the Atlantic crossing would take 24 days.

It's incredible how optimistic they were at the beginning. A day or two before their departure Elinore told the Perth *Daily News*, 'All we have room for is petrol, water and food. It is our honeymoon and we don't care how we look. We will live on cold food and concentrated chocolate. We have no cooking facilities. All our meals will be cold and we will love it.'

And for some reason they imagined it would be that easy, that they would just drive across the ocean like it was a weekend outing. But only a few hours out of New York things started going wrong.

Even with its new streamlined bow the brick-shaped jeep wouldn't hold a straight line. Instead it wandered drunkenly back and forth over the waves as Ben and Elinore alternated shifts at the wheel through the night, steering by the dimly lit compass, the constant struggle of course-correction draining them. A wind rose behind the jeep and Ben raised a small, square sail so they could move a little faster, but it didn't catch much wind, and its effect was negligible. He took it down and in the months ahead would unfurl it mainly for photos.

They drove through the night. At seven in the morning Ben turned off the engine, and he and Elinore curled up to sleep – Elinore on the cramped bunk, Ben across the two front seats with dirty clothes wedged in the gap between them. When they woke up a few hours later, the wind had died and the jeep rolled gently on the swells. They were just out of sight of the New Jersey shore, 14 miles due east of Manasquan, a beach town just starting to welcome summer tourists. Ben tried to radio Lynch with a progress report. No luck. He turned the ignition key, pressed the starter button on the floor next to the accelerator, and drove through a second day, and again they hove to – shut off the engine and stopped moving – and slept through the night. On the third day at sea Ben tried but failed to make radio contact with my grandfather, who stood by his receiver for a call that never came.

A headwind slowed the jeep, and Ben and Elinore took turns fighting the steering wheel, watching airliners flying high overhead along the flight path to Bermuda. That day the United Press reported that an army surplus amphibious jeep 'tentatively named *Carlin's Platypus*' had departed on a six-month voyage around the world and 'friends said the couple left secretly to avoid publicity'. That wasn't quite true. They just hadn't received much attention yet.

Australian newspapers were more effusive.

Wharfies Cheer Jeep Travellers On Way! exclaimed the Perth *Daily News*.

Transatlantic Honeymooners Set Sail – In Jeep! proclaimed the *Adelaide Advertiser.*

But a steady entropy was already engulfing the jeep. Its compass needle swung erratically. The engine radiator leaked badly, losing water at the rate of a gallon a day, which meant dipping into the fresh drinking water. And as the wind increased to 25 miles per hour, something ominous was developing, a dull thud emanating over and over from somewhere under the jeep as it chugged along.

Boom.

Boom.

Ben stripped, dove into the Atlantic and swam under the jeep amid the fish that schooled in its shadow. Through the salty blur of seawater he examined the six nylon straps that held the jeep's belly tank tight to its underside, three on each side, and saw they'd begun to stretch. As the jeep rode up and down over waves, the tank, full of fuel, would pull away and then crash back against the bottom of the jeep with increasing violence. The battering was taking a toll, already loosening the seam where the boxy cabin was bolted to the jeep's body. Seawater began seeping in.

The belly tank had seemed like such a good idea.

The sea grew rougher. Ben cut the engine and deployed a canvas sea anchor – a small aquatic parachute deployed from a vessel to keep it pointed safely into the waves while hove to, instead of turning sideways. But either it didn't work or Ben couldn't get it deployed properly, and the jeep kept spinning around and getting hammered broadside. *Platypus rides very badly at anchor*, Ben logged. The only solution was to keep the motor idling to keep the jeep's nose pointed into the waves, and that burned precious fuel.

At 9.55 am, with the wind rising and rain hammering down hard, Ben took a moment to log another disturbing turn. *Ellie has been out for an hour in a sort of trance. Wide staring eyes. I have been slapping her hands and face, her eyes showing no reflexes.*

Now *this* was worrying. Ben had no plans for this sort of thing, no medical training since a first-aid course a decade earlier, and the jeep was falling apart around them, petrol fumes and carbon monoxide venting into the cabin from undetected leaks as it wallowed wildly. Ben threw open the hatches to the dark sky above. It took half an hour for Elinore to become fully alert, complaining of weakness and *a filthy taste in her mouth.*

Ben suffered from the headaches too. He admitted defeat and turned back at 2.00 in the afternoon.

He didn't know it, but in the absence of radio communication since their departure two US Army bombers were soaring high over the Atlantic, dispatched on a futile mission to find the wayward jeep and its crew.

'If no message is received from them soon, we will throw our whole organisation into action to find them,' said a Coast Guard spokesman.

By 21 June the headlines had taken a darker turn.

Jeep Missing At Sea.

Bombers Search for Amphibious Jeep.

Round-World Jeep Lost: Air Search.

Ben was already heading back to New York, unaware of the worry his radio silence was causing the world, focused instead on learning how to handle his jeep in the ocean. *Half-Safe rides like a circus horse,* he noted in his log that evening.

Half-Safe. Now the jeep had a real name and identity. No more *Platypus*, no more *Carlin's Creation*, tentative names that had appeared in the press, names Ben never liked anyway. The new name was sparked by a radio ad for Arrid deodorant, and a slogan that had lodged in Ben's mind before departing: 'Don't be half-safe – use Arrid to be sure!' It was a defining moment.

Under a full moon, Ben tied *Half-Safe* to a bell buoy at the mouth of the Shark River near Belmar, New Jersey. He turned off the motor and he and Elinore slept. The next morning, on 21 June, they chugged slowly into the river and tied up at a jetty.

The first failed attempt at circling the world in an amphibious vehicle had covered 35 miles in a little less than five days. In the morning they sailed back up the coast to New York and moored at the Municipal Yacht Basin on the west side of Manhattan, just north of the Cunard pier.

A few days later a reporter tracked down Elinore's sister outside Chicago:

Dismayed surprise was the reaction of Mrs Alfred Novick, Winnetka, when she learned of the unannounced plans for her younger sister.

'I didn't think she'd do it,' she remarked at last. 'We have tried so hard to discourage her. We knew she was thinking about doing something like this.' How she would break the news to their mother, Mrs Caroline Arone, who lives with her in Winnetka, Mrs Novick didn't know.

Ben's army pay was now gone and there might never have been another attempt. But then the wider world started to take notice.

CHAPTER TWO

Another Start

Half-Safe chugged down the Hudson River on 13 July 1948, under the low clouds of a looming thunderstorm, past the towering steel hulk of *Queen Mary*, and through the traffic of Lower New York Bay. Rain was starting to fall and a wind hit the jeep from all directions. Ben wasn't happy with the conditions and knew it wasn't the best time to make another attempt at an Atlantic crossing, but for the first time he had to adhere to a schedule.

Publicist Ware Lynch had scored a coup: *Life* magazine had paid $500 for exclusive feature rights to the Carlins' story. The first installment was enough to get Ben's camera out of hock and pay for 90 gallons of petrol, but now they had to leave when it was convenient for a photographer to shoot them sailing down the Hudson, capturing stark images of the jeep looking incredibly small and frail and low in the water against the city skyline and the Statue of Liberty.

That evening, out in the Atlantic once again, Ben failed to raise anyone on the radio, and during the night a weld in the exhaust system cracked and again carbon monoxide leaked into the cabin. *Winds around the compass – sea confused – very unpleasant*, wrote Ben at 8.00 pm, and followed that two hours later with, *very tired – cannot keep eyes open & E is unfit so heave to.*

In the morning Elinore was still vomiting weakly into a tin cup, and the jeep was riding low under thunderstorms, water seeping into its hull. Ben ran the bilge pump for a while and resumed a course of 135 degrees. In the evening he launched a kite trailing a wire antenna, thinking that might help with reception. The kite flew beautifully but the radio received only static.

Again newspapers reported the lack of expected communication from the jeep, but Ware Lynch said, 'There is no cause for alarm. It is possible their radio signals are not strong enough to be picked up.'

By sunrise on 15 July, with the seas rising and Elinore suffering severe nausea, Ben aborted the second attempt. He swung *Half-Safe* back around to the north and slunk back to Brooklyn that night under cover of darkness.

Back in New York, they spent the next three weeks avoiding friends and the press as Ben rebuilt the entire exhaust system, hoping this time he'd found the source of the leak. They couldn't afford a hotel room for long, but they didn't want to impose on anyone or admit they'd failed again, so they quietly launched a third attempt on 7 August. And this time they were determined. Never mind the three men in a rowboat who stared at them and broke into laughter as they passed. Never mind the swarm of flies that appeared mysteriously from nowhere a few hours later, infesting the jeep. Never mind the dangerous debris drifting invisibly in the waters off New York. They were on their way.

Once more publicist Ware Lynch faced the press, once more said the Carlins expected to circle the world in six months, and when pressed for personal details said that while in New York the major had lived in a small Broadway hotel or visited friends in Greenwich Village.

'Looks like a comic-strip hero,' Lynch said, and then strangely started talking about Ben in the past tense, as if unsure he'd ever be seen again. 'He was a strange fellow. Sort of homespun, you know, like a lot of those Australians. He used to wander around New York in his shirtsleeves, a pair of pants and an old pair of moccasins with a bandanna wrapped around his head.' Elinore, he added, 'seemed to be quite phlegmatic about the whole thing'.

But the staid *New York Times* reported on 'the seagoing truck of F. B. Carlin and his lady' in an uncharacteristically enthusiastic manner.

Mr. and Mrs. Carlin prove by their try, if nothing else, that the spirit of Leif Ericson, of Magellan, of Columbus, of Captain Slocum, of those countless others who have dared the unknown of the trackless seas, still lives today. All shore-bound adventurers, who only make such trips vicariously, wish the Carlins, we are sure, a smooth voyage and a happy landfall.

Out at sea the entries in Ben's log became shorter, more to the point, like on 9 August when all he wrote was, *wind SW 10 mph* and *gassed up* and *altered course 130 degrees* and *dead calm*.

Late in the afternoon of the second day of their third attempt, 100 miles due east of Atlantic City, Ben and Elinore found themselves suddenly surrounded by five US Navy destroyers. Four sailed off, but one – the 2,600-ton Gearing-class destroyer USS *Robert L. Wilson*, based out of Newport, Rhode Island – circled the jeep a few times and at 6.10 pm radioed the odd sight of 'two women' in a strange boat before signalling *Half-Safe* to stop.

'I must put on my captain's hat,' Ben said to Elinore, and he donned a khaki handkerchief like a pirate, then politely declined the commander's offer of rescue and instead asked that a man named Lynch be contacted at a New York number and informed that he and Elinore were 'okay'.

When he received the message, Lynch told the press, 'They are in the hands of the gods now.'

After he'd convinced the *Robert L. Wilson* that *Half-Safe* didn't need help, Ben waved to the crew, who watched in mild dismay from the destroyer's deck as the jeep chugged away. Elinore willed herself not to be seasick, despite the 38-degree heat in the claustrophobic cabin and the petrol fumes, and let herself wonder what kind of meal they might have been treated to on the destroyer.

The next day, when it was her turn to take the wheel, she felt she was driving over a calm sea, *like a huge gelatinous mass that quivers now and again to show it's alive*. Her arms ached from holding the thin steering wheel, and on the morning of the second day at sea she stripped naked and lay in the sun on top of the cabin for 15 minutes to purge the stale, oily cabin air from her lungs and start her 'altogether' tan. They were going slower than expected and already had to start rationing food, cigarettes and water – just a quart each day. Every time Elinore sipped her share she couldn't help thinking of a ubiquitous magazine ad for Four Roses whiskey, the one with the red roses frozen in a big, beautiful block of ice.

When Ben decided it was time for a break he dove overboard and scraped barnacles from the bottom of the jeep while Elinore watched for sharks, and he stayed in the ocean until his ears hurt in the cold water, and later Elinore wrote 'Ode to Scraping Bottom of *Half-Safe*' while curled on the bunk.

> Oh joy, oh rapture, unforeseen
> And now our bottom is scraped and clean
> Barnacles gone – and seaweed too –
> It really did behoove us to.

Then Ben pumped water from the bilge until the pump handle broke off in his hand, and after a moment of concern he replaced the handle with a vise grip until he could get or craft a new one somewhere when they were back on land.

He always had a fast solution.

They'd entered the Gulf Stream, the world's fastest ocean current, and now *Half-Safe* got an extra nudge from behind, an extra knot or so as they headed south-east.

The next day it looked like rain. Ben spread a rubber sheet across the roof of the cabin to collect fresh water under the darkening sky, and Elinore looked out and saw the water was *cold and blackish blue*, and the waves were getting higher and the small jeep bobbed with less and less attention to the input of the steering wheel. The rain never came. All Elinore wanted to do was sleep, but she felt guilty every time she did because it seemed like Ben was doing all the work. Even worse, he had trouble sleeping when she was at the wheel, even though she herself could have slept for hours and hours if given the chance.

The sea was rising. They had to heave to and set the sea anchor, and Elinore couldn't believe that all Ben could say was, 'Yes, it's really building up to be quite a decent sea,' always understating things, as if even under the worst circumstances it didn't do to show emotion.

On 13 August the rain finally began to fall, soon hammering down in earnest. They tried setting out the rubber sheet again, but now it was too windy to catch water. They huddled miserably in the damp cabin, the rear hatch closed to keep out the rain, its rubber seal already beginning to rot and leak. Both of them were growing irritable with thirst, ironic given the torrent of fresh rain falling around them, and Elinore was always *on the edge of green*, trying desperately not to be seasick from the constant chop. The sea was even heavier the next day. Elinore struggled to fork hamburger meat out of a tin and thought about the syrupy ice-cream she used to eat at Ferrazini's Tea Room on Lindsay Street in Calcutta during the war, recalled the coolness upon entering from a sunbaked street. Even better was their tea, hot and fragrant. She tried to shake it from her mind.

In the evening *Half-Safe* rode monstrous waves like a roller-coaster, her engine running rough and stalling. Elinore was frightened, especially later that night when she couldn't see anything outside the jeep. She tried to hold a steady course while fighting the disconcerting sensation of hurtling through space at terrific speed.

After only a week at sea Ben realised they were going through their provisions much faster than expected. He climbed outside, clung to the exterior of the cabin and fished without luck until the weather forced him back inside. They ate crackers and drank sweet tinned milk from the SAFE packages they were supposed to be testing, and the water supply was now so low that Ben quietly realised they'd have to hail a passing ship to refill their tank, or die of thirst. He'd completely misjudged the jeep's stores.

The next day the seas calmed, but disaster struck.

Ben heard it as a clank; Elinore called it a terrific grinding noise. It was probably a lot of both, a metallic cacophony filling the cabin from somewhere down below the seats. Ben knew even before he looked exactly what was happening. The propeller shaft thrust bearing, which supported the shaft that transferred power from the jeep's engine to the propeller in the back, was disintegrating.

Ben winced and said to Elinore, 'This shouldn't have happened for ten years,' and for the first time she saw him look momentarily grim. *Looks pretty hopeless*, he confided in his log, and put the blame on bad wartime workmanship and worse luck. Elinore felt quietly devastated; to have the work of 18 months and the whole trip go down the drain simply because of something beyond Ben's control! But she admired her husband's stoicism, believed that *if Old Thing had made the bearing I'm damned sure it bloody well would* not *have gone fut!*

The next day Ben opened up a small inspection hatch between the two front seats to get a better look at the bearing. Taking it apart was a gruelling job never meant to be done at sea; first he had to disconnect the propeller shaft and slide it back 8 inches, which caused water to leak into the hull. Then he unpacked the bearing, saw it was coming apart, shrugged because there was really nothing he could do, repacked it, put it back in place and reconnected the propeller shaft. He didn't have a replacement, and he knew it was only a matter of time before the bearing fell completely apart. Would that be half an hour, a day, a month? He couldn't say. While Ben worked, Elinore climbed on top of the jeep to read *The Raft*, Robert Trumbull's 1942 account of three Navy pilots who survived 34 days drifting in the Pacific after ditching at sea. *Very shudder-making*, she wrote to an old friend back in Shanghai.

They were adrift in a leaking jeep 300 miles south-east of New York, their stores running low and their radio useless.

And so Ben did what he did best: he busied himself with mechanical work. As *Half-Safe* sat dead in the water, he fixed an electric fuel pump, cleared blocked fuel lines and found a loose connection in the radio, took care of the dozen small things that needed attention on a seagoing vessel. Elinore did laundry, hung it on the antenna wire to dry and watched their only pillowcase whip away in a gust of wind. Under the noon sun they jumped off the cabin into the Atlantic and swam around the jeep to cool off.

Despite Ben's tinkering he couldn't do anything more about the thrust bearing, and he decided they'd simply plough forward as long as possible until it fell apart.

Except now the engine wouldn't start.

They were bobbing aimlessly on 17 August, ten days at sea, when a gale-force wind picked up. *This is serious*, Ben wrote, and the rising sea tossed the jeep, waves slammed it and sometimes crashed entirely over it. The thin sheet metal sides took one violent blow after another, and Ben wondered how long *Half-Safe* could hold up. When the sun dipped below the horizon they huddled together in the damp darkness; without the engine to charge the jeep's battery they had to conserve electricity.

In the morning the sea was even wilder. Rain poured down and the wind whistled through the jeep's sparse rigging. Each time the waves smashed into the cabin the plexiglas windows bowed under the immense pressure of tons of water, and Ben prepared to launch the self-inflating orange rubber life raft as soon as one of the windows gave way.

It was also time for the oil bags.

The oil bag is an old marine safety measure. It's simply a canvas bag filled with a couple gallons of oil, and it's hung from the side of the boat. The oil seeps out slowly through small holes and coats the surface of the water, which temporarily quells the waves in the immediate vicinity. Oil bags are often carried in lifeboats, even today.

The first bag worked well for a while — *these damned side panels are liable to cave under the side blasts but at present oil bags are barely saving our bacon*, Ben noted — until its line tangled with the sea anchor line and both were ripped away.

They needed help.

At 7.40 on the morning of the 19th, Ben swallowed his pride, picked up the transmitter microphone and made a reluctant mayday call. He repeated it eight times without getting a response, even though he could hear the New York Coast Guard perfectly well. In the evening he transmitted in Morse code:

Amphib. named Half-Safe, NY to Azores, broken down with prop shaft thrust bearing gone – No danger, no immediate help required, we shall await casual ship pickup – Exact position unknown – Shall obtain fix as soon as sky clear and advise – Advise Lynch, Circle 6-1164

No response.

A freighter passed within a mile or two. Ben fired a flare and watched it arc across the sky. The freighter sailed on. The next day a plane flew overhead, unseen, the sound approaching and then fading somewhere above the clouds.

Ben tried without success to get a fix on their location. He hoisted the antenna by kite to make another radio transmission, and the kite soared into the sky, broke free and sailed off into the ocean.

He finally speared some of the fish circling the jeep, a dozen of what he and Elinore thought might be baby flounder. He cleaned them and tied them to the exhaust pipe with strands of wire and managed to get the engine to run briefly. Half an hour later a sweet aroma filled the cabin, and even Elinore felt her hunger return as they inhaled the crispy fillets.

Another ship appeared on the horizon. Ben was growing desperate. He poured a 5-gallon jerry can of petrol onto the surface of the ocean and tried to ignite the patch by tossing a handful of flaming kleenex into it, but the tissues fizzled and the petrol dissipated. This called for more serious measures. He jammed a flaming wad of kleenex directly into the spout of a second 5-gallon jerry can and dropped it into the water, like a Molotov cocktail. It blazed away, emitting clouds of black smoke that hung over the jeep, and then the petrol started spilling out of the steel can. This time it stayed lit on the surface of the water, the searing flames blowing back towards *Half-Safe* until the petrol burned away. As crazy as this seemed, they really, *really* wanted to get the attention of the passing ship, and so Ben did the same thing a second time. Six or seven minutes later the ship was gone, along with 15 gallons of petrol, and they were left staring at an empty horizon in the stench of burning fuel.

On 24 August, pilots and crews of Pan Am and TWA flights between New York and the Azores received an alert to be on the lookout for an amphibious jeep somewhere below. *Half-Safe* was adrift on a flat sea under an overcast sky, location unknown, Elinore reading on the roof, Ben trying to spear fish and taking pictures to pass the time.

Finally, late on the tenth day of drifting without power, a northbound tanker acknowledged the steady SOS signal from Ben's flashlight. The SS *New Jersey*, en route from Port Arthur, Texas, to Montreal, came alongside *Half-Safe* within minutes. Ben packed his cameras and film and steeled himself to scuttle the jeep. He had a hammer in hand to bash a hole through its thin hull and abandon it to the depths of the Atlantic, but when he clambered up a ladder to the tanker's deck, Captain Hans Brown offered to hoist the jeep on board with a pair of lifeboat davits. 'Hell, you're not going to leave that goddamned jeep lying around?' he asked in a thick accent that betrayed his Norwegian roots.

Suddenly, after nearly three weeks at sea, Ben and Elinore had hot water, soap and clean towels, coffee and whiskey. Captain Brown, 56 years old, his face creased by years at sea, called Elinore 'sugar' and told her he took his coffee black, his whiskey straight and his women wild. She was charmed.

On the ship's charts they saw they'd drifted backward several hundred miles after the engine died, and they were now just 80 miles from the American coast. Elinore wrote to a friend in Shanghai:

> I think no one has ever put to sea in a more abysmal state of ignorance of marine life and its connotations. In my saner moments (rare) I have worried a bit about this appalling lack of knowledge of the sea and such gloomy thoughts have sent me scurrying to the Enc. Britannica to look up such things as azimuth, keel, rudder, amplitude, etc. etc. ad infinitum.

But despite this third failed attempt – or maybe because of the couple's tenacity – the world was paying more attention. At 8.06 am on 26 August, the United Press sent a shore-to-ship radiogram to the rescuing ship:

> APPRECIATE YOU SEND US COLLECT A STORY UNDER SIGNATURES ON THERE EXPERIENCES SINCE DEPARTURE INCLUDING RESCUE WHAT ARE THEIR PLANS NOW ALSO WOULD LIKE QUOTES FROM YOU ON PICK UP ALSO PLEASE RADIO POSSIBILITY OF PICTURES

When they arrived in Montreal on 30 August, Ben and Elinore found that newspapers around the world had covered their misadventure. Tired but tanned, they posed for photos aboard the SS *New Jersey* with Ben looking like a young, muscled Marlon Brando in his tight white T-shirt and Elinore beaming. They told reporters they'd try again in two weeks, refusing to say anything specific about their ten days adrift other than Ben's observation that it was 'all in the game'.

That night, after *Half-Safe* was unloaded onto a Montreal dock, its neoprene coating already peeling like sunburned skin, someone broke into her and stole everything, from the life raft to the cameras and film.

It was too late in the year for another shot anyway, and Ben and Elinore were broke. Ben's US visa was going to expire in a few months, so he stayed in Canada and put *Half-Safe* in storage for $80. He found a job as a fitter in a Halifax machine shop, where he earned $45 on good weeks with a little overtime, did some side work as a maintenance man, and toiled through a dismal winter, reading *War and Peace* at night.

He also made two key decisions: first, somewhat arbitrarily, that Montreal rather than New York would mark the official departure point of the journey. Second, more practically, that the 1949 attempt would launch out of Halifax, cutting the first leg of the Atlantic crossing from 2,250 miles to about 1,700.

Elinore returned to New York to find secretarial work.

After the third failed departure, some critics were beginning to see what had at first seemed like a lark now seemed more like a selfish death wish. Alfred Loomis, writing for *Yachting* magazine under his nom de plume Spun Yarn, attacked savagely:

Since they are to try again to circumnavigate the world in their outsized kiddy car, I feel it incumbent on me to give a word of advice, namely, 'Don't do it, Major.' It is easier to defy death by walking a tightrope over the gorge below the Niagara Falls where facilities for recovering corpses are more highly developed than in mid-ocean. And it is a strain on the good nature of tanker skippers, coastguardsmen and other seafaring Samaritans to keep on snatching non-seamen from a watery grave.

Ben ignored the critics and threw himself into his work at the machine shop. He was still pleased with the jeep's belly tank and nose tank, which added nearly 350 gallons to the jeep's original capacity. But the storms of 1948 had shown the recklessness of setting to sea with just enough fuel.

He went back to an idea he'd had in 1947: towing additional fuel in some kind of tank that could be cast off when empty. He found exactly what he was imagining in a nearby junkyard – two scrapped 125-gallon drop tanks, the kind that attach to the underside of an aircraft and can be jettisoned when empty – and in the spring tried to figure out how to tow them safely behind the jeep. In trial after trial in Halifax Harbour the tanks spun crazily in the water and threatened to smash into and puncture the jeep's thin skin. Finally Ben cobbled together a steel-wire harness that held them side by side and seemed to keep them under control.

He also wrote long letters to Elinore, vacillating between loneliness, love and impatience.

On the way to work this morning I picked up 50 cents on the sidewalk.

After two weeks without a letter I was beginning to think you had finally managed a win in the park. If you step off the train here with breath smelling of caviar I'll beat your bottom.

I have been waiting impatiently to hear when you are coming. I can't put Gertie in the water until after you bring the neoprene. I crave to see that familiar fat face.

And always: *Love, Ben.*

Elinore flew back to Halifax in August 1949 to join Ben for another try.

On 1 September, as a black bird circled overhead in a grey sky, they cast off their lines and *Half-Safe* chugged into the foggy Atlantic. Only four people watched as they waved goodbye and headed for the open sea, towing new fuel tanks, bound once again for the Azores. They were heading into the Atlantic's storm season, with high winds already reported lashing the ocean along their projected course.

Ben refused all requests for interviews before the departure. The increasing skepticism after the cascade of failures in 1948 angered him, and now he resolved not to say anything to the press until he had a success for the bastards to write about. Instead, he left behind an antagonistic written statement that set the tone he would keep with the media for years to come:

We are trying to do something rather difficult. We have been accused, among other things, of pulling a stunt and being exhibitionists. While we have still done nothing we prefer to keep the idea to ourselves and will not change our decision against publicity. If and when we succeed in converting our idea into actuality, we may be persuaded to talk about it.

Less than a day out of Halifax the first tank ripped free of its harness, spewing fuel across the water. Ben leaped into the ocean to push it away from the jeep, and clambered back on board covered in fuel once the tank was safely drifting away. He dozed on the jeep's cramped bunk, exhausted. When he woke up most of the second tank was gone too, leaving just a scrap of steel attached to the towline. They could have tried for the Azores with one tank, but with both gone it was impossible. Ben gave up and, only 35 miles out of Halifax, turned around.

He didn't even take the 1949 attempt seriously enough to record it in his green logbook.

They were beaten down and depressed, and had just $80 left. They resigned themselves to a second winter apart. Elinore flew back to New York and distanced herself from the adventure, calling herself Miss Arone while working as a secretary in a law office – *they still think I'm a maiden, pristine and pure*, she told her brother, but there was a practical reason for her concealment. It was a time when the Help Wanted ads for typists could specify 'preferable age 21 to 25' or 'unmarried' or 'single preferred'. Elinore was married and 33. Why advertise it?

In Halifax, Ben paid $120 to store the jeep for another winter and looked for work.

And he remained focused on his mission. One thing had become clear during the attempts of 1948 and 1949: it would take more self-discipline to plan and execute a journey like this. It would take willpower. *Control.* Lodged in a boarding house at 76 Fairbanks Street run by an occasional bootlegger, Ben thought a lot about the art of self-denial as the fall days got shorter and darker and colder, and practised an essential asceticism to prepare himself for the next attempt.

When Elinore wrote from New York about her love of music, Ben responded that *such abnormal devotion merely indicates lack of balance – lack of self-control. Music has a place but it ranks way down below food, alcohol, football, cricket, a double bed and many other odds and ends.*

And when Elinore said a few weeks later that she'd spent five dollars one weekend, he raged.

We – you and I – are hibernating and hoarding for a simple, clear, specific purpose in which you have expressed as much interest as I. You are inclined to forget such things in a vague sort of way when you see a new magazine cover or something shiny in a window or somebody waving a bottle. We need money. Plainer than that I can't put it and please do not ever again give me reason to try.

Then he found a job that would replenish their funds.

On the first of November Ben joined a crew of nine as a 2nd engineer on the MV *Armoricain*, a 136-foot wooden schooner built in France shortly after World War I, converted to diesel and now operating as a freighter out of Halifax, carrying everything from fish to lumber to casks of wine. The ship creaked and crawled with rats, the skipper had a tight grip on a supply of rum but only a vague grasp of navigation, and the crew buzzed with a mutinous distrust. Ben toiled four hours on, four hours off as the ship worked the East Coast all the way down to the British West Indies and, in early 1950, across the Atlantic. Ben decided he knew more about the engine room after one month than the old Cape Breton chief engineer did after a lifetime at sea, and when their arguments turned into blows, the skipper had to pull them apart.

But Ben swore to Elinore that he was staying in control, that he was working with crystalline clarity towards the summer of 1950 and another attempt. *I have gone out of my way to avoid trouble*, he wrote to Elinore from a Newfoundland port of call, and he claimed he hadn't had a drink since she'd left for New York, except for strong coffee and one per cent beer. And he got the sense she was having a bit too much fun in New York without him: *would it really kill you to sign the pledge for a couple of months?*

Ben's resolve couldn't last.

Six weeks later the crew of the *Armoricain* came ashore in Madeira, a Portuguese island in the North Atlantic. Some went to brothels, some went to bars, but Ben went off alone to a dive with the cheapest cane alcohol in town, and drank until he blacked out. He woke up the next morning in handcuffs, his hands and feet bound with rope for good measure. *It appeared that I had passed out on my feet and run amok*, he wrote to Elinore afterward, saying it had taken eight police officers to restrain him, to fight the sheer physical rage he'd unleashed in his drunken state, to lock him up. There was an underlying pride in the telling, even though it contradicted everything he preached about saving money and staying in control.

Christ, he sighed in his letter. *I don't know.*

He paid $1.80 to get out of jail.

A few weeks later in Bordeaux, a woman picked a Canadian $100 bill from his wallet. *It's a long and involved story*, Ben wrote to Elinore without further elaboration.

At the end of his service the Canadian Department of Transport overlooked his questionable behaviour, and on 31 May 1950 stamped his Certificate of Discharge with a VERY GOOD for both Ability and General Conduct. Ben walked away with $600 in his pocket, a stronger feel for the sea, months of navigational experience and his reputation more or less intact.

A year later the *Armoricain* sprang a leak and sank off Saint-Pierre et Miquelon, the French islands south of Newfoundland.

                                                  ~

By the time Elinore returned to Halifax in early July 1950, Ben had fabricated a new bullet-shaped tow-tank with a capacity of 280 gallons, and he'd added vertical plywood stabilisers to the rear of the jeep – a pair of fins he hoped would address its maddening tendency to veer off a straight line. A few days later *Half-Safe* was fuelled, parked at the Royal Canadian Naval Air Station Shearwater on Halifax Harbour and ready to go as soon as the weather looked good.

One afternoon a passing Mountie stopped to examine the jeep and asked what they were doing. 'Going fishing,' Ben replied. *No one was fooled, but nothing could be done to prevent our suicide.*

With an area of high pressure approaching and the conditions nearly perfect, Ben and Elinore spent a last nervous night in the jeep. In the morning a light fog dissipated, and on 19 July 1950, after two years of failed attempts, separation, poverty and the wax and wane of public attention, with only a few airmen standing witness, and without any official permission to leave the country, Ben piloted *Half-Safe* away from the Canadian base. The jeep passed the cobbled shoreline of McNabs Island and headed south-eastward into the North Atlantic for one last shot.

CHAPTER THREE
The Ford GPA

By most accounts the Ford GPA amphibious army jeep was doomed from the start.

Built by Ford Motor Company during World War II, the GPA was essentially a basic army jeep dropped into a boat-shaped shell with cut-outs for wheels. It was 15 feet long and 5 feet wide – a little smaller than a modern Toyota Corolla – and it could carry four soldiers and their duffel bags. It didn't have a roof or trunk, or anything else beyond the essentials. But it had a propeller, and it floated. On land a soldier could drive it like a regular jeep, and if for some reason he had to cross a river or stream, he'd flip a lever that directed power to the propeller.

That was the plan, anyway. The GPA performed adequately during tests on the flat water of the Detroit River, but once it was in the field, soldiers complained it was too heavy to manoeuvre on land, that it wallowed clumsily on the water and, most damningly, that it was prone to sinking when waves kicked up. The GPA saw little wartime action, and production was cancelled after just 18 months.

So how did the Ford GPA amphibious jeep end up getting developed and built in the first place?

It began with the standard army jeep.

In his oddly readable 1943 government report about the genesis of the jeep, historian Herbert R. Rifkind explained that by the 1930s the US military felt the need for a vehicle that could ferry soldiers around the field, undertake cross-country reconnaissance missions and carry light weapons to support attacking infantry.

> The motorcycle, even when equipped with a sidecar, was recognized as a notoriously poor performer in this regard and dangerous to operate off the road except in the hands of a most expert rider. It was strongly felt that a machine was needed for reconnaissance and motor messenger service, which could be operated effectively under all conditions.

There had been some early experiments.

In 1932 the army bolted oversized wheels onto a two-seat Austin Roadster – the American edition of the baby Austin manufactured in England – mainly to show how a car could outperform a motorcycle. That experiment didn't go anywhere. Then it cobbled together the Howie Machine-Gun Carrier, better known as the 'Belly Flopper', a bizarre 1937 experiment manned by two crewmembers who lay flat on their stomachs. The vehicle had no seats – and no body, for that matter. The sole benefit was a low silhouette that made it hard for the enemy to see you and shoot. But the rear-engine, front-wheel-drive vehicle, steered by an awkward tiller, topped out at just 28 miles per hour, and one engineer dismissed it as 'a cross between a kid's scooter and a diving board on wheels'.

What if you could combine the small-vehicle benefits of the Austin with the low profile of the Belly Flopper and give it a bigger capacity?

In the summer of 1940, a tiny Pennsylvania auto manufacturer called American Bantam offered the army a design for a rugged new reconnaissance vehicle and offered to manufacture a first batch of 75 for $175,000. The army liked the simple, compact design but doubted Bantam's ability to scale up production. Almost immediately the army claimed ownership of Bantam's design and forced the company to turn over its plans to Toledo-based Willys-Overland, which had a bigger manufacturing capacity. Then the army realised Willys had just one plant, which seemed like putting all its eggs in one basket, and decided to split production 50/50 between Willys and the automotive powerhouse Ford, which had multiple manufacturing plants and an army of 100,000 workers.

In late 1940 Bantam, Ford and Willys all began working from the same standardised designs and blueprints. The very first vehicles, 1,500 from each manufacturer, were delivered the next spring. The new vehicle was officially known by the army as the 'truck, 1/4-ton, 4x4'. The name referred to its cargo capacity of about a quarter of a ton, though it could really carry more, and to its delivery of power to all four wheels. The Ford version was designated as GPW, in which G stood for government, P stood for the 80-inch wheelbase, and W reflected the design licensed from Willys, which in turn was based mostly on the Bantam design. The Willys-built version was called the Willys MB, for Military model B.

Regardless of manufacturer, they were all supposed to be identical, built to military spec, except Ford slyly stamped a subtle scripted 'F' onto its bolt heads, even though the army frowned on anything that smelled of promotion.

No matter who built the vehicle, everyone began calling it a 'jeep', a word that has neither official military status nor a widely accepted origin.

It was a sensation from the start.

It's hard to realise today, when the jeep is a ubiquitous icon of World War II and the military, how radically different it was from everything else on the road in 1941, how revolutionary. Soldiers and school kids alike became enamoured with its distinctive rectangular outline coated in a special lustreless olive drab enamel paint, its flat fenders, its folding windshield, its distinctive slotted grille, its beefy mud-and-snow tyres. As Rifkin put it,

The demonstrations it gave of climbing and leaping, and its all-round ability to push its way through tough situations, impressed all beholders. Neither sand, snow, nor mud seemed to hold any terrors for this quarter-ton Blitz-buggy, the tactical mission of which was to do a faster, harder-hitting job than any similar vehicle used by the renowned Nazi Panzer divisions.

It was instantly iconic and immediately successful on the battlefield. Armed with machine guns and anti-tank guns, the protean jeep fought against attacks by tanks and supporting infantry. It protected convoys from aerial strafing with anti-aircraft guns. It ran emergency telephone lines in the field and kept communications open under attack. Equipped with a searchlight, it picked enemy raiders out of the sky so anti-aircraft batteries could shoot them down. It shuttled medical supplies to the front and brought wounded soldiers to safety. It could do almost anything, even tow bombers into take-off position on the deck of an aircraft carrier in a pinch. By the end of the war 630,000 would be built.

It was a tough bastard of a vehicle.

'I don't think we could continue the war without the jeep,' said legendary war correspondent Ernie Pyle in June 1943. 'It does everything. It goes everywhere. It's as faithful as a dog, as strong as a mule, and as agile as a goat. It constantly carries twice what it was designed for, and still keeps on going. It doesn't even ride so badly after you get used to it.'

As production ramped up, Ford and Willys lowered their prices based on volume and their prediction that the jeep could be turned into a profitable postwar consumer vehicle. That was the beginning of the end for scrappy Bantam. The small company won orders for a few thousand more jeeps, but by 1943 it was squeezed out of the running. The company that had been responsible for the first prototypes of the remarkable jeep spent the rest of the decade manufacturing small trailers before going bankrupt in 1950, driven out of business by the soaring weight of back taxes.

ᕫ

From the start, there was a quixotic plan for a version of the new jeep that could tackle both land and water. The amphibious version was intended to have the road-going ability of the regular jeep, the capacity for three men and their equipment, plus one light machine gun with 2,000 rounds of .30-calibre ammunition, and all-wheel drive.

Development began in March 1941 and took on a greater urgency with the Japanese attack on Pearl Harbor on 7 December 1941.

The job fell to the National Defense Research Committee (NDRC), established by President Franklin D. Roosevelt in June 1940 to work in strict secrecy on developing new 'mechanisms and devices of warfare'. And the first thing the NDRC did was call on Olin and Rod Stephens at the New York office of Sparkman & Stephens.

In the middle of the 20th century, there was no more powerful partnership in the world of boating than Olin J. Stephens II and Roderick Stephens, Jr., brothers who designed, built and sailed America's best deep-water yachts. They were still in their twenties when they endured gale-force conditions to unexpectedly win the 1931 Transatlantic Race in their slender 52-foot yacht *Dorade*. When they crossed the finish line off Plymouth, England, after 17 days and 2,800 miles of sailing, their nearest competitors were two days behind.

By the late 30s, Sparkman & Stephens (Drake Sparkman ran the business side of things) was a naval powerhouse. In 1937 Olin and Roderick helped design, build and sail to America's

Cup victory the slender J-class yacht Ranger. Two years later, Olin designed the Lightning, a 19-foot centreboard sailboat that's still one of the most popular boats in the world, with more than 15,000 built.

In its first meeting with Sparkman & Stephens, just a few blocks from Grand Central Terminal in New York City, the NDRC stressed the urgency of the secret project and started off with a crazy idea: what about a *triphibian*, which could drive, sail and fly? The Stephens shot that down but got to work immediately on the challenge of designing an amphibious vehicle, sketching out rough plans for a hull that could encompass the new army jeep.

By late December 1941, Sparkman & Stephens was working with Ford to refine its design, which heavily leveraged the existing mechanics of the basic jeep.

Three pilot vehicles were hastily hand-built, the last one in late February 1942, and trials began on Michigan's icy Rouge River in the shadow of Ford's massive, eponymous Rouge River factory complex. Production began later in the year.

The new vehicle was called the Ford GPA, with the A standing for amphibious. Under their sheet-metal skins, the new amphibious jeep and its land-bound cousin shared the vast majority of their mechanical components, from their 134-cubic-inch, four-cylinder engines to their 16-inch, six-ply tyres. Even the cockpit looked pretty much like that of the basic jeep, except it had a greater profusion of levers. Like the basic jeep, the GPA had a transmission shift lever on the floor – three forward, one back. A high and low shift lever, the latter used for slower going. A front-axle engaging lever, for four-wheel drive. And a handbrake lever on the dashboard.

To these the GPA adds a few more: a winch control for the capstan on the bow and two shorter levers near the shift lever – one to engage the propeller and the other to engage the vital bilge pump.

By late 1942, word of the amphibious jeep started to leak, even though it was supposed to be a secret project. But it wasn't until 9 March 1943 that Ford was allowed to officially announce that the GPA had gone into high-volume production at the company's River Rouge Plant. Photos of the unusual jeep were now approved by the military censors, and a few appeared in newspapers. There were GPAs on patrol in Tunisia, looking tiny and fragile against dark blasts of dirt blown skyward by enemy bombs, and GPAs covered in netting, serving as make-shift camouflaged ambulances somewhere in North Africa. A young army photographer named Norman Harrington wrote home about a harrowing experience in a GPA after Operation Torch, the British–American invasion of French North Africa in November 1942. He'd been riding in the back of one when a sniper shot the driver in the head, killing him instantly. Harrington lunged forward and grabbed the wheel while an officer in the passenger seat stomped on the accelerator, and they sped away as more shots flew past, the GPA struggling to hit 60 miles per hour.

But the truth was that few GPAs ever made it to the battle-field. In July 1943 the vehicle saw its most notable amphibious use during the Allied invasion of Sicily, but by then its produc-tion had already been discontinued. When the GPA was mentioned in American newspapers it was usually a story about its use on domestic rescue missions during river floods, or its appearances in small-town parades, or its accidental sinking during training exercises. The brief burst of excitement around its introduction quickly dissipated. In 1944 the army issued a technical bulletin explaining how you could scavenge axles from the unloved GPA and use them for a standard jeep.

∽

I had to see a GPA for myself. Of the nearly 13,000 built during the war, fewer than 100 are still drivable, and of those, only 20 or so have been restored to their original condition. But incredibly, after a few days of emailing experts, I discovered that a GPA was parked in a driveway just 15 miles from my home in northern New Jersey.

And it wasn't just any GPA. Considered by some to be the single best remaining specimen in the world, Ford GPA serial number 1359 was restored over several years by David Welch, one of the top military restorers in the United States. Dave has a big walrus moustache and the quiet confidence of a guy who's lived. He studied psychology and spent a few years dividing his time between Oregon and Alaska, cutting firewood and working ski patrol. Then he came home to New Jersey, started a tree company, ran it for 35 years, retired a few years ago, and threw himself into his passion: restoring military vehicles.

As a member and eventual president of the Military Vehicle Preservation Association, Dave became fascinated by amphibians. And it's his Ford GPA, discovered in a Wisconsin barn, that most excites him these days. Dave calls the GPA 'a collectible home run' because of four things: it's a jeep, it's a Ford, it's amphibious, and it can fit in your driveway.

And it's incredibly rare.

Dave's GPA never left the United States. 'It was used in the Great Lakes for training, then it was used by Minnesota Fish, Game and Wildlife, then by a resort,' he says. Eventually a collector bought it, locked it up in a barn and apparently forgot about it. By the time Dave found it, the jeep was mostly rust. 'The jeep was original and straight, but there was a hole in the bottom so big you could drop a 55-gallon barrel straight through it. My restoration took about four and a half years and close to 3,000 hours.'

Today, parked on the grass in front of his house under soaring trees, Dave's GPA looks like it just rolled off the assembly line.

It's bigger than I expect, clad in a special matte olive drab paint with a big white star painted on the side, obviously military but surprisingly elegant, both timeless and an artifact of its time, industrial-age steel riding on brawny lugged tyres. The cockpit is a profusion of mechanical knobs, switches and analogue gauges.

Dave gives me a walk-around. He points to where Ford subtly stamped its name on the jeep, a script logo on a pintle towing hook in back and a script F on bolt heads. He shows me the registration number painted on the bow in a curiously light blue paint against the matte olive drab. The blue against green, he explains, wouldn't show up in black-and-white photos taken by the enemy, so they couldn't extrapolate from registration numbers how many we were building.

He points out a sloppy, rough seam above the left rear wheel. 'My dog Honey can weld better than that,' Dave grouses, and inside you can see spatter from other welds, a testament to the speed with which the jeeps were rushed down the assembly line. Military vehicles like this were built fast for short, dangerous lives.

But their bones were strong. During its development the underlying jeep had been subjected to the army's brutal Holabird Test Course in Baltimore, Maryland. 'That test course tortures a truck like an Inquisitional rack, and if a truck has anything to confess, it confesses,' said a Motor Transport officer at the time. Vehicles often came away from its rugged roads, steep 65-degree hills and sand courses with bent frames, broken springs and burned-out transmissions.

We climb carefully into the jeep, Dave pointing out a small step on the side and showing me how to swing my legs in without putting undue stress on any of its thin metal panels. He takes the driver's seat, turns the ignition key, presses the starter button with his foot, and the GPA comes to life with a rich rumble. On a winding road to a petrol station the wind blows through our hair, a woman in a Mercedes smiles at us, a guy in a Honda gives the thumbs up. 'People sometimes follow me home!' shouts Dave with a grin.

Everyone who knows amphibious vehicles knows about Ben Carlin, and as we chug up a hill Dave talks about Ben's mechanical prowess over the roar of the engine. He wonders aloud if Ben went to sea because the jeep was something he could control, something he could master. That's an interesting word to associate with Ben, *control*, one that comes up again and again, and it makes sense. Dave's also heard the story about Ben doing a complete valve job on the jeep's engine in the mid-Atlantic, a tale that's become legend among the tight community familiar with the GPA and Ben's journey. 'A valve job is hard enough on a workbench,' he says, and true respect comes through.

The ride is smoother than I expect, the rumble gentler. The GPA is about 700 pounds heavier than the basic World War II jeep, and that makes it more comfortable because the extra weight loads its springs and gives it a less bouncy ride. Its top speed, says David, is about 55 miles per hour, but we don't pass 30 or so on the two-lane roads of small-town northern New Jersey.

David rhapsodises about the GPA. 'Everything on this jeep has a purpose,' he says, and for the third or fourth time he uses the phrase, 'form follows function'.

Except no one knew exactly what the overall function of the GPA might be. In contrast, the bigger and better known DUKW, an amphibious vehicle designed soon after the GPA, succeeded because it had a clear purpose: ferrying materials from ship to beach and bringing wounded soldiers back to the ship, which it did well. Many of the 22,149 DUKWs built during the war are still in service around the world, including those ferrying tourists along Boston's Charles River, over the Lakes of Rotorua in New Zealand and down the Thames.

In the case of the GPA, says Dave, 'The army never really spent a lot of time figuring out what its use would be.' Its mission, its reason for being, had been oddly overlooked during development, aside from a passing observation that maybe the amphibious jeep could participate in invasion and landing operations.

And so the GPA program died an early death.

A 1945 army report confirms that 12,774 amphibious jeeps were built over 18 months until production was quietly cancelled. Adding insult to injury, the jeep's high-voltage electrical system turned it into an unwitting organ donor.

The GPA had been equipped with a 12-volt electrical system, a prerequisite for a two-way radio, while most regular army jeeps had 6-volt systems. So what did the army do when it wanted to upgrade regular jeeps in the field to radio jeeps? Nearly 4,000 amphibious jeeps rolled off the assembly line only to be ripped apart and scavenged for their 12-volt electrical parts.

It was no wonder so few American soldiers ever saw a GPA in the field. Ben once observed, 'Its military uses were pretty well confined to light amphibious reconnaissance, ferrying high-powered generals and serving as bait for nurses and Red Cross girls.' He was right.

A couple of weeks later Dave sends a short email: 'Don't plan anything for Sunday.' He's going to take his GPA out on the water.

Early in the morning my seven-year-old son, Henry, and I arrive at a boat launch in eastern Pennsylvania, next to a languid, coffee-coloured stretch of the Lehigh River upstream from a dam. It's a sunny 32 degrees under a blue sky, with tall trees arching out over the riverbanks and providing shade where the Lehigh narrows.

By the time we arrive a small crowd is gathered around the jeep. Dave helpfully points out that the seat cushions serve as life preservers.

A lot of people are hoping for rides, even a guy who shows up in a brand-new Corvette, and David obliges them all. On the first couple of entries, he rolls gingerly down the concrete boat ramp into the smooth water, as you'd expect in a meticulously restored vehicle once valued at $250,000. (David shrugs at that figure, says it was inflated for publicity.) After a few more entries he starts to peacock, hitting the water fast enough to kick up a spray from the flat bow as he ploughs in.

And then it's my turn for a ride.

As soon as the bow touches the water, Dave flicks the floor-mounted propeller-engaging lever forward, power is directed to the prop, and we're motoring into the river. We make a tight turn to starboard and head past narrow Turkey Island and under the Route 33 bridge that spans the river high above.

In the sun the GPA gets hot inside, even though it's open. It's not the heat of a car on a summer day but the machine heat of an engine room, hot air blowing into the cabin from multiple vents with the tang of engine oil. The steel body absorbs heat and radiates it back at the passengers. The heat in an enclosed cabin must have been brutal.

It's much louder in the water than on land and the low-frequency vibration rumbles through your body. Casual conversation isn't possible over the roar of the engine, a barrier to communication Ben and Elinore probably didn't mind after a while.

The front seats are ample enough, but the GPA has a rear seat the way a sports coupe has one, which is to say it's a notional space, not much more than a bench. It's fine for Henry but I can't imagine curling into a 5-foot space night after night.

Just as the GPA's weight gives it a smooth ride on land, its weight and low centre of gravity give it an equally smooth ride on water, and it rolls gently over the slight wake of a fishing boat. Still, there's only a foot or so of freeboard – the distance from waterline to deck – and that's without the weight of Ben's additions.

Exiting the water is even more impressive. We glide towards the ramp, and as the front wheels touch concrete David shifts the propeller lever and we thrum back up the ramp, dripping river water and trailing green strands of invasive weeds. Later, David will give the GPA a thorough cleaning.

On a second run David motions for me to get behind the wheel. We slide around each other and switch places. I grip the thin, hard wheel, Dave adjusts the dash-mounted hand throttle that's used on water, and we surge forward. The jeep feels steady and confident. After a minute or two I turn the wheel gently left, then right, trying not to alarm Dave. It's like steering an idling ski boat. Unlike a typical boat of its size, the GPA doesn't lean into its turns but stays flat on the water. Given its slow speed it doesn't matter.

Afterward Dave gives a ride to a stranger who's been taking photos the entire time, and the jeep stalls as soon as it hits the water. There's confusion as it drifts slowly towards the rocky shore just down from the ramp. A man in a fishing boat rushes to the rescue, throws out a line and pulls the jeep to safety.

Ben endured this on a daily basis, except without anyone to throw him a line.

As I'm getting ready to leave, Dave tells me the GPA has its own connection to Australia. After the war a lot of them were 'surplused out of the military', disposed of in auctions like the one at which Ben bid on his own jeep. Eventually quite a few wound up in Australia, where they were 'bobbed', which meant cutting off the bow and stern with a blowtorch and hacking doors in the sides, leaving the owners with a ragged but rugged vehicle that cost far less than a production jeep.

But by the time the mutilated amphibious jeeps had found a new life in his home country, Ben was long gone.

CHAPTER FOUR
Atlantic Crossing

When she chugged into the North Atlantic in the summer of 1950, *Half-Safe* was loaded far beyond capacity, carrying six weeks of food, 30 gallons of fresh water, 2,300 hand-rolled cigarettes, $240 in cash, 8 gallons of oil and 880 gallons of petrol in its internal and external tanks.

The jeep rode steadily but, as always, dangerously low in the water, with her deck just 6 inches above the surface. Light winds sloshed waves over the front and back, and stronger winds in the days and weeks ahead would send the sea crashing over the entire superstructure.

Ben and Elinore had stowed as much food as possible, an assortment of canned goods and fruit juices supplemented by biscuits, raisins, dates and jars of pigs' feet. As the army had made clear during its development, the army jeep was 'in no sense a cargo vehicle but is intended for reconnaissance and liaison missions only', and the GPA had scant room for storage.

The small cabin still reeked of fuel. Elinore's stomach lurched on the first day, and almost immediately she was curled fitfully on the jeep's short bunk, puking miserably into the same old tin cup.

Two years after the first aborted departure they were barely underway. Elinore noticed the first flecks of grey in Ben's beard and wondered how long the journey would ultimately last.

Yet Ben could be forgiven for finally allowing himself some optimism as the jeep chugged through a calm sea. On the second day, a school of porpoises swam alongside the jeep for hours. The winds stayed light, the sea calm, and the jeep made a 125-mile run on the third day. On the 23rd he even got the radio to work, contacting a Halifax operator with an 'all okay' message.

Ben's daily log entries are brief and focus on navigation and addressing a ceaseless daily drip of minor mechanical problems. He recorded the direction and speed of the wind, the duration of a refuelling stop, a new noise coming from somewhere in the engine compartment.

His entry of 1 August is typical:

Sea calm all night. Wind faded at daybreak. Sky has been particularly ominous since storm but this morning is clearing. Moderate SW winds came in about 1000 – changed course to 120. At daybreak found water leak – chafed hose. 1030 No. 3 cylinder missing, changed all plugs back to AR5s; OK. Sight at 1100 incredibly good. Engine stopped 2 1/2 hours altogether. 1200 wind SW 25 changed course 105.

His innate mechanical skill was essential. Every moving system makes its own unique sound; the jeep was a mechanical symphony and Ben knew when any note was off. He was a master mechanic, so attuned to the jeep he could judge engine speed without looking at the tachometer, and when the tachometer itself started making a grinding noise a few days out of Halifax, he simply dismantled it. He stayed especially focused on the rumbling from under the floor, where the thrust bearing remained a constant worry. When a familiar boom from below shook the jeep, Ben dove overboard to tighten the nylon straps holding the jeep's fuel tank taut to its belly.

And onward they sailed.

But what was Ben thinking, driving across the Atlantic, four years gone since he'd first seen the GPA? Was there a growing awareness that this thing was consuming his life? He expressed little introspection or wonder, and by this third summer, finally at sea, the entire journey itself seemed something to be endured rather than enjoyed, something to fight, something to get past. It had taken two years simply to make a successful departure.

Nor did he say or write much about fear, but at times he must have been afraid. As they sailed further into the wide ocean Ben and Elinore were astronauts, free climbers, fools stuffed into a bobbing can, lives entrusted entirely and absurdly to a machine purpose-built to live a hard but short life, powered by an engine pushed into running for weeks on end across thousands of miles of salt water. Between them and the rage of the sea was only thin, neoprene-coated sheet metal, old rubber seals and a boxy cabin built by a man who'd taught himself navigation in a basement from a textbook, whose engineering experience leaned more towards digging pits than drafting vessels. For anyone who stopped to think about it, it was entirely crazy. Almost unbelievable. Later Ben claimed people often refused to believe him when he said he'd crossed oceans in the jeep. And if you actually saw the jeep bobbing down the Seine, or parked by a Calcutta kerb, would you *really* believe? Or would you think it a stunt, a practical joke, the idea of this hard-drinking Australian and his seasick wife sailing the oceans in what a friend called an 'absurd contraption'?

The press scrambled to understand the meaning of the trip. Publicist Ware Lynch was out of the picture, and there was no more mention of Ben working on behalf of SAFE, so it was left to friends and relatives to explain things. The newspaper articles were shorter now and the Carlins no longer front-page news in this third summer of attempted crossings. Elinore's brother Domenic, now an editor for the CIA, told the *Washington Star*, 'Maj. Carlin said he wanted to go to India to collect some army pay. I think he's doing it the hard way. I don't know much about the trip. They just wanted to go around the world, I guess.'

Toward the end of July, near the 40th parallel, the wind picked up and *Half-Safe* rolled over a big sea. Ben hove to and streamed the sea anchor, and without heat from the engine the cabin grew chilly and damp. *Never been so cold, wet and uncomfortable*, Elinore wrote in one of the seven journals she kept during her travels with Ben. *Chilly, cheerless, choppy as hell. Can't read or eat or sleep. Damn the weather.*

But by the beginning of August the sea calmed, and they sailed on.

Every four or five days the nose tank ran dry and had to be refilled from 'Tillie the Tow-Tank'. It was a delicate operation:

first they hauled the cigar-shaped tank alongside the jeep, then Ben swam underneath it and attached a hose that ran from its bottom to the nose tank, and then he climbed on top of Tillie and pumped air into a valve on its top. The air pushed petrol from Tillie downward through the hose into the nose tank. And as Ben worked the hand pump he barked commands at Elinore, who made sure Tillie didn't smash into the jeep: 'Watch the tank! Watch the line! Don't let it get fouled out! Pull in the bloody slack!' The operation would have been easier with a boathook, but that was among the things they'd forgotten to bring.

Each time the process took hours.

On 4 August Tillie ran dry, all 270 gallons gone. The plan had been to jettison it, but now Ben thought it might make more sense to get rid of the jeep's belly tank instead, and he spent seven hours manually pumping all the fuel in the belly tank back into Tillie.

At the end of the operation *Half-Safe* had a $1,000 galvanised iron box of seawater strapped to her belly, doing absolutely no good. And it was big. Four hundred pounds empty, 10 feet long, 5 feet wide and 14 inches deep. It was a lot of unnecessary drag and, after days of consideration, on 10 August Ben decided to cut it away from the jeep and let it drop into the deep.

A light rain was falling, and it was cold, but Ben and Elinore stripped naked to undertake the delicate operation so they could keep their clothes dry.

Six nylon straps connected the belly tank to *Half-Safe*, three on each side. Ben clung to the side of the jeep to begin unfastening the straps, one at a time, while Elinore stood shark watch and kept an eye on the tow-tank.

Whatever plan Ben may have had in mind to jettison the belly tank, it didn't go the way he intended.

He'd released three of the straps when a sudden *boom!* shook *Half-Safe* and she pitched violently to the right, listing precariously at 30 degrees. When the jeep seemed to have stabilised, Ben dove to see what had gone wrong. The attachment points on the left side of the jeep had corroded and given way, and now the bulky belly tank hung vertically from the right side of the jeep by its two remaining straps, pulling downward with a force of several hundred pounds. At least there was no visible damage to the bottom of the jeep.

Ben shouted for a knife and dove under the jeep to sever the remaining straps, one after the other. As soon as he hacked through the second one the tank fell free and *Half-Safe* lurched back into a horizontal attitude. He stayed underwater as long as he could, watching in fascination as the boxy tank knifed downward into the blue-black, falling vertically until it was the size of a matchbox and then levelling out to plane off into the unseen, leaving Ben struck by the *terrifying awful finality* of its disappearance.

The operation took eight hours. When it was over Ben fixed their location as 40°41′N 41°50′W, or about halfway between Halifax and the Azores. About as far from anything as you could be, surrounded by an immensity of blue on even a world map, the Azores still 500 miles east south-east. For only the second time since leaving Halifax, they broke out a bottle of Scotch.

The jeep was easier to control without the belly tank, and its tyres, now more exposed, even served as crude fins to keep her on track. Oddly, however, the loss of the tank didn't make her any faster.

The weather here was unpredictable, and they had no way of making a forecast because, amazingly, the jeep lacked a simple barometer to measure atmospheric pressure. Cold gave way to heat again. Mid-August brought hot, glassy days as the little jeep rumbled slowly across a dead calm and the temperature rose to a humid 37 degrees in the hothouse cabin. Ben and Elinore began to stink, but somehow they'd neglected to pack soap. The toilet beneath the passenger seat was basically a tin chamber pot, so they hung over the back of the jeep instead.

As days and weeks passed, churning slowly across the vast sea in the tiny jeep, Ben and Elinore fell into a routine borne of two summers of failed attempts, taking turns at the wheel – two hours on and two hours off – staring at the compass until their eyes stung with salt. They inhaled an endless chain of cigarettes. Ben shot their location with a tiny pocket sextant he'd bought for $17.50 at a pawnshop in Washington, DC, and when the sun was hidden by clouds or fog he relied on dead reckoning, which means estimating your current position based on where you started, how fast and far you've travelled, and in what direction, taking into account things like wind and current.

They drove through day and night, rarely speaking, maddened by the monotony. They had only a few books with them, including Thor Heyerdahl's *Kon-Tiki*. Ben had become obsessed with Heyerdahl's 1947 Pacific journey on a balsa raft, which was supposed to prove long sea voyages could have connected distant cultures with basic technology thousands of years ago. Although Heyerdahl did demonstrate that such voyages were possible, his migration theories have little credence today.

They saw ships every few days, sometimes on the horizon, sometimes only a mile or two away, but never tried to signal them.

Midway across the Atlantic, Ben hallucinated that he was sailing over a Persian carpet that stretched to the horizon.

On the best days *Half-Safe* made 3.5 knots, around 4 miles per hour, the speed of a brisk walk. Sometimes Ben turned off the engine and they swam in the ocean to rinse the sweat and grime from their bodies, strangely oblivious to the terrifying miles of water below. The damp labels sloughed off all their cans of food, rendering the contents a mystery, and some days they ate syrupy fruit salad three times in a row. With blankets permanently wet and encrusted with salt, they developed raw sores from sitting so long in the same position. The 5-foot bunk provided little more comfort than the front seats.

The jeep suffered too, and by 17 August it was showing the strain, its engine *rapidly getting worse.*

As usual, it was the exhaust valves.

In an internal-combustion engine like the Ford GPA's four-cylinder power plant, petrol is mixed with oxygen in a combustion chamber, and the resulting mixture is ignited by the hot spark of a spark plug. This creates a gas that rapidly expands, pushing against a piston in the chamber. The linear motion of the piston is converted to rotational motion by the crankshaft, which, to keep things simple, is what turns the wheels – and, in the case of the GPA, the propeller too.

When the piston moves back upward to expel the exhaust from the burned petrol, an exhaust valve opens to let it out. But the marine environment in which *Half-Safe* operated created chronic problems. The engine ran for hours on end at a constant speed, which led to carbon build-up that made engine valves stick, which made the engine run poorly. Thus the entire trip was plagued by the need to open the engine to strip off the build-up, sometimes as often as every week or two. And it wasn't as simple as opening a hood. After the modifications to the jeep the engine could be accessed only through a 30-inch-square hatch, and each time the engine needed work Ben had to lean over the dashboard and contort himself through this opening into the engine compartment. It was grinding, gruelling work.

They had been at sea for 29 days. While working on the engine, Ben casually mentioned that they should be seeing Flores Island soon, as if they'd simply taken a weekend drive and he expected to see a landmark over the next hill.

And when it appeared, a tiny dot in the vastness of the mid-Atlantic, it was exactly where Ben had expected it would be. Elinore told a friend:

> Even remembering he'd learned his navigation in one week's reading out of a textbook, it never occurred to me to doubt it. Flores duly appeared the next afternoon and finally we'd completed the first lap of the Atlantic, after 3 years of effort and frustration. He reacted simply; he'd been expecting to reach the Azores in an amphibious jeep; he wasn't at all surprised. And, looking back, I can't say I was particularly surprised. It had only taken longer than was originally anticipated.

But with Flores on the horizon, after nearly a month of sailing, Ben decided to keep going. He was determined to reach Fayal, the next island over, another day or two to the east.

Even though she was in awe of her husband's navigational abilities, Elinore was furious at his lack of empathy.

Today settles it – the Azores are the end of the road for me, she wrote in frustration as Ben stuck to a course that would take *Half-Safe* past the southern edge of Flores.

But as Ben worked he realised it wasn't just deposits on the valves. Water was spilling into the jeep from a new leak in the deck ahead of the windshield. The heat turned the cabin into a sweltering hothouse every time the wind died. And even though Elinore had hand-rolled thousands of cigarettes in Halifax, they'd each been smoking 40 a day. After three weeks Elinore was smoking them a third at a time to make them last.

That evening, covered in oil, his knuckles bleeding from the hard work in the tight engine compartment, Ben gave it some thought and, for once, changed his mind. He swung back around to the north-east and set a course for Flores, the westernmost island in the archipelago, the westernmost point of Portugal and, you could say, the westernmost point of Europe.

A hard chop buffeted the jeep all night, and he knew he'd made the right decision. Elinore was ecstatic. Despite her hardships she wrote to Ben's sister, Jess, that *as far as I am concerned F.B.C. now stands for First British Christ – he just about performed every miracle in the book but parting the sea and walking on water.*

It took another 24 hours to reach Flores, the engine dying intermittently on the way. During the night they kept a lighthouse in view, and on the morning of 19 August, after 32 days at sea, the small amphibious jeep chugged around a seawall into the tiny harbour of Lajes das Flores, a village on the south side of the island.

A crowd gathered and people asked where they'd come from.

'Canada,' replied Ben, as if it was the most natural thing in the world. He'd been waiting two years to say it.

Half-Safe was only halfway across the Atlantic, only a fraction of the way around the world, but Ben had proven it could be done. The little Ford GPA had crossed nearly 2,000 miles of ocean. Ben's modifications had held up, and his navigation had brought them to exactly where they were supposed to be.

It was a huge milestone. Even though they hadn't yet crossed an entire ocean, even though the African coast was still a thousand miles to the east, they were in the news again. Page one around the world. Just when weeks of radio silence had everyone fearing the worst again, assuming the adventurers lost at sea, they'd arrived, dashing and insouciant, more interested in the local wine than talking about their adventure.

World Jeepers Safe!

Azores Welcomes Carlins!

Amphibious Jeep Reaches Azores!

Lajes das Flores was a cluster of simple whitewashed stone houses with red tile roofs and gardens in the back, a riot of wildflowers everywhere, the surrounding hills covered in hydrangea and cow pastures. Ben donned a beret and a pair of old white shorts from his prewar days in Peking to make a proper impression, and Elinore checked her lipstick, and they staggered off the jeep into a gathered crowd and a town so small there were no hotels or restaurants. It was hard to stand, and disconcerting to be on solid ground.

Soon a man named Senhor Soares, who spoke almost no English, led them up a steep, narrow cobblestone lane in the pouring rain, climbing to his family home. He insisted they strip off their wet clothes, take hot baths and sleep on his straw mattress in the only bedroom. Almost no one else spoke English either, but Ben had picked up enough Portuguese during his service on the *Armoricain* to get by. He had an astonishing natural facility with languages.

They stayed for a week, recuperating, making repairs to the jeep and being fed and feted until the town's electricity flickered off at 11.30 every night. After a month of thirst and canned food, Elinore's journal entries focused obsessively on the extraordinary meals the Soares family served them. At one lunch it was *tomatoes, eggs, cold meats, onions, etc & of course bread & butter – wonderful dark bread . . . followed by steak & eggs (2) & french fries & bread & butter & cheese & biscuits & jam & red table wine & port. We ate everything in sight & it was beautiful.*

On the morning of 26 August they sailed out of the harbour for Fayal, 126 miles to the east. It was an easy two-day sail. As they approached the port town of Horta, Fayal's main town, a motorboat sped out to meet them, bashing across low waves in the morning haze. To Elinore's slight dismay, a half-dozen men shouted out a raucous familiar greeting from the boat. Ben had met them all the preceding winter while crewing the *Armoricain* – engineers, whalers, raconteurs – and they were all ready to dive back into a barrel of booze at the town's legendary Café Sport with their old Australian friend.

A throng of islanders greeted the weary travellers as heroes with a rousing ovation, an exhilarating homecoming for Ben, who drank red wine until sunset, taking a break only when he remembered the jeep was still tethered in the harbour and went back to drive it up a beach.

The exhausted Carlins stayed on Fayal for a month. There were drunken dances where the locals cleared the floor for their esteemed guests, and Killer Carlin stumbled without grace across the floor.

That low, potato-eating Australian bastard is completely inept at dancing when sober, and when drunk his ability reaches a new low, said Elinore, but she was happy, and she was immensely proud of what Ben had accomplished. *The local Portuguese are mad about Ben – you have no idea of the respect and almost admiration they have for the beast*, she wrote to Jess. They befriended almost all of the island's British and American residents, most of them in some way attached to companies that managed and maintained the undersea communications cables that have connected North America and Europe since the 1850s. That meant even more dinner invitations and lazy afternoons at Café Sport, where locals dropped in, even if they weren't going to order anything. In between social obligations Elinore napped on the black sand beach or caught up on correspondence from a verandah looking out over the ocean towards the soaring 7,713-foot Mount Pico, 15 miles away. They stayed first with the acting British consular agent Brian Moorhouse, and then the Sociedade Amor da Pátria Masonic lodge opened its doors and gave them a place to stay. The Fayal Coal & Supply Co., which refuelled passing steamships, offered its repair facilities, and the general manager refused to accept payment.

Someone else always picked up the bill.

They got not one but two tours of the whaling factory, where 70-ton carcasses were dragged out of the sea and hacked apart by barefoot men who trudged through pools of blood. They were shocked both by the smell and the volume of oil that poured forth.

When asked about their plans they said they were in no rush; they thought they might stay in Horta until Christmas. Why not?

Ben became synonymous with Café Sport, where he ate a free lunch every day before working on the jeep, then returned a few hours later to begin drinking. Someone was always offering *um copo* at the café, even during the day, and Ben never said no.

Later on, when it was time for *Half-Safe* to leave Horta, Ben asked for the bill. Owner Henrique Azevedo hesitated, made excuses, didn't want to charge anything for a month of booze and cigarettes. When Ben pushed, Henrique jotted down some numbers and reluctantly handed Ben a bill for $13.

The café is still open, still accommodating transatlantic sailors behind its blue façade on the waterfront. Its third-generation owner, José Henrique Azevedo, still remembers tales of the Australian adventurer who spent so many afternoons in its cool interior, and is proud that Ben spoke 'very good words' about his grandfather.

After two years the Australian major and his amphibious jeep were getting more consistent media attention. *Life*, which had been there from the start, had lost its opportunity to really break the story, so its editors decided it was now or never, and the magazine ran its first and only feature about the Carlins' Atlantic crossing, without waiting to find out if *Half-Safe* would reach Africa. The short feature appeared in the 20 November issue, a three-paragraph summary of the crossing as far as the

Azores that emphasised the previous four failed attempts and Elinore's constant seasickness.

'Very peculiar,' said Elinore. 'Facts distorted and sometimes simply untrue.' Ben just called it an embarrassment.

Despite the drinking and social whirl, Ben managed to get work done. He ordered spare valves and gaskets from the US Air Force base on Terceira, the next island over. He rebuilt the exhaust system so that it went straight up through the jeep's cabin and out its roof rather than simply poking out in front of the windshield, where it had been more exposed to the elements. And he discovered a badly balanced section of the prop shaft that was sending a vibration through the jeep. A maintenance engineer at Western Union put it on a lathe and straightened it out.

They planned to leave Horta by 6.00 pm on 28 September. A crowd of friends kept bringing drinks to the waterfront until 9.00, and then someone arrived with a cake, and then bottles of champagne appeared. It was nearly midnight before *Half-Safe* chugged out of the harbour, bound for Terceira, 88 miles away. Ben passed out on his first watch and Elinore drove through the night, happy to let him sleep.

In the morning a US Air Force B-17 flew low over the jeep – on a reconnaissance mission, they would later learn, to take photos of the jeep that would help identify it in the case of a future rescue mission.

Ben aimed for a rotating aircraft beacon and *Half-Safe* reached Terceira in 26 hours, sailed into the harbour at Praia and tied up at a narrow dock, once again in pouring rain. Ben recalled the reaction of an American private, the first person to show up from the nearby Lajes Air Base:

'Just got in? Come by plane?'

'No . . .'

'Come by ship, huh?'

'No . . .'

'Howdja come?'

'In that,' Ben replied, pointing at *Half-Safe*.

'What is it?'

'Well, it's an amphibious jeep.'

'Uh-huh.'

Ben and Elinore stayed at the Officer's Club of the US airbase, stocking up at the commissary, giving talks about their adventure at the base school and answering tough questions from the young crowd – 'What would you do if a whale ate you?' A radio technician checked out the jeep's radio and couldn't figure out why it continued to give Ben so much trouble, but just to be sure he loaned Ben a bright yellow Gibson Girl – a waterproof emergency transmitter powered by a hand crank.

The British vice-consul asked for Elinore's passport and was shocked to hear she'd never got around to getting one before leaving the States. The American consul in turn insisted she put in an application immediately, but that would take three or four months.

They are agog as to how I shall get on in the interim, Elinore told her brother. *I shall probably do just that – get on.* As they always did. By now she and Ben had the sense things would just keep working out.

A week later *Half-Safe* sailed to Ponta Delgada on the southern coast of the island of São Miguel, the last and largest stop in the Azores. It was an easy 100-mile jog in 28 hours, and when they arrived at dusk church bells were ringing and the port captain, the press and a curious crowd were waiting anxiously to see them. They checked into the art-deco Terra Nostra Hotel, $3.50 a day for a room and meals. Oxford-educated owner Vasco Bensaude took pity, let them stay for free after their first two weeks and opened up his workshop to let Ben do more work on the jeep's propeller shaft. (Today, a room at the Terra Nostra runs about $200 a night and you can order lunch cooked over volcanic steam, but it's extra.)

Around now came the first hint that something was happening to their relationship. *I have a boyfriend of sorts*, Elinore wrote cryptically in a letter to her brother. *A gay young bachelor with plenty of escudos.* She said they stormed around São Miguel in his roadster, stirring up gossip, but it cheered her up and took her mind off . . . what? It wasn't yet clear.

Ben too had a wandering eye on the island. *Ma Reynolds. Dear Jesus. What a shocker*, he wrote to a friend, and *those Payne women . . .* In the eyes of the world press theirs was a great romance borne of a shared passion for adventure – the rugged Australian major and his adventurous, stereotype-smashing American wife – but there had been few hints of true romance since Ben's lonely letters from Halifax during their two winters apart.

Their finances weren't any better. Ben had always planned to help pay for the journey by exhibiting the jeep. Now he had a chance to try. He parked *Half-Safe* in an empty seaplane hangar, out of sight of the general public, and made $43 from a curious crowd the first day. Interest waned the next day, and by late November things were again grim.

It was time to move on.

They pushed off into a dead calm at midnight on 10 November. High pressure dominated, and although the hurricane season had been active it had just 13 days to go. Everything felt perfect. It was 520 miles to the island of Madeira, the last stop before Africa.

A little rain fell the first night and Elinore was sick as usual, but the engine was rumbling smoothly and they could make the leg in a week. Ben felt confident enough the next afternoon to nap under a clean blanket on the bunk while Elinore held the jeep on a course of 150 degrees. There was nothing but open sea ahead of them.

It was dark when Elinore shook Ben awake. He came to quickly, felt it before he heard it, a low moan keening up from somewhere beneath the seats. He stopped the jeep, streamed the sea anchor and traced the worrying sound to the propeller shaft thrust bearing, which was warm to the touch. That meant too much friction. Something was wrong.

As Ben crouched over the inspection hatch in the floor, examining the bearing, he heard Elinore shout from outside. More trouble: the towrope was tangled around the propeller. A little while later Ben thought she'd freed it, and he restarted the jeep's engine to test the bearing. As soon as he let his foot off the clutch the propeller spun, winding in the rope and yanking the big tow-tank towards the jeep, where it bashed into the hull with an alarming *thud*. Ben crawled out, cut the tank free and retied it with a spare line, and made Elinore dive in to hack the old line free of the propeller. That was enough for one day, and they went to sleep.

Sometime during the night the sea anchor disappeared.

Everything wrong to hell, Elinore wrote the next day. They turned back to São Miguel.

After a series of delays, and with a new sea anchor donated by the port captain, they left Ponta Delgada again on 18 November. A moderate wind was blowing and the troublesome thrust bearing was running warm. But otherwise things seemed good. The sun shone, and three days out they shared tamales and chocolate for dinner. When the towrope wrapped itself around a wheel and Ben kicked Elinore overboard with a splash to untangle it, it seemed more playful than mean-spirited.

On the other hand, they were making lousy time, with nearly constant headwinds from the south-east.

Things got worse very quickly.

November 22 was *a bastard of a day & night,* Elinore wrote, with the shifting wind making it hard to maintain a straight course and the engine dying sporadically as the jeep bounded over the waves.

Shortly after midnight on the sixth day out of Ponta Delgada, the seas broke into confusion and a beam wind, blowing at a right angle to the jeep, strengthened to a fresh gale force of around 40 miles per hour. Waves battered the thin side panels. The tow-tank bobbed dangerously and required constant vigilance in the black of night.

Ben streamed the sea anchor to stabilise the jeep, and as the waves got bigger he set out the oil bags to quell the surface around her. In the process he accidentally tore down the radio antenna and had to rig a replacement made of extra wire, a boathook and a glass jar that had once held pigs' feet.

The jeep kept getting pounded harder and harder, and while trying to fill an oil bag in the tight confines of the dark cabin even Ben got sick, the sudden nausea hitting him so fast he couldn't clamber out of the jeep. He vomited all over Elinore.

Every time they opened the rear hatch seawater poured in. Elinore was thinking about the safety of the inflatable rubber life raft strapped to the jeep's roof. Ben wasn't sure how many hits the cabin could take.

Later that night Ben poked his head out of the upper hatch to look around, and under a full moon enough light filtered through the clouds to illuminate a surprising amount of debris floating around the jeep. With shock he realised it wasn't debris at all; it was the entirety of their emergency gear – their only safety net – ripped from the roof by wind and waves and by a stroke of luck still floating in tight formation with the jeep. In a horrified panic Ben stripped off his clothes and dove into the dark sea to recover it all, piece by piece, struggling desperately in the waves under the silver moonlight in the middle of the vast ocean.

By 26 November they were nowhere near Madeira and conditions were getting even worse. A wave ripped the spare tyre from the back of the cabin, and then they lost the sea anchor. Ben sewed a new one from the jeep's sail, which he almost never used anyway. *Magnificent as long as it lasts!* he wrote. The old canvas began coming apart 18 hours later as a freshening gale blew like hell. They were getting low on biscuits and everything was rotten damp, with water dripping constantly down the interior of the cabin from condensation.

Very unpleasant day.

Day by day they hoped for conditions to improve. They ached from being cooped up immobile in the cabin, and they were filthy. Elinore kept throwing up. She read *Kon-Tiki* for the second time and gave it to Ben, who read it again without comment. The cabin was warm only when they ran the motor to charge the batteries to power the radio, but they still had a hard time making contact with Ponta Delgada when they transmitted every day at 1100 and 2300. They could barely make out the weather reports, although they were able to tune in the BBC with remarkable clarity and heard the alarming news that President Truman was considering using the atomic bomb in Korea, which seemed very far away.

By the start of December *Half-Safe* had been hove to in foul weather for nine days. Ben and Elinore took turns pumping out the sloshing bilge by hand every 60 minutes, the mechanical pump no longer working. Ben pencilled a growing list of leaks in his log:

Leaks in deck aft.

Leaks around exhaust.

Leak below starboard windshield.

After which he scrawled a reminder to *sharpen pencils*. He was writing down a lot of problems every day.

It was all they could do to keep the jeep pointed safely into the wind, and every time they used the motor to kick the nose windward they burned precious fuel. They began eating emergency rations to stretch out their canned stores.

A few days later at dusk there was a violent *snap* and *crack*, and they knew immediately the tow-tank had broken free. Ben threw open the rear hatch and caught a glimpse of the tank in the spray of waves – and then it was gone. Fortunately, it had been almost empty.

Three days later all hell broke loose. Heaping waves thundered over the jeep, submerging it under tons of seawater, testing Ben's backyard engineering. At its most furious, the storm whipped the barrier between sea and sky into an undefined haze of green spray. *Half-Safe*'s metal skin buckled with each hit, and its plexiglas windows, just 3/16 of an inch thick, flexed frighteningly under the force of the pounding waves. Failure seemed imminent. They were both acutely aware that once the jeep started taking on water faster than they could pump it out, they were dead.

They'd never even thought to buy life jackets.

The seas went absolutely mad, wrote Elinore. *We could hear the big ones coming from what seemed a long way off, boiling and hissing and churning, coming closer and closer, and then the resounding crash as the white water smashed against and over the jeep.*

They huddled in the dark, damp cabin, stale with cigarette smoke, anticipating each blow. They worried the emergency gear, including the life raft, would get torn off the jeep again, so Ben tied it all together with a rope. He then ran the rope into the cabin through the roof hatch, and they took turns gripping the end of it.

They shouted an escape drill back and forth above the howl of the storm:

'I shout out!'

'I get out and wait! You follow and grab the gear!'

'We stay in contact!'

'We stay in contact!'

But even as they shouted the plan they knew it was futile. No one knew where they were, and their chance of being discovered in the life raft was slim. They were still 260 miles from Madeira. And anyway, the raft would be ripped away by the wind as soon as they inflated it.

At that moment, in a savage coup de grâce, the engine sputtered and died. Once again Ben contorted himself over the dashboard to access the engine through its small hatch. As waves smashed over the jeep, crashing into the cabin with tons of force, Ben reached into the oily dark of the engine bay and discovered the fuel pump gasket had disintegrated and fuel was leaking over the hot engine. He worked for hours with excruciating care, taking apart the pump, cutting a new gasket from material he just happened to have onboard the jeep and reassembling it without losing a screw as towering waves and howling wind buffeted the fragile jeep.

When everything was back together Ben pressed the starter button and – *bang* – orange flame exploded from the engine compartment. Ben and Elinore thought this was finally the end, and when they'd recovered from the shock Ben crawled out into the storm to inspect the front of the jeep, expecting to see a hole blasted through its thin skin.

Half-Safe was intact. A flash of electricity had ignited a small amount of spilled fuel, but it had burned off almost immediately.

With the engine running again and disaster averted, they continued riding out the storm. They had one, maybe two days of fuel left. The engine kept stalling as water poured down the fan pipe, and it was getting harder and harder to restart it; Ben thought the starter might be jamming.

They were on their third day without sleep. Their eyes hurt. Ben tried raising radio operators at calls signs CTD and CTQ – Ponta Delgada, Azores and Porto Santo, Madeira – on the petulant radio. For his own call sign he used GO2HL. It amused him.

On each attempt Elinore stripped naked and crawled out of the top hatch onto the jeep's roof, holding the makeshift antenna aloft with one hand and the mast with the other, going out no matter how bad the weather. Ben made sporadic contact but couldn't make sense of anything through the static and howling wind.

There was one benefit to the lack of response: they had an unspoken understanding that rescue of any kind would negate everything they'd accomplished; *it meant the end of it all if we were rescued*, Elinore explained. To make sure they really agreed on this point, they took a two-person vote on 5 December as to whether they should try to contact Lajes Air Base, where they'd seen an Air-Sea Rescue plane sitting on the tarmac two weeks earlier.

Ben would later say that they'd both voted against calling for help. Through it all they were less afraid than tense and alert. They were extremely tired but unable to sleep. *Maybe we went through fear and beyond*, said Ben.

But by nightfall, calling for help was the only sane thing to do.

Half-Safe wallowed crazily, spun around her vertical axis, took direct broadside blows from the waves. The radio was wet but nothing could be done about that, and at 1600 hours, not knowing if anyone could receive him, Ben finally and reluctantly tuned the transmitter to 500 kHz – the international distress frequency for Morse code. Then he tapped out XXX. It's an old maritime distress signal, the equal of today's three calls of 'Pan-Pan', a step below SOS in urgency. It meant there was real concern for the safety of the ship, but it wasn't a plea for help. *Half-Safe* wasn't sinking. Yet.

Elinore once again clambered on top of the jeep naked and held aloft the antenna in the howling wind and spray while Ben tapped the Morse key clipped to his thigh with one hand and steered into the gale with the other.

There was no response to the repeated distress signal, nor to the Morse message AMPHIBIOUS JEEP HALF SAFE ALL OK, but their faint plea *had* been heard through the rage of the storm. The next day the Australian Associated Press sent a story over the wire:

LISBON, Dec 6: The Portuguese patrol ship *Flores* is combing a section of the Atlantic today for the amphibious jeep in which the West Australian, Mr. Ben Carlin, and his American wife, are attempting a world tour. The Lisbon marine radio reported signals from the couple around midnight, but could obtain no exact information from them. Earlier reports said the jeep was making for Funchal, on Madeira, after a breakdown at Ponta Del Gada. The reports said that Carlin had contacted San Miguel radio saying he was willing to return to the Azores, but Mrs. Carlin was not willing to head back.

I do remember thinking I must be mad to vote against the plan, Elinore admitted after they were safe. Even though Ben had finally radioed for help, she later explained, *I felt quite sure Ben wanted to go on with it*. And that was enough to keep her going.

And then it was over. The next afternoon the jeep floated in a sudden flat calm. The storm had passed.

Ben and Elinore collapsed in mental and physical exhaustion, and slept until the morning of 7 December.

Later the captain of the *Flores* confirmed that winds in the area had surpassed 70 knots at the height of the storm, agreeing with Ben's estimate; the naval patrol ship had sustained damage herself. While the wind speeds put the storm in hurricane category, there's no named storm on record for the vicinity; but in the days before satellite imagery that's not entirely unusual, and the area is notorious among sailors for its unpredictable weather.

The jeep's survival was extraordinary. During the fiercest 48 hours of the storm it had been savaged and smashed and submerged by wave after wave, tons of seawater hammering a home-built, steel-frame box on a fragile floating jeep. Even Ben, who had complete conviction in his abilities, was amazed by how well *Half-Safe* withstood the storm. Part of it, he thought, was the jeep's combination of rigid steel strength and masonite flexibility. She was a *steel fist in a plastic glove*. Part of it was how she sat so low in the water, bobbing along like a mostly submerged block of wood with minimal freeboard to take the brunt of the sea.

And, Ben would admit for the rest of his life, part of it was pure luck.

⌒

When the sky cleared and Ben took a fix, he found the storm had pushed them 140 miles to the south-west of their last known position. Between that and the disappearance of their tow-tank, reaching Madeira was impossible.

He picked up the radio microphone and contacted CTD. Could anyone in or around Ponta Delgada spare any petrol?

His message was relayed to the *Flores*, which sailed in the general direction of *Half-Safe*. Ben continued transmitting a series of Morse code Ks – *dah-di-dah, dah-di-dah, dah-di-dah* – so the *Flores* could home in on the jeep using its directional finder. On 9 December the ship steamed alongside.

Ben hitched his lines to her stern, boarded and inquired about the fuel.

The captain studied him. 'But . . . first you like to bathe, yes?'

They spent eight hours aboard the *Flores*, bathing, eating and telling stories while the crew siphoned two barrels of fuel into the jeep's tanks. As for being on another vessel, it wasn't cheating as long as they weren't moving. At 3.15, full of egg, bacon and coffee, Ben and Elinore paid $65 for the petrol, gave profuse thanks, clambered back down into the jeep and chugged onward until midnight. Madeira was 115 miles away.

Ben made a quick entry in his log the next day: *Me to sleep.*

And for some reason that was the last entry he ever made in the green logbook that had recorded every day of every attempt since 1948. Maybe it was because the journals Elinore kept were far more complete. Maybe it was because he switched to another logbook. But he *did* write something else in the log a few days and a few pages later. It was the pencilled draft of a letter to someone unknown, presumably meant to be typed up when they hit land.

In the language of the poets, the game stinks. I stink – you stink – Elinore stinks – everybloodything stinks. For the past 14 days we have been on our way, as it were, from Porta to

Funchal. For the past 14 days we have been on our fannies, as it is, from 0001 to 2400 – just going no place at all.

That was followed by a shot of jealousy at coverage of Edward Allcard, the British yachtsman who was about to set a record as the first person to sail solo across the North Atlantic in both directions, skippering a 7-ton yawl, enduring even worse conditions than *Half-Safe* on the voyage from New York City to Plymouth.

Allcard must have had quite a time but I did think the *News-Chronicle* overdid it a little in lashing him with 'six storms AND six hurricanes'. Rather windy, what!

Ben rarely voiced doubt and frustration and professional jealousy, and I wonder if the letter, written while Elinore was struggling to hold the jeep into the wind and Ben knew he'd loaded too little fuel and everything was wet and miserable, was mostly a way to exorcise frustration, to say things he couldn't admit to anyone else. Maybe he never intended to send the letter. Maybe writing it released feelings tamped down deep inside, so he could get back to work in the worst of conditions and turn his back on emotion. I don't know if he ever had it typed out and mailed.

Madeira appeared as a dark mass on the horizon late on 11 December, and *Half-Safe* followed the lights along the island's southern coast, towards the glow of Funchal. Twenty-three days after leaving the Azores, more than two weeks behind schedule, battered but moving under her own power, *Half-Safe* rounded a breakwater the next morning and limped into a harbour, the island rising rugged and green behind the main town's sprawl of red tile roofs and palm trees. Ben leaped from the jeep onto a flat-topped buoy to tie up near an Aquila Airways flying boat that ferried tourists from England. His bare feet squished into a thick deposit of seagull shit.

↶

The plan was to stay in Madeira no later than Christmas. They knew they weren't going to circle the world in a year, but they didn't want to repeat the languorous delay of the Azores. On the other hand, after two years of false starts and deprivation and suffering at sea, they were starting to enjoy their newfound minor celebrity and the comfort of life back on land.

While on Madeira the Carlins met a man who would change the trajectory of Ben's life in the distant mid-60s. Ben called him Creed, like the rest of his family did, but the man's full name was Major Charles Henry Creed Creed-Miles, and he was a 52-year-old veteran of the Royal Artillery now living in Madeira and running the family brewery. Sometimes he and his second wife, the Hollywood-glamorous Dorothy 'Scottie' Scott, sailed to Ireland where he jumped horses and she drank gin. They mostly left the handling of Scottie's nine-year-old daughter, Cynthia, the product of a first marriage to a Scottish colonel, to others.

Life on the island was a social whirl. The Carlins spent night after night drinking with Creed and Scottie and the island's dwindling British population, or floating lazily under a blue sky in the hotel pool at the Hotel Voga. One afternoon they lunched with the pianist Benno Moiseiwitsch, down from London on holiday.

Madeira was the most beautiful place Ben had ever seen, a technicolour splendour, and for a strange moment he found the prospect of returning to life in the jeep appalling. But that was okay; they had to have a new tow-tank made, and they had to find a way to pay for it, and that was enough to keep them grounded for a while.

Christmas passed, and then New Year's, with the explosion of fireworks over the harbour, and by the third week of January 1951 the collective weight of hangovers had reached a critical mass. They'd earned $166 from exhibiting the jeep at a fire station, but their hotel bill was nearing $400. By 24 January the new tow-tank was ready, and nothing was holding them back but the weather.

Then Ben got arrested again.

The way he described it, he went to bed early on the evening of 29 January while Elinore stayed up listening to the radio for weather bulletins. Around four in the morning a brawl broke out in the hotel lobby, loud enough to rouse Ben from his sleep, and he came downstairs to see what it was all about.

An hour later he was back behind bars even though he claimed he'd been completely uninvolved in whatever was happening, completely sober. He was in the same jail he'd been locked in a year earlier while serving on the *Armoricain*, and the only reason he was arrested, he said, was because a cop from that incident recognised him, presumed guilt and hauled him off.

It all sounded suspicious at best.

On 4 February, Ben and Elinore set off on the 370-mile crossing to Agadir, Morocco, the nearest African port with roads connecting it to the north. *Half-Safe* was loaded with Madeira wine, cheese, salami, ham and bread, packed on the roof in a new wicker basket. Ben topped off the tow-tank, and a crane swung the jeep out into the harbour, and a crowd waved them off after the usual series of delays.

They had a single dollar bill between them.

The wind blew hard from behind but conditions had been worse, and so it was a shock to find the tow-tank vanished at twilight the next day. A new hemp rope had given way during the night without a sound. A few hours later a huge wave crashed into the windshield and shattered the right pane, leaving its pieces held together only by the laminate film sandwiched between three layers of safety glass. It was strange, the jeep having survived far worse between the Azores and Madeira. But strange things happen at sea.

They turned back to Funchal, and Ben hocked the movie camera once again for $110 to pay for repairs. That wasn't enough to pay for a new tow-tank, so now they'd have to make an extra stop to refuel on the way to Morocco. Fortunately there was a convenient midway point, and a couple of days later they set out again on a course for Lanzarote, one of the Canary Islands off the southern coast of Morocco. It was smooth sailing on a calm sea.

The British consul in Lanzarote was alarmed that Ben planned to land at Spanish-controlled Cap Juby without asking for permission. 'I really think you should, old chap. I mean, after all, it *is* military territory.'

Ben ignored the advice and chugged out of the harbour on 21 February. The African coast was 75 miles away – an easy crossing, and the only one on which Elinore didn't throw up a single time.

They sailed through two nights and on 23 February 1951 saw a brilliant red sunrise through the haze of desert dust ahead of them. As *Half-Safe* neared the coast Ben and Elinore saw waves crashing onto an empty beach that stretched off to the north and south as far as they could see. It seemed surreal. Ben calculated that he'd hit the coast too far north, so he turned to starboard, sailing parallel to the shore for nearly 20 miles until a spit of land sprouting radio masts resolved in the distance, and when they saw the abandoned stone hulk of the old British fortress Casa Mar emerging from the sea on a stretch of reef, they knew they were in the right place. Beyond that was a brilliantly whitewashed compound with crenellated walls, an outpost in the middle of nowhere that had once served as a stopover point for Aéropostale flights from Casablanca to Dakar. Back in the 1920s author Antoine de Saint-Exupéry had been station manager for 18 months.

A rowboat approached. A Spanish officer tried to throw a towline but Ben waved him off, always declining unwanted assistance, and drove up the beach at the edge of the reddish desert that undulated endlessly east.

Half-Safe came to a stop on the hard-packed sand, and Ben and Elinore crawled out. It was chilly and cloudy, and they leaned into a hard wind. Great red clouds of sand billowed in the sky and wrapped abrasively around them.

The Spanish garrison welcomed them without hesitation, despite the British consul's warning.

Half-Safe had her wheels on African soil. Two hundred and nineteen days after leaving Halifax, they had crossed the North Atlantic in an amphibious jeep. The first part of their journey around the world, the most dangerous part until they reached the Pacific, was done. On top of that, according to some newspapers, *Half-Safe* had set a record as the smallest motorised vessel ever to cross the Atlantic.

CHAPTER FIVE

Prelude

Ben liked to say his grandfather had been born at sea to eloping parents on the long journey from England to Australia and bedded in the drawer of a chest. That wasn't quite true. His grandfather had in fact been born in London in 1847. Two years later, Ben's great-grandparents, Frederick Benjamin Carlin and Sarah Brooke Carlin, sailed for Australia on the *Stratheden*, which departed London on 6 November 1849 and arrived in Adelaide on 22 February 1850.

It *was* true, however, that three girls were born on the long journey, including the Carlins' daughter Hannah Mary. Maybe Ben thought being the direct descendant of a male Carlin born at sea better suited his personal narrative, or maybe he simply got it wrong.

Like so many others, the Carlins came to Australia seeking fortune and a new start. Frederick Benjamin Carlin spent a decade working as an ironmonger in Adelaide before moving the family to Port Lincoln, where he became a respected storekeeper, served briefly as the mayor of Norwood – now a suburb of Adelaide – and oversaw the laying of its original town hall on 23 July 1859. It was the first town hall built in South Australia.

Among his many children was a son named William Brooke Carlin, who eventually moved west and landed in the Perth suburb of West Leederville. He was a storekeeper and for a time was head of the Christian Endeavor Society at the Wesleyan Church in Fremantle.

William Brooke and his wife, Isabella, had five children, including a son named Frederick Cecil Carlin, born in 1875. Frederick Cecil joined the S.A. Railways as an electrical apprentice at 16 and spent five years learning the trade. When his indenture was complete he headed briefly to the Kalgoorlie goldfields before returning to the vocation he'd trained for. In 1898 he was hired by the Western Australian Government Railways as an electrician in the Midland railway workshops in the suburbs of Perth. Over the next 15 years his career took him from one town to another, and by 1912 he was in Northam, Western Australia, notable mainly as a stop on the train out of Perth for prospectors headed to the goldfields.

In photos taken in his thirties, the senior Carlin stares sternly at the camera, a heavy moustache obscuring the hard mouth that would make itself clear in his clean-shaven latter years. His wife, Charlotte Amelia Carlin, known to everyone as 'Lovey', is a skeletal presence, more shadow than waif, sickly and doomed with a bad heart.

Frederick and Charlotte Carlin had three children. Their first son, Tom, was born in 1901, and a daughter named Jessie followed in 1904. Then, eight years later, a second son arrived. Frederick Benjamin 'Ben' Carlin, named after his great-grandfather, was born on 27 July 1912 at the family's house on Forrest Street in Northam. Given his father's general coolness to children and his mother's declining health, it's likely that his birth was unplanned.

In 1914, when Ben was two, the Carlins auctioned off the contents of their Northam home – a bedroom suite and horse-hair mattress, a leather couch, even all the kitchenware – and moved into a few rooms in a house at 91 Blencowe Street in West Leederville. The house was situated on a corner lot, atop a hill that sloped down to Lake Monger, the site of weekend recreation and occasional drownings.

In the late summer of 1916 Lovey was weaker than ever when she wrote a letter to her son Tom, who was travelling somewhere with four-year-old Ben. 'Take care of Ben coming down, son. Don't get out of the carriage and leave him alone. Be sure to keep him warm.'

Lovey died three weeks later, on 24 September 1916. She was just 36 years old, but the *Eastern Districts Chronicle* said her health 'had been greatly impaired for a considerable period'. Family and friends were invited to a funeral at the Methodist portion of the Karrakatta Cemetery, with a recommendation that they take the 3.30 trains from Perth and Fremantle. The funeral was well attended.

In the years immediately after his mother's death, Ben suffered the dizzying one-two punch of loss followed by abandonment.

His father was unprepared to raise a young son single-handedly, and he mainly ignored the boy, though he found time to teach Ben to swim by throwing him off the end of the Rockingham jetty. He was oblivious to the need for babysitters. Years later, in a rare moment of admission, Ben described the quiet terror of being left by himself night after night in the family house, his father and older brother and sister leaving him to tremble with fear in the dim shadows and moonlight before he was even old enough to be in school.

> My mother died close to my fourth birthday. When the family went out, I was simply told to go to bed. Many, many nights I sat outside in the street, afraid to be alone in a dark house . . . and afraid of being found outside. I was so deadly afraid of the dark that I usually had no trouble keeping awake, but one night was terrible: I fell asleep, and around midnight was found sitting on the footpath with my back against the front gate. I was appallingly ashamed, not of being found asleep but of being afraid of the dark. My people were not cruel; they were simply incapable of envisioning fear of the dark. And why was I so afraid of the dark? Because my half-witted sister had filled me full of stories of bogeymen and what they did to small boys; the huge white bag carried by the Chinese laundryman was full of little boys being carried off to make chop suey.

These were the things that helped shape the man Ben Carlin would become. Abandonment. A deep shame in showing fear. Forced self-reliance.

When Ben was five, his father met Lucy Ruby Earle. She was married to a chemist named William Francis Earle, a veteran of the South African War who'd re-enlisted in 1915 and shipped off to Palestine to serve as part of the Australian Camel Field Ambulance unit, leaving Lucy to raise three daughters.

In January 1917, still raising her daughters alone, Lucy Ruby saw an ad in the *West Australian*:

LADY wishes to Let half House to soldier's wife or refined couple. 91 Blencowe-st., West Leederville

Lucy moved in with her daughters Lily, Norma and Alma.

The mourning widower Frederick Carlin and his three children were living in the other half of the house.

Earle returned later in the year with tuberculosis and a bad attitude, and spent the next two years convalescing as an inmate at the Wooroloo Sanitarium, east of Perth. When he got out he was angry and drinking heavily, and on occasion he threatened to shoot Lucy. It's unclear exactly what kind of relationship Lucy had developed with Frederick Carlin by this time, but in any case she left town, maybe to get away from Earle. She wandered through a series of jobs in the early 1920s across Western Australia, including a stint tending bar at the Royal Mail Hotel in Meekatharra, a gold-rush town nearly 500 miles north-east of Perth. Lucy was finally granted a divorce from Earle when he was found living with another woman and child. She returned to Leederville and eventually married Frederick Carlin, who now owned the house at 91 Blencowe Street.

Lucy's joining the family had a huge impact on Ben, I learned over dinner with Alison Carlin, a retired librarian, and Lynne Carlin, a fashion designer, at Lynne's home in Fremantle.

'I was under the impression that Ben's father remarried rather quickly, which was not uncommon,' said Lynne, who'd married Ben's nephew Andrew Carlin. And it was true; death in pre-antibiotic early 20th century was not uncommon. Families had to carry on, especially when there were children. But in this case there was friction.

'Ben and the stepmother didn't get on,' says Alison, who'd married another nephew, Eric Carlin.

'Oh no, they didn't,' agreed Lynne.

And so in 1923 Ben's father sent him off to become a boarding student at Guildford Grammar School, a prestigious private school north of Perth that advertised itself as 'a Secondary School, boarding and day, preparing boys for Commercial and Professional Life and the Universities'.

He was 11 years old.

For the time, it wasn't an entirely young age for a boarder. A lot of families who lived in rural farming communities and had the means would send their boys to schools like Guildford Grammar for an education that wasn't available outside the city.

Except Ben didn't live on a farm. He lived in a suburb 12 miles away from the school.

Maybe by 1923 his father simply didn't have time for him or feel capable of raising the boy without his mother. After all, Frederick Carlin's career was on the ascendant, and he'd been elected to the Perth Council, and his other two children were much older and much less demanding of his time.

Or maybe Ben was causing chaos at home.

'One of the stories I heard,' continued Alison, 'was that Ben was sent to Guildford because he was giving his stepmother such a rotten time.'

Ben's resentment had manifested itself in growing anger, an early hint of the rage that would simmer for the rest of his life. Still, imagine being sent away at that age, feeling less important than your stepmother, a woman you feel is below your father's station, a barmaid with an alcoholic, deadbeat ex-husband and the taint of scandal. It would have been tremendously upsetting.

But Guildford Grammar gave him structure, identity, a platform for success. For six years it was his home, and it was a huge influence on who he would become.

When I visited the school for the first time on an August afternoon in 2015, a damp spell and the low sun of late winter made the campus, on the banks of the Swan River, feel quite English. Packs of uniformed students jostled along paths between ivy-covered buildings, past the hundred-year-old Gothic Chapel of St Mary and St George. On the chapel's roof I saw a faded red cross, a reminder of three months during 1942 when the United States Medical Corps took over the campus for use as a base hospital, a precautionary move in case war spread into the Antipodes.

Until the 1890s there wasn't much demand for superior secondary schooling in Perth. If you wanted your kids to have an education based in the classics, or wanted to better prepare them for university, you'd send them to Adelaide or Melbourne for a proper education. But as Western Australia's economy and population grew, so did the need for a school that could prepare locals to compete with the better-educated immigrants arriving in droves. And so in 1896 Guildford Grammar School was established, modelled after the English system of elite, fee-paying public schools, with a focus on a liberal education emphasising classical languages and humanities, athleticism and disciplined competitiveness.

It was an outpost of the British Empire, buildings of dark wood and red brick covered with Virginia creeper, an establishment, in the words of author David Malouf, 'devoted to the making, through classical studies, music, sport, and very British notions of manliness and public service, of young men'. Many of the teachers were recruited from England and spoke in cultured accents the boys learned to imitate. Years later, Ben's accent was hard to place, stiff-jawed and vaguely continental, more British than Australian.

Ben resisted the discipline and rigour the school tried to impose, but he must have known they would prepare him well for life and set him apart from others.

Years later a schoolmate remembered that Ben 'had a satanic way about him, a satanic grin'. Another said he was brilliant but arrogant, 'contemptuous of people he considered fools'. Ian Bessell-Browne, a schoolmate who years later served as an executor of Ben's will, said, 'He used to drive his masters up the wall. He was a wild boy. If he didn't like a subject he'd just as likely not turn up – he'd be walking about somewhere dreaming.'

Rosemary Waller, who runs the school's archive, showed me where Ben slept outside on the dormitory's wide balcony, a wooden expanse where a line of beds under mosquito netting faced the river flats to the west, where boys could smoke without reprimand. Ben benefited from strength and power and a willingness to prey on the weaker students, and in his final year he was made a prefect in Stirling House, which meant he could mete out physical punishment on his peers, inflicting school-sanctioned canings for major infractions. One Guildford student who was a prefect around the same time as Ben in the 1920s said, 'Looking back, I think we were pretty sadistic.'

Ben grumbled about the pointlessness of the athletics that were so important to the school, but he rowed and swam and spent hours in the slow current and green glass water of the Swan River behind the school. The self-discipline and determination that later drove him onward, even though it bordered on pathological, was the product of both the 'will to win' evangelised by Robert Freeth, the headmaster during his senior year, and an innate survival instinct borne of a deep, hidden insecurity.

As Ben neared graduation, disturbances rippled through his family outside the placid campus. In 1928 Ben's father spent several weeks at St John of God Hospital for an unknown ailment, and in February 1929 he wrote to Guildford Grammar asking that Ben become a dayboy 'for financial reasons'. The school grudgingly approved.

It was odd that Ben was still in school. After all, in November 1928 he'd taken a leaving certificate exam administered by the University of Western Australia and got marks in English, Greek, Latin and French. He was officially done with his studies, and he'd done well enough to earn a Government Exhibition, or scholarship, in Latin and Greek to the University of Western Australia. Perhaps he was back for another year to take additional classes to better prepare him for university. None of his relatives could offer a reason, and there were no answers in the Guildford Grammar archives.

But he'd definitely graduated by 22 November 1929, when Headmaster Freeth wrote him a terse note: 'It has come to my knowledge that when you were visiting your old school recently you brought on to the premises intoxicants which were made available to boys now at the school.'

Ben replied promptly and proudly the next day.

'The subject of your note actually did occur,' he wrote. 'I trust, sir, that in dealing with the matter, you will remember that it was I who was entirely at fault as the prime mover and the means to the end.'

On 28 March of the following year Ben matriculated at the University of Western Australia in the faculty of law. At least academically, it seemed he had the best possible start you could ask for in Western Australia in 1930. He raced on the swim team, he took up rifle shooting, and he rowed with the Boat Club team, sitting bow position in an eight-person shell. He met a series of young women.

But he hated studying law and left after one year.

What happened next is less clear, straddling the line between fact and family lore, but the basic line is that Ben and his brother, Tom, got some money from their father and bought farms in the wheatbelt. 'It's what you did if you had money in those days,' explained Tom's grandson Michael Carlin on a call from Manitoba, where he was working as the production designer for Lasse Hallström's film *A Dog's Purpose*.

Tom made a serious go of it near Wickepin, described by the tiny town's *Wickepin Argus* in 1934:

Situated in a valley, which concentrates the wind on the town, Wickepin has for years been a dusty horror in the summer and a puddle in the winter. Hot winds laid the red dust from the main street over roofs, windows and stock, also played havoc with frocks and suits and generally leaving an atmosphere of decaying neglect.

Success on the red gravelly soil was short-lived. By 1935 Tom's 1,159-acre farm was for sale, along with its two wells and windmills, 5 miles of wire fencing and a four-room house. 'He bought the farm at a point when the wheatbelt was expanding into the sandy plain, but it was only good for a few years,' said Michael.

Ben was part of a similar farming venture, though the details are less clear. The story is that two of his partners fled in the middle of the night in the farm's truck, and Ben left the following night on the farm tractor and never returned.

He was restless, wanted to work with his hands, to live a physical life. He moved on to the desolation of the Murchison goldfields, lured by the demand for men at the Triton Gold Mine, which sat on a rich seam at Reedy, 430 miles north of Perth. Ben took snapshots of the mining town rising from the barren outback amid piles of lumber, and naked telephone poles along a dirt street wide enough to accommodate a U-turning camel train.

Men died at the mine with alarming regularity, but for Ben things went well enough until 1936. A series of disputes, sparked by boredom and alcohol, had been escalating between him and Murray Cheyne, a younger man who worked alongside him in the mine's mill. On 9 April, according to court testimony, Cheyne grew frustrated because Ben was interfering with his work. In anger, Cheyne swung a steel container at his face. Ben punched back. Cheyne lobbed the steel container at him and chased him outside with a jar of acid.

Two days later, still angry, Cheyne threw a billycan of scalding tea at Ben and ran at him with a heavy spanner. They were both briefly suspended.

The whole thing seems almost comical. Except Cheyne was smaller than Ben, less inclined to fight and afraid the violence might escalate. On Monday word reached Ben that Cheyne was planning to slip out of town. Just before midnight, Ben confronted him in front of Reedy Hall, the town's venue for everything from balls to concerts to boxing matches, and took a swing.

By the time a police constable arrived both men lay in the red dirt dripping blood. Ben thought he'd been smashed in the head by a rock. But when he reached for his face he felt a deep, ragged gash on his left cheek. An ambulance rushed him to Cue Hospital, 40 miles away, where a doctor stitched up his wound without much attention to cosmetic detail.

The constable arrested Cheyne. In the morning a man named O'Connell found a bloody knife on the ground outside Reedy Hall. Cheyne confessed it was his and was charged with assault. But when Ben stepped into the witness box in the limestone Cue courthouse two weeks later, with his head dramatically swathed in bandages, he refused to blame Cheyne for the fight or any of the bad blood between them. Instead, he said *he'd* been the aggressor, challenged Cheyne to fights, called him a 'Pommie bastard' and got both of them suspended.

It was a strange thing to do, an echo of his admission of guilt to the school headmaster seven years earlier. It was clear that Ben Carlin had decided no one would ever call him a victim, even if it meant he had to face the consequences. He alone was responsible. He determined his own fate.

The court was presided over by Colonel W. O. Mansbridge, magistrate for the northern goldfields, a man with his own connection to adventure; in 1929 he'd led the search party that found aviator Charles Kingsford Smith near the Glenelg River after Smith's emergency landing on a Kimberley mudflat.

Mansbridge dismissed the case against Cheyne. But a deep slash scarred Ben's face for the rest of his life.

Ben moved on to the Lake View and Star goldmine near Kalgoorlie. In the winter and spring of 1937 he suffered a bruised foot and a lacerated knuckle, according to the *Westralian Worker*'s monthly mine accident report, a gruesome and lengthy summary of cyanide rashes, contused eyes and amputated fingers. Ben must have wondered how in the span of seven years he'd gone from Perth's most prestigious school to risking his life to extract ore from tired mines.

And so the next year he tried to make a fresh start at the Kalgoorlie School of Mines.

Over coffee on the Perth campus of Curtin University, which today encompasses what was once the Kalgoorlie School of Mines, archivist Ursula Brimble explained why Ben, now 26, would make the choice to return to school after a seven-year absence, a school that didn't even award a prestigious degree.

'He went because that's where the action was,' she said. It was that simple. In 1938 the point of studying at the School of Mines wasn't about earning a diploma. It was a way to escape the dangerous grind of manual labour. If you had a certificate in hand that showed proficiency in a particular area, you'd have a better shot at a management position, and you'd be less likely to find yourself back on the accidents report. And while there were students as young as 15, Ben was by no means an old man among the hard-working and notoriously hard-drinking student body.

'In those days there were lots of students in their 30s and 40s,' said Ursula. Western Australia had been hit hard by the depression, and there were few jobs to be found. Except in the goldmining industry, which by 1939 had put 20,000 men to work in Western Australia.

But Ben's academic habits hadn't improved, and when his father visited Kalgoorlie he usually found him behind a pool cue instead of a desk. He cut off support, and Ben left school after one year, with passes in Mining I and Mine Sampling.

The trouble continued.

On 20 November 1938, the Kalgoorlie police fined Ben £2 after finding him at the Rising Sun Hotel after lawful trading hours. The establishment's clientele included 'women of evil fame', and the hotel, not far from the School of Mines, was subject to frequent raids and blamed for drunk drivers.

Maybe Ben was simply at the wrong place at the wrong time. After all, the proprietor argued it was one of the only places to get a drink after a long day, and could he really turn someone away if they arrived a little after closing at 11 pm?

But four months later came the last straw.

Ben was back in Perth. On 25 March 1939, a little after midnight, driving down a suburban road near his father's home, he felt a heavy thud. He stopped and turned around, peering into the dark. Two men lay on the road, their crushed bicycles beside them. One was bleeding from his head. Lawrence Chapman, a 24-year-old milkman, was hospitalised with either a concussion or a fractured spine, depending on whether the *Sunday Times* or *Daily News* got it right.

In a sworn statement Ben told the police he'd seen nothing before the impact.

Fights, fines and accidents: it was a lot of trouble for one man in a short period of time, and these are only the incidents serious enough to make the news.

Over a glass of wine before dinner, Alison tells me another story. Ben and a fellow student at the Kalgoorlie School of Mines were vying for the same girl. One night the two men were on a balcony at a dance hall, looking down at their mutual object of affection down below on the dance floor.

'There's only one way you'll get to her before me!' said Ben, or words to that effect, and he picked up his rival and threw him over the railing onto the dance floor below, where the man broke one leg, possibly both.

Trouble had followed Ben over thousands of miles across Western Australia. He kept moving, but he couldn't outpace it, couldn't escape his nature. I don't think it's any surprise that within a year he felt the need to disappear entirely. And he did.

A few weeks after the Perth accident Ben wrote a vague letter to his sister, Jess, saying he was headed to Sydney, telling her he had to 'get out and see something before he rotted'. On 27 April 1939, barely a month after hitting the cyclists, he boarded the *Westralia*, a liner bound for the eastern states. The ship pushed off from Fremantle's Victoria Quay early in the afternoon and steamed out of the mouth of the Swan River into the Indian Ocean on a warm, clear day.

The *Westralia* arrived in Sydney on 5 May and berthed at the No. 3 wharf in Darling Harbour. Twelve days later Ben was inoculated for smallpox and typhoid, though exactly how long he stayed in Sydney and what else he did over the next few months is unclear. He may have looked for work. Or he may have already had a job lined up. Sometime in the following weeks he boarded another ship that departed Sydney harbour and sailed north into the Pacific. Despite a detailed search of their outward passenger lists, the Sydney Office of the National Archives was unable to find any record of Ben's departure, but by August he was 5,000 miles from home, and he wouldn't return to Australia for another 16 years.

CHAPTER SIX

Landfall

The world's reaction to the Carlins' arrival in Africa on 23 February 1951 was muted.

The Australian Associated Press story didn't hit the wires until mid-March, and even then it was just a few short paragraphs buried deep in most newspapers. Ben had already proved *Half-Safe* seaworthy by getting to the Azores, and the brief window of calm and optimism that had followed the end of World War II was quickly closing. The news of *Half-Safe's* arrival in Africa was overshadowed by menacing headlines:

Countering Threat of Red A-Bombs.

Seoul Taken as Reds Move to New Defences.

Red Barrage Slows Yank Advance.

There were more serious things for the world to think about than a strange journey in a stranger vessel.

The one hotel in Cap Juby was full so the Spanish army gave Ben and Elinore the use of a simple bungalow with a bucket of water. That night they drank wine and ate camel steaks and fell into bed at midnight.

The usual repairs took ten days. Elinore wrote to her brother to say they'd arrived safely in Africa and apologised for sending the letter surface; they couldn't afford airmail postage. By the time they drove into the desert on 5 March, heading north towards the Strait of Gibraltar, their net worth came to $21, a bottle of 100-year-old madeira, a bottle of a cheap Azorean spirits and two cameras.

There were conflicting reports about the condition of the road to Tan-Tan, the last Spanish post before French Morocco. An American-built supply truck made the 230-mile trip every two weeks, but an overloaded amphibious jeep? The fort commandant shook his head, said he wouldn't let them travel alone and assigned a robed Berber soldier named Bessahri to ride with *Half-Safe* and guide the way.

Ben and Elinore expected a sea of sand, but as they travelled north the Sahara was mostly a bleak, rock-strewn plain, the path unclear unless you knew where you were going. *Half-Safe*, as small and insignificant in the vast desert as she had been in the sea, made just 12 miles the first day, crawling along the stony ground in first gear and ploughing in four-wheel drive over the occasional 50-foot dunes that dwarfed her. Elinore and Bessahri jumped out to push as Ben rocked the jeep back and forth each time it sank to its belly.

A cold wind blew when they stopped at twilight. Ben and Elinore bedded down in the jeep and Bessahri huddled on the ground outside the jeep, his rifle next to him, wrapped only in a single thin blanket in the lee of a ridge. Ben took pity and tossed down the canvas sea anchor for a bed and his oilskins to keep out the wind. He smiled as he drifted back to sleep, wondering if any other Berber had ever slept in the desert on a sea anchor.

A series of small desert outposts followed. They reached Tan-Tan on 7 March, crossed a barbed-wire perimeter into French Moroccan Goulimine on 10 March, and arrived in Agadir, on the Atlantic shore, on 11 March. The city was just beginning its tourism boom, hotels were rising along the beach and they'd missed the Grand Prix d'Agadir by six weeks.

The driving got easier with every mile, until they were rolling along smooth roads built by the French, and the glow of colonial familiarity obscured the nationalist sentiment simmering across Morocco. As *Half-Safe* forged forward, Ahmad Shukeiri, assistant secretary general of the Arab League, was declaring, 'Imperialists have gone from all Asia. It's Africa's turn now. It's time for every free man to say, "Leave Morocco to the Moroccans and Africa to the Africans."'

Yet in Ben's mind the native population and the colonisers were perfectly symbiotic. *I have never encountered such a healthy relation between rulers and natives as was evident in Spanish Sahara*, he wrote. *Such a fine mutual respect and genuine easy friendship.* Maybe he really did see it that way. It's easy to be judgemental from a modern vantage point.

Half-Safe raced onward along a curving coastal road, Elinore smoking Azorean cigarettes and staring out the window as hundreds of miles of surf passed on their left, the jeep hitting 45 miles per hour for the first time since leaving Halifax. They arrived in Casablanca on 14 March, driving down the wide, palm-lined Boulevard du 4ème Zouaves, past modern apartment blocks, cafés, and shops offering brass, carpets and leather goods, down to the bustling port where ships from around the world were docked.

After checking in at the British consulate to see if there was any mail waiting, Ben went to the yacht club and ran into Edward Allcard, the Englishman who'd just become the first person to sail solo across the Atlantic in both directions in his 34-foot yawl *Temptress*. A few weeks earlier Allcard had discovered a Portuguese stowaway on his boat after sailing out of Madeira. Otilia Frayao was 23, and she called herself a poet, and Elinore found her ravishing. The story made international headlines.

Ben called the shy, bearded Allcard 'strange', but their meeting sparked a Reuters story claiming they would sail together to Gibraltar. They posed for a photo on *Temptress*, smiling in the glare of the sun with Elinore and Otilia, and they were joined by the French sailor Marcel Bardiaux, who was sailing solo around the world in his own sloop, *Les 4 Vents*. It was an extraordinary coincidence, all three men being in Casablanca at the same time, and Ben wore his suit and tie for the photo. But despite the promise of an all-star adventurers crossing, nothing came of it and they all went their own ways.

'I guess the chemistry between Carlin and Edward just didn't work,' Clare Allcard told me in an email from their home in Andorra, where she and Edward – at 101 years old – were working on a book about his voyage around South America. 'I remember from way back – we've been together almost 48 years now – that Edward had been a bit disparaging of Ben as a publicity seeker. As long as I have known him, Edward has done his best to avoid publicity.'

And it was true. In 1953 Allcard had said of Ben's quest, 'It taints rather of stunt.' He and Ben were very different men.

～

During their days in Casablanca the Carlins ate and drank and shared stories with diplomats and fellow adventurers, then slipped out to the edge of the city to sleep in the parked jeep in vacant lots, eating tins of tuna and sardines for dinner, embarrassed to admit they couldn't afford a hotel. A quick exhibit of *Half-Safe* at the Place de France, a square in the city centre, drew some visitors the first day – *see the jeep that sailed the Atlantic!* – but after paying for flyers and other materials they only broke even. They were luckier in the capital, Rabat, where they caught the attention of Diana Racine, who worked at the British consulate.

'Ben Carlin and his wife arrived at the consulate in their jeep, rather tired and without any money,' recalled Diana's son Michel Racine, today a landscape architect in Versailles. His mother was immediately taken with the jeep – and even more so with its rugged driver.

Diana convinced her French husband to host Ben and Elinore for nearly two weeks at their home at 4 rue de Midelt, where *Half-Safe* jutted from the small garage out into the street.

'It was great fun for me and my young sister to have them at home,' said Michel, 'and to show the jeep to all our neighbours.'

Over breakfast one morning Diana had an idea: why not show *Half-Safe* at Rabat's annual fair? Ben was reluctant but the crowd was curious; the first day some 200 people paid

25 francs each – 10 francs for children – to get a glimpse of the jeep hidden behind a tantalising screen. Four days later they'd earned 11,000 francs. If they kept sleeping in the jeep beyond Rabat and could cadge enough free meals and fuel, the windfall might be enough to get them to Lisbon.

In Tangier they found a deserted beach and slept in the jeep in the shadow of a luxury hotel. The next day Ben sat on a stool for two hours, waiting for a cobbler to resole his only pair of shoes.

Europe lay just 20 miles away, across the Strait of Gibraltar.

A wooden ramp at a small Norwegian-owned whaling station in Ceuta, a Spanish enclave surrounded by Morocco on the north coast of Africa, offered the easiest way into the water for the crossing. Ben inched backward onto the ramp. *Half-Safe*'s tyres skidded in the whale blood and oil, and the jeep turned dangerously sideways. Ben hit the brakes and came to a slow, lurching halt. He attached a rope to the stern and let the jeep get winched down slowly into the Strait of Gibraltar, past a soon-to-be-butchered blue whale just hauled out of the water. Not until they were well out to sea did the greasy stench of offal and boiling blubber vent from the cabin. Elinore threw up anyway on the choppy ride.

The crossing took six hours against a north-west wind, and early in the evening, a few hours after passing the dramatic southern tip of Gibraltar, Ben followed the harbour police towards Royal Air Force station Gibraltar, located on the isthmus connecting the towering limestone Rock to the mainland.

He aimed for a wide seaplane ramp, but as he rumbled closer a police sergeant eyed *Half-Safe* with suspicion.

'We are going to land at the slipway!' Ben shouted from the open hatch. No response. Ben climbed back inside the cabin, hit the gas and drove out of the water as two young RAF officers joined the policeman. It was 21 April, and *Half-Safe* now had her wheels on the third continent of the voyage.

They were in Europe.

And they could see a car park just 300 yards away. Couldn't they just park there for the night and sleep? The officers conferred. It was all right for a man and a jeep, they decided, but you couldn't have a strange woman spending the night on the base.

A boarding officer filled out a pratique form that spelled out the rules. F. B. Carlin was the master of a vessel with a crew of two, it said, and would occupy the berth or mooring assigned by the Captain of the Port, and moreover would place a tin rat guard on each mooring rope to prevent the introduction of vermin to the port. On the line where he was supposed to write the name of the vessel, the boarding officer scrawled something that might have said 'Australian' or possibly 'amphibian'. One thing was sure: the vehicle might have wheels and it might be parked on the tarmac in front of him, but it had arrived by sea and that bloody well made it a boat, subject to the rules of the Port of Gibraltar. It had to go back in the water.

Ben snatched the form without looking at it and walked off to the nearest bar with Elinore.

Moments later more police arrived. 'You're to re-enter the water and go around to the regular small-boats anchorage!'

commanded an officer. It was Saturday. They could return on Monday and request permission to land.

'That is impossible,' replied Ben curtly. He was finally in Europe, and he had a beer in his hand, you see, and the small-boats anchorage was two miles away.

'May I ask what you intend to do?' the officer asked.

'We are going to drive to the public car park for the night.'

Under further questioning Ben showed driver's licences from Australia, Canada and the US – all expired. Jeep registration? Didn't have anything. Passports? Yes, he had one. Elinore still didn't.

The police ordered *Half-Safe* into the water again and threatened arrest if Ben failed to comply.

Elinore popped out of the top hatch. 'Do you provide soap and towels?' She was secretly relieved when they were detained and fed sandwiches and tea. After three hours of conferring and telephone calls to higher-ups the verdict came: the jeep could stay.

Two days later a story about 'Crazy Carlins' in the *Gibraltar Chronicle* reported that Australian-born Benjamin Carlin and his pretty American wife, Elinore, awoke in the car park the next morning to a crush of sightseers gazing through the jeep's plexiglas windows. Mrs Carlin had remarked in her lazy American drawl that 'being ashore is like being in a goldfish bowl'.

On the morning of 27 April the British naval armament ship RFA *Bedenham* exploded while unloading ammunition at Gibraltar's Gun Wharf. Ben and Elinore felt the blast that killed 13 people and shattered windows across the British territory. Later that day Ben hocked his small sextant to a friend of a friend for £10, and *Half-Safe* was on her way through Spain and into Portugal, arriving in Lisbon on 30 April. A quick stop at the

British consulate yielded a $100 check sent by Elinore's worried mother. They checked into a hotel for the first time in weeks, and Ben sent payment to Madeira to retrieve the movie camera he'd hocked. They'd never shot a single frame before arriving in Madeira, being too poor to afford film for the camera.

All sense of urgency was gone. They were taking things day by day, relying on the fascination of strangers and the odd income from exhibiting the jeep. Life in *Half-Safe* was less a journey than an existence. But in Lisbon British consul John Selwyn made all the right connections and the Automóvel Club de Portugal arranged an exhibition of the jeep at the sprawling Estoril Casino, the inspiration for Ian Fleming's *Casino Royale*. The Carlins were outrageous and exotic to the faded and exiled European royalty – 'the kings of yesterday, whose only subjects are memories,' the *Daily Mail* called them – who golfed and played tennis and drank the nights away around the casino's roulette and baccarat tables. Don Juan Carlos Teresa Silverio Alfonso de Borbón y Battenberg, son of King Alfonso XIII, heir to the Spanish throne, summoned the Carlins to dinner, climbed into the jeep and sat on the passenger seat that hid a toilet.

'You won't believe this, sir, but you are the first prince of blood I have ever seen sitting on a toilet,' Ben said from the driver's seat.

'Well, you know, we *do* call them thrones!' roared the count, a Royal Navy veteran delighted by Ben's lack of pretence. 'If you go to the Coach Museum in Lisbon, you will see there the coach of my ancestor Philip II. If you look carefully you will see under the king's seat a commode.'

'History repeats itself!' replied Ben.

A few nights later Ben and Elinore found ex-King Carol of Romania, living in exile in Estoril since 1940, gazing curiously at the jeep. Ben beckoned him into the cabin but immediately regretted it. Carol, who'd be dead of a heart attack two years later, was in bad shape, and it was embarrassing to have to help the once-king in and out of the jeep.

Then King Umberto II of Italy paid five escudos to see the jeep and invited the Carlins to dinner at *his* seaside home, Villa Italia, to learn about their adventure. He was thrilled to hear that Elinore, given a seat of honour to his right, shared Italian blood. *Calabrese!*

Ben and Elinore left Estoril on 23 May, spent the night in an olive orchard, crossed into Spain at Badajoz and spent a second night by the bank of the Tagus River near Navalmoral, where Ben swatted away mosquitoes as he bathed in the river's cold water.

⌒

When *Half-Safe* arrived in Paris a week later, she was disintegrating. Katherine Verco, a young visitor from Adelaide, was so surprised to see the clattering amphibious jeep on the Champs Élysées that she described it in a letter to her parents, Sir Lavington and Lady Bonython of Adelaide, that was subsequently summarised in the *Adelaide Advertiser* on what must have been a slow news day. 'The jeep was covered in rust, and piled high with petrol tins and water tins.'

There was a litany of very specific problems that only Ben could understand, a *broken buffer spring in the drag link* and *kingpin bearings that needed slight prior loading*, not to mention the persistent shimmy and an alarming amount of corrosion. The jeep required constant attention and the kindness of garage owners, Jeep dealers and mechanics along the way to lend him tools and make the more complicated repairs or give him a greasy bay in which to do it himself.

Half-Safe needed more, though. She needed a complete overhaul before the next leg of the trip. England held the most promise for facilities, and maybe they could finally make some real money from jeep exhibitions, even if, Ben said, they were a 'donkeys-on-the-sand' sort of thing.

It wouldn't come to that, at least not yet. In the biggest break so far, London's *Daily Express* offered to hire *Half-Safe* for a month for the extraordinary sum of £500, during which time the paper would have exclusive access to the jeep, the Carlins and their story. The paper flew Ben and Elinore from Paris to London on 6 June to discuss the deal, which came with a caveat: *Half-Safe* couldn't arrive in England until mid-August, when there would be a late-summer lull in the news cycle and the paper could use a big human interest story.

That meant killing two more months on the continent. They could do that, even if it meant their journey around the world was turning into a curving jaunt rather than a direct shot. They decided to head north into Scandinavia – when would they get to see it again?

The next two months were entirely inessential to the journey, but *Half-Safe* received its warmest welcomes and most profitable exhibitions the further north it travelled. In Brussels the jeep earned $30 a day on display at the Bon Marché department store, and after three weeks they had $320, the most they'd had since leaving Halifax. Elinore wrote proudly on 14 July that they'd been able to buy their own lunch for the first time in days. A local Goodyear dealer replaced the spare tyre lost in the North Atlantic. They drove onward to Antwerp, and Amsterdam, and more displays and more free nights in hotels and press receptions and drinks with diplomats in consulates.

One month Ben and Elinore had been sleeping in the desert, broke; the next they were the toast of faded royalty; now they were approaching something like minor celebrity status. They shared a chameleonic ability to adapt.

Except while Ben was always happy to get back on the road, Elinore was increasingly less enthusiastic about climbing back in the jeep. *More and more difficult to leave places*, she wrote, wishing she could stay a little longer, spend time with new friends, sleep another night in a soft hotel bed, visit another museum. Ben knew the nomadic and unpredictable life in the claustrophobic jeep was precisely the thing that gained him attention, and in the world's eyes he and *Half-Safe* were synonymous. Elinore on the other hand was seen less as an equal partner than a brave and loyal wife, and increasingly she knew the unasked question was, *How do you put up with this?*

She just did.

At the German border on 18 July a customs officer combed the entire jeep, kicking its tanks, crawling underneath and examining the emergency equipment before allowing it to pass. An hour later the right front wheel broke off, which Ben had been expecting, and *Half-Safe* drifted to the side of the road where he switched it out for the new spare.

They spent 11 days in Hamburg, a city still shattered by war. The local Socony-Vacuum head of public relations gave them 500 Deutschmarks on behalf of the oil company, and on 21 July the *Hamburger Abendblatt* called the Carlins the most daring people to cross the Atlantic since Columbus. Ben was a young man with laughing eyes and Elinore a graceful, feminine yachtswoman, living in a jeep cabin that resembled a cramped, colourless repair shop. The paper paid them 150 Deutschmarks to chug around the Alster River, flying a pennant with the newspaper's name, the demonstration ending abruptly after five minutes as water pooled on the jeep's floor from another unseen leak.

They were headed to Denmark when, on 29 July, Ben stopped at a police station in Flensburg, Germany, just south of the Danish border. He went inside and asked if anyone was familiar with an estate called Dallacker or a man named Willy Plath, a *Korvettenkapitän* in the German Navy during the first war, who must be nearly 80 years old now?

Armed with vague directions, he drove down a series of winding cobbled streets as the sun went down, getting further directions from a man on the street – *ja, Kapitän Plath* – who directed them south through Süderbrarup and down a series of narrow dirt roads winding towards the Schlei, an inlet of the Baltic Sea surrounded by farmland and villages.

The roads got worse and Ben felt a leaf spring break with an alarming *crack*, but he continued slowly into the dark, Elinore shining the jeep's spotlight ahead of them. At 10.30 a huge villa appeared in its beam, high on the banks of the Schlei, the grounds unkempt and overgrown.

An old couple appeared at the door, curious about the late-night arrival but not afraid. And then they heard the name.

Carlin. Kapitän Plath stood a little taller, and he and his wife invited Ben and Elinore to come in.

The four of them retired to a formal sitting room and sat in worn chairs surrounded by dusty artifacts from around the world. A bronze figure of Hermes, an ivory-inlaid table from China, every free surface cluttered with miniatures. They drank a bottle of Macon. The old officer and his wife listened to stories of Ben's travels and showed a photograph of their son Fritz in his Nazi uniform and sighed; he'd been killed somewhere on the Eastern Front during the war, no one knew quite where. Their daughter Getrude had remarried, they said, was living in Reno and had two daughters, but they didn't hear from her very often.

And then *Kapitän* Plath apologised that he couldn't offer them a bed, but he and his wife shared the house with 28 refugees from the Eastern Zone. All of the family wealth had been lost during the war; even his military pension had stopped. Ben and Elinore went out into the warm night and slept in the jeep.

Ben had never met the old German couple, but he had once been their son-in-law. It was a marriage further back in time and far away, when Ben had first tried to reinvent himself far from Australia, a marriage even his own family knew almost nothing about. I would learn more about Ben's brief marriage to Gertrude Plath later.

༄

The Plaths insisted they stay two more days. *Kapitän* Plath, who'd instructed engineering personnel during the Great War, took a keen interest in the jeep and sent to the village for a blacksmith to help Ben repair the broken leaf spring. Every so often as Ben worked on the jeep he appeared with a bottle of aniseed-flavoured Kümmel and asked hopefully, 'How about an eye-opener?' And of course Ben said yes.

Eventually the Carlins left and drove north into Denmark on 31 July but made it only as far as Aabenraa, just 45 miles away, when a grinding and thumping and shimmying stopped the jeep. Ben found a garage and crawled under the jeep to make repairs, working until dark, and when that wasn't enough they spent three nights sleeping in the jeep behind garages in Nyborg.

On 3 August they passed the town's medieval castle on their way to the Nyborg Strand, where they would sail 15 miles across the Great Belt, the strait separating the islands of Funen and Zealand, on the way to Copenhagen. Hundreds of children swarmed around Ben as he attached the propeller, coming from all directions along the wide beach – fair-haired and tanned and laughing and shouting – and even though they all had to touch the jeep with their *foolish little hands*, Elinore looked at them with a painful longing. It was her 34th birthday.

The jeep leaked during the crossing, and every ten minutes Elinore drained the bilge with the hand pump. More children swarmed them when they reached the beach at Korsør, and when Ben struggled to drive over the rocky expanse to a road on the other side, the children were thrilled to lend a hand and haul the odd amphibian up onto flat ground by a rope attached to her capstan.

They were getting more attention than ever. A carload of reporters flagged them down outside Copenhagen and one of them – Paul Hammerich, who years later became famous as a writer for the Danish TV series *Matador* – jumped into the jeep and told them to pull over, and a waiter appeared from nowhere with a tray of beer. *Half-Safe* arrived in Copenhagen under a grey sky, and an editor at the newspaper offered $100 for three days of the Carlins' time, including daily runs down the harbour flying two *Politiken* banners as long as the jeep. The next day while it poured a photographer shot *Half-Safe* on the rain-slicked City Hall Square, surrounded by a crowd, and snapped a photo of Elinore tipping back a bottle of Carlsberg, looking like an Italian star in her dark sunglasses as they waited for the rain to stop.

For the next three days *Half-Safe* chugged up and down the harbour flying the *Politiken* banners, giving rides to reporters, new friends and children, Ben and Elinore amazed by the ever bigger crowds that appeared to wave and cheer. On 7 August *Half-Safe* did a victory lap around The Lakes in the middle of Copenhagen, and *Politiken* reported an astonishing if exaggerated crowd of 20,000 people. The newspaper covered their hotel bills too, while Goodyear and Socony-Vacuum paid sponsorship fees and filled their fuel tanks.

When Elinore saw a Christian Dior suit in a store window, marked down to 500 kronor, Ben insisted she buy it, and she did.

They were becoming famous, at least in this part of the world.

But not everything was perfect. They had an agreement to keep with the *Daily Express*, and on 18 August they were back in Calais, ready to make the triumphant Channel crossing to England, and more importantly to collect £500. That afternoon a satisfied Ben went drinking with a new friend, Belgian

Mobil advertising executive Theo Dufresne, and suddenly they'd drained five bottles of wine. A little later, when Ben went to park *Half-Safe* at a garage, the attendant refused him entry. Ben, unsteady and slurring, called him a *cochon* – a dirty pig – and a loud argument followed. The police showed up and summoned Ben and Theo to the police station. They let Ben return to his hotel after a few hours, and they were *vastly amused*, said Elinore afterward, but were they really? She'd said the same thing after Ben's two arrests in Madeira, and after his police detention in Gibraltar.

And that made an astonishing four incidents with the police in three countries in the span of a single year. Ben believed in control, but anything could happen when he drank. It had to be getting hard for Elinore to rationalise the increasingly erratic and unsafe behaviour that was beginning to mar his reputation, even though the press was still too proper to mention it.

She said nothing.

Two days later a wire arrived from the *Daily Express*. The deal was off, with no explanation. No press, no payment. *Bastards*, wrote Elinore. *Such a mess. We could have gone to Norway and Sweden and made a pile.*

They thought about taking legal action but there had never been a signed agreement, so they decided to sail to England anyway. They stayed for a few nights in the Hotel Metropol on the Quai du Rhin, which was cheap and tired, but at least it had bathtubs. They spent their last night in the jeep to save money, parked in front of the hotel, and woke early on 24 August to uncurl their bodies from the cramped space and pick up Theo. They cleared customs in Calais and drove past the rubble of bombed buildings, still shattered after the war, to the beach. Elinore fought another hangover with a packet of harsh French cigarettes.

'They're made to be smoked in French toilets,' sneered Ben dismissively, but Elinore lit another, trying to wake up.

The weather report wasn't good, but at 11.00 they drove into the Channel with almost no one to witness their departure. Two hours later a fuel line clogged, as it had so many times on the Atlantic crossing. Ben blew into it to clear the blockage and gagged on a mouthful of fuel.

The sea grew rough, and by evening Theo crawled out of the bunk to vomit off the jeep along with Elinore as they motored onward over the waves and into the low sun. Closer to England they saw white cliffs ahead, and then a throng of reporters watching them approach the beach at Deal, a few miles north of Dover. A lifeboat appeared to offer help as they passed over the shallow, wreck-strewn Goodwin Sands, but Ben waved them off adamantly and steered straight towards the beach to make a triumphant arrival in the long, late-summer twilight. The front wheels touched the beach, the crowd cheered, flash-bulbs popped – and the jeep sank to its belly in the steep, rocky shingle. Ben emerged, scowling from the cabin in his black beret and oil-stained khakis.

'We weren't rescued! Make it clear we weren't rescued!' Ben shouted to the reporters.

A lifeboat crew winched the jeep out of the shingle and a group of young reporters dragged the exhausted crew across the street to the ancient True Briton pub, where they collapsed on the floor in front of an electric heater. A crowd of regulars, customs agents and police filed in to congratulate them and buy endless rounds of beer, gin and whiskey.

But the press was stumped. The story lacked the drama of the Atlantic crossing.

'To this intrepid pair, the Channel must have seemed a mere paddling pool,' said the *Perth Countryman*. So reporters focused instead on the mid-Channel breakdown, the anticlimactic grounding on the beach and the wretched state of the crew. A smiling shot of Elinore in the *Daily Express* was captioned, 'Aspirins . . . Give me aspirins!' while the *Daily Mail* had her moaning, 'I'm bad, I'm bad!'

Other newspapers ran a photo of the jeep sunk into the shingle, Ben standing next to it, shovel in hand.

'Lurid tripe,' Elinore complained.

It was an ignominious arrival, but their lives were about to change forever.

CHAPTER SEVEN

Transition

Nothing could prepare them for London.

It had been more than three years since the first failed attempt, a year since they'd sailed out of Halifax to make the successful crossing. By the time they got to England, Ben and Elinore had less than 100 dollars and the jeep needed a complete overhaul. They were just a fifth of the way around the world.

But suddenly they were famous, or at least notorious, and everyone wanted a piece of them. They'd spent an hour signing autographs before leaving Deal, where the pub owners refused payment. Then a man named David Graham said he was going to London too, took them under his wing and recommended they stay at the Royal Over-Seas League clubhouse in central London. They arrived to a chilly reception; the doorman told them to park their shabby jeep elsewhere, but Graham didn't care. He swept them off to Simpson's Restaurant, the oak-panelled one-time haunt of Sir Arthur Conan Doyle and Charles Dickens, where he bought them round after round under the heavy chandeliers and introduced them to Cecil Clavering, the architect who'd perfected the Odeon Cinemas in the 1930s, then dragged them to the Strangers Club for more drinks, and then back to the Over-Seas League to introduce them to its director, who was *most* apologetic for the initial reaction to the jeep and offered *more* drinks and had an assistant find them affordable accommodation in London. When they asked Graham what he did, exactly, he said something about being a writer, then something about being involved in Persian oil, and left it at that.

Four days after they landed in London they were interviewed on the BBC radio show *In Town Tonight*, just before the world table tennis champion and an armless pianist who played with his toes. A few days later the BBC rang again, asked if the Carlins would drive the jeep to the television studio – actually drive *into* the studio, under the bright lights – hop out and do an interview. They did.

They were the bright young(ish) things, the new blood. They found themselves at one moment downing pints at a pub with writer Michael Sadleir, who'd just written *Fanny by Gaslight*, then in a club with a 'very drunk, very young, very spoiled' Oswald Berry, heir to England's biggest newspaper chain, who would be dead of pneumonia within a year, then at lunch with one Lady Willingdon, who commanded the table to keep drinking as she talked about her 49 years of bliss with the late Major Freeman Freeman-Thomas, 1st Marquess of Willingdon, former Viceroy and Governor-General of India.

From club to club they swam across London on a sea of gin.

But the Carlins were dead broke and relying on the generosity of others, and when they found a Chelsea flat on Draycott Place, they were barely able to scrape together the rent of £6.60 per week.

Elinore parked herself in the office of London-based *Melbourne Herald* reporter Noel Hawken and typed fruitless letters to seaside resort towns proposing they put the jeep on display and charge admission. *Nothing happening very fast to further the Carlin finances*, she wrote with panic, and she pounded the pavement in London, spent weeks looking for secretarial work and interviewing at NATO, the US Navy and US Air Force. All of them struggled to make sense of her strange story and her marriage to an Australian, until finally in September the US Air Force hired her to work in an office on Bushy Park in Teddington. Like Ben, when she wanted something she didn't stop until she got it.

The job was more than just a steady paycheque. London's postwar food rationing limited citizens to a single egg per person, a piece of cheese the size of a matchbox, two small lamb chops per week. Elinore's new American job entitled her to shop at the PX and Commissary, a pound of butter and a carton and a half of Philip Morris cigarettes every week.

But Elinore felt increasingly uncomfortable with her compatriots. In a letter to her brother, she wrote,

In all our travels we have met many Americans abroad. We have met most of the consular people in all of the islands and countries we have visited. We have met business people, State

Department people, travellers, etcetera ad infinitum. The regretful conclusion is that we – the USA – send only morons to represent us in foreign places.

Except, fortunately, for the Basses of Annapolis, Maryland.

Four years earlier my dad had watched Ben put the final touches on the jeep, and my grandfather had helped him learn how to operate a radio. By great coincidence, my grandparents, my father and my uncle Bob were all in England now, and in Elinore's journal entries I saw the Basses and Carlins all weave in and out of each other's lives.

My father was 19 years old in the autumn of 1951. He was in England for an undergraduate year at Exeter, having completed a freshman year as an English major at Johns Hopkins University in Baltimore. He was uncertain of his future, checking his draft status at the American embassy, thinking he might want to crew a yacht to New Zealand. When he visited Ben and Elinore at their flat on Draycott Place on 13 October he told them excitedly about how he'd just careened through France and Spain in a used taxi with a group of friends. *Young Georgie Bass*, Elinore called him, and said he was *the most intelligent & un-painful young American I've met in a long time.*

'They treated me royally when I was in London,' Dad told me. It was a transitional period for him, too. A few months later he'd travel to Italy and watch the sun set over a Roman theatre in Taormina, sparking a lifelong love affair with classical archaeology and a career that would lead to his founding the Institute of Nautical Archaeology, pioneering a new kind of archaeology that studied the past scientifically through shipwrecks, and earning just about every award and accolade an archaeologist can receive, including the National Medal of Science bestowed in a White House ceremony.

On Poppy Day, Ben and Elinore took a bus to Cambridge to spend a long day with the Basses. They strolled until dusk through narrow streets and across the college campuses, with a scattering of leaves on the ground and mist rising from the river. Elinore found my grandfather *fat and very American*, and with his heavy South Carolina accent she had a hard time imagining him as an English professor. She didn't know he was one of 11 children raised poor on a farm, the only one to go to college, never mind get a PhD; she just knew he was spending a few months at the British Museum to research *The Green Dragoon*, a biography of the British soldier and politician Banastre Tarleton. He was already thinking about his next book, *Swamp Fox*, a biography of Revolutionary War hero Francis Marion that would spawn a Walt Disney TV show starring Leslie Nielsen.

Elinore found my grandmother a quiet, soft-spoken Southerner, and Ben took a special liking to her: 'Virginia is a bloody peach; if she were a month or two younger I would slip down south and snare her,' he said a few years later in a letter to my grandfather.

He probably meant it.

Uncle Bob, my dad's brother, was in his early twenties, a Rhodes Scholar at Oxford, on the first marriage of an eventual eight. Handsome and intellectual, he announced to Ben and Elinore, 'My ambition is to become a physicist and contribute to the development of atomic energy for interplanetary travel.' That was long before he worked on a space-based laser cannon for the

US government, before he joined and then fled a cult, before he claimed the 'men in black' were after him because he knew the secret to nuclear fusion and limitless energy. Of course, we think to ourselves today, maybe he *did* know too much.

In a photograph taken that November weekend, across the River Cam from the Trinity Hall boathouse, Ben, Elinore, my grandfather and Uncle Bob stand side by side, the men in coats and ties, all of them looking at the photographer, probably my grandmother, with the hint of a smile. Elinore, wearing gloves and the slim Christian Dior suit she'd bought in Copenhagen, stares at something down the river, lost in her own thoughts.

~

In November, Ben took the train to Birmingham to convince the automaker Rover that they should build an entirely new amphibious vehicle for him. He slapped down a series of hand-drawn plans on large sheets of paper and made a case for a vehicle vastly superior to the Ford GPA.

They declined.

Before leaving the city Ben went to Hardy Spicer and Co., which manufactured universal joints and drive shafts for loco-motives and Land Rovers and Le Mans racecars. He'd met John Hardy in Madeira, and Hardy had offered use of a space and tools in the company's Birmingham-based two-storey brick factory if Ben needed a place to rebuild the jeep once he got to England.

Birmingham was three or four hours from London, depend-ing on whether you took the bus or train, so it was too far for a daily commute. But by December Ben and Elinore were falling apart. They were drunk every night, and the more Ben drank the more he insulted Elinore and the less he worried if she saw him looking at other women. On 25 November, after the latest in a string of cocktail parties, she asked if they could please go home early just once, and Ben lashed out at her once more in front of their friends. Humiliation was wearing her down. *The home front presents such an unattractive vista I keep away as often as possible*, she wrote that night, and Ben was a *bloody drunk*, although when she balanced their accounts she realised she was spending an awful lot on her own booze too.

And so when Ben left London and moved into a Birmingham boarding house on 7 January 1952, to spend the next year and a half working on the jeep, they simply got on with their own lives.

Over that time Ben lived and breathed the jeep, wholly immersed in its reconstruction in a greasy corner of a busy factory. Clad in overalls and the black beret he'd started wearing in Madeira, he stripped *Half-Safe* to her chassis, and when she was reduced to a pile of disassembled body panels, drivetrain parts and an engine block sitting on the oil-stained concrete floor, he was shocked at the devastation wrought by the first leg of the trip. The overhaul, he said, became an 'autopsy'. As Dave Welch told me when we went for a ride in his restored GPA, the vehicle was never designed with a long life in mind, and *Half-Safe*'s condition proved the point. Ben observed that the 'flimsy mass-produced shell . . . was reduced to a rusty colander serving only to distend the paper-thin neoprene skin which alone has kept us afloat of late'.

In some places rust had completely penetrated the hull, and there was almost nothing left of the jeep's original gunwales – the part of its body extending above the waterline around the cabin. Ben removed as much rust as possible by soaking steel parts in electrolytic baths, patched the hull where necessary, fabricated new gunwales and brushed on 27 coats of fresh waterproofing neoprene, totalling an eighth of an inch thick, which renewed the jeep's weirdly spongy texture.

He removed the cabin frame and lengthened it so that it extended farther fore and aft, and replaced the masonite panels that formed its top and sides with lighter holoplast, a fire-resistant, moisture-resistant laminated plastic developed during World War II. He gutted the interior, with only the two front seats and steering wheel remaining from the original vehicle; the roomier and less boxy cabin was outfitted with a warren of storage bays fashioned from aluminium and plastic and painted a pale hospital-green that made it look like the interior of a spartan military spaceship designed by a madman.

At no point did Ben put pencil to paper during the rebuild.

I simply started at one end and worked to the other, he wrote, *the reason being congenital laziness and devotion to doing things the hard way.* He worked through an absolute and intuitive understanding of every element of the jeep and what he needed to do. Since each step required knowing what would come next, it was like playing a mental game of mechanical chess, always thinking two steps ahead as the jeep came back together piece by piece.

He installed bigger brake drums meant for a Jaguar, a bigger rudder controlled by a tiller mounted above the driver's seat rather than by the steering wheel, eight new internal aluminium tanks with a capacity of 240 gallons of fuel and/or water. He filled difficult-to-access bilge spaces with custom-cut blocks of hard foam rubber so they couldn't flood, replaced the axle housings, overhauled the electrical system. And when all this was done, and the jeep reborn phoenix-like from its debris, he painted the exterior a shocking yellow.

∽

Alone for a year and a half in London, Elinore threw herself into the life she felt she'd always deserved. She saw Emlyn Williams' magnificent reading of Dickens. She attended the ballet and theatre, saw Gladys Cooper in Noël Coward's *Relative Values* and John Gielgud in *Much Ado About Nothing*. She went to a modern dance performance but it left her agitated.

She played tennis, took French lessons and German lessons and fencing lessons and photography lessons. She bought a bike and explored London, which she found a lot like Boston, although Christopher Wren's painted hall left her cold and the National Gallery was shabby and badly lit, and she didn't care much for Rubens' earthy and unclothed creatures, but she absorbed it all, gave herself up to beauty and richness. When she thought too hard about what her life had become, about how the years were passing, about eventually climbing back into *Half-Safe* and leaving this more refined life behind, it left her so depressed she couldn't get out of bed for days.

On Fridays Ben took the train down for weekends that turned into a blur of drunken, lost nights followed by boozy lunches to recover. Their lives continued to diverge as their shared adventure faded into the past, and Ben would often stay for only a few hours before heading back to Birmingham.

The stress was caused by more than fighting and drinking.

From the day they arrived in London, Elinore had begun noting in the margin of her journal pages the number of days they'd been there – 23 days, 34 days, 49 days – as if she were counting towards something.

And on Thursday, 27 September, after 32 days in London, Elinore made a cryptic note in her journal, next to her summary of the day's activities: FELL OFF ROOF. She wrote it in large capital letters, a dark rectangle drawn around the words.

She wrote it again on 25 October, FELL OFF ROOF, in big letters.

And again on 20 November.

And on 19 December.

The cadence was clear. Elinore wanted to get pregnant.

In 1952 she was turning 35. The women she knew who were her age had started families years earlier. Elinore adored children; she gushed about friends' and neighbours' kids, always so smart, polite and charming. But she wasn't getting pregnant, and she didn't know why. Every month she hoped, and every month she had her heart broken.

On 19 June 1952, she saw a doctor at the Chelsea Hospital for Women in Hammersmith. He found her fallopian tubes 'blocked'. Two months later she had some small cysts removed, to no effect.

Elinore was mad-keen to have a child, Ben recalled years later. *Patiently I explained she couldn't cross the Pacific with a baby; she was going to do both, she said. Of course she couldn't.*

But he too wanted children, and he shared her pain. Sometimes he even felt guilt, however fleetingly, for the way he'd been treating her. In 1964 he recalled,

Working on the jeep at Birmingham at the end of 1952, I guess I was depressed. I said to myself, a) maybe I don't deserve any better, and b) maybe there are worse women around. Unknown to E., I bought a wedding ring and, very early on the morning of 25 December 1952, while she was still asleep, slipped it on her finger.

When Elinore awoke on Christmas Day she gasped. She felt really married for the first time, felt they were in it together, felt a redoubled desire for a child.

That evening, Ben went out drinking without her.

They spent the first day of 1953 at the Chelsea Hospital, where they got a verdict about Ben's side of the equation: 'Sperm by the million, all alive and kicking.' Which meant the difficulty in getting pregnant, as Ben saw it, was entirely Elinore's fault. But they kept trying, doing everything possible according to the best medical advice of the 1950s.

On 25 June 1953, a doctor gave them the news. *With some major surgery stand a 10% chance*, wrote Elinore. *Definite tube blockage.*

Ben, with his millions of fighting sperm and his antagonistic ego, fell back on his anger, blamed Elinore, theorising she couldn't get pregnant because of her abortion during their time in India. (In a letter years later he engaged in revisionist history, suggesting Elinore had actually fallen pregnant by someone else and he'd simply been gallant enough to pay for the termination. It was a brutal, horrendous thing to say, and utterly unconvincing. Nothing about Ben suggests he'd ever take responsibility for another man's seed.)

Or maybe it had been the next abortion. It turned out Elinore had become pregnant again in Shanghai in 1946, and she'd come back to the States for the procedure in early 1947, shortly before joining Ben in Annapolis for the trials of *Half-Safe* on Weems Creek.

'The San Francisco abortion had left her barren,' explained Ben in 1964. 'Burned up her fallopian tubes.' Anything to fault her, to belittle her, to put the blame squarely on her shoulders.

A decade later Ben's old friend Richard Battey tried to set him straight: 'Your idea that "barrenness" is caused by abortion(s) and that you have never heard of any other reason shows both your ignorance of medicine and refusal to learn the truth.'

In late 1953 Elinore decided to have a salpingostomy, an operation that repairs fallopian tubes so they can carry a mature egg from the ovaries to the uterus. The surgery was performed in November and the results looked promising. Elinore stayed in the chilly hospital for days, annoyed by the lack of staff attention, visited occasionally by Ben, who was usually on his way to drinks with someone else. The surgery was a final shot, and after a weekend with Ben she hoped to be pregnant by her next visit to the hospital on 15 December.

Christmas Day, 1953: FELL OFF ROOF.

On 8 May of the following year, Elinore made one last visit to Chelsea Hospital. The doctors were kind but clear. In her journal, in sad, small script, she wrote her final words about the subject: *Verdict – negative. No babies – ever.*

Sadness and stress weakened her, and now Elinore was constantly sick, fighting colds and sinus infections that dragged on for months. She suffered bouts of depression. She complained about *the filthy weather and sheets of rain*. She hated her office. *I don't understand American girls*, she said. *One can't make a rash, original or risqué statement without squeals of surprise, shock or horror forthcoming. They feel they must be some damnably, stupidly sweet. They are a synthetic carbon copy of some make-believe ideal.*

They were all *the living dead types*.

The months in England unreeled and turned into years.

Ben drove *Half-Safe* back to London for good in June 1953 and moved in with Elinore in a comfortable basement flat at 106 Regent's Park Road, just north of Central London, across from the grassy Primrose Hill public park, for £6 per week.

During happy periods Elinore loved life on Primrose Hill, a working-class neighbourhood just starting to acquire a bohemian air. She wrote that she and Ben were embraced by a *mad crowd full of television and theatrical people*, complete with *an expatriate American writer*. They lived in the orbit of their landlord, Louis 'Büdi' Hagen, who owned the building and lived on the top floor. As a teen, Hagen had been rescued from a concentration camp, fled to England and during the war served as a British Army glider pilot. After that he was a journalist, writer and children's film producer. His 1945 book, *Arnhem Lift*, was a bestseller. Now he was producing films and, with German animation legend Lotte Reiniger, founded Primrose Film Productions, which made dozens of children's features, mainly for the BBC.

Everyone was someone in the Primrose Hill building. Actor Ralph Michael's career spanned four decades and films from *A Night to Remember* to *Empire of the Sun*. 'What a flirt,' said Elinore, noting his roving eye. Muriel Smith was an American singer riding on the success of her 1953 Top 10 single 'Hold Me, Thrill Me, Kiss Me'. Patrick Barr was in the middle of a career that lasted all the way through a small role in the 1983 Bond film *Octopussy*.

The Carlins bought a TV, the first in the building, and friends and neighbours gathered around the small set to watch Wimbledon and old movies and variety shows, drinking gin in a haze of cigarette smoke until long after midnight and then waking up with hangovers and doing it all over again.

Beverly Barry was one of the many people who passed through the Carlins' London flat. She was 22 years old, a young Australian on a working holiday visa who'd arrived in London in 1954 after a nearly month-long voyage on the *Orontes* from Perth via the Suez Canal. She lived with friends in a cold flat on Albert Terrace, a few minutes' walk from the Carlins, and one Saturday afternoon in October she met Elinore at a market.

'She was an attractive, friendly American,' Beverly said of Elinore. 'Our flat was in a basement with a tiny coal fire, so it didn't take too much encouragement to coax us to their cosy ground-floor flat where it was warm.

'Ben did not suffer fools. But he had a real charm about him when it suited him. He was a great raconteur and good company.'

He spun such good stories that, in the spring of 1955, Beverly and a friend briefly considered an invitation to join the next leg of the trip. 'I'm not sure why we decided not to,' Beverly said. 'I still find it one of the biggest regrets of my life.'

Maybe it was the tension that now crackled around the couple – Elinore's growing unhappiness, the sense the trip would have a new layer of difficulty.

Ben has developed nausea for me, Elinore wrote. *Antipathy. I just want to bloody well die. Last six months pure unmitigated hell.*

'We all got the feeling that she and Ben were drifting apart,' Beverly recalled. 'She was certainly not as keen as he was to finish the circumnavigation.'

There were more visitors. Scottie Henderson and her husband, Creed, who they'd met while in Madeira, were often jetting through London and stopped in for drinks and dinner, sometimes with Scottie's daughter Cynthia in tow. Ben and Elinore were charmed by the girl, who turned nine years old in the summer of 1951. Cynthia's father, Colonel Thomas Robert Henderson of the Royal Scots, sometimes came down from Scotland to see her for a few hours, and Elinore found him 'full of acid and caustic comments'. He was an eccentric man, divorced from Scottie for years; he'd tried and failed to get his fellow soldiers to sign a pledge against the evils of alcohol during World War II. (Henderson had gone to war with a small brown teddy bear named Teddy Girl at his side that shattered records when sold for £110,000 at a Christie's auction in London in 1994, but that's another story.)

Scottie, Creed, Colonel Henderson and Cynthia would re-enter Ben's life years later and change everything, but there was no way he could know that now.

$\backsim$

While their own adventure was on hiatus, they paid attention to the competition. When they saw a documentary about the Kon-Tiki raft expedition, Elinore thought Thor Heyerdahl had 'shifty eyes' and sniffed at the 16mm footage shot by the crew on the raft, even though the film won a 1951 Academy Award. Ben expressed suspicion that things weren't what they seemed, without elaborating. On the other hand, when he heard about Hillary and Tensing summiting Everest on 29 May 1953, he wept at the achievement.

The Carlins still had no clear plan for the future, and at times Ben wondered if the journey was worth continuing. On the one hand, 'the jeep had carved her tiny notch on the Pillar of History' by crossing the Atlantic, and had proved it could be done. And even Ben felt an unexpected longing for stability.

> Now aged 39 I had lived from suitcase or kit-bag for 13 years; the travel urge was long satisfied and I yearned for a permanent hat-peg, a lawnmower, the pit-a-pat of little footsies. If beforehand I had been persuaded that the trip would take longer than a year I would have dropped it; now five years later I was barely started.

But, he admitted, 'Although a sweet-enough aria, *Half-Safe*'s feat was no opera. Neither an Atlantic crossing nor even a 99-per cent circumnavigation compares with a complete trip all the way round.' He had to finish.

And once again the pieces fell into place.

Among Hagen's coterie was 35-year-old André Deutsch, who'd just formed a small but increasingly influential eponymous London publishing house. Born in Budapest, he was arrogant but insecure, described by one of his writers as a 'mid-European leprechaun'. When Deutsch met Ben he told him he'd followed news accounts of *Half-Safe*'s travels with great interest, and in the summer of 1954 he took Ben and Elinore to lunch with his partner, editor Diana Athill, to talk about the potential for a book and drink bottle after bottle of wine. Deutsch stressed that he published only stories he liked, and he liked the *Half-Safe* story very much. The next month a formal meeting followed, over prodigious amounts of gin.

'It is quite remarkable that I still remember every detail of our discussion,' Deutsch wrote afterward, and officially proposed that Ben write a book about his Atlantic crossing:

> I think it's time you had something in writing from me, so here goes: We would like to publish your book. Naturally, we shall want an option on your second volume. That we are enthusiastic about your book perhaps I need hardly repeat.

Ben had been thinking about writing a book, but assumed he'd do it at the end of the journey. But now, with an offer dangled in front of him, he saw it as a way to help finance the rest of the trip. The income he'd once expected from sponsorships and exhibitions clearly wouldn't be enough, and Elinore's income – by 1954 her annual salary was $3560.72 – would end once they were on the road again.

The terms were good: a £1,000 advance, the first half payable as soon as Ben signed the contract. It was financial salvation.

Ben set up a space at a table in front of the flat's fireplace and wrote quickly through the fall and early winter of 1954–1955, using his logs and Elinore's detailed journals to weave a narrative that focused on the preparation of the jeep and the Atlantic crossing. He fed his handwritten pages to Elinore, who stayed up late typing out the pages, and a first draft was complete in January.

Diana Athill, who would later become famous for editing Norman Mailer, Philip Roth and V. S. Naipaul, began working with Ben to polish his workmanlike prose.

'Ben and I got down to editing, and it went like wedding bells,' Athill told me in a letter from London when she was nearly 90. 'A bit too literally so, since Ben and I were in bed together by the end of the first session.' But both of them knew the score: 'No romance involved, just amiability and pleasure.'

André Deutsch quickly sold the first serial rights for Ben's book to a newspaper called *The People* – 'a bit of a rag,' said Diana, 'but lively.' The £500 deal meant *The People* could publish four excerpts from the book before any other newspaper, and that in turn would help draw attention to the book and drive sales.

Almost immediately there was a hiccup: just after arriving in London in 1951, Ben had written a long article about the Atlantic crossing for the UK newspaper *Sunday Express.* 'The World's Craziest Honeymoon', by Major Ben Carlin, was essentially a condensed version of the story he'd just sold to André Deutsch. The problem was, Ben had neglected to tell Deutsch about this article before signing his book deal. Deutsch was furious when he learned about it.

The People wanted out of its serial rights deal entirely.

Ben didn't understand the publishing world and thought he could bluster his way through the situation the way he talked himself across borders and into free drinks. He couldn't. 'Ben went paranoid,' said Diana, 'convinced it was some sort of mad conspiracy against him between us and the newspaper. I ended up in such a rage with him that he became the only person at whom I have ever thrown something. It was only, and ineffectively, a book, but if a heavy rock had been to hand I wouldn't have hesitated to use it.'

The People terminated its deal in June. In a letter to André Deutsch's lawyer, Ben called Deutsch 'an ambitious, unbridled egotist', going on to say, 'He has little or no taste, his general knowledge is microscopic and is devoid of mental flexibility; he cannot think on his feet.'

'It does not do to get on the wrong side of the press,' warned Ben's own lawyer. 'After all, they have the power if not to kill the book at least to mar its chances of success.'

Ben didn't listen.

As Diana got to know him, she felt his lifelong anger and suspicious nature were fuelled by deep insecurity. 'I had always been aware of a slight tendency in him to suspect the English,' she told me. 'They might be seeing him as an Australian hick and try to take him for a ride, so he'd better be smart and get in and take them for a ride first.'

Despite these early troubles, André Deutsch was still convinced the book could really sell. 'I do believe this is the biggest book I have given you so far, and perhaps it will remain so for a long time,' Diana Athill wrote to Odette Arnaud, a literary agent in Paris who was seeking a French publisher for the book.

Ben had already begun the book by the time the deal was formalised, but he was three months late in delivering the manuscript. That forced Deutsch to push back the publication date and got the relationship off to a rocky start.

'This sort of thing happens in the publishing world every day,' explained Ben to his lawyer. He had no idea what he was talking about. For the first time, Ben was out of his element and punching above his weight. He didn't understand Deutsch's influence and he was oblivious to the implications of pissing him off.

When Ben was finally done writing, and the last page had been dutifully typed up by Elinore, he delivered the manuscript to André Deutsch. Then he turned his focus to crossing Europe and conquering the rest of the world.

'Off he flounced,' said Diana, 'and we never saw him again.'

On 30 May 1954, Ben drove *Half-Safe* into the river at Bray-on-Thames, just above London, and did tight circles in the placid water with friends sitting on the cabin and watching from the riverbank. For the first time in three years she was back in the water. All of Ben's new modifications and repairs performed flawlessly.

Two weeks later he failed a driving test in London.

As the date of departure drew closer, Ben decided he needed a support vehicle to carry equipment and fuel at least as far as India. He bought a powder-blue Ford Thames 5cwt van – which to modern eyes looks like a cross between a car and a very small SUV – for £355. He decided Elinore couldn't possibly drive the van by herself. He had to find a third crewmember.

In March, Treyer Evans, who illustrated books by children's author Enid Blyton and others, introduced Ben and Elinore to Frank Ringland, a quiet 39-year-old Londoner who'd suffered a broken engagement in 1949 followed by a bad marriage in 1950. He was in the midst of a divorce and selling his family business, and he wanted to get as far away from London as possible.

Frank agreed to sign on as a driver and cameraman in exchange for getting all of his expenses paid on the way to Calcutta. He was 'intelligent, smallish, slim, dark and well-educated', according to Elinore. He'd been in the Royal Air Force Volunteer Reserve, noted Ben. They agreed he was perfect.

That was the last time they saw Frank sober. In the weeks that followed, Elinore smelled alcohol on his breath every time they raced around London collecting the visas they needed for all the border crossings on the way to India. But it was too late to find a replacement.

On 20 April 1955, Ben and Elinore woke early to pack the jeep, parked in front of their flat on Primrose Hill, with a trio of heavy steamer trunks and dozens of bags, bedrolls and cartons, boxes of kleenex, and tins of rations from Campbell soups to corn – everything they'd need on the long drive to Calcutta. The trees were still bare, and a late-spring chill was in the air as hundreds of friends and neighbours crowded around the jeep, freshly painted a brilliant yellow with red trim, trying to get a last look. Children in their school uniforms swarmed over *Half-Safe*, whose right side was covered with a map of the Carlins' intended route, and more than a dozen sponsor logos plastered the left side. Newton

Shock Absorbers. Lockheed Brakes. Perspex. Holoplast. GACO Oil Seals. Goodyear. Shell.

The mast and two wicker baskets of supplies were lashed to the jeep's roof.

The BBC interviewed the Carlins and photographers shot them loading their supplies. Elinore was stylish in black slacks and sweater, while Ben sported the usual scowl and a heavy red plaid work shirt. A cigarette hung from his mouth. The two of them climbed onto the back of the jeep, dropped into the cabin through the roof hatch, and they were ready to go.

But as they prepared to pull away, Elinore said something Ben didn't like. The gathered crowd saw the jeep lurch to a stop. They couldn't hear Ben lashing out at Elinore for some perceived slight – hurling *a stream of abuse and invective*, she wrote – but they saw her climb back out of the jeep for no apparent reason and get into the van with Frank for the grand departure.

Elinore was more than embarrassed. She was again humiliated.

Everything must be crushed, everything must be reduced to its most miserable terms, she wrote that night. *I'm so ashamed of this shameful state of affairs. Life is hell again in all directions.* It was an ominous start to the trip.

'Mine was not a gracious performance,' Ben later admitted, and blamed his bad behaviour on building stress. A newspaper strike was in its third week, and Deutsch was panicking about the lack of press coverage for the departure. The timing was terrible, but their flat had been rented to new tenants who were anxious to move in, and the Carlins had to go. Grim resolve on his face, alone in *Half-Safe*, Ben pulled away from 106 Regent's Park Road with children running after the jeep and the van following. He took a quick lap of London for the benefit of the press, around Trafalgar Square, past the Houses of Parliament and over Westminster Bridge. Then he turned the overloaded jeep down the Dover Road.

After a hiatus of nearly five years, London was finally behind them and the journey was back on.

CHAPTER EIGHT
Overland

The Atlantic crossing had been the big draw, the death-defying high-wire act that put *Half-Safe* in the spotlight and drew the attention of the world media. Ben didn't anticipate that there would be much drama in the drive eastward to Istanbul, so the plan was to get it done as quickly as possible, then head to India, loop around South-East Asia and launch the Pacific crossing from Japan, which would be the dramatic highlight of the second leg.

To this plan a detour was added: André Deutsch believed Australia was a key market for the book, so Ben revised the journey to include a quick deviation to Australia, by ship, for a book tour.

Ben and Elinore drove across a rocky beach into the English Channel against the backdrop of brilliant white cliffs after breakfast on 22 April 1955. There were two passengers aboard.

Photographer John Simmons was taking pictures for the *Picture Post*, and Richard Kaplan, a 30-year-old American film producer who worked at Primrose Productions with Hagen, was filming the event for Ben, who'd supplied him with £69 of film and explained he was going to make a documentary when the trip was done.

Richard nearly walked away before the jeep even hit the water. Conditions were perfect for a crossing, the Channel a sheet of glass under a clear blue sky, but inside the cabin a storm raged as Ben argued with Elinore from the moment the jeep touched water.

'I thought it was a gas!' Richard told me from his home in New York. 'But it was very confined and claustrophobic in the jeep, and those two were not terribly pleasant to be around, frankly.' He shot *Half-Safe* entering the water and a few moments of Ben and Elinore looking unhappy as Ben swivelled the tiller, but for most of the crossing he and John sat on top of the cabin to escape the fighting. It was uncomfortable for both of them, especially when halfway across the Channel Ben called John into the cabin and let him take a turn at the wheel. Elinore stared ahead in anger, having been told to stay put in the passenger seat.

The 22-mile crossing took six and a half hours – seven and a half, counting the hour spent stuck at the water's edge in Calais under the gaze of two policemen and a small crowd that eventually helped push the jeep onto dry sand. Frank brought the van separately on a ferry, and they all sped to Paris and a night in a cheap hotel. Richard gave his exposed movie film to Ben and parted ways with the Carlins a few days later, flying back from Paris to London. He was followed soon afterward by John. 'Ben wanted me to continue with him around the world, and I said, "I'm crazy but not that crazy!"'

A decade later Richard would win an Academy Award for his documentary film *The Eleanor Roosevelt Story*.

Ben was behind schedule when he arrived in Paris and already sabotaging early publicity for his upcoming book. On 21 April a panicked Odette Arnaud – the Parisian agent described by author Daphne du Maurier as 'terrifyingly efficient and businesslike' – wrote to André Deutsch, wondering why the intrepid adventurer hadn't arrived on time for a series of planned press events.

'We all feel very desperate about Ben Carlin. We had been expecting him every day since April 7th. We are also in a most awkward position vis-à-vis the big press because we had managed to get demands for exclusive interviews from *Match*, *France-Soir*, and *Constellation*.'

The immediate response: '*Entre nous*, organization does not seem to be his forte and after the numerous rumours of his departure I was really very much relieved to see him leave.'

Anxious for attention after an ill-attended press event, Ben drove down a ramp into the Seine near the Eiffel Tower. Aside from a kiss blown at Elinore, the promenading Parisians mostly ignored the strange yellow vehicle.

Ben bought a new rubber raft for £14 and stowed it atop the jeep, and then they left Paris, Ben alone in the jeep, Frank and Elinore in the van, and drove through the countryside to Switzerland. In Geneva representatives from Rolex and Shell invited Ben and Elinore for drinks at a lakefront café under a brilliantly clear sky. Ben basked in the attention and accepted two watches and 173 litres of fuel in exchange for a photo opportunity. He looped around Lac Léman a few times, flying a big green Rolex flag, with television and newsreel cameras rolling as yet again the jeep lodged itself in the sandy shore at the end of the demonstration.

But it didn't worry Ben, because with the book advance he had his own money for the first time in years. He had a new Rolex on his wrist, replacing the one he'd lost in the Delaware River in 1947, and now he decided he needed not one but *two* new cameras. He dropped $500 on a 16mm Bolex movie camera and another $200 on a 35mm Alpa camera for colour transparencies. The great irony was that Ben was a terrible photographer. It concerned Deutsch, who told Ben the photos for *Half-Safe* were mostly lousy. 'You realise that we are really stuck on the photographic side,' he complained.

How do you cross an ocean in a jeep and fail to get good photos? In Perth I spent days looking through hundreds of Ben's photos, negatives and contact sheets, many of them blurred and badly composed. In the early 1960s my father, who was writing his first articles for *National Geographic* about the ancient shipwrecks he was excavating in the Mediterranean, asked his editors why they had never published anything by or about Ben. 'They said they knew him well,' he told me, 'but he just didn't have any good photographs.'

Elinore may have seen the purchases differently. While Ben considered the cameras essential, it was *her* years of grinding, frustrating work as a secretary that had kept them afloat in London, that had paid for all the gin and wine, all the late nights, all the rent. She kept a detailed list of expenses that outlined what they'd spent almost every day since the summer of 1948. At one point she broke down how much each of them contributed to the bankroll. During nearly four years in England, Ben's entire income prior to selling his book had been £103 – half from writing the *Sunday Express* story in 1951 and half in compensation for a couple of BBC appearances.

During the same period Elinore earned $11,539, or a little more than £4,000.

It wasn't until 1961 that she felt compelled to mention the money. *You seem to have forgotten so very many things*, she wrote from an office on Madison Avenue in New York. *Small things, such as your passive acceptance of over 10 years of quiet and comfortable support from me. You also have long since forgotten many, many loans, in 1946, 1947 and 1948, in varying amounts from $25 to $100. Certainly I have never mentioned this before.*

But Ben kept spending. Where they'd once slept on the side of the road or let strangers take them in, now there were hotels and fancy dinners. Between Paris and Geneva alone Ben spent £76 for food and accommodation. It made a huge dent in his advance.

Maybe Elinore said something about the cameras that day in Geneva. Maybe she gently reminded him they had to be careful with their money. Maybe she simply glanced at the new gear with a certain look on her face. Whatever it was, something ignited Ben. After their drinks by the lake were drained, and they were back in their room at the Elite Hotel, he lashed out. He shouted and unleashed the unpredictable latent anger that could erupt at any time and kept Elinore on constant alert.

And then he hit her. Not hard enough to make a mark, but he said the worst was yet to come.

When he'd exhausted his rage Elinore fixed her make-up, and later in the evening she smiled pleasantly through dinner with the man from Rolex.

More socialising and drinks followed. Ben swapped stories with Guy Piazzani, who'd just written a book about his expedition to Africa. He dragged Elinore and Frank to Rue de la Fontaine to drink more and watch gyrating girls in G-strings at the Ba-Ta-Clan nightclub until three in the morning. And then he made them hit the road at sunrise and drive through the fog of hangovers, headed through the Alps and into Italy via the Simplon Pass at 6,578 feet – the jeep's highest elevation for the entire trip.

The next morning Elinore recorded it all in her journal. FELL OFF ROOF.

They kept driving eastward, now sharing the road with trucks, donkeys and buses hauling German tourists to Greece. This was no adventure, just the monotony of grinding motion punctuated by borders and breakdowns. They had a flat tyre entering Zagreb, Yugoslavia. On the other side of the city they hit a dismal milestone when they passed through a longitude of E 16° 26'. It had been five years since leaving Montreal, which after the years of failed starts Ben considered his official Mile 0. He and Elinore were only one quarter of the way around the world. At this rate they would complete the journey in 1976.

During an interview in a loud bar in Venice, two Italian reporters had grilled Ben with skepticism. 'Is it true that your jeep has crossed the Atlantic alone?' asked one. When Ben answered yes, the reporter shot back, 'Prove it.'

And then there was Frank.

His ineptitude was becoming more obvious, which at least had an upside: it absorbed some of the simmering hostility between the Carlins, who both had a litany of complaints about him. He tried to speak the local language in every country but didn't admit he didn't understand a word when given directions. He drank heavily, which was saying a lot considering his travel companions. He forgot instructions. He was hapless when it came to mechanics. Elinore couldn't stand him. *For sheer stupidity he takes all prizes*, she wrote, dismayed that he didn't know much about the parts of a car, despite having supposedly come from an automotive background. He referred to 'the thing on top' or 'that chap there' or 'the what do you call it' when trying to talk his way through repairs and maintenance, and working with him was *like playing mother to a 10-year-old moronic child*.

Onward and onward. Getting stuck behind sheep, stopping at roadside cafés for wine with lunch and again for slivovitz with dinner, beating over cracked paved roads that turned to dirt and back again, clouds of dust everywhere in the jeep and van, Ben alone with his thoughts, scowling over the steering wheel, Elinore banished to the van with Frank, everyone angry at everyone else when they were together.

In Niš, Yugoslavia, Ben acquiesced to the overland nature of the journey, finally dismounting the jeep's rudder and propeller and lashing them on the roof, away from potholes and traffic.

In southern Macedonia, on 7 May, the narrow dirt road ahead of the jeep disappeared into a crumbling cliff face where a single-lane tunnel punched through bare rock. It was a dramatic spot, so Ben flagged down the van and told Elinore to park it out of sight while Frank filmed the jeep driving down the road and entering the tunnel. Simple enough.

As always, it was hard to tell what set Ben off. As soon as Elinore had parked the van he leapt out of the jeep under the glaring sun and stormed towards her, screaming at her at first, then *throwing physical blows to match each filthy & abusive accusation of I can't remember exactly what*, she wrote. *What comes over him is difficult to understand – but he's quite sure everyone else is stupid, is willfully doing the wrong thing to obstruct his purposes – oh – better to be dead.*

Frank stood back and watched, helpless. But when the fighting was done he got the shot Ben was looking for.

They drove on.

The road matches Ben's anger, wrote Elinore. *Tank tracks, deep holes, ditches, gravel patches – anything but a road.* The further they drove, the hotter and drier it got.

⁓

Half-Safe was unique, but it wasn't alone on the road. In the 1950s a steady stream of adventurers were setting off on various overland 'expeditions' into the not-really-unknown of Africa and Asia. They were mostly British, mostly of means, setting out to see their Empire in its waning years. They wrote books with common tropes: a wife who is too delicate for the trip but insists on coming; curious locals and suspicious guards at every border crossing; a litany of fouled plugs and broken steering arms as mid-century machines struggled over crumbled, potholed roads.

There were so many of them that they ran into each other along the way, in Istanbul and Tehran and Cairo. 'World travel by motorcar is becoming almost a commonplace,' sniffed the *Melbourne Argus* on 22 June, noting the current field included 'a one-armed driver travelling from London to Melbourne in a Standard Eight'.

In late 1955, one of the more notable journeys launched from London: the Oxford and Cambridge Far Eastern Expedition. Six students set off in two Land Rovers, determined to make the first overland drive to Singapore. They were media savvy in a way that Ben could only dream about; not only did Land Rover provide their vehicles for publicity, but the students landed a BBC deal and a book deal before they left, and sponsorships that provided supplies from electric shavers and typewriters to a crate of Dewar's. The drive, organised with military precision, took six months, and *First Overland*, an account by expedition member Tim Slessor, became a bestseller.

From London to Calcutta, the Far Eastern Expedition took the same route as *Half-Safe*. It was, after all, 'a drive that had been done as early as 1937,' Slessor told me. The expedition's real challenge would come later in South-East Asia, especially tackling the abandoned Stillwell Road in Burma, which *Half-Safe* would avoid by taking to the Bay of Bengal.

When I spoke to Slessor by phone he'd just come inside from mucking around in his garden in France. I asked him what he knew about Ben.

'He drove an amphibious DUKW around the world in the 1950s, I believe. He wrote a book, didn't he?' So much for my hope that the two men had once traded stories over beer in some dusty corner of the Middle East.

But as we talked, I recognised similarities in the two men. Slessor attributed his own drive to a quality Ben would have understood and respected: 'I'm a bit bloody minded. As a friend once said, "Tim, you're very much of the *take it or leave it, but don't fuck me about* type."'

Why, I asked, was the early 1950s a golden era for this kind of adventure?

'Young men – and maybe women too – began to have enough money to do this sort of thing,' offered Slessor. 'The kind of vehicles that were competent enough to do long journeys – across the Sahara, across the Middle East – were coming on line. And it was only five or ten years after World War II. So in the 50s there was a window of opportunity, which hadn't really existed before. Then by the mid-60s, most of it had been done!'

Slessor demurred. He's not sure the route from Alaska to Cape Horn, the farthest southern reach of Chile, has *really* been done yet, because Panama's notorious Darién Gap remains dangerous, roadless and nearly impenetrable, the sole break in the 19,000-mile Pan-American Highway. To do the route properly you'd need an amphibious vehicle, sort of like *Half-Safe*.

Which brings us to the *other* great amphibious jeep journey of the 1950s. Helen and Frank Schreider, Californians who met as students at UCLA in 1947, decided they were going to drive the length of the Americas after graduating and getting married, before settling down. Just like Ben and Elinore. But during their planning they looked at the map and saw a mountain barrier across their path near the Guatemalan border, east to west across Central America.

'And so I thought, *well, that's it*,' Helen tells me on a Skype call from a friend's home in Santa Fe, New Mexico. She's 90, a smiling spark of energy with a grey bob. 'But Frank said, "Oh no, we're going to get an amphibious jeep. I think I can still find one somewhere." I said, "What do you mean? Why'd they stop making them?" And he said, "Because they all sank."'

So they found a Ford GPA in a junkyard, its hull rusted through, and Frank spent three years patching it up. He built a cabin on top, dubbed it *La Tortuga*, and in 1954 he and Helen drove out of Circle City, Alaska, bound for the southernmost tip of South America. Where they couldn't go by land they took to the water, including a hop across the Strait of Magellan. The 18-month trip and subsequent adventures through the Indonesian Archipelago and down the Ganges and Amazon turned into books, lecture tours and articles in *National Geographic*, which in 1967 hired the couple as a journalistic team.

In 1957 Ben cut out a newspaper article about the Schreiders, and I found it, yellowed and brittle, among the clippings of his own adventures. Helen tells me she and Frank didn't know about *Half-Safe* until they'd completed their own journey and the media began comparing the two couples and their adventures.

'The first time we heard about Ben was when we came back from our trip,' she says. 'I gathered he and Elinore had had problems because he was difficult,' she adds diplomatically, and leaves it at that.

For Frank and Helen, like Ben and Elinore, the amphibious jeep was a means to freedom and a shot at doing something no one else had ever done at the dawn of the 1950s. There was a difference, though: Helen and Frank were equal partners, in it together in every possible way. Life in the jeep was good. Helen used to love falling asleep in the jeep as it rocked gently in the water at night.

～

And there was one more significant overland expedition during this period, long forgotten but of note because it fortuitously crossed paths with *Half-Safe*. Around the same time as Ben and Elinore were preparing to leave London and the Far Eastern Expedition was locking up its sponsorship and the Schreiders were southbound down the spine of the Americas, a 47-year-old Australian writer named F. J. Thwaites, who cranked out more than two dozen mostly forgotten adventure and romance novels like *Whispers in Tahiti* and *Oasis of Shalimar* during the 1940s and 1950s, left London on his own adventure. He was bound for Sydney in a Hillman Husky, an anemic two-door station wagon with a top speed of 65 miles per hour. It was ostensibly a trip to gather information for future novels, but he'd secured a promotional deal that subsidised fuel and repairs, paid to fly the car over the English Channel, and promised media interest. His wife, Jessica, and their 11-year-old son, Roger, came along too. They followed a route that nearly matched that of *Half-Safe*, and on 8 May the Thwaites found themselves in Salonika, a Greek port city at the northern end of the Aegean.

That day a shimmy stopped *Half-Safe* in the same place. While Ben tracked down a Ford garage, Elinore and Frank wandered down to the harbour esplanade, where photographers stood around waiting for tourists, and a dead dog floated in the green water under a beating sun. They parked themselves under a café umbrella for drinks and noticed a car parked across the street: a dusty and dented two-door Hillman Husky station wagon, its front door emblazoned with a map of the world and the words 'England – Australia'.

Elinore crossed the street and introduced herself to the driver. F. J. Thwaites found her attractive, 'tall and olive of complexion', but noted that 'dark circles showed under her deep brown eyes, and she smoked quickly, as one does when unconsciously fighting against frayed nerves'.

'While we talked I kept wondering where I had heard the name "Carlin" before,' wrote Thwaites in *Husky Be My Guide*, his 1957 book about his family's odyssey. 'My mind associated it with something spectacular.'

Frank explained who they were, and said he was accompanying Ben and Elinore as far as Calcutta. They all had dinner together that evening, and Thwaites sized up his fellow Australian.

Ben, the strong silent type, had Great Public School stamped on his fine features. His physique, less than a decade ago, probably would have come under the category of athletic, but on our first meeting, could only be described as powerful. Thick jawbones, aggressive chin and lips which curved down slightly at both corners, revealed a character easily stirred to anger.

Thwaites paid for the beers but couldn't get Ben or Elinore to say anything about the Atlantic crossing other than vague admissions that it was 'a bit tough'.

171

When they talked about the road ahead, though, Ben was combative, as if sensing in Thwaites the threat of a potential competitor. 'You're not in the hunt!' Ben said. 'Chose the wrong car to start off with.' He predicted the ten-horsepower Husky would be stopped dead by the unforgiving terrain between Damascus and Delhi.

They drank until midnight and walked along the waterfront. The light of a waning gibbous moon reflected on the water, and the rattle of rigging and voices of fishermen floated across the harbour. Ben grew increasingly argumentative and dismissive. 'If you get stuck we'll tow you as far as Baghdad,' he spat, and they parted ways for the night.

Half-Safe arrived in Istanbul on 14 May. The next day Ben drove into the water for the first time since the English Channel, crossing the Bosporus in an hour with a reporter from the afternoon newspaper *Istanbul Ekspres* riding shotgun. Frank shuttled the van across by ferry.

They were in Asia.

They stopped for small glasses of tea and then drove onward into Turkey, towards the modernist expansion of Ankara, where portraits of Mustafa Kemal Atatürk hung in every tea house and café. Elinore admired the handsome policemen with their puttees and moustaches but was shocked to see men walking hand in hand down the wide boulevards lined by new buildings. Then they turned south into the vast barrenness of the Anatolian steppes, crunching along the gravel of rough, narrow roads. Somewhere near Lake Tuz they hurtled into a looming steel-grey sky that turned black by afternoon, ferocious gusts kicking up clouds of dust and grit that pelted the vehicles, then through a downpour that washed the sky clean as they passed under a towering thunderhead. The air smelled of lightning and dry dirt shocked into momentary life by the pouring rain.

Later, in the dark of night, it was like being at sea again. The jeep and van were tiny and insignificant in the sweep of the rolling, treeless landscape. They felt alone in the world. The easy part of the overland push was behind them.

They climbed the Taurus Mountains in low gear at 10 miles per hour, and when the van's radiator overheated, Ben wrapped it in wet rags to cool it down so they could keep going. On the descent they coasted for miles in neutral, around hairpin turns, down to the sprawl of Adana, and onward to Iskenderun and their first glimpse of the blue Mediterranean.

On 20 May they reached the Syrian border and the next day drove into Damascus on a day so hot the asphalt road was melting into shining wet patches. At midnight the city erupted in celebration at the end of Ramadan.

After checking out of the Orient Hotel the next morning, they ran into Thwaites, who'd just arrived with his family. Ben remained argumentative and cagey, refusing to discuss his plans or route towards Iran.

'Taking the desert track?' asked Thwaites. No answer. 'Why all this stupid secrecy?' But Ben wouldn't give anything up. Thwaites thought Ben didn't know where he was going. Or maybe he kept quiet out of paranoid caution, afraid of giving up insight that would help Thwaites or anyone else follow in his tracks.

'He won't even tell Elinore,' said Frank when Ben was out of earshot. 'Damn fellow's awfully difficult to get along with.'

They crossed into Jordan at the Nasib border crossing, where a smiling official gave them sweets and said, 'Today is

Christmas!' Elinore stocked up on cigarettes and tea before they turned into the country's great eastern desert, a scorching badland of stony plains, driving on rutted roads that sometimes dissolved into near nothingness. Baghdad was 500 miles away. As the road deteriorated into serious washboard, the corduroy-like ridges that plagues unpaved roads everywhere, the jeep and van shook furiously, the jerry cans and cases and tools and gear rattling and banging, screws loosening, bones jarring. Ben had to stop every few hours to tighten up his wheel bolts, but he never slowed, instead stomping hard on the accelerator. The worse the surface, he believed, the faster you had to drive to get over it, the way it had worked for him years earlier on the rough corrugated dirt roads of Western Australia.

'You just grit your teeth,' he said. 'Above 50 mph the car flies and one has little sense of contact with the road.'

Interestingly, Tim Slessor made an identical observation a few months later while travelling the same route: 'The faster one drives, the smoother the road seems to become.' He also wondered why dirt roads become so corrugated in the first place. The expedition's cameraman, Anthony Barrington Brown, had a theory that it was 'some function of the harmonic frequency of lorry springs which, over the years, had pounded out the ripples', and fifty years later he was proven correct. A 2007 study published by the University of Cambridge determined ripple formation is caused by the speed and weight of passing wheels and the density of the road itself. When a wheel hits a random bump in a soft road, it rises up and comes back down, shoving material out of its way to create a trough that's followed by a second bump as it bounces back up. As more vehicles pass the process is repeated, the troughs get deeper and the ridges higher, and a pattern of ripples and corrugation soon emerges.

And the expert drivers fly over them.

Then Elinore tried the same thing in the van. Ben raged at her excessive speed, even though she was doing the right thing, and Elinore forced herself into a stoic silence as a defence against his growing brutality. *I never open my mouth for even the smallest thing,* she wrote that night, *but am called a half-wit, a bitch, all manner of filthy names with gestures of impending physical violence.*

Everything got steadily worse. The jeep became hellishly hot under what Elinore described as a 'murderous sun'. Ben had never been able to get it ventilated properly, and engine heat radiated into the cabin. He stripped down to shorts and rope sandals and sweated off ten pounds. Between Damascus and Baghdad the cabin soared past 65 degrees, and in the back of the jeep his toolboxes softened and collapsed, sealing their contents inside plastic sarcophagi.

It was almost as bad in the van. *Suffocatingly hot,* Elinore scrawled weakly in her journal. *Dead air. No wind.*

Great drifts of sand covered the broken road as they drove eastward under a scorching sun. *Half-Safe* ploughed through, but the van repeatedly bogged down, and Ben and Frank had to stop, get out and push. At night they slept on bare rocky ground, slathered with insect repellent to keep the swarming mosquitoes at bay. They woke up before the sun rose and rattled onward towards the dusty heart of Iraq's western Al Anbar Province.

In Fallujah they found brief reprieve in an invitation to a private club where American and British engineers quaffed

Pepsi and gin. Frank and the Carlins got smashed under slowly spinning fans, shared their adventures and left with a donated bottle of gin that helped them ignore the wind and mosquitoes when they bedded down in the desert at midnight.

On 26 May, 4,270 miles out of London, they crossed a bridge over the muddy Tigris into Baghdad and collapsed in air-conditioned rooms at the Semiramis Hotel on Rashid Street. It was a favourite of foreigners and home to a motley assortment of permanent residents who never seemed to go much further than the dining room or the tree-shaded terrace overlooking the Tigris. Elinore called Baghdad a *rat-bag of a city*, dreary and depressing, and tried to distract herself with a prewar Abbott & Costello film in a theatre where it was hard to hear the words.

For a third time *Half-Safe* crossed paths with the Hillman Husky. Thwaites ran into Frank at the Semiramis, and they compared notes over cold beer.

'I've had it!' complained Frank, looking notably thinner than in Damascus. 'If anyone mentions the Jordan–Syrian desert to me again I'll shoot them.'

Meanwhile Ben fitted the van with a bigger four-bladed fan to help cool its engine more effectively, and Elinore stocked up against the ailments of the desert: anti-mosquito cream, anti-constipation tablets, antibacterial Asepso soap to fight prickly heat, quinine tablets to prevent malaria.

They drove north-west towards Khanaqin, near the Iranian border.

It was dark and they were bedded down on the rocky desert ground next to their vehicles, greasy with anti-mosquito cream, when they heard the crunch of horses approaching, and then low voices. Ben signalled for Elinore and Frank to remain silent and motionless. The horses drew nearer. Two men dismounted.

'Stand up! Stand up!' shouted one of the men. He issued commands in Arabic, then said something about the jeep and car in halting English. It was unclear what they wanted, what they intended. In the moonlight, Ben saw that the two men were Iraqi soldiers, or at least were dressed like Iraqi soldiers. And they were carrying military rifles. He thought fast.

'Yes . . . no . . . okay . . . *salaam*,' he said, responding to the commands but not moving, repeating simple words over and over as the soldiers continued shouting. He was buying time and hoping the soldiers might think more people were sleeping in the jeep and van. The commands kept coming: *Stand up, stand up!* But Ben, Elinore and Frank remained on the ground, passively refusing to move.

The journey could have ended then and there, but this was Ben at his best. Reading the situation correctly and applying logic. Acting decisively in the face of danger. Being brave but not rash. The soldiers grew frustrated, seemingly uncertain about what to do next. Finally, after almost half an hour of getting nowhere, they gave up, got back on their horses and rode off into the night, their intentions forever unknown.

෨

On 29 May, *Half-Safe* arrived at the Iranian border. Women and children gathered around Elinore in the sweltering customs hall, watching her write in her journal as Ben filled out endless forms under the gaze of the Shah and Queen Soraya, whose portraits hung throughout the building. Outside, a sweating official climbed inside the jeep. Its military pedigree worried him. So did its radio and photographic equipment. He called two more officials into the cramped cabin. They examined its contents. Maybe the odd-looking jeep was some kind of military reconnaissance vehicle? They sealed the radio and all of the jeep's photographic equipment, pending further examination in Tehran.

But just to be sure: 'Do you carry guns or ammunition?'

Ben said no.

Ten miles past the border in Qasr-e Shirin, a small city that had once been a stop on the Silk Road, the police detained them again. It was late afternoon. They were ushered into a police station and offered cigarettes and small glasses of water in an office with whitewashed walls while the jeep was examined further. After several hours of indecision the officials told them to stay the night on the open balcony of a local hotel, above a crowded main street where music blared through loudspeakers until past midnight. They could leave in the morning, provided a guard rode with them as far as Kermanshah.

The next morning an Iranian official wearing a heavy wool tunic joined Ben in *Half-Safe* for the drive. Ben closed the rear hatch, turning the jeep into a rolling oven. It got so hot that a few hours later petrol vapourised in a fuel line passing through the cabin and the jeep stalled in the middle of the road. They rolled to a stop and Ben opened the rear hatch. The official took the opportunity to stagger out and immediately collapsed on the side of the road.

They were free to drive on alone after that.

Officials in Kermanshah unsealed the radio and cameras and waved them eastward, through fields of pink and purple

Above: The Carlin family in West Leederville, WA, around 1914. Standing, from left: Ben's older brother, Tom; his mother, Charlotte; his older sister, Jess. Seated, from left: Ben; his father, Frederick Carlin; and an unidentified girl. *All photos courtesy Guildford Grammar School unless otherwise noted.*

Right: Ben in his final year at Guildford Grammar School in 1929.

Below: Ben and his soon-to-be first wife, Gertrude Plath, in Mentougou, China, in 1939. Camel caravans carried coal to Peking, a few miles to the east. *Betty Halvorsen*

Ben during his service in the Indian Army, 1943.

Ben's as-yet unnamed Ford GPA with modifications complete and the belly tank strapped to its roof in 1947.

An original Ford GPA at Blythe Army Air Base in California in 1943. The military found the amphibious vehicle ineffective and cancelled production after 18 months. *John Funk*

Ben at the wheel and Elinore curled onto the cramped bunk. Photographed for *LIFE* magazine in 1948.

The jeep's interior in 1948. One early visitor called it a 'floating workshop'.

The jeep approaches Weems Creek in Annapolis, Maryland, for a sea trial in August 1947. A few days later it sank.

More testing in Annapolis in 1947.

Half-Safe sails past the *Queen Mary* on 13 July 1948, on an attempted launch from New York City.

Half-Safe departing Flores Island in the Azores, 1950. *José Henrique Azevedo*

Days on Fayal Island ended with drinks at Café Sport. From left: Café owner Henrique Azevedo; Tomás Alberto Azevedo; Elinore; Ben; Henrique's son José 'Peter' Azevedo; António Dutra; Mestre Costa. *José Henrique Azevedo*

Heading north into the Spanish Sahara in March 1951, with Berber guide Bessahri showing the way.

Visitors in the Spanish Sahara, March 1951.

The Carlins earned $30 a day by displaying *Half-Safe* at a Brussels department store in the summer of 1951. *George Bass*

Ben found some of his most enthusiastic fans in Scandinavia. Copenhagen, August 1951.

Carlins and Basses in Cambridge, England, November 1951. From left: Ben; my grandfather Robert Bass; Elinore; my uncle Bob Bass.
George Bass

GG 7753

Le tour du Monde en Jeep

Stripped down for a complete rebuild in Birmingham, England, February 1952.

Ben working on *Half-Safe* in London in 1954.

In front of the Primrose Hill flat, packing to leave London, April 1955. *Deirdre Carlin*

Crossing the English Channel, 22 April 1955. Shot by John Simmons for *Picture Post*. Ben steers with the newly installed tiller and Elinore pretends to operate the radio. *Deirdre Carlin*

Landing at Calais, just before *Half-Safe* sank into a sandy beach. *Deirdre Carlin*

Ben, Elinore and Frank slept on the ground while crossing Iran, slathered in insect repellent. June 1955.

Ben and Barry Hanley, a draftsman from Perth who joined *Half-Safe* in Burma and went as far as Japan. Date and location unknown.

Arrival in Calcutta, India, July 1955.

Barry Hanley on *Half-Safe*, somewhere in Burma, 1956.

Half-Safe and the new tow-tank fabricated in Japan for the Pacific crossing, 1957.

Ben and Boyé De Mente, a Tokyo-based American journalist who crossed the Pacific with him in 1957, made frequent stops on their way to Wakkanai.

In the North Pacific, 1957.

Naked in the North Pacific, hacking the propeller free of Japanese fishing nets on 26 June 1957.

Landing on Shemya Island, Alaska, in the far western Aleutian Islands, July 1957.

The crew of a Reeve Aleutian Airways flight examines the jeep on Shemya Island, July 1957. *Dick Reeve*

By 1957 Ben resembled a rugged, nomadic Ernest Hemingway.

No more oceans to cross. Outside Whitehorse, Canada, in October 1957. *Deirdre Carlin*

Ben married Cynthia Scott Henderson in 1963. She was nearly 30 years younger than him.

Ben and Betty Halvorsen, daughter of his first wife, Gertrude Plath, in Nevada, 12 November 1957. *Betty Halvorsen*

Half-Safe today, in her protective shelter at Guildford Grammar School outside Perth. *Gordon Bass*

opium poppies and into brown hills that Elinore saw as *soft and billowy as a fat woman's curves*, heading towards the mountains in the distance. When they arrived at Hamadan, 6,070 feet up in the foothills of Mount Almand, they were shocked by a chill in the air.

The sun hung low in the sky when they arrived in Tehran and checked into a small hotel run by an Austrian woman. Elinore crawled into bed, her head aching. She didn't know if it was the heat or the altitude or Ben; the threats and physical blows came ever more frequently now. *Even Frank looks good by comparison*, she wrote on 1 June, *and that is a new low.*

> It goes on. No instructions and never any explanations. If one asks a question one is bitingly referred to as a simple moron. If there are two routes and one asks which one (we have no map, and Ben never offers info on route), one is scathingly referred to as a bloody fool, and if one asks to look at the map – *why? You won't understand it.* To be shouted at in front of large crowds of people is now common but still shattering.
>
> Misery.
>
> Why? To what end this eternal Bligh manner?
>
> Fraud.

She awoke the next morning wracked by vomiting and diarrhoea. She skipped breakfast and collapsed into the van's passenger seat. Her eyes hurt. Insect bites covered her skin.

Later, driving south from Tehran to Isfahan, the van sputtered and coughed. Frank stopped, studied the engine, found nothing and got back behind the wheel. More halting progress, more stopping and starting.

'You're the engineer who claimed to know all about cars!'

Elinore screamed at Frank with what energy she had left. It was the sad fact that only Ben could fix things.

He was waiting ahead at a three-table mud-hut café.

While Ben worked under the hood on the van's ignition coil, a small crowd gathered around the foreigners and decided Elinore should ride on a donkey. Frank pulled out the Bolex and started filming her. She looked casually glamorous in a white T-shirt, khakis and sunglasses. She smiled at the children gathered around her in the glaring sunlight as the donkey took a few steps past the dusty yellow jeep. Mountains rose in the background under heavy grey clouds.

The footage appeared in 1964, when Ben was the featured guest on two episodes of *It's a Small World*, a short-lived real-life adventure TV series that ran for a few years in the Los Angeles area opposite *The Alfred Hitchcock Hour*. Host Donald Curtis was a minor character actor with a pencil-thin moustache, near the end of a career that had peaked with a role in *Earth vs. the Flying Saucers*. He lobbed simple questions through an obsequious smile as Ben narrated a documentary edited together from his years of travel.

'Well, you know how women are,' cracked Ben when they got to the scene with Elinore astride the tired animal. 'Just never satisfied. Some demand a Cadillac, others demand a second-hand donkey, but always wanting something.'

Curtis smirked knowingly.

Watching the footage today, and knowing the pain behind Elinore's forced smile, is heartbreaking.

Darkness fell. Ben continued working by the hissing light of a kerosene lantern while Frank looked on helplessly and sighed.

'That's about all we can do,' Frank said.

Will we ever reach Calcutta and be rid of him? thought Elinore. The owners of the café summoned her inside to sleep on a pile of carpets while the men slept outside in the vehicles. She felt insects crawl over her body in the dark.

In the morning they continued south to Isfahan and stopped for days of repairs. The jeep had a violent shimmy and damaged left front wheel, and the van still lacked power.

After that the roads devolved into unmapped scratches in the arid soil on the long drive further south-east towards the Pakistani border. They started running low on water, and what was left tasted of petrol.

Somewhere between Yazd and Kerman the jeep's left front wheel flung itself into the desert, and then the steering arm snapped. Ben left Elinore and Frank in the desert with the crippled jeep and drove the van to Yazd to get the parts welded.

Elinore lay in the shade next to the jeep until the sun rose higher and the temperature hit 38 degrees, and then she collapsed next to Frank under a blanket strung up from the back of the jeep, looking out across the arid landscape, empty except for patches of thorny scrub. The occasional breeze felt like a hot blast from a furnace. Here in the middle of Iran they were just as aware of the wind as they'd been at sea, oddly dependent on its direction as they endured this hottest part of the journey. When it blew from behind, the jeep's air intake became less effective and the engine overheated, so as they drove further into the desert they hoped for headwinds, then started driving by night to avoid the heat. There were millions of stars overhead, more than they'd ever seen, the Milky Way splashed wide across the sky. They slept on the ground during the day, hugging the vehicles for their shade, trying to ignore the small ants that swarmed over them.

The Carlins' seventh anniversary came and went. *Neither thought of it, as usual*, wrote Elinore. *Can't envision an eighth.*

On 11 June they arrived in Kerman and found a cheap hotel at the end of a long, narrow alley with a single pomegranate tree in its dusty courtyard. But even here there was socialising to be done. The first night, Brewster Wilson, a young Near East Foundation official in horn-rimmed glasses, invited them to dinner. The next night an invitation arrived from Kevin Carroll, a director of the United States' Point Four aid program, and his wife, Anita, who Elinore found *young, pretty and painful*. There wasn't much to Kerman, but the Carrolls lived in comfort; their home was palatial, strewn with carpets, and had a pool and tennis court. An American diplomat joined the dinner and lent Elinore old copies of *Life* to help pass the time.

Less than two years later, *Life* reported on the murder of Wilson and the Carrolls, who were found shot dead by their jeep along a desert trail. Bandits had fired on their car, according to the official report. Anita survived the initial ambush, even though a bullet had entered her chest and exited her back, but was dragged away from the jeep and shot again to ensure she wouldn't survive as a witness.

The desert could still be a dangerous place. Ben and Elinore realised how close they'd come to death outside Baghdad.

At night Elinore escaped into books, finding parallels to her own life in their pages. In Richard Aldington's just-published

Lawrence of Arabia: A Biographical Enquiry, she identified with the ferocious attack that portrayed its subject as a self-important liar who wrote badly. *A schoolboy who drugs himself on hazy heroics*, she wrote. *A complete fraud.*

Fraud.

She read D. H. Lawrence's *Sons and Lovers* too, feeling all too familiar with its cast of men who were unable to love. *Quite a true picture*, she wrote. And then she read Aldous Huxley's *Brave New World*, where falling in love was a sin.

It wasn't the best selection of books for escapism.

While Elinore read, Ben worked on the jeep. First, he removed two of the clear perspex panels from the sides of the cabin and replaced them with air scoops covered with chicken wire to help cool the cabin. Then there was the hastily repaired steering arm, which had already broken again; he ordered a replacement from Tehran. The neoprene sealing the deck was peeling under the brutal sunlight. Nothing to do about that, really. One of the U-bolts that attached the suspension springs to the jeep had broken and needed to be replaced. The intense heat of the desert had cracked two of the holoplast panels of the jeep's superstructure.

There was always something to do to the jeep, and Ben tended to it like a nurse, no, like a *lover*, more aware of its mechanical rhythms and sounds and needs than to those of any person, his hands often bloodied with the work. More than any woman, *Half-Safe* was the greatest relationship of his life. Ben had imagined it . . . imagined *her*. He had conceived her and nurtured her. He understood her, even if he didn't ever love her. He was happiest with her grease under his nails. Her shimmies and sounds told him where she was weak, where she needed attention. He knew her smell, a peculiar tang of oil that even in the middle of the desert was as much boat as car.

And Frank? He kept to himself during the days in Kerman, beginning to realise how incredibly much Elinore despised him. Had he looked at her journals when she was off at the baths? Read her description of him as a *weak and fawning clot*? Her complaints that he was an *incompetent imbecile and braggart*? Or her observation that, *He's waking up to the fact that his presence is not exactly exhilarating or even tolerable*?

Until this point Ben had mostly ignored him, but as the two men stood in the shadow of a Kerman garage, their own relationship finally began to splinter as well.

'Drain the oil,' Ben asked. A simple request of someone who claimed to know all about cars.

Frank breathed in the sweet scent of oil and dust as he studied the mysterious inner workings of the jeep, its engine, the various hoses and wires. He had no idea where you might drain the oil, but he saw a promising plug and unscrewed it. Fluid poured forth, but it wasn't the right plug or the right fluid.

Ben shook his head. 'You can get off here or carry on to Calcutta,' he said, 'but we can't pay any further expenses for you.'

'I'm doing my best,' protested Frank.

Which meant, according to Elinore, *drinking beer, drinking tea, finding ways of putting extras on the hotel bill, and generally bragging and boasting of his capabilities to any English-speaking person he can find.*

That night Frank pulled Elinore aside. 'I made a very bad mistake this afternoon,' he admitted. He offered to pack it in once they reached Quetta. But first he'd have to wire home for money – and by the way, was Quetta still in the Commonwealth?

Since he was supposedly broke it's unclear how Frank got hold of a full bottle of vodka a hundred miles down the road in Bam. But it was a pleasant anesthetic against the worst hotel so far, a nameless building where they slept on a bare concrete floor among other weary travellers and washed with water from a communal jug. Goats and chickens shambled about in the dirt of an interior courtyard, and Elinore awoke at sunrise with a rabbit hopping lazily across her body.

Beyond that the road was lost in drifts of sand. A fine grit filled both vehicles and entered their noses, ears and eyes. The vehicles bogged down repeatedly. They passed an 80-foot brick tower built hundreds of years earlier, once a desert lighthouse with a fire burning at the top to guide camel caravans travelling by night through the desolate landscape.

At one lunch stop Elinore waited quietly for more than an hour after Ben's omelette was served before daring to ask if her own was being prepared. Ben hissed at her to stop 'begging'. And now that Frank had been terminated from the dysfunctional expedition ahead of schedule, he turned equally rude and critical. He refused to show Elinore how to put new film in the movie camera, making her figure it out for herself.

Is no one going to be happy & polite again? she asked. *Why, why, why?*

She had come to hate it all. Hated that she'd wasted seven years on this damned venture, still only halfway around the world. Hated Ben's anger and violence. Hated Frank's helplessness. Hated that it would be years before they returned to a normal life. Hated that she would never have children. She'd suffered enough.

Elinore made her final journal entry on 22 June 1955, at the Hotel Kalfides, a small inn run by a 70-year-old Greek man in Zahedan, a tan sprawl of mud-brick buildings near the three-way border with Pakistan and Afghanistan, an area described in *Time* magazine as 'a triangular no-man's land'. Her words show her escaping into fantasy in her final weeks on the hot, dusty roads of the Middle East, imagining herself a tourist on an exotic vacation rather than a merciless journey that was crushing her body and soul. In the stifling, still heat and quiet of a windowless hotel room that day, she wrote page after page about the stooped old Greek proprietor and his wife and their 'confirmed bachelor' son Dimitri, who ran a local garage. She wrote about the servant in striped pyjamas who rushed to attend to every need, and about the soft water and perfect temperature of a hot bath. She wrote about the expensive cold beer and the cheap wine spiked with vodka to give it a kick. She wrote about the young American 'fly-boy' pilots for Persian Airlines, the handsome maître d'hôtel who used to be a 'smoky Joe' but had kicked the opium habit, and about the two young maids who still slipped away every few hours to return in a haze. She wrote about a boy dropping a bucket into the hotel's well, and how the maître d'hôtel gallantly took off his shirt and climbed down to retrieve it without complaint.

There was no more to write. After this last entry she closed the last of her seven spiral-bound notebooks, in which she'd recorded seven years of joy and anguish and hope and disappointment, and she thought with fear and excitement about being free for the first time in nearly a decade. Yet to come was the detour to Australia, a necessary obligation to help promote the book. But after that she was going to buy a single ticket to some place far away.

~

The series of mechanical breakdowns meant it had taken 28 days to drive 1,450 miles across Iran. They were going too slow.

Ben tapped into a stash of 'emergency' methedrine and ploughed across Pakistan in ten days, driving through day and night, roaring past the landmarks that in happier days he'd once promised to show Elinore.

They stopped in Quetta just long enough to unload Frank. He made his way to Bombay and sailed for Australia, arriving in Fremantle on 20 October, then headed east for a temporary stay at the Morris Hotel on Pitt Street in Sydney.

Despite three months on the road with the Carlins, Frank remained, and remains, mostly a cipher. He was born in Ireland in 1915, the son of a wealthy motor-body builder who'd moved to England and inherited part of a £100,000 estate in 1928. Two world wars killed off most of the males in the Ringland family before they had children, so there wasn't much competition for what remained of the fortune, and in the summer of 1955 the family business, North London Engineering Company, was being liquidated. Money never seemed to be an issue for Frank. He was living comfortably in London when he decided to head east in *Half-Safe*.

F. J. Thwaites portrayed Frank as a nervous man second-guessing his decision to join the Carlins and trying to avoid their wrath. Ben seems mostly to have ignored him until the very end; in the sequel to *Half-Safe* he mentions him only in passing.

Maybe he originally had more to say but thought better of it: when I read Ben's original manuscript for his posthumously published book *The Other Half of Half-Safe*, I found half a page cut off, physically *missing*, leaving just a single factual sentence about Frank's departure: 'Frank left us at Quetta to take ship to Australia from Karachi.'

Other than his 90-odd days with the Carlins, Frank left virtually no mark on the world, save one. In the May 1937 issue of *Speed* magazine, published by the British Racing Drivers' Club, there's a pencil sketch of an Alfa-Romeo 2.3 in a section about overseas motoring activities. There's nothing else remarkable about the simple drawing of the open two-seat sports car, except this: it's credited to Frank W. Ringland. He was 20 years old and already dreaming about automobiles and motion and faraway places.

I showed it to Tony Clark, a British authority on automotive art. 'He looks to be an amateur artist,' he judged, 'from the way the front wheel is drawn.'

But Frank was more than a mediocre artist, hapless driver and punching bag. He shot almost all of the footage of *Half-Safe* between London and Quetta. He drove the Ford van across Europe and the Middle East. His DNA is forever part of the story, even if Ben took pains to minimise his supporting role because it didn't fit into the narrative of a single vehicle tackling the world.

While the world never really heard about Frank, I wondered how he remembered the long drive of 1955. As the adventure of a lifetime? As a mistake? As the catalyst for change after an unhappy first marriage? He stayed in Australia, settled in the Sydney suburb of Sylvania and married dressmaker Winifred

Mary Keough in Springwood on 20 April 1957. She was 40, a 'spinster' according to the marriage certificate. Frank was listed as a widower, which might or might not have been true, but so what? His old life was half a world away. According to voter rolls he became a 'sales executive', and in 1969 he joined his local sub branch of the Returned and Services League in Miranda, badge No. N97017, made eligible by his service as a flight lieutenant in the RAF.

I tracked down a few people who'd lived near him on Crystal Street in the early 1970s. None of them, not even a man who'd lived just two doors down, had more than a vague memory of his name, nor had any idea that he'd once journeyed across Europe and the Middle East tending to a record-setting amphibious army jeep and its bickering crew. When Frank Ringland died on 10 June 1973, he was just 57 years old. I'd like to think he found happiness in those years far from home.

CHAPTER NINE

Mutiny

On 15 July, a punishing 86 days and 8,550 miles out of London, *Half-Safe* rolled into Calcutta. It was steaming hot, and upon seeing the crowded city for the first time in a decade Ben complained, 'India is not the sort of country one returns to voluntarily.' Yet this was where he'd spent his years in the army, and where he'd met Elinore, and where he'd first seen a Ford GPA and dreamed up the circumnavigation a decade earlier. It was a sort of homecoming.

The dusty, beaten amphibious jeep pulled up in front of a grand house at 9 Camac Street. It was home to the Shellims, a prominent Jewish family that had arrived from Baghdad in the late 19th century and built a successful import–export company that traded mainly in jute, a strong textile fibre. Ben and Elinore knew the family from their time in India during the war, and when they appeared at the door the family's Nepalese maid Maily greeted them as if not a day had passed.

Maurice Shellim, a London-trained doctor, self-taught artist and frequent figure at the Bengal Club, invited them into his ground-floor apartment, where he tended to caged birds and entertained around his grand piano. He worried privately that Elinore looked quite 'scruffy'.

Maurice's niece Valerie Collis lived in the Calcutta house as a young girl in the 1940s, before her parents and most of the extended family migrated to England in the early 1950s. She'd left India by the time Ben returned, but her memories shed an interesting light on him.

'India then was free and open and welcoming, and there was no anti-Semitism,' she recalled over coffee during a visit to New York. By the early 1940s, she said, around 5,000 Jews lived in Calcutta, although with India's independence in 1947 and the creation of Israel the following year most would soon leave.

Despite the general tolerance, social codes were complex.

'There were three groups in India,' said Valerie. 'The British, who ran the show, protected their clubs and mores fiercely, and kept to themselves. The Jews, who were quite a close-knit community, moderately religious and dealt mainly in trade. And the Indians, who were not allowed into British establishments unless they were influential and rich.'

This talk of social strata and ethnic division was interesting, because based on Ben's letters and unedited book manuscripts it could be easy to attribute to Ben much of the prejudice that was a hallmark of the era.

I have never known the French to resist anything but the display of valour, honesty, sobriety or chastity.

191

Aimless and ineffective, the Cambodians were a good-natured troupe of comedians devoid of the deceit that characterizes Siam.

The tendency to give way to or affect addiction to the musical drug is generally popular among such frustrated and irrational people and peoples as spinsters, pansies, Jews, Poles and American Negroes.

But the reality was more nuanced. Ben, I realised, would have been comfortable in all the social circles Valerie told me about. His friends and colleagues were Christian, Hindu and Muslim. He drank gin in elegant British clubs and beer in Burmese army camps. He worked alongside Spanish sailors and Chinese miners who considered him a close friend.

And a few years later he told the *Los Angeles Times* he found people essentially the same everywhere he went. 'I came to that realisation while sitting in a tea house in Persia,' he said. 'The people I saw followed certain types, and those types are universal. While there are such things as national characteristics, basically people are the same.'

So while Ben undeniably shared some contemporary notions about ethnicities and nationalities and wrote some awful things over the years, in his day-to-day life he judged people on their abilities and by the way they treated him. His actions spoke louder than his words, even though his words were loud.

Knowing this about Ben was a happy revelation.

⌒

An introduction soon led Ben to the Calcutta office of Blackwood Hodge, a British company that sold and serviced heavy equipment around the world. India had recently implemented a five-year development plan, which included dams and canals, and there was a huge market for Western tractors, bulldozers and trucks.

At Blackwood Hodge Ben was among his kind of people, people who worked hard and knew their way around machinery. He met Jerry Jowett and Colin Wardle, the company's works manager and service manager, a pair of young Britons who'd just taken a short leave from work to set a record for the overland Calcutta to London run, travelling the same route as *Half-Safe*, but in reverse, in 12 days, 12 hours and 39 minutes in a stock 1947 Studebaker Saloon. The three men compared dates and routes, and realised they'd unknowingly passed each other somewhere in Syria going in opposite directions.

A Blackwood Hodge historian told me Wardle was living in Northampton, England, and while a phone call might not be productive given his hearing loss, he'd be happy to get a letter from me. I wrote and received a response almost immediately, pages of handwritten memories and an apology for any lapses in grammar or readability – *the onset of dementia*, you see, *although you learn to live with it.*

Wardle was a seasoned mechanic with an extraordinary handlebar moustache – an '*abu shanab*,' he said, 'father of the moustache' – and he managed a well-equipped workshop.

He remembered Ben well. 'I personally welcomed him on to our Calcutta premises,' he wrote. 'We allocated a work area for his exclusive use for an indefinite period. He was a great man and good friend, and like me he greatly valued independence. We regularly shared a beer and a Chinese meal at a simple restaurant in some Calcutta backstreet – he was not a great spender.'

I'd opened the floodgates of memory for Wardle, who followed up with a series of letters over the next few weeks that ranged beyond his friendship with Ben to his own record-breaking drive, to a career that took him to Calcutta, Beirut and Manila, to friends around the world lost too early to 'bottleitis'. He sent me a photo of the old 1924 three-litre Bentley roadster he and Ben used to roar around in, taken right around the time Ben was in Calcutta. Wardle's at the wheel of the open-cockpit car in a flat cap, resplendent in his *abu shanab*, a pipe clenched in his teeth. I can imagine the two men out in the heat of Calcutta, talking about the jeep, trading stories of travel, each a little jealous of the other. Years later Ben sent Wardle a copy of his book with the inscription, 'Some go fast, some get wet.' The lives, I think, these men lived. And now . . .

'I live with a few personal health problems – total loss of smell, nearly total loss of taste, type II diabetes, arthritis and hearing loss. I wonder how I achieved so much in life and am now very dependent on others.'

Wardle's friend and co-driver Jerry Jowett, who lived in Calcutta for eight years before returning to England, was more mysterious – 'dangerous and secretive,' according to Wardle – one of the mythical characters briefly caught in Ben's orbit before flinging themselves out to parts unknown. He'd been a commando, landed on Normandy in the D-Day invasion, later fought in Burma. There were rumours he'd been involved in black-market trading somewhere in South-East Asia before arriving in Calcutta. Ben called him 'a most remarkable bird' and said, 'I get on with him like a house fire and wish he could come with me.' He was especially fond of Jowett's wife, Margaretha, who was born of Dutch and Javanese parents.

Jowett's own daughter, Linda Johnson, who lives in England, hasn't been able to find out much about her father, who left soon after her birth in 1959. 'My mum said he was "involved in something". He visited a couple of times when I was small and said we were in danger.' In the 1970s Jowett simply vanished, although in the years afterward his family and Colin Wardle spoke of people coming to look for him.

'I don't know what my dad was involved in. He was obviously fearless and charismatic. My mum said MI6, also the Profumo Affair. I really don't know.'

~

Ben found nothing wrong with the jeep during his initial examination at Blackwood Hodge, but given a first-rate workshop he stripped the engine for good measure and repaired the rudderpost, which he'd bent by backing into a cliff in Switzerland.

Outside the rain poured down. Monsoon season had begun, that late-summer season when a foot or more of rain falls every month, and for the two months Ben and Elinore were in Calcutta heavy torrents soaked the city. Their cigarettes were too damp to light and Elinore got sick from everything she ate.

But then Ben was in his element, even after he left the workshop. He floated between cocktail parties and charmed the expatriate crowd with drunken exaggerations. *Man cannot live by bread alone*, he said. *He cannot thrive without leavening or lubrication by nonsense; adultery, alcohol, the weather, and other such sports. When such inanities are made capital offences I shall hand in my chips.*

When the rain paused he rolled around Calcutta in Wardle's Bentley. He dined with the maharaja at Burdwan Palace. And in the evenings he stumbled back to the house on Camac Street. Even for Ben it was almost too much. *Sporting activity is pretty well limited to dancing, air-conditioned bedrooms, and especially alcohol. I have no criticism, but what little life was left in Elinore and me by the trek was just about annihilated by Calcutta's social shenanigans.*

One night Ben navigated *Half-Safe* through Calcutta's crowded Chowringhee neighbourhood, driving home drunk with Elinore from another party, the rain blurring the world beyond. The jeep had no wipers. Up ahead in the dark, a stalled car had been abandoned sideways across the street, its lights off. Ben hit the brakes at the last minute, but it was too late, the jeep too heavy, the road too wet. Her wheels locked up and *Half-Safe* slid into the car with a crunch.

It wasn't a hard collision. No one was hurt. But it pushed Elinore over the edge. She unleashed months of pent up anger, frustration and shame, momentarily unafraid of the consequences. 'You did it!' she screamed at Ben. 'You were driving! You did it!'

Ben couldn't take that. Not in public, anyway.

'I hit her only once,' he said coolly, years later, recalling the event without shame or regret but as a matter-of-fact statement of what had to be done.

Elinore woke the next morning with a black eye. The humiliation was no longer bearable, no matter what forces had so long bound her to Ben. She resolved again to leave him.

But why had she insisted on joining him in the first place in 1947?

Ben always had dismissive stock non-answers ready when asked about his motivation. But when a reporter finally asked Elinore, a few years later, why *she'd* embarked on the journey in the jeep, she gave only a cryptic answer: 'My reason for going was of course obvious and simple.'

She rarely said more than that. And it wasn't that obvious, really.

Ron Shaw, whose father had helped Ben in Annapolis, told me, 'Theirs had been a wedding of convenience since Ben needed companionship on that miserable voyage,' and he said it like it was the most obvious thing in the world, like all of their friends knew it. Maybe he was right. Maybe from the start Elinore simply wanted adventure. After all, she'd volunteered for the Red Cross and sailed to India just before her 28th birthday. And maybe she thought there would be a financial reward. A key part of the plan had been to secure sponsorships and shoot film for a documentary Ben hoped to sell.

But Elinore's heartbroken journal entries of the 1950s show that she truly and deeply loved Ben, at least early on, at least some of the time.

Maybe in her mid-thirties she saw him as her last hope for children. Or maybe he had convinced her that no one else would ever love or accept her.

On 19 September, after two months in India, Ben and Elinore boarded the MS *Carpentaria*, a British-India Steam Navigation cargo ship carrying just nine other passengers. They invited their Calcutta friends on board for a round of drinks before departure, and Shellim was happy to see that Elinore was for once in good spirits. She knew the end of her journey was near. After the drinks were done and their friends had gone, the ship steamed down the Hooghly River, making stops at Madras and Colombo, and arrived in Fremantle on 9 October.

It's unclear why Ben was wearing a black eye-patch when he walked down the *Carpentaria*'s gangplank onto the wharf, but it made for a strong impression and dramatic photos. Among the crowd gathered to greet them were several Carlins – his sister, Jess, beaming at him; his nephews Eric and Brian in suits; and Brian's wife, Joan.

Ben smiled broadly for the cameras, but he was panicked about the appearance of arriving with *Half-Safe* lashed to *Carpentaria*'s deck like common cargo. He wrote pre-emptively to his Australian publisher:

> This jaunt to Australia is purely a sidestep: we shall ship *Half-Safe* back to Calcutta at the end of the year to resume the round trip. In leaking to the press, please emphasize that steamer-board is NOT our normal method of ocean crossing.

The Carlins stayed in Perth for two weeks with Jess in the old family home on Blencowe Street, which she now owned. Ben made a triumphant return to Guildford Grammar School, where a photo shows students swarming around *Half-Safe*. Among them was head boy David Malcolm, who was suitably impressed by the man and the jeep, and would years later become Chief Justice of Western Australia.

They drove east to Kalgoorlie, and Ben signed the six copies of his book at the only bookseller in town. He felt the town had become seedy, even though it had seen 'the best years of my life and . . . remains my spiritual home'. At heart, he was still a miner. A man who worked with his hands and was most comfortable in the company of like-minded men. Naturally, he tracked down old friends and got roaring drunk and revelled in the past. Elinore listened in boredom and frustration.

From there he packed *Half-Safe* onto a train bound for Port Pirie and continued eastward.

～

Half-Safe: Across the Atlantic by Jeep arrived in bookstores on 10 October 1955. It was a straightforward, linear telling of the Atlantic crossing – day by day, hour by hour – starting with the first sight of a GPA at the tail end of World War II and ending with the arrival in London. Ben wrote in a stiff-jawed manner that betrayed little emotion and downplayed most of the danger. It's as if he'd imagined himself telling the story at a club over cocktails, admitting it got a bit rough in patches but focusing mostly on his mastery of navigation and mechanics. A random paragraph, mid-Atlantic:

> All evening we bowled along smoothly but before daylight on the 25th – seventh day – a breeze sprang from SE. By midday it had raised such a chop that we changed course to 105°, where *Half-Safe* ran more easily. Late in the afternoon came a ninety-minute stop for refueling and oiling up. The sea continued to rise during the evening and at midnight I changed course again to 75°.

It was like this for 279 pages.

To hear Ben tell it, he was confident and capable from the beginning. It was just a matter of getting it done. The few moments of fear and doubt, and of human discomfort, came in occasional quotes from Elinore's meticulous journals, which were essential to Ben's reconstruction of the story.

The book tour of Australia was a disaster.

The obvious problem was that by 1955 the Atlantic crossing was old news. The drive from London to Calcutta was merely an interlude, the arrival in Australia by ship an anticlimax. In the hands of a gifted writer all of this might not have been a problem, but there was only so much Diana Athill could do to add warmth and humanity to Ben's prose. And there was another shortcoming: while he could charm almost anyone when he wanted, Ben's more formal presentations on his book tour were marked by a reserved stiffness. He came across as a lecturer and his bookstore appearances underwhelmed. Worse, he was increasingly belligerent with the press and brushed off their questions, and he arrived late or not at all to media events.

In a letter to Ben's lawyer, André Deutsch blasted his author's behaviour:

Carlin's tour of Australia was a complete failure. In his own home town of Perth he refused to cooperate with the leading bookseller, who suggested that Ben should have his jeep outside his shop, come in and sign copies inside the shop, drive around the main street, etc. Instead Carlin locked up the jeep and asked for 2/6 from people to go and see it.

I had to reread the letter to make sure I'd understood it correctly: instead of cooperating with a bookseller who had his book in stock, Deutsch fumed, Ben had parked down the street and set up a competing attraction, trying to replenish his funds by charging people to climb inside the jeep.

It wasn't just belligerence. He really did need the money, and he couldn't wait. After all the months on the road, all the repairs, all the drinking across three continents, Ben was broke. In November he wrote to Deutsch: 'This Australian jaunt has cost us a packet & after repaying AU$600 borrowed earlier from my sister we are low again & shall need more funds for passages back to Calcutta.'

No deal. Deutsch was already distancing himself from the chaos of *Half-Safe*. 'Carlin won't have a dog's chance of selling the second volume,' he told a colleague.

Ben blamed poor sales on everyone but himself. There weren't enough copies in the bookstores. Display materials and author photos were behind schedule in Sydney. The media didn't show up as promised. In Adelaide, *Half-Safe* had to compete for coverage with the Melbourne Cup. Alistair's MacLean's debut novel *HMS Ulysses* was getting more of a promotional push. Ben had to do everything himself, he complained, including organising a display of the jeep at Mark Foy's department store.

But more truthfully, the critics were not kind to his book.

'*Half-Safe* (which tells of the crossing of the Atlantic in a Jeep) is, in fact, only half-interesting,' said the *Times Literary Supplement*.

In the *Sunday Times*, critic Richard Hughes compared Ben unfavourably to famous adventurers like Joshua Slocum and Thor Heyerdahl, who'd been more than brave; they'd had something to prove. But Ben?

> Maybe this exploit will lead to the better designing of amphibians in the future, a wider utility for them . . . but is that all, *really* all this expensive, hazardous and uncomfortable trip is in aid of? If so, it looks perilously like a mere nautical variety of pole-squatting – at least, by the cold light of a reviewer's midnight oil.

Jim Hodge, writing for the Sydney-based newspaper *The Farmer and Settler*, savaged Ben's purpose and prose equally:

> Carlin selected a pretty painful way of gathering material for 279 pages of shaky grammar, superficial description and inconsequential comment. *Half Safe* is a racily written diary which one would think would be of interest mainly to the writer's friends . . . A great number have made long voyages in small craft and published books about their travels. Dwight Long, the American, and Gerbault, the great French yachtsman, were a couple. These men sailed their boats single-handed around the world. They were fine seamen and competent and thoughtful writers. Carlin's original thought is confined to: 'The valves took only a few hours to grind in but the inaccessibility of the valve chamber entailed placing the sixteen half-moon keeps by finger tip at arm's length and blind.' . . . Mr. and Mrs. Carlin hope to drive up onto an Alaskan beach on the last stage of their world trip towards the end of 1956. They will then be the only people to have taken an amphibious jeep around the globe. So what?

One especially sensitive critic winced at 'the exclamatory use of the Holy Name'.

And so it went.

The harsh reviews went beyond Ben's literary limitations. They indicted the endeavour itself, reducing the whole thing to a pointless journey in an absurd vehicle.

A stunt.

But Hodge and other critics were misguided in their criticism of the journey. No matter your opinion of the man or his writing, Ben's achievement, even after the Atlantic crossing alone, was every bit as impressive as that of any other adventurer. Dwight Long circled the world in the 1920s in a 32-foot ketch explicitly designed for the open sea. Alain Gerbault's circumnavigation a decade later was made in a 39-foot racing cruiser designed by a noted British naval architect. Neither was the first to sail around the world, and neither had any motivation other than a thirst for adventure. You might as well ask 'so what?' of any venture without a scientific purpose. Why balloon around the world? Why jump from space? Why submarine under the Arctic ice? Why bag the highest peak on every continent?

The essential fact remained: Ben had crossed the Atlantic Ocean in an 18-foot jeep – a bloody *jeep*! – patched together in a driveway, and he was going to cross the Pacific next.

Ben had his fans. Richard Gordon McCloskey, who founded the Slocum Society in 1955 to support long-distance passages in small boats, called Carlin's journey 'a classical example of the triumph of man over machinery, not the pathetic dependence of a boob on equipment'. Modern sailors, he said, suckered themselves into thinking equipment could replace cunning, but a few like Ben became master mariners by *conquering* their equipment – which, in the case of *Half-Safe*, had been boiled down to the essentials, and nothing more. A temperamental transceiver – which generally failed to transmit but reliably tuned in the BBC from almost everywhere – a compass, a sextant, a wristwatch.

Anyone who's actually seen a GPA – and anyone who visits *Half-Safe* today, on display in its protective glass-sided shelter at Guildford Grammar in Perth – understands the sheer audacity of heading to sea in the flimsy vehicle.

Ben's own personality overshadowed the very thing he was doing.

Certainly the critics were right to point out the emotional slightness of his storytelling. No matter how huge a feat he'd accomplished, the book failed to give a sense of the human side of things. What was it like for two people to share the cramped confines of a jeep for a month straight? What about the madness, the anger, the fear, the fights? Did they shout at each other across the endless expanse of ocean, or did they steel themselves in silence, thankful for the roar of the barely muffled four-cylinder engine? What kept them together and threatened to tear them apart? What were they thinking in the horror of the storm that nearly crushed *Half-Safe* around them? How did they feel when they stepped onto the beach in Morocco? Ben all but ignored the emotional side of the story. When he began talking about a sequel, publishing executive Anthony Clarkson told him it wouldn't work unless he focused on Elinore and their relationship. 'It is absolutely vital,' warned Clarkson, 'that a warm, sympathetic feeling of the husband-wife team on this extraordinary journey comes in along with the adventures and the interesting technical material.'

A critic for *The Spectator*, Jeremiah Ashe was one of the few who understood Ben and his book. He'd once leapt from a sinking GPA moments before it disappeared into the murk of a Venetian canal, and he had a sense of the fragility of the vehicle and the courage it took to drive one across an ocean. 'It is an extraordinary tale, in a way more remarkable even than Kon-Tiki,' he wrote.

But with the critical consensus markedly lukewarm, the damage was already being done. The next month Diane Athill wrote with a new formality, 'It is a long time since we heard from you and we wonder how things are going in Australia.' And then she got to the point: 'There have been some nice window displays of the book, but the reviews have been disappointing on the whole.' She wrote again in January 1956: 'There is a theory that saturation point has been reached, temporarily at least, in the market for strange journeys.'

I like the book for what it is, not least because with each reading you find more of Ben unwittingly revealing himself between the lines. But it was competing with *Kon-Tiki*, *The Spirit of St. Louis*, *Seven Years in Tibet*. With big adventures. With writers who captured not just a sense of time and place, but of what it meant to be human.

Half-Safe just wasn't selling. 'By the end of 1955 the book was patently a failure,' admitted Ben. In February 1956, Diana told him there were nearly 20,000 unsold copies sitting in a warehouse. The Quality Book Club was interested in buying a few thousand at a price that wouldn't even cover production costs, and as for the rest? 'If you want them,' said Diana, 'they are yours.'

It was more than a publishing failure. The indifferent reaction to the book and Ben's fast-souring relationship with everyone in the publishing world, from André Deutsch to Odette Arnaud, dimmed Ben's star before it ever had a chance to shine. It's a huge part of the reason almost no one remembers Ben today. It's why his book sold so poorly. It's why his bigger dreams of a Hollywood blockbuster were crushed by subsequent years of bitterness, accusations and eventual lawsuits.

Once Ben left London he never again gained the world's attention in quite the same way as he had during and immediately after the Atlantic crossing, even though the most brutal travel was still ahead.

Ben and Elinore parted ways in December. He began preparing to return to India. She sold the van for £580 in Melbourne and kept the money. She was free.

CHAPTER TEN

China

In late August 1939, the heaviest rains in 80 years were falling hard on northern coastal China when Ben Carlin, seeking a new start on a new continent after years of disillusionment in Western Australia, walked down a gangway at the port of Tientsin, a major city 95 miles south-east of Peking. He was 27 years old.

An embankment on the Chingtzu River collapsed that summer, flooding the foreign concessions in up to ten feet of murky water, severing train service and communications, and creating a food shortage and subsequent black market on which butchers sold their dwindling supplies of meat to the highest bidders before being arrested. Free cholera and smallpox inoculations were administered to prevent epidemic disease from taking root. The *South China Post* predicted a bleak winter of damp houses, coal shortages and unemployment.

Westerners flocked to China for the first half of the 20th century, seeking fortunes, seeking converts, seeking adventure. And with the Depression decimating their home job market, thousands of Australians sailed to China in search of work, economic migrants rather than bohemian hedonists. There was never enough work for them, but they kept coming, some of them having been out of work for years, all of them eager to believe the rumours of something better far from home. Fares were cheap on the ships that steamed back and forth between the Australian east coast and China, and if you couldn't afford the trip you could stow away. The Australian expatriate population grew into the thousands and unemployment soared. The Anzac Society of Shanghai started handing out cash to the growing number of Australians and New Zealanders who needed help, and in more serious cases paid to send them back home. By 1934 the situation was serious enough that the Australian government issued an official warning against further migration to China, urging that 'persons known to contemplate going there should be warned not to do so'.

Ben may have been aware of the dire employment situation in China, but he'd run out of options. He figured wherever he wound up, he'd land on his feet.

And he was still obsessed with the idea of war as the ultimate test of manhood. In China, he thought, he might be able to somehow involve himself in the Second Sino-Japanese War. But until he could find a way to get into uniform, he'd go back to the thing he knew better than anything else: mining.

'The story I heard,' said Alison Carlin, Ben's niece by marriage, 'is that before he left he got a job in China, but by the time he got there, China was at war with Japan. And it was soon after that that he went off and joined the British Army or something. But again, that's another of these family myths.'

She was close. The truth was more impressive.

It was a strange time to get into the mining business in China. While lots of foreign countries had acquired rights to mine large areas of the country, tensions were rising because of a growing Chinese nationalism and Japanese aggression. Ben strode through Peking, felt the uncertainty, took photos of the banners that hung across roads and on the sides of trolley cars. *Down With Britain. Exclude the British.*

To learn more about Western involvement in coal mining in China in the 1930s, I emailed Tim Wright, Professor Emeritus of East Asian Studies at the University of Sheffield and the author of *Coal Mining in China's Economy and Society, 1895–1937.*

Wright was intrigued and curious about Ben, having himself lived in Perth for 20 years before moving to the UK. He agreed it would have been a 'somewhat strange' decision for an Australian to take up a position in China in 1939.

And then he found something unexpected in his files.

It was a report, dated 18 August 1939, to the British ambassador to China from the general manager of the Anglo-Chinese Finance and Trade Corporation, which ran the Zhong-Fu mine at Jiaozuo in northern Honan Province. Tensions were rising between the Chinese and Japanese, and foreigners were caught in the middle. The desperate letter outlined the situation:

Our British staff at Tsiaotso . . . have been detained in my house under armed guard since the 20th July and completely isolated so that they have no contact with our Chinese staff or business affairs. The Mines have been confiscated and taken over completely, I presume, by nominees of the Honan Provincial Puppet Government organized under Japanese auspices.

There was something even more interesting a few paragraphs later:

My representative in Peking is Mr. G. Rodgers assisted by Mr. Frederick B. Carlin.

Within months of arriving in China, it seemed, Ben was working for a mining company in Peking. It was impressive, but perhaps not surprising. By 1939 he had years of experience in the goldfields, and he'd taken a few courses at the Kalgoorlie School of Mines, which by the 1930s had established a solid reputation that would have reached China. Even without a certificate Ben could have turned on his charm and talked his way into a managerial position.

There was more.

Wright found another letter dated 22 August, four days later. It was a communication sent from the British Embassy in Peking to the British Embassy in Shanghai, and it was marked SAFE HAND, meaning it contained confidential information. The letter raised further alarms about threats by the Chinese to take over mines run by the British. Things were especially bad at Tsiaotso, where the local press was reporting the imminent expulsion of the British and immediate takeover by the Japanese-led Provincial Government.

According to the most recent information, the advisability of the temporary withdrawal of the foreign personnel at Chiaotso . . . is under consideration. On the other hand, another member of the Syndicate staff, Mr. F. B. Carlin, a young Australian mining engineer, has just arrived in Peking with the intention of proceeding to Chiaotso.

But Ben didn't leave Peking. On 3 September 1939, in response to Hitler's invasion of Poland, Britain and France declared war on Germany. And upon hearing the news, Ben knew immediately that this was the opportunity he'd been wishing for, his destiny, his chance to prove himself. The next morning at 9.00 sharp he presented himself at the British consulate in Peking and volunteered for military service.

He was told that volunteers weren't needed in China. If he wanted to fight, he'd have to go to Europe. And by the time he arrived the war might already be over.

His hopes were crushed.

It's possible Ben headed next for the Mentoukou Coal Mine outside Peking; he took half a dozen photos of mining operations there in 1940.

And at some point, while all of this was going on, Ben met Gertrude Plath.

Gertrude Gondela Mathilde Maria Plath was born into privilege. When she told people she was from Dallacker she wasn't talking about a town; she was talking about her family's estate in Schleswig, Germany, 20 miles south of the Danish border. The house was so big it appeared on local maps, and its grounds rolled down to the Schlei, a narrow inlet of the Baltic Sea where the children fished for eels in the cold water.

Her father, Willy Plath, served in the Imperial German Navy for nearly 30 years, resigning in 1920 with the rank of *Korvettenkapitän* and a *Dienstauszeichnung* award for long service.

Gertrude arrived in China in the summer of 1939, having sailed from Hamburg on the U.S. Lines passenger liner SS *President Roosevelt*, travelling westward via New York and Los Angeles and then across the Pacific. She was 26 years old.

There was never any expectation Gertrude would work. Instead she travelled extensively and expensively. She'd come to China because her American uncle Paul Plath was working there for Frazar Federal, a company that distributed Chrysler vehicles in China. Life was comfortable for Westerners cloistered in the walled foreign concessions.

Paul and his wife, Winnie, didn't have children, so maybe they were happy to have Gertrude stay with them. And of course there were likely other considerations for her trip; by the summer of 1939 things were heating up in Germany.

At some point over the next few months, while the wider Peking area was still recovering from the floods and a hum of uncertainty was buzzing in the close-knit expatriate community, Gertrude and Ben crossed paths, voyagers from opposite sides of the world, both of them confident and convinced they were destined for bigger and better things.

They were married in Peking on 22 April 1940.

In the wedding photos Ben wears a dark suit with a carnation in the lapel. Gertrude is on his arm in a simple wedding dress, carrying a bouquet of flowers. The two of them walk out the front door of a nondescript brick building in a Western-style neighbourhood, Gertrude beaming, Ben looking serious. They walk through a sprinkle of rice, press through a small crowd and duck into a black Plymouth sedan with two small 'Just Married' placards on the front bumper.

The marriage lasted less than a year.

Ben still yearned for battle. Soon after the wedding, he volunteered for the Royal Air Force, but was turned away because, he said, of his flat feet. There was one last chance. In October he successfully enlisted in the Indian Army, which was made up of European officers and Indian soldiers. He resigned from the Anglo-Chinese Mining Corporation, and his years of labour, he thought, were forever behind him.

On 28 December 1940 Ben reported to the Cadet College in Bangalore, India, for infantry training, without much thought, it seems, to what Gertrude would do in his absence.

Gertrude stayed behind for a while in China before packing up in the spring of 1941. On 28 April she sailed out of Kobe, Japan, aboard the SS *President Coolidge*, bound for Los Angeles. The marriage might have failed, but the ship's passenger manifest revealed Gertrude had gained something valuable in her short time with Ben: British citizenship. That made emigration to the United States much easier.

Gertrude stayed briefly with an uncle in Beverly Hills, California, who directed her to Reno, Nevada, famed for the quickie divorce. You only had to live in the city for six weeks before being granted a divorce, and there were even boarding houses where women could rent a room and count off the days before they could collect their papers. On 7 July Gertrude issued a summons against Ben to recover a judgement 'upon the grounds of extreme cruelty'. Ben was half a world away, and the divorce was granted in August.

I assumed at first that the claim of 'extreme cruelty' was a stock phrase on a form, a choice meant to expedite the divorce Gertrude knew Ben would never contest.

But then, through diligent searching and extraordinary luck, I discovered Gertrude's copy of *Practical Chinese*, which she'd bought upon her arrival in Peking, in a used bookstore in Eugene, Oregon.

Inside the front cover she'd written her name in tight fountain pen script, spelling it without an 'e', as she did until she moved to America.

Gertrud Plath
Peking, Sept. 39

I flipped through the pages of characters, grammar and dated phrases. Gertrude would have been able to practise sentences like, 'Quickly, call the rickshaw boy to come' and 'Chang, have you locked my trunks?' and 'It will not be long before the kidnapped persons will be out of danger.' The book was written in 1931 by the Peking-based Chinese Language Officer of the United States Army, and it was more than a textbook. It was an unintentional glimpse into the social mores and strata of Western expatriates in China at the twilight of the golden years.

It also hid something darker in its acid-yellowed pages.

At first the book appeared unused, an impulse purchase made with all the best intentions upon arrival in a new country and then, as usual, relegated to a shelf to receive the occasional guilty glance.

But as I leafed through it, I noticed a series of words pencilled lightly on some of its pages, in tiny letters no bigger than the printed text that surrounded them. There weren't many, but together they carried a particular weight, especially when the pattern emerged.

Lately.

Angry.

Impatient.

Women.

It was like a secret message from the past, a long-dead lament, Gertrude's dawning awareness of a marriage going bad, hidden for 80 years in the pages of a musty lexicon.

Was this the only way she could express her growing fear? Was she confiding in a teacher, another student, a friend?

The deeper I dug, the more I saw there was something broken deep inside of Ben. Maybe the rage that fuelled his anger was the same rage that once drove him to seek war, the rage that made his father banish him to a boarding school a dozen miles down the road, the rage that manifested itself in physical violence over decades and continents.

In *The Other Half of Half-Safe*, Ben wrote, 'Growing up during the 20s and 30s I was miserably aware of having missed World War I; there could never be another in my lifetime. I regarded war as a supreme (if painful and expensive) experience.'

Deep down, Ben had to fight.

He completed infantry training on 4 May 1941, and on 8 May received an emergency commission as a second lieutenant in the Engineering Brigade of the Indian Army. But even in uniform, disappointment lay ahead. As an engineer, he spent years digging latrines and building warehouses and airstrips across the Middle East, travelling through Iraq, Israel, Lebanon, Iran and Egypt. In 1942 and 1943, desperate for action, he took bomb-disposal courses, and between 28 February 1943 and 17 March 1944 he served in the 2nd Regiment Bomb Disposal Unit.

There was never a single bomb to dispose of.

Next he was shunted off to a heavy bridge corps in Italy. That post lasted less than three months before Ben was shipped back to Delhi via Cairo.

He had one last hope. In the spring of 1944 Ben talked himself into Force 136, a Calcutta-based clandestine branch of the British Special Operations Executive (SOE), which was created during World War II to promote sabotage and subversion, and assist resistance groups in enemy-occupied territory. But the reality, at least in India, was less glamourous. By 1944, Force 136 had established a network of legitimate businesses posing as fronts for intelligence-gathering activities, and Ben said it was a disappointment, 'all cloak and no dagger'. His frustration was growing.

Most SOE documents were destroyed towards the end of the war, but Ben's personnel file, 14 pages of documents complete with a red SECRET stamp on its manila cover, survived and was declassified on 1 January 2013, after being sealed for 66 years.

When I got scans of the files from the National Archives, I hoped for surprises, for signs that Ben had taken part in secret missions he'd never spoken about, maybe even something that might suggest a covert subtext for the later jeep journey itself. But Lieutenant F. B. Carlin's personnel file, a series of brief, acronym-rich communications, mostly concerns the logistics of his transfer to Force 136. It confirms a brief and uneventful service, and supports the narrative in his Officer's Record of Service.

Still, it offers interesting insights. By 1944 Ben could read and write French and Urdu and had a working knowledge of Mandarin Chinese. Five years of mining experience in Australia and one more in China had given him 'extensive incidental experience with explosives, I.C. [internal combustion] engines and engineering generally'. His special knowledge included 'map reading and field sketching'. His sporting achievements were noted as 'Sailing, Shooting, Driving, Swimming'.

In other words, the traits and skills that drew the SOE's attention were also forming the perfect background for driving an amphibious army jeep around the world. You couldn't craft a better curriculum for a would-be adventurer.

Ben lasted less than five months in the clandestine unit. On 4 November, he was reposted to the No. 1 Engineers Depot in Lahore, and then on 8 January 1945 to the GHQ Pool of Engineers, where he spent the remainder of his service.

As the war wound down, disillusionment and drink were taking a toll. Ben's file shows he spent ten days in a hospital in May 1944 for undisclosed reasons; a decade later he admitted to periods of being laid low during his years of service by 'a state of low morale compounded by boredom, lack of exercise, frustration and worry'. At such times, he said, he broke out in 'quinsies and boils', and I had to turn to the dictionary to learn that a quinsy is a now-rare complication of tonsillitis in which a painful, pus-filled abscess forms behind a tonsil. The only cure, said Ben, was to regain a sense of mental control and do strenuous 'setting up' exercises in the morning. Penicillin wasn't yet widely available to Allied forces, and without antibiotic treatment the quinsies would have been particularly painful and possibly responsible for Ben's hospital stay.

Japan surrendered on 15 August and signed the Japanese Instrument of Surrender on the USS *Missouri* in Tokyo Bay on 15 September at 9.18 am.

The war was over.

And Ben, languishing in India with the Pool of Engineers, sweltering through another monsoon summer and suffering through hangover after hangover, prone to depression, had never fired a gun in battle, never defused a bomb, never taken part in a covert mission behind enemy lines. He was back where he'd started as a field engineer, worse for wear, in his words, *ravaged cruelly by wartime Indian gin* and *in pretty bad shape*. He was 33 years old, 'a passionately interested student of hangovers', well past the age when other Australian men were settling down, getting married, starting families, joining the family business.

He hadn't yet seen the Ford GPA that would shape his life.

And then he met Elinore.

She knew what she was getting into when she met Ben in September 1945. 'Tales of one Major Carlin had reached me long before I ever set eyes on him,' she told an interviewer in 1951.

She'd been born Teresa Eleanor Arone, one of six children, in Watertown, Massachusetts, in 1917. Her parents were Italian immigrants, her father a farm labourer, and the 1940 census said they still couldn't speak English. And like so many second-generation Americans in the early 20th century, she wanted to distance herself from these poor roots, from her home in a working-class neighbourhood of immigrants from Italy, Germany, Armenia and Turkey.

'Before the war she was a clerk in a Watertown bank,' her brother Nicholas said in 1948, 'but the workaday routine never appealed to her so she joined the WAC.' That was the Women's Army Corps, the women's branch of the US Army. 'She was sent to the west coast, but when she volunteered for foreign duty she went to India. That was where she met Major Carlin. I have never met him, but I suppose he is the same adventurous type as she.'

Arriving in India was her opportunity to reinvent herself as a woman of the world, and as soon as she'd left her hometown she ironed the curls from her hair, changed the spelling of her name from Eleanor to Elinore, and shook her working-class inflections for an affected blue-blood accent.

In April 1945 she arrived in Calcutta, moved into a hostel where she slept in a pool of sweat under mosquito netting, and in June became secretary to the Director of Club Operations in the American Red Cross Headquarters. In November she was transferred to the American Red Cross Central Warehouse where, with the help of four assistants, she oversaw the closing down and inventory of Red Cross installations in the India Burma Theatre that were no longer needed at the end of the war.

She worked hard and she was efficient.

And only a few months after arriving in India, probably somewhere you could buy a bottle of cold beer for a nickel, she met Ben.

Photos show them lying on a beach somewhere on the Bay of Bengal, Ben reclining at pugilistic ease, solid, his sandy blond hair movie-star perfect, expression always tending towards a smug scowl. Leaning against a jeep in Midnapore, a scarf around Elinore's neck and a rare smile on Ben's face. Among a group of Ben's army friends, the couple looking at each other with the intensity of early passion.

Years later, when he felt Elinore had betrayed him, when unbridled anger at the world consumed him, Ben wrote a letter that described the start of their romance in brutal if questionable terms and shone an ugly light on his relationships with women:

In September 1945 in Calcutta, for two bottles of Haig, I bought from Lieut. Wilber F. Andrews, USA-CE, who was going home, a portable gramophone, about 200 records, a portable radio, and Elinore. Andie guaranteed they'd all work.

In the first days and weeks, Ben liked the confidence of the dark-haired American who wasn't like the others, who didn't care about idle chatter and gossip, and who wanted raw experience like he did. Elinore liked the toughness and conviction of the Australian major, liked his absolute self-sufficiency, and they moved in together.

By early 1946 Elinore was pregnant.

'I took the blame,' said Ben, 'and had her aborted by the best British surgeon in Calcutta.'

Which may be why Elinore left Calcutta less than a year after she'd arrived. She sailed to Shanghai in April 1946 to work for the United Nations Relief and Rehabilitation Administration, and that was supposed to be the end of things.

And not long after she'd gone, Ben saw a strange version of an American army jeep under the scorching sun at the Kalaikunda Airfield in West Bengal, and a stranger idea formed, emerging from the fog of drink, fatigue, sickness and disappointment, something that could provide redemption and give his life meaning.

When the army released Major Frederick Benjamin Carlin from duty, the idea had taken the shape of something approaching destiny, and the final entry in his Officer's Record of Service shows that instead of returning to the familiar goldfields or quiet suburbs of Western Australia, he was *proceeding to USA on release*, heading straight to the source of the Ford GPA, his passage paid by the government of India.

CHAPTER ELEVEN

And Then There Was One

In November 1955, the *Half-Safe* book tour wound down with a final press appearance on Bourke Street in Melbourne. And though it would be years before Ben and Elinore were officially divorced, their marriage was over too. Ben began preparing for his return to Calcutta, and Elinore started planning her own future.

Alone for the first time in eight years, Ben had to secure the visas, stock the jeep, type his own letters – all the things that Elinore had done without complaint. He went to a market and bought £45 of canned food for the upcoming leg between Calcutta and Hong Kong. He stowed his supplies in *Half-Safe* and loaded her on the cargo ship *Chakdina* for the voyage back to India on 15 December to resume the journey proper.

He'd almost landed a new copilot at a party back in Calcutta, when the New Zealand-born doctor and experienced

Himalayan climber Donald Matthews had expressed interest in filling Elinore's spot, but days before *Chakdina's* departure Matthews cabled Ben:

MUCH REGRET UNABLE PERU EXPEDITION
BOOKED ME PITY THANKS

Matthews had joined a British expedition to the Cordillera Blanca range of the Andes. A few weeks after summiting Huagaruncho, a difficult and isolated peak in Peru, he dropped dead of a heart attack on a dusty Lima street. He was just 39. When Ben heard the news he couldn't help wondering what he would have done with a dead body in the middle of the Pacific.

And so with just days to go before *Chakdina* left Fremantle, Ben got a story placed in Perth newspapers:

Ben Carlin Requires Crew Man
The West Australian-born author-adventurer, Ben Carlin, will leave for Calcutta today and he wants another man to make the year-long journey with him to New York by way of the Far East and Alaska.

Would-be applicants for the 'Half-Safe' job must be able to swim well and must not be susceptible to seasickness. Mr. Carlin will pay all traveling and living expenses, but the successful candidate must be able to transport himself to Calcutta and repatriate himself if necessary.

Applicants would be favoured if they had a knowledge of radio operation and maintenance, driving and mechanical experience, and 'unlimited patience.' Any West Australians who want to go with Mr. Carlin can communicate with him aboard the motorship *Chakdina* at Fremantle before she sails today.

Two men showed up. Neither impressed Ben, but at least Barry Hanley, a quiet 23-year-old draftsman from Perth, had some mechanical experience. Ben decided he'd probably do, and said he'd cable Barry from India and make arrangements to meet somewhere in South-East Asia. He bade Australia goodbye once again.

Chakdina steamed slowly northward, and on 22 January arrived back in Calcutta.

And Elinore?

The way Ben explained it to friends, she was going back to New York via London to wait for his arrival. The two of them had thought long and hard, he said, and *with infinite reluctance we had decided that beyond Calcutta Elinore would be replaced by a male. After her courage in tackling the Atlantic, in braving its repeated trials, and in suffering (me and) the Middle East and India in summer, it was a crying shame that she couldn't be in at the kill . . .*

There was, in his parenthetical, a hint of responsibility.

Other than that, the story was pure fabrication.

On 17 January, Elinore boarded the Orient Lines SS *Oronsay*, bound for London via the Suez Canal. Because of attention surrounding the book, people recognised her, among them 40-year-old Jim Marshall, a fellow passenger from Australia.

'Jim was impressed with her, as well as her celebrity,' his widow, Betty Marshall, told me 50 years later in a letter from Terrigal. 'She was a big news item.' He was impressed when Elinore told him to order Irish whiskey instead of Scotch because the stewards watered down the latter; he found her sophisticated, worldly and attractive, and maybe their meeting turned into something more. 'It would be easy to imagine a shipboard romance,' Betty said, the decades softening any sense of the jealousy she might have once felt. 'I might even wish it for these two dead people.'

It was a generous sentiment, but when Elinore wrote to Ben from Egypt and was compelled to tell him about Jim to stir his jealousy, she denied anything other than a friendship: 'We have every opportunity but don't take them – and there's nothing wrong with his impulses.'

It was her turn to push the knife, to twist it, knowing just how to inflict pain, to let him know that she was all right, that she'd survived, that *she* was now in control of her life. And it worked, stirring up strange feelings inside Ben, something unfamiliar, something hard to confess, even when couched in stiff-jawed bravado.

'Call it primitive animal jealousy or what you like,' Ben replied, 'but boy, it's strong.'

Elinore, it turned out, wasn't going all the way to London. She got off the *Oronsay* at Port Said, Egypt, took a train to Cairo and flew to Beirut. A man was waiting at the airport. David Parks, who represented the Cummins Diesel Export Corporation in the Middle East, was a handsome Texan she and Ben had met during the long, rainy months in Calcutta when Parks was in the city on business. Parks, like Ben, was larger than life, if even more accomplished. He wrote for *Skin Diver* magazine. He'd just appeared in an ad for Cornelius Compressors, posing with his scuba gear by the Gulf of Aquaba. He ran in a circle with Jacques Cousteau and Arthur C. Clarke. During World

War II he'd earned two Purple Hearts, one of them for getting wounded when he landed behind enemy lines as a paratrooper with the 101st Airborne Division. He was younger than Elinore. He was her kind of man: adventurous, charismatic, an absolute womaniser.

I heard the best story about Parks from his son David Parks, Jr, a director at FedEx in Memphis, Tennessee. 'Dad was at the Eagle's Nest, Hitler's retreat, when it was captured by the Allies in 1945. While he was there he grabbed a dachshund from the garden. He brought that dog all the way back to the States on the ship with him, but he didn't have any money to get the rest of the way home to Texas. Some flyboys in a C-54 said, "Hell, we're going that way and we'll fly right over if you want to jump out." So over Corpus Christi he quite literally jumped out of the plane with all of his stuff and the dog and landed on the beach. A man from the local paper showed up and said, *Who are you?*" Papa said, "I'm Sergeant Parks and this is Hitler's dog!"'

The dog made the news when it died.

After the war Parks travelled the world, stopping to work whenever he needed money. 'In Bangkok, he and his second wife started Tex and Wendy's Dancing School in a pub,' said David. 'It was a big goddamn success!' Parks arrived in Beirut in 1954 and was soon in charge of Cummins's international network. The job regularly took him to Calcutta.

When I asked David if he'd ever heard Elinore's name, he laughed deeply. 'I know where this is going,' he said in a rich Texas accent. 'When I got your email yesterday I told my wife, "I don't remember if Dad was having a poke with Ben's wife, or if Ben was having a poke with Dad's wife!" Pappa had six wives – married one of 'em twice. He got rid of one in Beirut, then he and Elinore shacked up.'

I was happy to know I hadn't exposed a dark family secret.

By the time Elinore moved into Parks's flat overlooking the Mediterranean, the years in *Half-Safe* had taken their toll. Over the following year she spent nearly £1,000, a huge amount then, to begin undoing the physical damage. Two months of penicillin, streptomycin and erythromycin injections for infections of the ear and thumb. A cap on a front tooth. Three more infected fingers. Treatments for a sty, abscesses and boils. A vitamin prescription. Elinore paid for it herself, as always. For most of 1956 she worked for the wealthy Australian businessman and inventor Sidney Cotton, who was living in Beirut while trying unsuccessfully to drum up interest in Tectonite, a material that was going to revolutionise the building industry.

Later in the year she broke up with Parks, but she was ready to go home anyway. On 20 October 1957, nearly nine years after setting out to circle the world in *Half-Safe*, she arrived back in Boston on Pan American flight 5/20 from London. She found an apartment in an 1844 brick Federal-style townhouse at 10 West 10th Street in New York City, in the heart of Greenwich Village. And although she moved a few more times, she remained within a few blocks of that apartment for the rest of her life. Two years after leaving Calcutta and the jeep, her journey was over.

ᕲ

Alone in Calcutta in early 1956, Ben wove himself back into the social fabric as he made final preparations to resume his adventure. Colin Wardle picked him up in his Bentley every morning after breakfast, and long days in the Blackwood Hodge workshop blurred into long nights of drinking afterward. 'I strove to keep my head above alcohol,' Ben later recalled, but he loved the struggle.

In a city of five million people Ben moved in small circles, and through friends at Blackwood Hodge he soon heard about Elinore's affair with Parks. He seemed unsurprised. He called the American man Elinore's 'latest love' and warned Elinore, 'If you MUST play with him, for Christ's sake put the fear of God into him on the subject of talking – much as I like him, I have reason to doubt his discretion.'

He signed off with 'Cuckold Carlin'. He knew the score. He just didn't want anyone else hearing about it.

By 18 February *Half-Safe* was fuelled, loaded and ready to go. Friends and locals gathered as Ben drove down the hard-packed clay of the riverbank and into the muddy water of the Hooghly River at Dai Ghat in Kidderpore.

As soon as the jeep was afloat, water seeped into the cabin and pooled on the floor. Ben backed out of the river and found a leak in the steering system. The sun sank to the west as he made careful repairs and the disappointed crowd dispersed.

Under a darkening sky he drove once again into the river, backing in this time to protect the rudder. It was now too late in the day and the tide too low to get underway, so he and Jerry Jowett, who'd come to see him off, opened a bottle of gin and settled in for a drinking session atop of the jeep in the still, humid heat of the night. They weren't alone for long. As darkness fell a new crowd appeared on the riverbank, one completely oblivious to the jeep and its pilot. The crowd of revellers, increasingly boisterous, grew in size as the evening progressed, placing life-sized wicker-and-plaster statues of the goddess Saraswati into the holy waters of the Hooghly on the day of Vasant Panchami, the coming of spring. They kept arriving late into the evening, their shouts and laughter carrying over the river as their colourful statues dissolved down to their wicker frames and drifted one by one past the bright yellow jeep.

Ben and Jerry drank until two in the morning, slept in sweat and roused themselves at sunrise. As Jerry climbed out of the jeep to head home, Wardle arrived in his Bentley bearing tea and ham sandwiches, and moments later another Blackwood Hodge acquaintance, sales director Herbert 'Bert' Samek, arrived. In a fit of boozy exuberance a few days earlier, Samek had volunteered to copilot *Half-Safe* as far as Akyab, on the west coast of Burma. Maybe he half hoped to miss the departure, but the jeep was still waiting, so Samek boarded with a basket of roast pheasant and German beer packed by the Calcutta Club.

Samek was a dapper man with a neat moustache and dark hair swept back from a receding hairline, and this morning he looked more like he was headed to a golf course than an adventure. But he had a formidable past: he'd escaped Austria and the Nazis in 1938, volunteered for the British Army and taken part in a mission to reach prisoners of war near the border of Burma and Siam. When his team's raft disintegrated in the Salween River, he swam for six hours straight to stay alive, the sole survivor. He was the kind of man Ben respected and wanted in the copilot seat, if only for a short leg of the trip.

At 6.46 am, as the tide turned and the river began flowing back towards the Bay of Bengal, Ben steered downriver, where, he observed, 'The sweetest thing sailing is a week-old corpse.' *Half-Safe* trailed a wake of empty beer bottles.

Less than 48 hours later, after spending an uncomfortable night with Ben waist-deep in water trying to free the jeep from a tidal mudflat in pitch-black darkness, Samek suddenly remembered a critical company meeting back in Calcutta. Ben detoured to deposit him on a light ship where the Hooghly entered the Bay of Bengal, quietly seething at the inconvenience and loss of a capable copilot.

And now he was alone.

This was the first time *Half-Safe* had been at sea since the English Channel crossing nearly a year earlier and, more seriously, the first time in the entire journey Ben had sailed solo on open water. But despite his initial worry about Bert's change of heart and his worries about being alone, he began to relish the solitude.

Although, given the choice, he wrote, *I would have taken Bertie, having done something the hard way (with a crewman), one looks for a still harder way. At sea the jeep was a complex and fragile tin can. I hated the idea of sleeping without a mate on watch . . . I knew that strain of steering for more than 3 or 4 hours, yet I was confident that methedrine would enable me to battle along for 18 or 20 hours daily.*

Akyab was a week away, across 325 miles of open sea, and Ben felt exhilarated and alive. 'It was a joy to be free of social entanglements,' he said. 'Again life was real and earnest.' But the thrill of motion was tempered by a growing sense of loss and jealousy, and strange emotions swirled inside him. He couldn't stop thinking about Elinore, and his letters to her got longer and longer, scrawled in a loose handwriting fuelled by a peculiar combination of amphetamines and loneliness.

I am a bit jittery at the moment, he wrote the night he dropped off Bert and prepared to sail into the Bay of Bengal, nearly a million square miles of sea stretching from India in the west to Burma in the east.

His letters reminded me of those he'd written from Canada in the late 40s, when he and Elinore were younger and still dreaming and planning and shaking off two years of failed attempts. It was as if the months of abuse and anger on the long slog from London had never happened.

Deah, he began, or sometimes *ma biche*, my pet:

I miss you more than considerable – particularly when I regard my mound of dirty clothes . . .

For two pins I'd cable asking you to fly here – not just because I'm short of crew, and in Dutch all around, but because it's just as painful living without you as with you. And don't let that go to your head, or I'll change my mind . . .

If the beauty and poetry of Beirut haven't percolated to your pants they have at least gone to your head. Come off it ducks – feet back on the ground . . .

I miss you considerable, you witch.

He even quoted C. J. Dennis's 'The Songs of a Sentimental Bloke', like its narrator wanting to leave his rough past behind and settle down with an 'ideel bit o' skirt'.

The world 'as got me snouted jist a treat;
    Crool Forchin's dirty left 'as smote me soul;
An' all them joys o' life I 'eld so sweet
    Is up the pole.
Fer, as the poit sez, me 'eart as got
The pip wiv yearnin' fer – I dunno wot.
I'm crook; me name is Mud . . .

Once he was in the Bay of Bengal he turned east toward Burma, sailing across a flat brown sea. He started popping ever more methedrine, four or five tablets a day, to stay alert. He gripped the tiller for 20 hours at a stretch until collapsing into restless, sweaty sleep on the short bunk and hoping an alarm clock would wake him after a few hours. He usually slept through it. The beating sun and drugs diminished his hunger, and he had to force himself to eat. He heated cans of beans on the jeep's exhaust manifold and sometimes forgot about them; after 30 minutes the cans exploded and sprayed the engine compartment with baked-bean shrapnel.

With no one to stand watch while he slept, or to spell him at the tiller, or to talk with him, he was shocked into a renewed awareness not just of his feelings for Elinore but of the world around him. He motored across the flat water and was moved to poetry as he watched the sun dip into the bay.

Over a dust cloud, the lemon sunset turned to pink and brown.

He was alone. Able to fall into his own rhythms. Life reduced to its essence in the jeep's small, noisy, hot cabin. Drive, sleep, eat. Two raw eggs for breakfast, sucked from their shells, followed by half a can of pears. Half a can of beans and biscuits for lunch. Half a tin of hamburger for dinner. He tossed the empties into the sea and watched them slip under the surface and disappear, each one a tiny jeep vanishing into the deep.

The thought of sleeping at night made him nervous, so he always drove until dawn and took more methedrine at sunrise. His heart pounded, his jaw tensed, he struggled to focus. After one 36-hour stretch without sleep, Ben watched the jeep's compass, salvaged from a military aircraft, swirl and shift. The lubber line down the centre of its face morphed into a spear in the hands of Saint George, who attacked the symbols around the perimeter of the compass – did Ben remember, subconsciously, that Saint George was famed for slaying a dragon in Beirut? And then the lines reformed as *tilaka*, the lines painted on the face of a *sadhu*, a Hindu holy man free of all material attachments. Ben stared into eyes that burned back into his own, glowering as the *sadhu* leaned towards him, frowning –

No, he had to stay awake! He shook himself out of the fugue, lit another cigarette and rumbled onward towards Akyab.

On the fifth day out of Calcutta a wind picked up from the south-west and kicked up a chop that made it increasingly difficult to maintain a steady course. By midnight Ben decided it was a sign. He was exhausted. He turned off the engine, switched off all the lights except for the one atop the mast, deployed the sea anchor and passed out on the bunk at one in the morning as the jeep rolled over the waves. He slept for three hours, and when he reached into the sea to pull in the sea anchor jellyfish stung his arms.

On 25 February, with no land in sight, a butterfly alighted on the windshield.

Ben kept going. More methedrine. More cigarettes. More canned food. The sun beat down mercilessly on the jeep, and even with its hull slung low in the water the cabin temperature hovered at 38 degrees.

Then disaster struck a week out of Calcutta.

It was late and a strong wind had finally subsided. Around 10 pm Ben spotted the signature *ten seconds on, five seconds off* flash of the Oyster Island Lighthouse, which sat on a scrabble of rocks ten miles off the Burmese coast and marked a safe approach to Akyab, just south of the Bangladesh border. Pleased to see that his navigation had once again kept him on course, and only a few hours from port, he ate a dinner of canned sardines and crushed pineapple, set his alarm clock and collapsed on his bunk to sleep.

Suddenly he awoke, a chemical taste like batteries in his mouth.

He could hear the gentle slosh of water in the jeep's wheel wells, but otherwise everything was oddly still. Including his breathing.

He wasn't breathing.

Goddamn it, you're not breathing!

Somehow he could think clearly, or at least clearly enough for a deep-seated survival instinct to kick in. Within seconds he pulled himself off the bunk, threw open the hatch above the passenger seat and stuck his head out into the salty night air.

He still couldn't breathe.

Why in hell must you go to sea alone?

He pressed his chest against the hatch coaming as hard as he could, trying to expel the noxious gas he believed had flooded his lungs. He had no instinctual desire to breathe, but logically he knew he had to. He pushed as hard as he could. He tried to ignore the strange taste in his mouth – acrid, metallic, chemical – because if he couldn't squeeze out the bad air he'd die, alone and adrift. As he finally felt his lungs begin to move, waves of nausea hit him. Eventually he began gulping in fresh air, and then suddenly the nausea was overwhelming and he began vomiting over the side of the jeep, violently, heaving until there was nothing left inside him, even as he tried to catch his breath.

When the convulsions subsided he lowered himself back into the jeep, weak, shaking with fear and relief, and gripped by a horrendous headache. He was aware of being entirely alone.

It was the closest he'd come to death since the raging Atlantic storm of 1950.

The next morning Ben decided it was something he'd eaten, that spoiled food had somehow produced a gas that seeped into his lungs. He dug through his stores and tossed overboard a dozen cans of suspect Iranian sardines.

Blaming it on spoiled food didn't make sense. Years later a doctor suggested it had probably been carbon monoxide poisoning. That would account for the nausea and respiratory arrest, and could have triggered the earlier hallucinations – Ben had struggled over the years with exhaust-system leaks. It's likely the methedrine factored in as well. He'd started taking the amphetamines in earnest out in the desert, when Elinore called them his 'wake-up pills', but alone on the sea he'd been taking them by the fistful, pushing himself for almost a week and sleeping just two or three hours at a time when he collapsed. A few hours after his near-death experience, Ben tried to pull himself out of the scare by taking three *more* methedrine tablets. His tolerance was so high he fell asleep anyway.

When Ben awoke in the morning the Burmese coast was ahead, a horizon of thick jungle shrouded in mist, his first glimpse of South-East Asia, where rugged mountains, dense jungle and wide river deltas put travellers and their vehicles to a gruelling test.

Ben steered for Akyab, a city at the mouth of the Kaladan River, and dropped the jeep's 12-pound Danforth anchor near a beach. As soon as it dug into the seabed, he jumped over the side of the jeep and scrubbed away the sweat and grime of his solo week at sea. That night he stayed with a British harbour pilot, who told Ben there were just two other foreigners in town, an American priest and British nun dutifully saving souls on the flat, tropical estuarial island.

On 2 March, Ben's new copilot, Barry Hanley, arrived in Akyab. Born in Kalgoorlie in 1933, Barry had moved to Perth to live with his grandmother after his schooling. Now 23, he had been working as a draftsman for Western Australian Government Railways when he saw Ben's newspaper notice for a copilot.

Ben's assessment of Barry: shortish, slim but muscular, quiet-spoken. Lacking in mechanical experience, but had spent time on the water. And 'hasn't once proclaimed he's "a dinkum aussie"', he wrote to Elinore with relief. 'No oil painting, just a bit steak-and-eggsy, like an overgrown jockey, but not at all repulsive. I'll be surprised if he doesn't make out well.'

He never said or wrote much more about Barry, just like he'd never said much about Frank. Barry was simply a means to an end, a body in the passenger seat.

Barry was quiet, and to Ben he seemed detached, but he was searching and curious. He observed and absorbed the world around him. He was fascinated by the philosophy of Buddhism.

'You ask about what might have impelled Barry to join Ben,' Barry's widow, Luceille Hanley, wrote to me in 2016. 'His mother was an alcoholic and his father a functional drunkard. As a kid he would often come home from school needing to search the bush to find his mother and carry her home. I suspect that the only way he had of coping was to dampen down or deny his emotional self. The opportunity to break away from his parents when Ben advertised for a crewman was something he saw as a way to freedom.'

In short, he'd been driven to the jeep by the same powerful need to escape, to leave things behind, that drove Ben. And that had driven Elinore and Frank before him.

And like Elinore and Frank, he got the adventure he thought he was looking for. The next day *Half-Safe* was on the water, heading 90 miles down the thickly jungled Burmese coast towards sleepy Taungup. Halfway there, with the sun going down, Ben anchored in shallow water near a stand of mangroves at the edge of Cheduba Island, a few miles off the mainland. He laughed when Barry shyly put on a bathing suit before jumping into the water to bathe; Ben always swam nude, and on the hottest days he sometimes drove that way too.

Eleven years earlier the Allies had fought the Japanese here in a ferocious battle, part of a campaign to push them out of Burma and keep them away from India. Vice Admiral Arthur Power of the Royal Navy described the area as 'dark during the day as well as during the night; acres of thick impenetrable forest; miles of deep, black mud, mosquitoes, scorpions, flies and weird insects by the billion and – worst of all – crocodiles'. Legend has it that scores of fleeing Japanese soldiers were eaten alive by crocodiles in the very waters where Ben and Barry now bathed.

By midnight they were asleep, Barry on the bunk and Ben lying across the front seats. The night was pitch black around them, and the jeep floated nearly motionless under a canopy of stars on a dead-calm sea miles from any sign of civilisation.

In the morning they navigated slowly inland, trying to find Taungup via a maze of coastal mangrove swamps and twisting channels, the water sometimes so shallow the jeep's tyres skimmed the muddy bottom. They passed a motley assortment of junks; on one a man held up his arms as if holding a rifle. It was a warning – this was bandit country. That night in Taungup three policemen stood guard as Ben and Barry slept in the jeep. The deputy superintendent of police had been shot 48 hours earlier.

⌒

When it came to his route around the world, Ben knew the big picture. From the beginning he'd had a pretty good idea of the major stops along the way – London, Baghdad, Calcutta. But beyond that, everything was a little looser. He'd never planned to set any speed records anyway.

By Ben's calculation the simplest route to the next stop, Rangoon, was the longest. It meant weaving back down the twisted channels from Taungup back into the Bay of Bengal, sailing down around the Irrawaddy Delta and up the Rangoon River. But he heard there was a shorter overland route. As he told Elinore in a short letter sent care of David Parks in Beirut, 'It is a long way around the corner by sea, and I should like to see something of the interior, despite the insurgents.'

Today an all-weather road winds from Taungup over the rugged Arakan Mountains to Pye, a small town on the Irrawaddy River. But in 1956 the road was little more than a new idea, freshly cut into loamy clay as it wound up steep slopes through dense jungle and bamboo. Higher up, the road wound tightly back and forth, following mountain ridgelines to avoid the necessity of building bridges and tunnels. The road was closed to civilians, but the Burmese officials said *Half-Safe* could attempt the road with a military escort.

They made eight miles in the first hour on the rough road, led by 15 men in an army truck, and it took a dozen men to push *Half-Safe* up the steepest sections, choking in exhaust and the dust of the dry season. Burmese soldiers marched ahead of the vehicles, occasionally firing their rifles at unseen threats in the dense growth that choked the narrow road. At night they stopped at a camp surrounded by barbed wire to protect against the tigers that prowled the hills.

After two days and 100 miles of slow going, the road began curving down out of the mountains until – at last, up ahead – they saw a glint of the Irrawaddy River, Burma's main artery of commerce, flowing slow and flat through a wide alluvial plain in the centre of the country to the Indian Ocean.

In this part of the world every river crossing meant wide, muddy banks, and Ben avoided them wherever possible. Here, there was no alternative. During monsoon season the Irrawaddy would be a mile across, but now it had narrowed by half. From the high-water mark to water's edge the jeep had to cross two hundred yards of loose sand followed by a quarter mile of sunbaked clay riven with deep fissures, followed by wet, sucking mud nearer the water. Ben gunned the jeep. On the first attack it got stuck in the mud. A tractor pulled it free. Ben tried again, floored the accelerator and made it to the water's edge, where the softer wet mud was stained by spills from oilfields far upriver. Far enough. He parked, mounted the jeep's rudder and propeller, and bedded down in the cabin with Barry. The sound of music from the village echoed out across the water, and in the evening water carts arrived at the river, each cart no more than an oil drum on an axle pulled by a pair of bullocks. The drivers led their bullocks into the slow current, scrubbed themselves and their animals, and filled up with water, the animals ignoring the odd vehicle in their midst.

In the morning *Half-Safe* had settled to its belly in the mud, and a crowd watched Ben dig for two hours on his knees, trying to shovel the mud away from the wheels so he and Barry could push her into the water with their help. It took another hour to cross the Irrawaddy, fighting eddies and sandbanks under the burning sun. Ben and Barry slaked their thirst by drinking brown water straight from the river.

Getting *Half-Safe* back out of the river on the other side was a brutal operation that required winching, digging and the aid of a water-carter's bullocks.

As the worst was almost over, an outboard-powered skiff pulled close.

'What are you doing?' called the helmsman in English.

'I'm getting out of the water!' shouted Ben.

'Why are you doing it!?'

'Because I don't wish to stay in the river! I wish to drive up the bank!'

'Then why are you not landing on a riverbank? This is only an island!'

Christ.

It was late again. Ben always felt safer on water than on land, so he and Barry winched the jeep back into the river and anchored for the night, exhausted by their Sisyphean battle.

In the morning they hauled themselves back onto land, this time making sure it was actually the far side of the river, then made good time along a paved road to Rangoon, 175 miles to the south. On the outskirts of the city they passed the odd and incongruous sight of an abandoned Ford GPA – a Detroit-born sibling to *Half-Safe*, far from home, stripped and rusting by the roadside.

Until independence in 1948, Rangoon had been British Burma's capital, an outpost of ostentation in the tropics, with grand buildings laid out on a grid of broad avenues, a bustling port and huge population of Indians. Now, to Ben's eyes, the city was falling into post-Colonial disrepair. It had never really recovered from the Japanese bombing raids and occupation of World War II, and a decade later saplings sprouted from rooftops, paving stones were stolen wholesale from the city's footpaths, and open pits served as public toilets in the once-magnificent public gardens. At least the extraordinary Shwedagon Pagoda still gleamed in burnished golden glory on a hill, so prominent a landmark that Ben used it to navigate into the city.

During a few days of socialising, the Australian legation minister donated two bottles of Scotch to the venture and the local press watched *Half-Safe* chug around a small city lake.

A few days later Ben and Barry sailed 30 miles down the Rangoon River to Burma's turbid Gulf of Martaban, and continued eastward for two days across the bay to the city of Moulmein (today Mawlamyine) in eastern Burma. As they approached the city by water they saw small golden pagodas glittering on a ridge that rose above a dense green expanse of palm and banana trees.

It would get more difficult from here. Burma was 'impassable by land', said Ben, trying to map a route to Bangkok, the next major port of call.

The notorious Death Railway, built across rugged terrain by the Japanese using forced labour during World War II, extended from Moulmein almost all the way down to Bangkok. Nearly 13,000 Allied prisoners of war had died during its construction, including 2,802 Australians. But the railway had been extensively bombed by the Allies in 1945, and anyway, *Half-Safe* had to travel under her own power. That left only one long, practical alternative: *Half-Safe* would have to sail down the Burmese coast to Victoria Point, cross the Malay Peninsula, enter the Gulf of Thailand and sail back north to Bangkok. It was a long and indirect route, some 800 miles.

Except once again Ben heard reports about a possible shorter overland route. Forty miles upriver from Moulmein was a small Burmese army post at Kyondo, nothing more than an outpost in the jungle from which a mythical road cut through the Dawna Mountains to Myawadee, just across the border from Mae Saute, Thailand. The road had been built decades earlier by the British but hadn't been maintained since 1941. Its current condition was a matter of conjecture. Attempting the road, allowed one source with British reserve, would be a 'novel approach'. Officials at Rangoon's immigration office said the road was simply impassable – and besides that, the surrounding jungle was crawling with Karen National Liberation Army insurgents. If Ben insisted on tackling the road in his battered yellow vehicle, he'd have to sign a waiver absolving the Burmese government of responsibility. It was suicidal.

In Moulmein the district commissioner reiterated a stern warning: 'You are about to enter a military area in which your welfare will be no concern of mine. Many men have been shot along the road that you propose to take. Your famous vehicle has not the slightest chance of covering the road successfully. Gentlemen, please turn back.'

Ben had limited patience for officials and their opinions, and this was no exception. The road, no matter how bad, would shave hundreds of miles off the journey. He sighed. How could it be any worse than the road he'd just driven from Taungup to the Irrawaddy? Or any more dangerous than crossing the Atlantic?

He signed a document, strolled to the local market, filled a basket with bananas and ducks' eggs, stocked *Half-Safe* and left Moulmein on the afternoon of 17 March.

The jeep chugged 40 miles up the wide, shallow Gyaing River towards Kyondo, and the beginning of the road he hoped would take them to the Thai border. As night fell the river narrowed and was choked by small islands and sand-banks. Ben gave the tiller to Barry, climbed on top of the cabin and shouted down commands as he navigated through the dark jungle by the beam of a spotlight. They spent the night anchored off the riverbank for safety and in the morning, after a breakfast of fruit and raw eggs, arrived at Kyondo, a ramshackle waterfront of buildings elevated on stilts to stay clear of seasonal floods.

A captain from the town's small army compound greeted Ben and Barry and invited them to dine in the mess with his men, who examined the jeep with curiosity. Ben gave thanks by opening one of the bottles of whiskey from Rangoon, and when that was gone the Burmese broke out their own bottles of moonshine, telling the Australians with wry smiles that they were insane to head east on the road to Myawaddy. Ben and Barry passed out on tables in the mess and slept through the roar of cicadas.

In the morning Ben climbed under the jeep to make repairs. The seal around the front-axle drive shaft had leaked, and the transfer case and gearbox were full of water instead of transmission fluid, but he'd seen worse. They hit the road in the afternoon, and the first 15 miles to the village of Kawkareik were easy running through flat paddy land. *Maybe the reports had been exaggerated*, thought Ben. *Maybe this wasn't the heart of darkness after all.*

But it *was* dangerous territory. The Burmese hold on the area was tenuous at best, and Karen rebels, who demanded an independent state, staged regular attacks against the government. In Kawkareik, where another tall golden pagoda poked out from the tops of the palm trees, more army officers pled with Ben to turn back, explaining that the road was impassable and the Karen insurgents were a very real and deadly threat. Four years earlier Kawkareik had been the site of a bloody battle between the Burmese Army and Karen troops, and the violence continued.

'Look,' said an officer, pointing to fresh bullet holes in the ceiling.

Besides, the Burmese officers were under orders to escort *Half-Safe* if she made the attempt, and they didn't especially want to go. Ben shrugged off their warnings again. The Burmese broke out a bottle of Mekhong sugarcane whiskey. Ben opened his last bottle of Rangoon whiskey. They drank into the night.

In the morning 15 armed Burmese soldiers piled into the 4x4, 3-ton truck that would lead the way. Its massive tyres gave it a clearance of nearly 20 inches; in comparison, *Half-Safe*'s flat, boat-like belly scratched the ground at half a foot. The jeep simply wasn't designed for the kind of gruelling terrain that lay beyond the village of Kawkareik.

Drunken camaraderie gave way to a sombre mood. Seven miles east of the village lay the foothills of the Dawna Mountains that rose, steep and rugged, above the plains – and what Ben described for the rest of his life as the most hellish part of the entire journey.

What wound into the mountains was less a road than a tortured, twisted, violent gash through dense jungle. At first there were remains of the stone soling that had once been sealed with bitumen, but as the road steepened its condition became increasingly bad until it was just dirt and, where that was washed and scoured away, jagged bedrock.

So that's what the district commissioner was nattering about, thought Ben. *Hell, that's nothing much.*

Soon there was less soil and more bedrock, and within a few miles all that remained of the road was its rocky shadow, almost all of the soil washed away by 15 years of torrential rains. In some places the road was hemmed in on both sides by walls of encroaching jungle, the roar of bird and insect life, and the howls of gibbons. In others it fell away to one side, with nothing but a crumbling edge between the narrow track and a sheer tumble into the jungle below. Like the road from Taungup to Padaung, this one wound back and forth along ridgelines; even today, in satellite images, its path through the mountains resembles a long, twisted viral strand devoid of logic.

*Now I see what the district commissioner was talking about.
Well, it isn't killing us anyway – not quite.*

Ben pulled out his chart and looked wistfully at the sea route
that would have taken them down the Malay Peninsula. He
choked on dust, mopped the sweat from his face and wondered
if he'd made a terrible mistake, but it was too late for regret.
Anyway, maybe it would get better ahead.

Press on.

Barry staggered ahead of the jeep in the heavy jungle heat,
shoving boulders and debris out of the way while Ben struggled to stay on track. The jeep's wheels spun, its engine revved,
and Ben cringed as *Half-Safe* crashed forward over the rocky
track in the green light of the primeval growth. They averaged
less than 4 miles per hour. Ben's shoulders tensed and knotted
as he gripped the steering wheel. When he looked at the ther-
mometer it was nearly pegged at 63 degrees, an extraordinary,
suffocating heat.

The drive became choreography as Ben crept forward, navi-
gating the jeep around obstacles and trying to make sure its
belly wasn't punctured by a shale outcrop. Barry crouched in
the heat, dust and exhaust of the escort truck ahead of them,
studying the topography, thinking of the jeep's tyres like chess
pieces on a fractured board and shouting commands to Ben:
'Eighteen inches forward on full-right lock. Straighten. Back six
inches. Half left. Forward nine inches. Straighten. Backward
two feet . . .'

If you whisk me back to Moulmein, sir, thought Ben, *I will go
through two typhoons for you on the way to Victoria Point.*

And with that thought dissolving from his mind he realised
Half-Safe was resting on its nose in a giant hole. He'd blacked

out, hadn't even felt the crash as the jeep plunged into the void. The army truck pulled out the jeep. It was dented but drivable, and they struggled onward.

It was 'by far the worst road I have ever been over,' Ben said later. 'A giant's rosary of granite boulders. The trip was almost comparable with the driving of an ordinary jeep up a dry creek's bed to the top of Mount Everest. Impossible.'

Eight miles from Myawaddy the road improved slightly as it unspooled out of the mountains, and they drove into town at twilight to collapse in a Burmese Army dormitory. Ben later looked back on it as the most exhausting day of his life. Barry was in bad shape, refusing to eat anything he didn't recognise, and on a diet of rice and water he'd become whippet-thin, looking in photographs like a prisoner of war emerged from the jungle.

The brutal going had been hard on *Half-Safe* too. 'I don't think she took any major damage,' said Ben, 'but she can never be the same girl again after that terrible wrenching, twisting, bouncing, bashing.'

The army escort turned back and left *Half-Safe* at the border.

A few weeks later an internationally syndicated article reported the mountain crossing: 'The jeepsters believe they are the only persons ever to take a vehicle through this roadless area that is sometimes virgin jungle, sometimes mere footpaths or elephant trails.'

In the same article, Ben was asked when he would complete his journey. He shrugged. It seemed a lifetime since he'd arrived in New York City with a jeep and a dream. He'd told a reporter back then that he planned to leave in February 1948 and be back in five months, give or take. By the second summer of failed launches he'd revised the travel time to one year, and on leaving London in 1955 he predicted finishing in 1956.

But now he was beyond guessing at an arrival date. The journey was all that mattered. It had been nearly eight years so far, and how could he say how much longer it would take? He would finish when he finished. All that mattered was the broader cycle of seasons, the rhythms that ruled the deserts and tropics and oceans of the northern hemisphere. Ben was the jeep, and the jeep was Ben, and together they moved slowly eastward, year after year.

'Major Carlin will make no prediction.'

The next morning they drove across the shallow Moei River, and they were in Thailand.

On the way out of Mae Saute, Ben looked over and saw a man on a bicycle pedalling furiously to keep up with him. He pulled over and stuck his head and shoulders out of the hatch. A panting official told him he'd driven past the customs and immigration office, and directed him back to complete the paperwork necessary for the jeep to enter the country. Confusion followed: the jeep lacked the proper documents for an arrival from Moulmein because vehicles simply didn't enter the country that way. (Ben later claimed *Half-Safe* was the first vehicle ever to cross all the way from Moulmein into Thailand; it's a hard one to verify.) After a few cigarettes and fruitless phone calls the official shrugged and waved Ben out of his office, and that was that. Ben drove down the street and parked in front of the police station for the night.

One last hard stretch of mountain road lay ahead, 60 miles between Mae Saute and Tak, where they would finally get on the Phahonyothin Road leading straight into Bangkok. This time it wasn't the condition of the surface that slowed *Half-Safe* so much as the steepness. Ben had to stop and winch the jeep up steep slopes a dozen times.

Ben seemed to know people everywhere he went, and in Tak it was Harry Marshall, an Englishman who logged teak for the British Borneo Company, which still used elephants to haul logs to the nearest river and float them down to Bangkok. The company had tried Caterpillar tractors, but the pachyderms proved more effective on the rough terrain. Marshall had sent Ben advance information about Asian roads, and that night he put up Ben and Barry in a teak house built by Louis Leonowens, a teak trader who inspired a character in *The King and I*.

In the morning they awoke to a gunshot. They went downstairs where Harry stood over a nine-foot python he'd killed under his desk.

⌒〜

Before they departed for Bangkok, Harry suggested what should have been an obvious modification to the jeep: The top hatch, above the passenger seat, was hinged at the rear; why not fashion a latch to hold it partway open so it served as an air scoop to cool the cabin? It worked.

Straight down to Bangkok, through forested country that slowly gave way to paddy land, *Half-Safe* arrived on 27 March. In the 36 days since leaving Calcutta, she had covered 630 nautical miles by water and 709 miles by land.

They stopped for two weeks to drink, make repairs in a garage owned by a West Australian and collapse in a guest-house owned by a cousin to the king of Siam. Where Ben didn't already have friends, he made them fast.

The Colonial era was fading away, nowhere more visibly than here. The French had just transferred consular responsibilities to new Cambodian and Vietnamese consulates. Ben was unimpressed. 'Bangkok's once-picturesque street-side canals now function principally as sewers, mosquito nurseries and road hazards,' he said.

But he was greeted warmly by the local representatives of Shell – mostly British and all *bloody nice folks*, he told Elinore in a letter, and they made sure the jeep was fully fuelled and opened a guesthouse for Ben and Barry.

Although it wouldn't expire until 1960, every page in Ben's passport was crowded with visas and entry and exit stamps, so before leaving Bangkok he was issued a new one at the Australian embassy. *Australian Citizen and a British Subject. Engineer. Six feet tall, green eyes, fair hair. Scar on left cheek.*

Half-Safe crossed the border into Cambodia uneventfully at Aranyaprathet and kept going, winding through mountains and rice paddies. Ben was back to taking methedrine and they made good time. At night they slept in the jeep by the side of the road but more often benefited from the hospitality of friends, or friends of friends, or strangers.

⌒

Since their parting in Australia, Ben had been writing to Elinore almost every time he stopped somewhere for more than a day or two, his thoughts alternating between jealousy, pride and proclamations of love in the course of a single scrawled page (with Elinore gone, there was no one to type his letters). From Bangkok he wrote reassuringly, *Please don't worry about money for me – I'll get along*, even though the advance money was long gone and he was almost broke, and across the entire country of Burma he had managed to scratch along on just £30. They were still married, at least on paper, and despite the wound of Elinore's affair he tried to provoke her guilt by claiming at least *he'd* been loyal: *I'm a bull virgin since Calcutta*, he claimed.

Elinore's replies from Beirut got more succinct, then slowed, then stopped altogether in the spring.

Despite having sworn off rivers after the Irrawaddy, Ben was unusually compelled to detour to Angkor Wat in north-western Cambodia, which required crossing the Tonlé Sap River afterward. The sprawling, elaborately carved complex mesmerised him. He spent the day wandering the ancient temple strangled by the roots of banyan trees, pausing by waterlily-choked ponds while Barry shot film, marvelling at the engineering, maybe even feeling humbled.

When it was time to leave he dosed himself with methedrine to drive through the night, but his tolerance was now so high that he collapsed at dark and parked by the side of the road to sleep.

The next morning he and Barry arrived at the river, 300 yards wide, a muddy bank sloped steeply down from a cluster of buildings. With hundreds of shouting, shirtless children swarming around the jeep, Ben drove 50 feet down a precarious embankment and sank the jeep into riverbank mud. A ferry tried pulling him out but the nylon rope tore free and the ferry snapped back violently. The metal attachments at the end of the rope whipped towards the jeep, whistling through the air like incoming artillery, and punched holes in the cabin and the aluminium rear fuel tank. A blow to Ben's head would have killed him.

Always prepared, Ben plugged the biggest hole with a fid — a long, tapered wooden tool used to pry apart knots in rope.

Who carries a fid in a jeep?

Then, out of sheer frustration and exhaustion, he collapsed in a sliver of shade in the mud and water next to the jeep to catch his breath. From above, the children laughed and dropped pebbles on his head from a half-collapsed wooden landing.

By the time *Half-Safe* rumbled up the far bank the sun was dipping towards the horizon, and another day was almost gone.

As Ben thought about whether he should try for Phnom Penh, only 20 miles away, waves of nausea washed over him. He pushed himself out of the jeep and vomited at the edge of the road, heaving over and over under the hot sun. He couldn't go any farther, not even after taking more methedrine. The heat and heavy humidity had drained him. He closed the hatches to keep out the mosquitoes that swarmed from the river in clouds, doused himself liberally with DDT-rich Flit for good measure and knocked back the day's quinine tablets to ward off the malaria endemic to the region.

The next day they made Phnom Penh, but there was no good reason to stay. After pausing to repair the jeep's knuckle assembly in the Shell Oil compound, Ben drove on, now racing along on good roads built by the French, past brick towers built during the Indochinese war of independence. Onward through the fertile Mekong Delta, where bananas, papaws and breadfruit grew incredibly fast and chickens and pigs wandered across the road, and Ben reckoned you could feed a family off an eighth of an acre.

In the evening, at the border between Cambodia and Vietnam, they arrived at a barbed-wire barrier. A customs official slept in a rough structure under a mosquito net, his sweltering office lit by a dim oil lamp that threw faint shadows of flying, flittering insects onto the walls and ceiling.

Once he was roused by the unwelcome travellers, the official examined their Australian passports, flipping through the pages with exaggerated purpose, and when he was satisfied with them he pulled out a stamp and thumped it into a pad of ink. But the swarm of insects drawn to the lamplight was so heavy it was hard for him to get a clean shot at stamping the passports.

He aborted three swings, Ben wrote later, *but even then nailed one small bug to my passport.*

During a trip to Perth I'd photographed every page of all of Ben's passports to double-check travel dates and border crossings, and now I wondered: Did Ben really remember that evening with such an eye for detail? I was happy to see that, on page 11 of the passport issued just weeks earlier in Bangkok, there remains near the centre of a blue *Sortie de Bavet* stamp the faint impression, in yellow and brown, of a tiny insect crushed by a sweating border official on 11 April 1956.

The official waved *Half-Safe* across the border, and Ben drove through the hot, humid night towards Saigon. The last light of French rule was flickering out but, at least as Ben saw it, the Vietnamese were gracious victors, and he thought they felt no lingering resentment to the departing French.

Saigon was a milestone. After eight years Ben was exactly halfway around the world. And now, after having headed generally south-east all the way from London, he planned a dramatic change of course.

The shortest distance between two geographic locations isn't described by a straight line drawn on a flat map, but by a great circle route, which is the shortest distance between two points on a sphere. If you look at an airline map you'll see an example of this; the arcing routes roughly reflect the concept. And if you map the great circle route from Saigon to Vancouver, you'll see it arcs up through the South China Sea, passes Hong Kong, follows the Sea of Japan into Russia's Sea of Okhotsk, leaps over the Aleutian Islands and cuts just south of Anchorage before arriving at its destination.

This was the route Ben planned to take.

In other words, his last big push was almost perfectly efficient. From Saigon he would turn 90 degrees to the north-east, follow the great circle across land and sea to Vancouver, and drive across North America to Montreal. The journey would be over in eight months. The end was in sight.

But first *Half-Safe* needed attention. She'd been beaten to hell by the brutal mountain crossings, the weeks in water and a series of small accidents caused by the unwieldy nature of the vehicle. The original GPA had been extended from 15 feet to 18 feet with the addition of the bow and stern tanks, and had terrible visibility. After Ben had rebuilt her in England, the windshield sat a full eight feet forward of the driver's seat. As one reporter said, it was a little like driving a rolling duck blind, and Ben smashed into things on a regular basis. On his first day in Saigon he backed into a parked steamroller and buckled the rear tank, but fortunately there was a Ford garage in the city where he spent a week patching holes, hammering the rear of the jeep back into something approximating its original shape and overhauling the recalcitrant radio. Shell had always been good to Ben, and its Saigon office put up him and Barry in a modern employee apartment building near its imposing headquarters.

An Italian journalist interviewed the adventurers over beer for a local French-language newspaper and described Ben as having 'the strong and fierce visage of a medieval Viking', while Barry was *petite et mince* – 'small and thin' – which Ben found hilarious. But in general, even after crossing South-East Asia with him, Ben said little more about Barry. 'He's doing pretty well considering his age and background.' He shrugged. 'He could be very much worse.'

Before leaving Saigon on 18 April, Ben consulted Colonel Fergus MacAdie, the services attaché for the Australian Army in Saigon. MacAdie had surveyed every major road in Vietnam, knew which ones were maintained and which ones had fallen into disrepair, and where the bridges were still out in the wake of the war against the French. His recommendation: drive north up the centre of the country to Dalat, turn east towards the coastal city of Nha Tran and then sail 272 miles along the coast to Da Nang.

On the way out of Saigon *Half-Safe* passed miles of refugee camps in the rolling fertile countryside, home to hundreds of thousands of people who'd fled North Vietnam in 1954 and 1955. They crossed single-lane bridges, climbed slowly into the mountains towards Dalat in the central highlands, past elegant and deserted French villas.

Upon arriving in Nha Trang, a coastal city in southern Vietnam, Ben staggered out of the hot jeep into a Chinese restaurant, and after his first sip of cold beer the recurring nausea hit him again. He went outside where the heat shimmered off the asphalt, collapsed against a leaning lamppost and vomited onto the street. It was happening more frequently now, the nausea and sickness, but it didn't seem to worry him. He blamed the heat, the stress, sometimes the water. It never occurred to him that he was pushing himself too hard, drinking too much, staving off too much sleep with too much methedrine.

He purged himself, wiped his mouth and returned to the beer.

When *Half-Safe* sailed out of Nha Trang into the South China Sea the next day, the sea was calm, the wind at her stern. For once life inside the jeep was tranquil. Ben navigated and Barry boiled water for hot tea on one of the two electric water heaters built into the cabin in front of the passenger seat. They sailed into the night, taking turns at two-hour shifts at the tiller. They steered along the dark-green Vietnamese coast, punctuated by rocky headlands and natural harbours, past endless fishing boats, the occasional dolphins swimming alongside the yellow jeep.

They reached Da Nang Bay just past noon on 24 April, having covered 272 miles in three days. They tied up next to a freighter and set out to find the coldest beer possible. Soon they ran into the local Shell manager, who insisted on inviting them to his home and then a whiskey-soaked reception the following night at the Cercle Sportif, attended by the French consul, the mayor and the town's notable names. Ben returned the favour by demonstrating *Half-Safe* the next day in front of city hall, then topped off its fuel tanks and hit the market to provision the jeep for the 530-mile run to Hong Kong. He stocked up on eggs, fruit, cigarettes and 16 gallons of drinking water.

On the way out of the harbour, *Half-Safe* sailed over a string of fish traps and tangled a line around an axle. Ben ordered Barry to dive in to untangle it.

April turned into May. Now the cabin was a floating hothouse, sweltering and sticky, and they gorged themselves on bananas, trying to eat them all before they softened into brown rot. Barry swore he saw sharks circling, but Ben laughed that off and after a few days they stopped for the luxury of a bath in the ocean; they took turns lathering themselves on the bow and then dipping into the ocean to rinse off. Now they were clean and the sea was still smooth, and Ben was uncharacteristically relaxed enough to remember two bottles of Châteauneuf-du-Pape donated by a friend in Nha Trang. He turned off the motor, and he and Barry clambered on top of the jeep and drank warm wine under the hot sun until the bottles were empty and their heads were light, and they slept through the night and well into the next day.

CHAPTER TWELVE
Out of Empire

A mysterious glare appeared on the horizon the night before they were to reach Hong Kong, growing brighter as they sailed north. Ben checked his charts. It wasn't the lights of Macau or Hong Kong – it was coming from nearer the Wanshan Archipelago, a scattering of more than a hundred islands off the coast. A thickening mist smudged the strange glow. Ben held his course but heightened his caution; he still knew the islands by their old Portuguese name, the Ladrones. Thieves Islands.

He slowed as he approached the glow, then hove to and climbed slowly out of the top hatch for a better look. For the first time since leaving Halifax, he told an interviewer a decade later, 'I'd have given my left leg for a rifle. Piracy still thrives on the China coast, and those boys could have wiped me off without leaving a trace.' Slowly the glow resolved itself into separate points of light, dozens and dozens of them, and as the jeep drifted closer Ben saw the distinctive silhouettes of junks and sampans ahead. From each one a bank of high-pressure sodium-vapour lights shone straight down into the water, the glow drawing squid from the black depths up to the surface and waiting nets.

They were simply fishing boats.

Ben restarted the jeep's motor and wove slowly through the glowing armada that stretched nearly to Hong Kong.

Late in the afternoon of 6 May, guided in by the flashing light on Green Island, *Half-Safe* chugged through Sulphur Channel into Victoria Harbour, where traditional junks still sailed, and in a steady downpour tied up near the Star Ferry Pier as waiting passengers watched curiously.

Ben invited a reporter from the *South China Morning Post* to climb into *Half-Safe* and took pleasure at the young man's reaction to the damp, cramped space. As usual he dismissed the all-too-expected questions. Tell us about the journey? 'I think I'll be glad when it's all over.' Why go? 'Oh, just to see if it can be done.' And your wife, Elinore? 'One of the worst sailors in the world.'

What Ben really wanted was directions to the Royal Hong Kong Yacht Club.

'Do you have any friends there?'

'No,' replied Ben, 'but I'm going to make some.'

He hadn't shaved since Saigon, and as he strode off into the narrow, crowded streets of Hong Kong in a yellow skirt-like Burmese *longyi* and green-and-black plaid shirt, looking for a cold beer and new companions, he pretended to be oblivious to the stares that followed him.

Barry stayed behind to watch over the jeep and answer more questions from the reporter, sounding like a politician delivering an uncomfortable soundbite.

'I have always wanted to go to America,' he said unconvincingly. 'I can think of no better way than this. I will achieve my ambition and I will also get adventure.'

By evening the Royal Hong Kong Yacht Club was in love with Carlin. The sailing secretary gave him permission to drive *Half-Safe* up the club's ramp to a parking spot, and invited him and Barry to stay in the club's small dormitory – 'sort of a bum's shelter for visiting odds and ends', said Ben. A night dragged into a week, and then two, and then three.

One of the club members who became besotted with Ben was Neville Fullford, Hong Kong service manager for The Standard Motor Company, the British auto manufacturer that owned Triumph. He raced his TR2 regularly in the Macau Grand Prix, and *Half-Safe* fascinated him. Without hesitation he gave Ben full access to the Standard workshop in the Far East Motors building, right on the harbour overlooking a clot of sampans and racing boats. Ben spent his days there doing small jobs on *Half-Safe*, and in the evenings washed up back at the club's bar. His plans to catch up on correspondence mostly failed. *Bloody near impossible to settle down to writing in the club*, he complained in a letter to Elinore. *Hospitable booze-hounds galore.* He managed, at least, to write one of the semi-regular circular letters he sent to friends, family and people he'd met along the way; in three pages he summed up his travels from London to Hong Kong and had 150 copies made.

Elinore, he wrote, had settled temporarily in Beirut.

Ben discovered a handful of old friends in the city, pre-war companions from his brief mining career in China and subsequent service with the Indian Army. Nobby Clark had survived a Japanese prisoner camp; R. J. 'Con' Crokam had endured internment; Edwin Pennell had done forced labour on the Death Railway. All of them had wound up in Hong Kong, working in various ventures, and they liked to drink and relive the past. 'Their hospitality did nothing for my health.'

⌒

Saigon had marked the halfway point, but Hong Kong carried its own bittersweet meaning. From the start, Ben had never been far from the influence of Europe and European Colonialism. There were always British clubs and gin, French cafés, familiar accents and old friends, or friends of friends, in the most remote reaches of his journey. Even the Middle East was familiar territory from his army days. Now, in leaving Hong Kong, he was leaving behind one of the few remaining strongholds of the fading British Empire, and by extension sailing past the edge of the world he knew.

A handful of new and old friends gathered at the yacht club on 1 June to watch *Half-Safe*, laden with fresh provisions and 200 gallons of fuel, cast off at 6.30 pm. The club fired nine salvoes from its big starter gun as the jeep chugged slowly away, and the reports echoed across Victoria Harbour. Ben steered towards the South China Sea via the short passage between Kowloon and Hong Kong Island, headed to Taiwan in unsettled weather and a hard rain.

Out in the open sea the winds picked up. Ben gripped the tiller and stared alternately at the compass and the waves through the salt-whitened windows while next to him Barry silently counted the hours, seasick and unable to eat, a helpless passenger on a long journey across 414 nautical miles of rising sea.

As the sea grew rougher Ben tried raising Hong Kong on the jeep's radio – no response. Four days later, through the static, he caught a fragment of a warning from Radio Hong Kong: *a tropical depression is forming at E 112 N 18.*

Just 270 miles to the south, and moving a lot faster than the jeep.

And the last thing Ben wanted was to be caught in another storm. He knew surviving the Atlantic squall in 1950 had been as much about extraordinary luck as nautical skill. As for *Half-Safe*, nearly a decade after he'd welded a boxy cabin over the seats she was still running, but the brutal going beyond Europe had worn her down, even after the overhaul in England.

And there was one more risk. Although the rough sea seemed vast and empty, the Taiwan Strait is heavily trafficked, and *Half-Safe*, floating low in the water, was easy to miss, especially at night. At twilight Ben pointed the beam of the jeep's searchlight straight into the stormy sky, a frail warning beacon, and hoped for the best.

The jeep battled a headwind, rough seas and the south-flowing China coastal current. Lightning ripped across the sky as thunderstorms passed overhead, hammering the jeep with sheets of rain. Water from the sky and sea leaked through seams that seemed to be opening up throughout the cabin, and waves sloshed in through the open vents that gave some relief from the heat, soaking their clothes and bedding. It was miserable. 'Every goddamn thing leaked, and we shipped more water than in the whole of the Atlantic,' said Ben.

ം

Six days out of Hong Kong, the island nation of Taiwan appeared on the distant horizon, but at 3 knots it was nearly midnight before they arrived at Kaohsiung, a port city of half a million people in the south. The harbour's signal station displayed three red lights; the entrance was closed for the night. Ben streamed the sea anchor, and he and Barry settled in for a night of difficult sleep.

At two in the morning a bright beam cut through the darkness. Barry shook Ben from a deep sleep: 'Company!' A Chinese pilot boat escorted them into the harbour, past rusting merchant vessels, Chinese and American naval vessels and brought them into a floating hostel, which Ben soon realised was actually a beached brothel for American sailors, where 'a sinful symphony reverberated nightly through all steel-cabins'. Police and reporters plied the Australian adventurers with questions and drinks until the sky lightened in the east.

Taiwan's reception astonished Ben.

Half-Safe always made its strongest impression when emerging from the ocean at the end of a long voyage, when the sheer absurdity of its amphibious nature and the audacity of Ben's odyssey were perfectly clear. On land, 'She was just another weird-looking vehicle, perhaps an armoured car, perhaps a garbage truck,' said Ben. 'Only on islands do they realise fully you've arrived by sea.'

In the morning a huge crane swung *Half-Safe* out of the water and onto the concrete wharf, with Ben standing triumphantly atop her in his *longyi* to the delight of a crowd. Vice Admiral Liang Hsu-Chao, commander-in-chief of the Nationalist Chinese Navy, welcomed Ben in person. The Tainan chief of police presented Ben with a banner that read, 'Triumphing by spiritual intensity over insurmountable difficulties.' Chiang Wei-kuo, the adopted son of Chiang Kai-shek, summoned him to lunch. The British consulate offered accommodation in Taipei. Ben fell in with a crowd of Australians who worked for the Civil Air Transport, the putative Nationalist Chinese airline that provided covert support for CIA operations, and gave Ben a place to make repairs in a 'magnificent' airline workshop. The days devolved into *endless food, booze and natter*, he complained unconvincingly in a letter to Elinore. It was the last letter he would write to her for a long time, or at least the last one she kept. Few of her letters back to Ben survive, but he was finally getting the message that things were serious in Beirut.

Ben and Barry worked slowly northward, staggering from reception to reception on an island country that was fascinated by the bizarre vehicle and its crew. The days were idyllically unproductive, devoted to socialising with foreign diplomats, dining, drinking and 'swapping lies', and nearly three weeks had passed in a haze when Ben woke up in a small room at the Keelung Hostel, in a port city near Taipei, his head throbbing with another hangover. It had been days since he'd done anything productive to prepare for the next leg. There were so many outstanding invitations, so much socialising yet to be done, but he had to leave. It was 27 June, and typhoon season loomed. The window of opportunity was closing if he was going to make Japan and launch a Pacific crossing from Hokkaido.

He carefully adjusted his Rolex to the correct time by a radio signal and packed his bags.

There was a knock at the door: John Ogle, lieutenant commander of the Royal Navy at the British Consulate, bore a hamper of sandwiches and gin. 'No bloody picnics today!' said Ben, but a bit of gin eased the hangover, and by the time he arrived at Keelung's city dock he wasn't quite sober.

Thousands of spectators were gathered at the city's main dock, where the jeep was now moored, to watch the departure. A brass band in white uniforms played a thunderous rendition of 'Auld Lang Syne', and when they were done the PA system blared Eartha Kitt's rendition of 'C'est si Bon' for no apparent reason.

Two young girls hung garlands of flowers around Ben and Barry's necks, and Ben gave a short speech as the Australian Red Ensign and the flag of the Republic of China whipped behind them in gusts of wind. He gave a quick, sloppy salute to the crowd, clambered into the jeep followed by Barry and sailed slowly out of the harbour to the bang of firecrackers.

Half-Safe sailed uneventfully across the East China Sea to the Japanese island of Okinawa, making 375 miles in four days. On 1 July she sailed straight into the Naha Military Port, controlled by the United States, between two long wharves towards a moored army tugboat. A newspaper reported:

> Seaman and dock workers were startled to see a yellow jeep chug through the water and tie up to the AG31's mooring line,

but this only prepared them for the sight of Carlin rising from the small hatch on top wearing a T-shirt, yellow sarong and a big, red Davy Crockett beard. Carlin . . . inquired as to the whereabouts of the nearest cold beer.

He found it half a mile down the wharf at the blissfully air-conditioned Seaman's Club, at the south end of the island. By chance Ron Shaw, who'd watched Ben work on the jeep in Annapolis a decade earlier as a high school student, was now a maintenance officer with the 16th Fighter Interceptor Squadron, stationed at Naha Air Base. He was stunned to see Ben again and introduced him to the club's manager, who offered a spare room and a spot for the jeep in the crushed-coral car park that glared in the bright sun. He arranged for Ben to have the use of a revetment, a protected parking space for one of the base's North American F-86D Sabre all-weather interceptor jets, as a workspace.

'Ben and Barry basically housed themselves there during a rather extended stay on Okinawa,' Ron told me. 'I was proud that we were able to help Ben as much as we could, and in return Ben gave an outstanding talk to the fighter pilots in my squadron regarding survival at sea.'

Actually, Ben had given the lecture because he'd been promised a ride in an F-86D, but the offer was somehow forgotten the next day.

'He had a heart of gold, and he'd do anything for anybody,' said Ron. But his relationship with Ben was complex. 'You had to test him to get information from him. And if you challenged him he thought you were an idiot. He defended his position. He had a way of talking down to people.'

And he held grudges. After a long dinner one night he brought up *Half-Safe*'s maiden voyage on Weems Creek back in 1947, when the jeep had taken on water and sunk.

'He never forgave me for not bailing out the damned jeep faster,' said Ron.

Ben worked on the jeep through the hot weeks of July, too close to the cool interior of the Seamen's Club, just 20 yards away, to avoid the temptation of frequent beer breaks. He was again broke, so he put *Half-Safe* on display at a Fourth of July event, charging 15 cents for the chance to crawl inside. Fourteen people paid for admission. *Stars and Stripes* reported some of them muttering, 'They must be crazy,' as they walked away from the jeep. When Barry was asked about the trip, he just shrugged his shoulders and smiled awkwardly.

'Ben and Barry drank an awful lot of my gin during their stay,' said Ron.

Through the fog of another hangover, Ben piloted *Half-Safe* out of Okinawa on 18 July. Under a high summer sun the cabin was again brutally hot, 50 degrees or more when the winds died. He'd lost his wallet somewhere the night before, and water trickled into the jeep past a bad seal where the steering system passed through the hull. To hell with it all: there was no money in his wallet and he'd fix the leak later. He steered north. The crossing was hot and humid. He and Barry had little to say to each other, and sailed on in their own worlds.

Six days later *Half-Safe* rumbled through glassy water under a starlit sky towards the volcanic cone of Sakurajima and into the harbour at Kagoshima, at the south-western end of Kyushu, the southernmost of Japan's four main islands. Ben hitched the jeep to a barge moored to the breakwater, and as they fell asleep both he and Barry were amazed at the unexpected pungency of Japan's soy-sweet smell.

The next morning he saw he'd tied up to a honey barge laden with raw sewage. Barry would tell the story for years afterward.

∽

The worst thing about the drive to Tokyo was the abysmal road system. In 1956 an economic advisor told the government bluntly, 'The roads of Japan are incredibly bad. No other industrial nation has so completely neglected its highway system.' Just 23 per cent of the national roads were paved. Not that it made much difference for the majority of traffic; in the years immediately after the war, more than 90 per cent of registered vehicles were bicycles, carts and other non-motorised vehicles. By the time Ben arrived the ambitious Five-Year Highway Improvement Plan was underway and vehicle ownership was about to explode, but long stretches of the 1,000-mile route to Tokyo ranged from shattered postwar disrepair to tracks in the dirt.

Sometimes there were a few miles of concrete and Ben could push *Half-Safe* into top gear, but then the road turned back into dirt without warning and Ben had to hit the brakes and judder over rocky, rutted tracks. It took three days to drive the first 175 miles across farmland, over hills and through stands of pine to Fukuoka, where a reporter for *Stars and Stripes* described Ben and Barry as looking like characters from

Kipling's *The Seven Seas* as they ravenously consumed rice cakes during an interview.

'It's not really as dangerous as most people imagine,' said Ben between mouthfuls, depriving one more reporter of a dramatic quote. 'It is sheer misery and hard work for the most part, with some very bright highlights in between.'

'Would you advise anyone else to attempt an adventure such as this?'

'No. I don't bear that degree of enmity to anyone.'

A sergeant from the US Army's port at Moji helped Ben reconnoitre the best place to cross the Kanmon Straits that separate Kyushu and Honshu, and covertly slipped 55 gallons of fuel out of a depot and into *Half-Safe*. The jeep was across in an hour.

The road on the other side, the optimistically named National Highway One, was even worse and, crawling along between trucks, three-wheeled vehicles and bicycles, Ben thought maybe he should have just sailed up the coast to Tokyo.

Ben learned to say *o furo wa doko desu ka* – where is the bath house? – before almost anything else, and on the grinding drive north he visited the steamy baths as often as he could, scrubbing and sweating away the miles of hard travel. He laughed because Barry was still embarrassed to take his clothes off in front of strangers. One night, through the steam, he noticed four small scars dotted across the buttocks of another bath visitor, the bullet wounds a reminder of a war ended just 12 years earlier.

It took nearly a month to get to Tokyo, a drive you could do in 15 hours today, and they arrived far behind schedule in August 1956. The rice-planting season was over and the rains were coming. It was too late to cross the Pacific.

Barry took a job as an architectural draftsman for an American engineering company. Ben rented a room in a private home. He picked up some Japanese, learned to love miso and tried to get used to the minor quakes that rattled the city. The country felt foreign to him in a new way; he was beyond the orbit of his Colonial friends. He tried to understand Japan, but the closest he could get was to observe that the bleary-eyed, late-night drunks on the subway reminded him in some way of scenes in the goldfields of Western Australia 20 years earlier.

And in the midst of the overwhelming confusion all he wanted to do was stop and rest. *Suddenly I was terribly tired after six months of leapfrogging the sun all the way from Calcutta,* he wrote, and *I couldn't go on without a few weeks of rest.*

Curt Prendergast, *Time* magazine's Japan correspondent, interviewed Ben on 17 August. Like everyone else, he failed to get anything interesting from Ben, and the short article that appeared a week later was a recap of the adventure for a readership that had mostly forgotten about Ben in the first place. *Life* planned a follow-up to its coverage of the Atlantic crossing, and a photographer spent a day with Ben and *Half-Safe* soon after the Prendergast interview, but a few months later an editor sent a terse letter stating the story was being killed. Ben claimed it was because the magazine had just run a series on great adventures, and his own would 'blow them sky high'.

In October, in between recuperating and exploring the locals' bars near his rented room, he gave a dinner lecture at the Propeller Club at the Port of Yokohama, and he talked his way into a workshop at Sumisei K. K., a manufacturer of automobile bodies just south of Tokyo. That gave him a place to take out the jeep's engine and transmission, and when he stripped them both he found them in surprisingly good condition. On the other hand, the propeller shaft had always annoyed him with a slight wobble, and the Sumisei workshop didn't have the tools for that job. But Ben had run into a Scandinavian captain overseeing the construction of a ship at Kawasaki, and he had a new one made for Ben – no problem!

Finally, he had a new 16-foot, 372-gallon tow-tank made and shipped to northern Hokkaido for his eventual Pacific launch. When all of that was done, he drove *Half-Safe* back to Tokyo and at the end of 1956 parked in a garage at the home of Nevil Stuart, the Australian trade commissioner in Tokyo. Nevil had a two-storey house with two servants in Azabu, within walking distance of the Australian embassy. Ben had an especially good relationship with Nevil's wife, Isla, a tall and once-prolific Sydney journalist who was fascinated by the underworld and loved sharing stories over a pint with colleagues.

'She would have relished yarning with such a maverick character,' Nevil's son Stephen said of his stepmother on a call from Melbourne. 'She was rather a colourful woman herself. She knew how to judge corduroy in the markets of Tokyo; she hooted with delight when she came back from her first lesson in Japanese, where the first sentence they concluded with was, "What colour is your mother-in-law's container?"'

On the morning of 9 January 1957, a uniformed chauffeur drove Stephen, his younger brother, Guy, and their father to visit Ben. In photos taken in front of *Half-Safe* that day in the corner of a dimly lit workshop, the visitors all look serious, wearing long coats against the winter cold. Ben looks like he'd rather be doing something else, and he's put on a suit jacket over his ubiquitous plaid work shirt. Young Stephen is smiling as only a 16-year-old could in the presence of such a blunt, charismatic character.

'I remember he was a very genial bloke. He didn't say anything like, "Oh, would you like to sit in the jeep and pretend to drive" – he was just a sort of guy who was telling us about some of his adventures. He did say he was working on a book, taking pictures and recording all sorts of things that were happening along the way.'

At the Stuarts' house Ben continued to fuss over *Half-Safe* obsessively, repairing corrosion in the nose tank, reinsulating the generator coils and checking the rigging. She was ready.

But his finances weren't. Ben was desperate to sell foreign rights to his books, mainly because he needed the money, so he reached out to several American publishers, going around André Deutsch. His reputation, as usual, preceded him. Around the same time Elinore got a letter from William Morrow & Company, which had published the American edition of *Half-Safe*:

Not knowing where to reach Ben, I am writing him in Tokyo and sending you a copy of my letter so that he will be sure to get it eventually. I like you and Ben, but after receiving the letter from him dated May 31st, I am perfectly sure that our relationship in the future would be much more friendly if we did not try to do any more business together.

There was one lucky break. The Standard-Vacuum Oil Company – a short-lived Asian joint venture of Standard Oil of New Jersey and Mobil Oil – agreed to have Ben fly its banner from *Half-Safe* on his drive north from Tokyo to Wakkanai, where he planned to launch into the Pacific. The company distributed a memo alerting its service stations along the route to prepare for the jeep's arrival, urging them to drum up local curiosity. In exchange, the company would provide all necessary fuel and oil for the Pacific crossing, and they loaned Ben a credit card – 'which he should return to us on his departure from Wakkanai' – to buy fuel in Japan.

And then the hammer fell. At the end of January, Ben received a short letter from Barry, who was on assignment in Hong Kong.

I'm sorry that I have to give you this news by letter & not in person, but as I'm not sure when I will be back in Tokyo it's only fair that I should tell you of my decision as soon as possible. The decision is that I'm not going to carry on any further with the trip. I'm sorry that it has to end this way Ben.

It had been nine months for Barry. It was a good run, and he'd seen and done things that had been unimaginable a year earlier. He eventually returned to Australia, and over the years he thought less and less about his life's amphibious detour. He became a principal of the architectural practice Silver Thomas Hanley in 1985, a firm that has designed more than 2,000 hospitals and health-care facilities around the world.

In 2006 the ABC show *Can We Help?* broadcast a short segment about *Half-Safe*. Barry, his voice deepened with time, his body thickened a bit by good living and his white hair swept back stylishly, spoke briefly about Ben and his nine months on the jeep, appearing a bit surprised at the interest. He explained how they'd lived on canned food and 'left a trail of cigarettes across the Pacific', how *Half-Safe* was immensely uncomfortable and 'couldn't really be described as seaworthy'. He said nothing about any pain Ben had caused half a century earlier. 'He was a special person, and there are only a few that I've met. I was lucky to meet him.'

A few years before he died in 2010, Barry made clear that 'whilst I shared some of the adventure, the dream was never mine. My only contribution was to assist in Ben's quest.'

'Barry never railed against Ben,' Luceille Hanley told me. 'I perceived that Ben was a bit difficult, as you say, but I think Barry would just turn away, or walk away if they were on land.'

That had happened one night shortly after *Half-Safe* landed in Japan.

'One night, stumbling with exhaustion, Barry went back to their overnight digs to find Ben "entertaining" a woman in their room,' Luceille told me. 'He turned around and went away again. He slept in the street and I suspect was not feeling kind. But he told the story with a smile.

'The adventure of it all gave him confidence. Once he and Ben parted, he seemed to be more relaxed in himself, more powerfully self-determined. He watched and thought and enlarged himself.'

⌒

Ben was stunned by Barry's departure, his plans thrown into disarray. He couldn't cross the Pacific alone. For a third time he had to find someone to fill the passenger seat. He wrangled a newspaper story to find a new copilot, and it led to a syndicated article that appeared in newspapers around the world and stressed the need for a man with 'unlimited patience' to join Ben on the Pacific crossing.

Boyé De Mente, an American editor at the English-language *Japan Times* in Tokyo, met Ben shortly afterward to write a story about the Australian adventurer. Ben said he was still looking for a copilot, then paused and sized up Boyé.

'Care to join me on the rest of my trip?' he asked.

Boyé said yes.

He was 28. Everyone called him Jingo. He'd grown up in Mayberry, Missouri, a farming and logging community of a few dozen people tucked into the Ozark Hills. He joined the Navy in 1946, studied cryptography, and from 1949 to 1952 served with the Army Security Agency in Japan and operated code-breaking IBM machines. He became fluent in Japanese and enrolled at Sophia University in Tokyo, where he paid for his studies by helping manage a downtown nightclub and taking bit parts in Japanese movies. He earned a Bachelor of Science in history in January 1956. He looked sort of like a beatnik, with a jazz-club beard and earnest expression.

Boyé's reputation for drinking and womanising impressed even Ben. But he was bored, and pressure from a growing number of unhappy young women and their fathers had him ready to hit the road, and you couldn't do better than fleeing the country by amphibious vehicle. 'If I make it to New York,' he told a reporter from *Stars and Stripes*, 'I'll fly back to Japan to continue my editorial work, and I promise you I'll never be bored again.'

Boyé immediately began studying Morse code, with an emphasis on emergency signals. He planned to take a prayer book on the journey.

In late April, Ben sold what little he'd accumulated while in Japan, and on 3 May 1957, he and Boyé posed for the press atop *Half-Safe* in front of Tokyo's *Mainichi Shimbun* newspaper building, surrounded by a crowd of 500 people.

The reporters asked the usual question: *why?*

It was always a hard one for Ben to answer. Today, nearly nine years after his first aborted Atlantic departure, was no different. In a slightly reflective moment Ben had told *Time* reporter Prendergast, 'It's pure sport. Every Saturday you have thousands of guys kicking themselves up a football field. In the end they're covered with mud or in a hospital. Nobody asks them why they do it.' Usually he answered more succinctly: 'Any idiot can sail across the Atlantic. It takes a good man to cross in a jeep.' None of which really explained why you'd want to tackle something as mad as crossing an ocean in a jeep in the first place.

What he couldn't say was that he was driven by the over-whelming sense of growing up thousands of miles from anything of importance, and the need to escape, and by the quiet fear of being considered an Australian bushie. He always felt the urge to prove himself better and braver and smarter than the next person.

Even though Ben was jealous of Edward Allcard, who he'd met in Morocco, I'm certain he read his 1953 book *Temptress Returns* and approved of what his fellow adventurer said about the need to be free:

I decided to escape the masses of regimented people who appeared to be content to exist in little concentric circles, clinging to life but afraid to live it. People would say to me,

'I wish my ties and responsibilities did not prevent me doing what you have done. If only I had the time –'

Ben had the time.

Even before he sailed out of New York in 1948 he'd escaped the regimented masses and seen a lot of the world, travelled from the goldfields of Western Australia to the coalmines of China to the barracks of the Indian Army, all by the time he was 30. He kept moving and seeking new experiences, driven by a constant and extraordinary need to test himself.

But when it came time to answer his Tokyo interrogators, Ben simply scowled, ducked inside *Half-Safe*, turned the key in the ignition, pressed the starter button and rumbled northward, cheered on by the crowd.

The northern roads were easier. Ben was back on the big circle, bound for the city of Wakkanai on the northern tip of Japan, the end of the journey seemingly within his grasp. They stopped at petrol stations and schools, where Boyé gave passionate speeches in Japanese and Ben waited impatiently in the jeep, not understanding a word.

Half-Safe rumbled along on a month-long, booze-soaked joyride. At one stop, Boyé recalled, Ben disappeared with a bottle of cheap gin and a young woman, only to return in the middle of the night to wake him and show off his scraped knees. 'It's your turn now, mate!' he said. Boyé rolled over and went back to sleep.

They made good time, up to 100 miles a day, and each time they stopped Ben liked his new copilot a little more. *I never saw a more stylish operator on Japanese girls than my new rutting mate,* he wrote, and every night there were dinners and drinks and geisha, with Socony representatives along the way taking their sponsorship duties very seriously.

Half-Safe reached the northernmost point of Honshu and on 17 May drove down to the beach to cross the Tsugaru Straits to Hokkaido, the northernmost of the main Japanese islands. The police held back a curious crowd, and as soon as the jeep hit the water the leaks began again, and the engine was over-heating and burning fuel far too quickly, but Ben kept going. The tanks ran dry 200 yards from the beach in Hakodate Bay, and the jeep bobbed maddeningly close to shore as a customs launch loaded with photographers recorded the embarrassing arrival. An old fisherman rowed out 8 gallons of petrol to save the day.

Half-Safe continued northward into Japan's frontier country, through forests and mountains and rolling farmland, through wide-open spaces that even today are a world away from the push and crowd of Tokyo. They arrived in Wakkanai on the bleak, rainy afternoon of 23 May. The land ran out here at the far northern end of Japan, and the Sakhalin penin-sula lay just 25 miles to the north. It was the ideal location for an American surveillance site with huge antennae that eaves-dropped on the Soviets.

The base commander took an interest in the old amphibious army jeep and invited Ben and Boyé to stay a few nights in a bungalow. The base, surrounded by a chain-link fence topped with barbed wire, was legendary for its barren remoteness, and Ben half-believed a story that the previous commander had been carried away on a stretcher.

It had been almost seven years since the Atlantic crossing, but Ben applied its lesson as he prepared for the Pacific. He smeared hundreds of cans of food with a thin film of grease to protect the edges from saltwater corrosion and prevent the labels from getting damp and falling off. He took three days to provision the jeep properly, stowing everything as far down as possible in the jeep to keep its centre of gravity low, under the bunk and in the storage areas he'd crafted in England. He fashioned a new rear hatch from transparent plexiglas, checked the jeep's electrical connections and overhauled the critically important bilge pumps that were the only way to purge the jeep of the steady seep of seawater that inevitably penetrated its seals and seams. He sent the jeep's radio for an inspection in the base's workshop. Once again he removed the engine's cylinder head and once again he checked the valves – the No. 2 exhaust valve was slightly burned but it would do. It had got him this far.

The emergency gear was a mess. The two-man rubber raft lashed to the roof had baked in the sun for two years, and Ben had no real idea of its condition. Along with the raft were a meagre 2 quarts of drinking water and an old flare pistol, plus a handful of flare cartridges that had been opened by a customs inspector years earlier in India and were probably ruined. Ben repacked them and hoped for the best. That was it.

It was time to go.

CHAPTER THIRTEEN

Pacific

On 10 June 1957 a throng of reporters from *Stars and Stripes*, the Far East Network and NHK gathered in a steady rain to cover *Half-Safe*'s departure. But when a crane lowered *Half-Safe* into the sea, with Ben standing majestically on top of her wearing a Japanese headband, she leaked immediately through her dried seals. Back out she came. Ben caulked up the leaks and had her lowered back into the cold waters, and this time she remained dry enough. Her tanks were topped off, a total of 572 gallons of petrol, 24 gallons of water and 16 gallons of oil. The jeep was so full that the usual 6-inch freeboard was reduced to three. But by now the sun was setting, and again it was too late to leave.

The next day a dazzling blue sky bode well for departure. Ben exuberantly leaped from the dock to *Half-Safe*'s roof and smashed a leg straight through a holoplast panel when he landed. He sighed at another lost day and bolted a piece of fibreglass over the hole. He was long past counting the days.

Finally, on the drizzly morning of 12 June, *Half-Safe* headed north into the Sea of Okhotsk, grey and bleak and forbidding, with nearly a thousand Japanese spectators in attendance for the third attempt in as many days. And Ben was relieved to leave them behind.

'The bearded pair, confident that they will make Shemya within three weeks, were delayed several days by a blown head gasket in their 1942 Jeep engine, a leak in the hull, and bad weather and customs,' reported *Stars and Stripes*, adding a bit of vague drama: 'During most of their trip to Alaska, the two will be sailing their jeep, the *Half-Safe*, through Russian-dominated waters in which 15 Japanese fishing ships have "disappeared" this year.'

Years later Ben described his emotions as he sailed slowly northward into the Sea of Okhotsk, and his words waxed poetic, perhaps as close as anything to a personal manifesto as he'd ever make, a statement of just what it was to be Ben Carlin.

With each departure by sea my sense of relief and freedom was overwhelming: freedom from the post office and the telephone; freedom from jackasses and their jerkess mates; freedom from the need to scratch a living; freedom from the thousand petty requirements of social existence around which so many people build their lives. Nothing but the sea to live with and beat; the excitement softened even the yearning for women.

And so despite Ben's need for women, despite his longing for Elinore, or at least the *idea* of Elinore, the farther he pushed himself into the vast, cold greyness of the Pacific the more he could shut away hunger and the thoughts of soft flesh, and he could be in control. People who knew Ben always told me that he never spoke about women, which surprised me, and I pressed and questioned their memories until it was clear that they were in fact recalling it all clearly, that Ben had indeed compartmentalised that part of himself, shut it away when he was on the sea and far from everything.

He could simply *be*.

And so Ben took his place in the driver's seat in his woollen underwear, gripped the tiller once again and pointed the yellow jeep north-east along an arcing route to Shemya Island in the Aleutians in the grey drizzle. The engine knocked because Ben had opted for a fuel with too little octane; the carburettor silted up; the oil-warning light flickered; petrol fumes filled the cabin. The first few days were warm and humid, and when the temperatures dropped into the single digits condensation formed inside the jeep after sunset and the cabin grew damp and miserable. They passed within a dozen miles of Sakhalin, the large Russian island to the north of Japan, with blue whales sailing beside the jeep, and then turned into the wider Pacific, the days growing colder and the sea rougher. Waves smashed against the windshield as they had in the Atlantic. The jeep chugged slowly northward, and the first light in the east appeared a little earlier each day, now 2.00 am, now 1.30.

With nothing but 1,300 miles of cold, dark Pacific ahead of *Half-Safe*, Ben turned to navigation, maintenance and keeping an eye on the cigar-shaped tow-tank – longer than the jeep itself, loaded with 3,000 pounds of fuel and helpfully labelled *Fuel Tank For Jeep Half-Safe*. He communed with the jeep, trying to understand why she was burning too much oil, taking off the cylinder head and adding a second gasket to lower the compression ratio; resetting the engine's distributor cap. This is what Ben was thinking about, a week at sea:

Alkaline nickel-iron batteries require a slightly higher charging voltage than do lead-acid, and voltage regulators tend to lower the voltage gradually with time. Now our voltage is a shade too low for a full charge; once or twice daily I was running in second gear for a few minutes in attempts to top the batteries.

But for Boyé, it was another story entirely.

He was hit by the lunacy of it all, the sheer impossibility of the situation he found himself in. The petrol vapour in the cabin stung his eyes and made him nauseous, and within hours of departure he was vomiting over the side of the jeep like so many before him.

'Riding in the jeep was like being in a coffin,' he told me. '*Half-Safe* was a tiny cage with two front seats and a bench in the back.' For the next three months this would be the extent of his world.

Worse, after nine years Ben was increasingly withdrawn and bitter. He struggled with the nightmarishly slow pace of his journey, raged about perceived slights, silently missed Elinore. The worst part of it, he later wrote, was the 'awful endlessness' of the sea. 'It seemed that one was confined to that greasy little mouse-trap – 2 hours on and 2 hours off – for ever and ever and ever. There was so little sign of progress; no mileposts, no mountains, no change in the countryside.'

But he couldn't stop.

And while Boyé felt an immediate wave of regret, Ben was already back in dictatorial captain mode, more concerned about the jeep than his copilot. He wondered whether he should have asked Socony for something stronger than 55-octane fuel; he panicked as the jeep burned through a gallon of oil in just 24 hours. And now the cabin was actually filling with *smoke*. It rained that first night, and when nature called Boyé had to strip naked, crawl up through the top hatch and over the slippery, gear-strapped roof of the cabin towards the back of the jeep, where he could grab onto the spare tyre and hang his arse out over the ocean as cold rain pelted him.

The temperature dropped below 5 degrees in the cabin but Ben had to leave it ventilated or the fumes would overpower them. To stay warm they wore all the clothes they had; by now Ben had on four wool shirts, two pairs of wool pants and three pairs of socks. Boyé had a wool cap pulled down low, and in photos they resembled survivors of the 1972 Andes flight disaster, shivering and stuffed into layers of filthy clothes, huddled grimly in a sooty cabin.

They drove onward, past blue whales and bleached Siberian driftwood, past huge pieces of hewn lumber drifting from some sawmill hundreds of miles across the ocean and up some unknown river.

Before dawn on 15 June the wind gusted to 40 miles per hour and Ben streamed the sea anchor. Inside the cold, damp cabin, Boyé fell into a state of depression. Ben tried to cheer him by saying it could be worse – hell, he'd drifted for 13 days straight in the Atlantic with Elinore, and what do you think about that?

As usual, Ben's telling of the Pacific crossing focused on the mechanics, and he wrote little about his relationship with his copilot. But Boyé himself was less reticent, and years later painted an unflattering picture of Ben in *Once a Fool*, his 2005 self-published memoir of the Pacific crossing. When I reached him at his home in Arizona, he'd agreed to talk to me with some reluctance. I got the sense he thought his book could speak for itself, and he'd rather talk about what he'd done since then. But once he got going, he didn't hold back.

First, there was the jeep itself. More than half a century later, Boyé's memories remained vivid.

'*Half-Safe* had extremely low visibility because you rode so low in the water,' he told me. 'There were only seven or eight inches of freeboard. And because it was totally enclosed, the only time that you felt you were in a relatively normal situation is if you were out on top of the jeep or standing up in the passenger's seat with your head and shoulders sticking out of the hatch so you could look around.

'We didn't bathe, but it didn't smell because it was cold all the time.' And they didn't use the jeep's toilet, a bedpan tucked in a cut-out under the passenger-seat cushion. 'We hung off the back.'

The roar of the four-cylinder engine made conversation difficult, but even when it was off Boyé learned to avoid saying anything that would spark Ben's anger.

'You wouldn't initiate a personal conversation with him because of his response. It was invariably, at the beginning, very hostile. Often insulting. Only after a certain period of time would he mellow to any extent and have a conversation. The only thing it was safe to talk to him about was his skill as a mechanic and a few other topics that were relatively neutral and didn't have anything to do with personal relationships, like Australia.'

At least the conditions in the jeep didn't lend themselves to unnecessary conversation. 'The severity of the situation, of being four on and four off every day, will put you in a kind of a trance. You are not in a mood to talk or to associate in a normal way. You go for hours and hours or days and days with very few words. *Very* few words.'

I asked what Ben said about Elinore, or other romantic interests, when they did talk.

'He did not talk about women. He did not talk about much of anything. That was his way.'

They passed Makanrushi, an uninhabited volcanic island in the northern Kuril Islands, on 23 June. They had been at sea for 11 days, following the chain of the Kurils in a north-easterly direction towards the southern end of the Kamchatka Peninsula. Boyé looked longingly at the island rising black and steep from the cold sea, and from a distance they saw a small, snow-covered rocky beach, but Ben decided it was too danger-ous to go ashore, even with the life raft.

'Jingo was so keen that I suspected desertion,' Ben said later, but he too wished he could put his feet on solid ground, even for a moment.

And so they turned eastward.

A sudden near-silence woke Ben at 1.30 in the morning on 26 June; the only sound was the soft gurgle of water in the wheel wells. He pulled himself out of the bunk and into conscious-ness as Boyé described 'some sort of rope stretched over the sea'. It was a trawler's net, miles long, its upper edge stretching invisibly along the surface of the ocean. The nets were supposed to be flagged, even lit by a string of lights at night, but this one hadn't been.

Ben leaned over the back of the jeep and saw a hemp line tangled around the prop shaft. He hacked off what he could, but the prop still wouldn't turn.

Around two miles to the south he made out the silhouette of a trawler, which was apparently hauling in the net and slowly coming closer. Ben stripped naked and dove into the darkness of the early-morning sea to cut away the rest of the net line from the propeller. In the cold it was impossible; he lost the sense of touch as soon as he was underwater. After another try he was more than numb; he was in pain.

By now the trawler was just 100 yards away, and Ben made an impulsive decision – the trawler had to be warmer than the jeep. And so he lunged towards it, forcing himself across the low waves with what little energy remained as Boyé looked on in dismay. When he reached the trawler he saw the net being winched on board, so he grabbed a hold and it pulled him up and over the rust-streaked gunwale, dumping him onto the transom, slick with salmon blood.

The shocked fishermen hauled him into the small deck-house, thrust dry underwear and a fur coat upon him, stoked the coal stove and produced a bottle of sake. They were alarmed. They tried to understand what he was doing, and Ben tried to explain that, no, he hadn't *fallen* in – he'd simply got caught in their net.

And that he was driving around the world.

As soon as he was sufficiently warmed and armed with a borrowed fisherman's knife, Ben threw off the fur coat and dove back into the ocean to finish clearing the prop. He failed again, returned to the trawler and helped himself to a full litre of sake. Now warmed inside and out, he dove in a *third* time, hacking over and over blindly around the propeller with numb hands until he'd cleared every fibre of rope.

In thanks to the trawler's crew, he gave them a can of ham, potatoes and gravy, a US quarter, five Iranian rials and a Hong Kong fifty-cent piece.

Three days later Ben felt another *clunk* shudder through the jeep, followed by the silence of a stopped engine; *another* net. He pulled a bottle of Johnnie Walker Black Label from the jeep's stores: 'Diligently I worked my way to the bottom of the bottle in a vain search for courage.'

Fortunately the net belonged to a trawler that was closing in on the jeep, and once again Ben boarded to warm himself before getting to work.

He shouted out to Boyé to take a colour photo as he worked.

He could just hear the faint reply: 'The camera fell overboard.'

The hard-earned 35mm Alpa was tumbling to the bottom of the North Pacific.

Ben exploded in fury, shouting helplessly from the water while clutching the rear of the jeep. Not just the camera gone, but every bloody colour photograph taken since Wakkanai! Later he said, 'I am a free man today only because, maddened by pain and knife in hand, I was 10 feet from Jingo and unable to reach him.'

By now Ben realised that Boyé had less nautical experience than he'd suggested. The Navy experience meant nothing; he'd been to sea just once. Ben was infuriated by his perceived incompetence and brooded silently on top of the jeep, flying into a rage every time Boyé did something wrong, screaming that he was a son of a whore, had no business being at sea, was a bastard who kept steering straight into Japanese driftnets – the goddamned lines were everywhere! – in the world's biggest ocean.

Boyé feared for his life. 'He was a physically strong man with extraordinary stamina, *unbelievable* stamina given his drinking habits,' he told me. It was only the realisation that Ben couldn't survive without him in the middle of the Pacific that diminished his fear. 'He was not going to kill me in my sleep or push me overboard and leave me.'

After this latest net incident Ben lashed a long boathook to the front of the jeep, like a cowcatcher, to scoop up net lines before they tangled around the propeller. It worked most of the time and they sailed into July, and on the first warm night Boyé slept on top of the cabin without a blanket. A few days later the tow-tank ran dry. Ben painted 'Jettisoned by *Half-Safe* N52°43′ E168°39″' on the side and cast it off. It may be rusting on a deserted beach somewhere today.

⌇

Two days later, as *Half-Safe* bobbed across the North Pacific with its barnacled tyres suspended two miles above the seabed, a United Press International article suggested she was lost at sea. The premature eulogy said the jeep had been expected three days earlier at Shemya Island and, more worryingly, it hadn't been heard from since leaving the Japanese mainland. Nor had Northwest Orient pilots, who'd been on the lookout, seen anything on its presumed route.

The jeep *had* veered off course in the Pacific storms and fog, but on 7 July 1957, Ben saw North America for the first time in seven years. Attu Island rose nearly 3,000 feet above the sea, windswept, treeless and barren, the very last of the Aleutian Islands, the westernmost point of the Americas. Snow shone on her peaks. On his map Ben read place names – *Murder Point, Massacre Bay, Terrible Mountain* – that spoke to the bloody fighting of May 1943, when more than 3,000 American and Japanese soldiers died on the island's jagged landscape and boggy tundra.

But they couldn't stop. They'd told the press they were going 50 miles further to Shemya, home to an American air base, and Ben wouldn't let anyone think they'd failed. Attu disappeared in the mist behind them.

⁓

A fox watched curiously as *Half-Safe* touched the black sand of a Shemya beach. Ben tied up to a jetty, and he and Boyé trudged across the beach, through soft bog and past a series of deserted huts until they came to a lighted building a mile away. He knocked on the door.

A tall, gaunt man, 82 years old, opened the door.

'You spik Roosian?' growled Ben in his best Russian accent. 'Me Rooskie. Escape. Come America.'

The old man, a plumber, was not amused. He pointed them to the Northwest Orient Airlines accommodations; the airline used the island as an emergency stopover for its flights to Tokyo.

The *Anchorage Daily News* treated *Half-Safe*'s arrival like the biggest news of the year. JAPAN–ALASKA TRIP

COMPLETED BY JEEP, read the massive front-page headline, and the paper reported the appearance of a 'grimy yellow craft no longer than an ordinary automobile and packed with a great conglomeration of supplies', and said that Ben planned to be in Anchorage on the mainland by the end of July. Even though they were in the United States, they were only halfway from Wakkanai to Anchorage. They had 1,600 miles to go.

Ben scavenged 144 gallons of fuel from rusting drums abandoned in the tundra at the end of the war, accepted two cases of expired C-rations from the US Air Force, and a few days later headed back into the Pacific, travelling eastward along the stepping stones of the Aleutian Islands, trailed by porpoises, through fog and under low, grey skies. They would occasionally stop on small islands to explore abandoned wartime buildings or work on the jeep or watch herds of caribou – or simply to feel solid ground under their feet. The bleak landscape agreed with Ben.

The jeep ran rougher now. A clogged carburettor. A jammed starter. Prop-shaft vibration. A new leak that left the blankets wet with seawater. As always, Ben made repairs as if by second nature, and *Half-Safe* kept chugging across the ocean. And at the end of August, in the black of night on a glassy sea, the rotating flash of an aircraft beacon at Homer, Alaska, guided them in. They were at 'the end of the road', done with the Pacific.

('Ben really never crossed the Pacific,' Ron Shaw told me in an email a few years before his death in 2014, still stung by the lack of thanks and credit from Ben for the help he'd given on Okinawa. 'He went up the China Sea to Japan, hugged the coastline to the Kurils, then went down the Alaskan highway and ultimately to California.' It was certainly a far cry from the route Ben had initially proposed, which would have launched from the Philippines and stopped at Hawaii, but Ron was apparently the only person to raise the issue – and in any case, it was good enough to help qualify Ben's amphibious circumnavigation for the record books.)

Boyé walked away soon after *Half-Safe* drove into Anchorage on 4 September.

'Ben was one of the most stubborn people I've ever met,' said Boyé. 'He was stubborn to the extreme. Once he made up his mind he was going to do something, he was going to do it come hell or high water. He was fantastically proud of his ability to do things, and once he made a commitment, he was going to keep it. All of those things led him to do his one great adventure. He just didn't suspect that it was going to take up so many years of his life.'

Boyé claimed he never gave much thought to what shaped Ben, or what drove him. I pressed.

'He got a great deal of satisfaction from all the media attention, all the attention of ordinary people who came upon the jeep. It was an *extraordinary* amount of attention. He had to feed on it to a considerable degree. Because without the attention, without the public taking notice, would he have continued to expose himself to extreme danger in pursuit of the goal?'

The attention didn't just feed Ben's ego; it was essential because publicity generated continued support. 'His trip took a fantastic contribution by other people. It was the magnanimous side of society. If they had not been supportive, he wouldn't have gotten anywhere. Some adventurers go off on their own, say to the North Pole, and depend only on themselves and maybe some dogs. He had to depend on hundreds of people.'

At least, I said, he could be charming –

'It was an act! It was a selfish act, pure and simple. If he hadn't been so charming, the trip would have ended many years earlier.'

CHAPTER FOURTEEN

The End

The feeling hit him like a punch to the gut.

'Reaching Alaska – no more oceans to cross – should have been my biggest thrill,' Ben told the *Washington Star*. 'I had been looking forward to it for years. Actually, I never felt so flat and depressed in my life.'

Ben had imagined champagne and celebration, but now it meant only that he was getting closer to the end of the journey, and the only way of life he'd known since leaving Australia in 1939. *I faced a return to the jungle of life as a civilian*, he wrote. *I would have to learn to be polite to painful numbies and to either rhapsodize or lament over every tiny thing.*

Bob Reeve, a legendary bush pilot who'd launched an eponymous airline, hosted Ben for six weeks of repairs, dinners and drinking in Anchorage, but when snow began falling hard in October it was time to move on. High above, the Soviet satellite Sputnik was entering its second week in orbit, transmitting a faint signal that could be heard around the world.

Ben headed south, *Half-Safe* passing incongruously through snowy mountain passes, dwarfed by the Alaskan ranges and drifts piled 10 feet high on the side of the road. During his years in Kalgoorlie he'd met men who'd panned in the Klondike and returned with stories about the cold, rugged Yukon, and now he thought about driving 500 miles east to Dawson City to see what they'd described. But the snow-covered roads were too questionable for a tired amphibious jeep. Ben turned south onto the Alcan Highway on 13 October. The road alternated between asphalt and gravel, and at night, parked on the side of the road, Ben gave himself to the wonder of the Aurora Borealis draped across the northern sky. He crossed into Canada and spent 24 hours in Whitehorse, then drove on and stopped by the banks of the Morley River near the border with British Columbia. He slept in the jeep and the bitter cold pressed through sheet metal into the cabin.

In Taylor, a boomtown on the north bank of the Peace River, Ben pushed the starter button and, for the first time since 1948, the engine refused to turn over. The timing chain was slipping. It took a week to order the parts and make repairs, and when it was done Ben discovered the bridge was out, so he sailed *Half-Safe* across the frigid river in the dark of night, dodging icefloes. The unexpected crossing marked her last time on water before the end of the trip, cathartically rinsing the salt residue of the Pacific Ocean from her chassis.

With no windshield wipers he was forced to pull over every time it started snowing, but otherwise it was just a southbound drive down a rough highway in a strange vehicle. He made

Vancouver on 1 November, found old friends and tolerated an interview with *The Sunday Sun*. The reporter asked why he was piloting an amphibious jeep around the world, still at it after nearly a decade.

'Why not?' snarled Ben. 'If you don't mind my saying so, that's a foolish question.'

∿

Ben crossed into the United States at Blaine, Washington, and arrived in Seattle on 5 November. He was closer to the end.

The next stretch took him 700 miles south, through Washington State, over the 5,335-foot McKenzie Pass in central Oregon, down through the north-eastern corner of California into northern Nevada. In Sparks, in the high desert just east of Reno, he paused and struck a deal to exhibit *Half-Safe* in front of the new, low-slung Nugget casino for $100 per day.

SEE IT – IN PERSON!

'HALF-SAFE'

The amphibious jeep that has travelled around the world . . . on land and <u>sea</u>!

MEET HIM – IN PERSON!

BEN CARLIN . . .

'Half-Safe's' owner and skipper, who has guided his sea-going home-on-wheels during the past seven years . . . and the author of the book describing these adventures!

THROUGH SUNDAY

DICK GRAVES' NUGGET – SPARKS

Locals and tourists stopped by to get a glimpse on their way to lose money at the slot machines and gorge themselves at the casino's prime rib cart, and Ben made several hundred dollars.

But he had another reason to route himself through Nevada: a detour into the past.

He hadn't seen his first wife, Gertrude, since leaving her for the Indian Army in 1940. But in Germany in 1951 her parents had told him she was living in Reno, that she'd become Gertrude Halvorsen after marrying a lumber mill worker in 1943. She had two daughters, Britta and Betty.

He was too close not to look her up, or maybe too lonely.

Betty Halvorsen was born in 1946 and today lives in a small Nevada town half an hour west of Reno. She was thrilled when I called out of the blue to ask about her mother and Ben. It was the first time she'd ever been contacted about him.

Betty painted a picture of her mother as a severe, private woman who'd never quite fit into American society, even later in her life. She never lost her heavy German accent, though she spoke English with impeccable precision.

'She was extremely domineering,' said Betty. 'I don't remember ever getting a hug from her. She only ever told one joke. She didn't have a sense of humour at all. She chose our clothes until we were in high school. She was cold.

'We grew up in Reno until I was in seventh grade, then moved to Sparks after we tossed my dad out. My mother went to the University of Nevada and got a degree so she could teach foreign languages. But she was so cold and unfriendly, I could never imagine her being a teacher, and eventually I think she was fired.'

What stories had her mother told, I asked, about her early life in China, and about her brief marriage to Ben Carlin?

'Ben was the best-kept secret my mother ever had,' laughed Betty with a warm rasp. 'We knew nothing about him when I was a kid. Nothing!' It was as if Gertrude's short time in China had never happened. She never said anything to anyone about her Australian first husband, certainly not to her daughters, not even when they were older.

But by her teens Betty was growing curious about her mother's past. 'My mother played piano beautifully, and I started noticing the name "Carlin" on a lot of her sheet music. I asked, "What does this mean?" And my mother replied, "Oh, it's just a name."'

Betty suspected there was more to the story.

'I went snooping in her personal papers in her desk until I found a wedding picture of Ben and Gertrude. It was dated April 20, 1940.'

What did you say to your mother when you told her about it?

'I never mentioned it to her! You just didn't do that!'

And so for the next year or two the secret remained intact.

But on 12 November 1957, Betty told me, there was a knock on the front door.

'A man was standing there. "I'm Ben Carlin," he said. I already knew who he was. I invited him in and yelled, "Mother, your first husband is here!" She came running out, and she was just furious. There he sat. She had a little explaining to do.'

Gertrude eventually softened enough to let Britta and Betty ride in the remarkable vehicle parked out front. She even took a photo of her girls sitting on top of the jeep, Betty and Britta in cardigans and long skirts, Ben in khakis and his favourite heavy plaid shirt, cigarette in hand, his beard shaved off. He was still handsome, though the strong line of his chin had softened with time and drink.

'He was a very rugged character, but calm and kind to me. He called me "Bet-Bet". That's interesting, to get a nickname from someone you've just known for a couple hours. I really enjoyed what few hours I had with the guy. I enjoyed all of my mother's ex-husbands! She had great taste in men.'

Ben stayed in Sparks long enough to give a program at the junior high school.

'After that,' said Betty, 'I never saw him again.'

With his wallet fattened by the Reno display, Ben rumbled over the Donner Pass towards California and dreams of Hollywood. He arrived in San Francisco via the Bay Bridge on 19 November and found a cheap hotel. He was floored by the scenery but said, *Much of San Francisco and most of Marin County crawls with psychos.*

In early December, Ben went to a dinner party at a house overlooking the bay and drank until five in the morning. On the way back to his hotel he misjudged a curve and slid off Tiburon Boulevard into a ditch, and only a telephone pole prevented *Half-Safe* from overturning completely. The next day a reporter asked if he'd been drinking. *Did the man think I drove that way all the time?* Local papers pointed out the irony of *Half-Safe* crossing two oceans only to sink into a roadside ditch, and tactfully attributed the accident to a 'giddy spell'.

Three days later Ben arrived in Riverside, California, just outside Los Angeles. He wasn't done with the Plath hospitality; he stayed with Gertrude's uncle and aunt, whom he'd met in China in 1940.

Ben talked to TV producers and movie producers – and anyone else he could get to listen – but despite four months in Hollywood he couldn't make a deal. No one knew what to do with the story, or the journey that had dragged on for years and still wasn't done. They didn't know what to do with his shaky footage either. Depressed, Ben climbed into *Half-Safe* on 16 April 1958 and headed east on Highway 60 to make the final push towards Montreal and the end of his odyssey. The first night back on the road he camped in the dry, hot desert near the Arizona border. The next day he stopped in Phoenix to see Boyé, but found his former copilot had returned to Japan. (Boyé went on to write a slew of guidebooks to Asian culture, including the *Lover's Guide to Japan: Where the Action Is . . . and How to Get Some.*)

Ben pressed onward through New Mexico and the wide, flat expanse of west Texas until two-lane roads gave way to the wide highways approaching the Dallas skyline, just beginning to bloom with sleek modern skyscrapers. In the city a police officer pulled up next to *Half-Safe* and shouted out, 'You hit any water with it yet?'

A few hours later Ben had a flat tyre, and that night he slept by the road near a small town 50 miles outside of Oklahoma City.

The End

The car park surrounding the gleaming new glass-and-steel Ford World Headquarters building in Dearborn, Michigan, was filled with shining new cars: low-slung, finned Fairlanes; black Lincoln Continentals; long Country Squire station wagons with faux woodgrain panels. This was the spiritual home of the GPA, which had been assembled a few miles away at the River Rouge Plant. Ben rolled up in late May and talked his way into a meeting with the head of public relations, from whom he expected a hero's welcome. Instead, he said, 'The man refused to turn and look on the most extraordinary automobile (judged on performance) that Ford or any other manufacturer has ever produced.'

So Ben got back into *Half-Safe* and drove on.

A few days later he stopped at the Goodyear Tire and Rubber Company in Akron, Ohio, and got a similar reception, with a promise of four free tyres once he arrived in Montreal.

Well, he thought, *Let's go to Montreal and get it over.*

And there was nothing else left to do, so he did.

Ben Carlin spent the last night of his journey on the side of the road on the outskirts of Montreal, which nearly ten years ago he'd chosen as the official starting point of the journey. In the morning, for the last time, he uncurled himself from the hard bunk, lit a cigarette, crawled behind the wheel and made the final push into a city he hadn't seen in almost a decade. It looked just the same to him, but he was older now, and alone, and almost forgotten.

MONTREAL, May 14. – Australian engineer Ben Carlin drove his amphibious jeep *Half-Safe* into Montreal yesterday, completing a round-the-world trip that took him 10 years to complete, covered 50,000 miles and cost him £17,850. Carlin, 45, said he had proved his point – that he could cross land and sea with the 18-foot United States army surplus vehicle. But he had little affection for 'Half-Safe'.

'I can't get rid of her fast enough,' he said. 'It's been a tortoise shell on my back for many years.'

– The Age, Melbourne, 15 May 1958

And here at the end there was no celebration, no feeling of accomplishment, nothing other than a vague sense that it was over.

The job was done.

Ben recuperated for ten days in Montreal before meandering south, and he arrived in New York on 30 May. There were no crowds waiting for him there either, and the slight media interest was quickly evaporating after his arrival in Montreal. He was 45 years old and broke, a worn-out man with a grey beard in a battered yellow amphibious jeep. The journey that had shaped his life since 1946 was now complete, and he had no idea what to do next.

He had Elinore's phone number, GRmrcy 3-3211, and when he called she agreed to let him stay in her apartment at 119 Bank Street in Lower Manhattan for a few weeks until he found his own place to live.

She wasn't home when he arrived, so he parked the jeep in front of her building to wait. He turned off the engine and closed his eyes.

And suddenly I was tired, and I was asleep when she returned.

The End

Ben had spent years sneering at anyone who dared ask about the point of the journey, but now he was desperate for a greater sense of completion, or at least some sense that it had all meant something. He arrived unannounced at the Gates Engineering Company in Wilmington, Delaware, a producer of chemical products, and insisted he had to see company president Arthur J. Seiler to personally thank him for donating the Gaco N-200 neoprene he'd used to coat *Half-Safe* back in 1947. A surprised Seiler inspected the jeep for the sake of the local press and pronounced himself impressed.

'The last time you told me goodbye, you thought it was for good,' Ben muttered. Then he drove into rush-hour traffic bound for Maryland and the US Army's Aberdeen Proving Ground, where he'd bought the jeep, thinking maybe the ordnance men there would be interested in seeing how the jeep had fared. There's no record of their reaction.

He went to the US Army Transportation Command Research Center at Fort Eustis, Virginia, insisting he should be hired as a consultant on the design of amphibious vehicles. A naval architect who'd met Ben in Annapolis in 1947 was stunned to see him, looking 'considerably older than I had remembered him to be, perhaps because of a weary stance from all his hardships'.

Ben didn't get a job.

A few weeks later *Half-Safe* fell in line with antique cars and marching bands at the Big Sea Day parade in Point Pleasant, New Jersey. A hometown crowd clutched balloons and cotton candy along Arnold Avenue and watched the odd vehicle rumble towards the boardwalk and the Jersey shore, followed by waving contestants for the title of New Jersey Seafood Princess.

Maybe Ben tried to sell a few copies of his book afterward.

He found an apartment in Falls Church, Virginia, near where *Half-Safe* had been born. Aside from Perth, it was the closest thing he had to a home.

⌒

A year later Ben was still trying to figure out how to monetise the trip around the world. In 1959 he approached Socony Mobil Oil Company with a pitch for a story to run in the company's magazine for employees and stockholders and hand-delivered a box of his best photos to editor Willard Colton in New York. After all, Socony had sponsored him for years. The company bit and paid $300 for the right to use the photos, but nothing came of it.

'We never did have room to run the story. Maybe one of these days,' wrote Colton a year later.

How quickly you become old news.

Ben wanted the photos back, but Colton had lost them. For the next four years Ben would write increasingly desperate letters, trying to track them down.

May 1960: *Assuming that my box of photos is with you, I shall be grateful if you will be good enough to mail them hither.*

July 1963: *A television-plus deal has come up, and I need those damned pictures.*

September 1963: *Again I apologize for troubling you, but I MUST have those photos immediately.*

By 1964 Colton said he'd been promoted and no longer had anything to do with the magazine – maybe Ben had actually got them back and lost them himself? Ben filed the correspondence in a folder labelled EVIDENCE.

The End

He started writing a sequel to *Half-Safe*, but without Elinore's help and journals it was harder to piece together a strong narrative. He wrote two chapters in 1960, decided it was putrid and gave up.

He was humbled and anonymous. He drove a cab for a living while trying to figure out something else, ferrying passengers from Washington National Airport to destinations in and around the Capitol.

'Such liberal display of such virtuosity for only 40 cents a mile galls me no end,' he complained to a friend, but he had to support himself. He usually drove two shifts in a row, 16 hours straight.

In 1960 he found a job that played to his strengths and paid fairly well. It was a part-time position abstracting articles – taking long academic articles and condensing them to their essentials – for the National Academy of Sciences in Washington, and he was good at the job. After four years of that, in June 1964 he became a full-time assistant editor at *Science*, a weekly peer-reviewed publication of the American Association for the Advancement of Science. 'Very high-class stuff,' he said. Although his name appeared near the bottom of the masthead, and the job was by his admission not much more than 'a rather superior type of proofreading', he was proud of the work he did, especially since he'd never taken a single class in physics or chemistry, or most of the other hard sciences the magazine covered.

He began driving around the country on wandering lecture tours during the early 60s, always happiest when he was moving – 19,000 miles through the winter and spring of 1961–1962 alone. He presented a colour film called *Half-Safe Around the World*, edited in Los Angeles from footage shot during his decade of travel. He brought his adventures to the Exchange Club in Winona, Minnesota; the Lions Club in Decatur, Illinois; the Montague-Whitehall Rotary Club in Montague, Michigan; the Newport Harbor Kiwanis Club in Southern California. On and on, unreeling the past to polite applause in high schools, churches and civic centres across the heartland of America. In Janesville, Wisconsin, he filled 250 seats in a high-school auditorium, 'in spite of several conflicting activities,' according to the local paper. Tickets for two dollars, a buck for students.

Ben was in California to give another lecture when he was in the crash that nearly killed him.

At 5.10 in the morning on 15 April 1962, an hour before sunrise and long after his appearance the night before, Ben was riding with George Cresswell, a Harvard PhD who worked for the Tiburon Oceanographic Institute, to Cresswell's home at the north end of San Francisco Bay in Marin County. They were in Ben's car but they'd been drinking, and Creswell was driving. They sped toward San Francisco's Golden Gate Bridge, which spans the foggy strait through which Ben had first sailed into America in 1946. On the entrance ramp to the bridge, according to police reports, Cresswell fell asleep, smashed into a concrete abutment and flipped Ben's small station wagon.

It was almost an hour before the California Highway Patrol extracted the men from the wreckage, both of them bloody and unconscious. Ben was in serious condition, with a broken femur, fractured jaw, facial lacerations and a concussion. Cresswell was in critical condition with severe head injuries.

An ambulance rushed the two men to Mission Emergency Hospital. Despite his significant injuries Ben recovered sufficiently enough to move around the hospital within a week, his belligerent attitude intact. A few days later one of the attending doctors said something he didn't like, and Ben decided he was well enough to leave.

He limped out of the hospital on crutches, bought another car and drove across the United States back to Annapolis. While the injuries to his face required plastic surgery once he was home, the signature knife-fight scar remained intact.

But Cresswell never fully recovered. He lingered in a coma for months with brain damage, and when he awoke he was a different man. His fledgling academic career was over. He never married or had children, and when he died 40 years later, a relative told me, he was destitute.

CHAPTER FIFTEEN
Cynthia

Ben spent nearly a year recovering from the California accident. He remained restless, needed to keep moving, and hit the road again as soon as he could. And in early March 1963, driving through Canada, everything began to fall apart.

The temperature hovered just below freezing and there was a trace of snow on the ground when he drove into Toronto, on his way, he later said, to somewhere in a hurry. That was all the explanation he ever gave, but he had friends and acquaintances everywhere, and Toronto was no exception. He rang Gerald and Ann Mason, whom he'd met in London in 1951 through Madeira friends. He was hoping to stop by and say hello, maybe get a place to spend the night before he moved on.

A young woman answered the phone. She told Ben she was staying at the Masons' house while they were away. The accent was strangely familiar, and Ben felt he'd heard it somewhere before. Then she said her name, and Ben realised with a shock who he was talking to: Cynthia Scott, the daughter of Colonel Thomas Robert Henderson and Dorothy Louise Scott; the stodgy old retired Scottish officer who lived in Edinburgh and his ex-wife who lived a wine-softened life on Madeira. Ben and Elinore had socialised with Scottie and her second husband, Creed, in Madeira and later in London, where they'd met Henderson, too, when he came to pick up his daughter.

Cynthia had been just nine years old, a child, when Ben first saw her on Madeira. He'd seen her a few brief times after that in London, and he had a vague idea that in the years since she'd become a wild child, a delinquent. He'd heard stories about how her parents didn't know what to do with her, about how in her teens she was shunted off to stay with various relatives and family friends in Paris, Lisbon and London, about how she ran up debt and called mummy to pay the bills, and about how in the past few years she'd been sent ever further away, to Rhodesia, to Tanganyika. And along the way things had happened, *dark* things not spoken about.

And now she was in Toronto, barely 20 years old, and her voice got into his head and he couldn't shake it. He had to see her. He drove to the Masons' brick house at 125 St Germain Avenue and knocked on the door. Cynthia invited him in and he stayed for only a few minutes, but two days later he returned. He was obsessed. He spent most of the next two days with her; *I watched surreptitiously her every word and action*, he said, *and I liked what I saw and heard.*

Ben was 50 years old. They were not quite 30 years apart, he later pointed out, just 29 years and 347 days. And look, Charlie Chaplin had done it, married Oona O'Neill when he was 54 and she was just 18, and they'd had *eight children*. So he could do it too, dammit! A few weeks later he picked up the phone, called Cynthia and asked her to marry him.

She said yes.

Ben felt compelled to write an explanation to Scottie. It began with a statement of love but turned into an admission that his life had not gone as expected.

> I am 50, and not such a bad sort of bastard as men go. Despite affection of the contrary, I am highly responsible . . . and this includes the present marriage. I have promised to love, honor and cherish Cine, and more than that no man can do. Economically, I have forfeited what professional status I ever had. I had a pretty tough trot after the end of the trip; not many people were hiring jeep drivers.

A little further down the letter Ben escalated his brutal campaign against Elinore with an attack that heralded a new phase of his legendary anger and would spare no one over the years to come.

> More or less of necessity, you have been misled to the nature of me and my relations with Elinore. I took her with me in the jeep only in preference to an alarm clock. Lest you be overcome with sympathy with Elinore or in condemnation of me, I tell you (for your own ears) that I have a document signed 8 June 1948 which reads: 'The marriage we have this day contracted is purely for the purpose of (regularizing) the current project. It may be terminated at any time by one party giving six months' notice to the other party.'

The contract.

Although he would mention it several more times in the years ahead, he'd quote it slightly differently each time. I never found any real evidence it ever existed. That was surprising. In years of poring through journals, manuscripts and thousands of letters and documents, and in interviewing dozens of friends, family members and acquaintances as I dove into Ben's life, I'd been able to piece together a pretty comprehensive timeline. And I'd found I could confirm almost everything he said he'd said and done, no matter how outrageous or unbelievable or egregious. Perhaps in a quest to make sure his life was properly documented, Ben even held on to letters that painted him in a terrifically unflattering light, letters he could have easily thrown away.

But after the California crash and his marriage to Cynthia there was a change in Ben's behaviour, an even greater tendency towards extremes, and I began to wonder if the contract with Elinore was a manifestation of that, something imagined, something Ben wanted so much that it had become real in his memory, an imagined version of the purely financial agreement Elinore had made him sign in 1948. Maybe it helped him defend his own behaviour towards Elinore and, more importantly, explain the ease with which she left him when they were barely halfway around the world.

Or maybe the contract was real, and simply didn't survive.

In any case, what he said about his relationship with Elinore began to stretch and mutate over the following years. Ben wrote to a lawyer in 1969: 'While I was married to her she was bedded by seven other men that I know of. I deserted her in December 1955.'

The first part might have been true. The second was clearly not.

After their 1 June wedding the young bride moved to Ben's apartment at 1309 North Pierce Street in Arlington, Virginia, in a nondescript low-rise brick complex built mainly for workers and servicemen stationed at an army post near Arlington National Cemetery.

The night of their wedding, Cynthia started to undress. And then she paused. She had to tell Ben a few things. The truth began tumbling out.

About the time she slashed her wrists in 1959, when she was 17 years old. About the subsequent psychiatric treatment at Guy's Hospital in London. About getting pregnant and having the illegitimate child of an American serviceman in February 1961, and giving up the child for adoption.

When her dress came off it exposed the rough scar across her belly, the permanent mark, the *evidence.*

It shocked Ben. It stunned him. But it didn't deter him. He paused long enough to tell Cynthia she was a fool not to have had an abortion, but he *had* to have a child. He took her to bed and in the next few days said little about her revelations.

Two weeks later Cynthia told him more, about how she'd been shipped off to live with her godmother in Kenya after giving birth to the baby boy in London; about how she did something terrible in Kenya and was sent off again, this time to live with her aunt and uncle in Dar es Salaam; about how while her aunt was away, and she was alone with her uncle, *Cynthia deputized for her in all respects*, as Ben put it. And how after that she was sent off to Montreal to live with family friends, sharing a cabin with the ship's captain on the way.

Ben saw his life spiralling out of control, the stories getting ever more shattering. His last chance at marriage and a family was collapsing in ways he could never have imagined. After the years in the jeep and the life he'd led, to have it all falling apart like this, instead of a storm at sea, instead of insurgents in the jungle?

But he was desperate to have a child. Within weeks of the wedding Cynthia was pregnant. And if this was as close as he'd ever get to the domesticity he'd so long sought, so be it. Ben tried as best he could to return to a sort of normalcy, and refocused on his editorial work.

It was hard. Even in the quietest moments Ben felt the span of years that separated him from Cynthia more than he wanted to admit. Thirty years. That was a long time. A generation. And the years had worn on Ben in so many ways, despite his claims of perfect health. He wore a truss for his hernia. He walked with a slight limp. His teeth had gone to hell and he was already wearing dentures, and he was embarrassed. He tried taking them out when Cynthia wasn't looking, padding quietly into the apartment's small bathroom to brush them before bed, and when Cynthia came into the bathroom he had to quickly hide them. *Have you ever tried brushing your teeth behind your back?* he said, *Have you?*

And there was another thing: when he got up in the night to go to the bathroom it was his habit to keep his eyes tightly closed on the way there and back, so he wouldn't quite wake up, he explained. *Often when I returned to bed you would reach over to me affectionately, but I would gently rebuff the advance; with any playing around I would have been wide awake . . . Every time this happened I resolved to explain the rebuff in the morning and every damned morning I forgot.*

Cynthia just didn't understand. Everything had a reason. Even the beatings.

It wasn't Cynthia's past, she had to understand, it was that she told his friends everything she'd been through, *everything*, and that drove him mad. Cynthia said she was only doing it because it was her policy to tell all, *because from the time of my leaving Dar es Salaam I vowed that I would tell everything to anybody who showed any interest in me whatsoever, male or female, for only then could I prove once and for all if they would stick by me or not. In most cases I was not disappointed.*

Ben told her she talked too much, and that she should keep her mouth shut, and that she was showing off shamelessly. She didn't listen.

Rage consumed him. He was spinning out of control. He drove to Annapolis and saw his old friend Paul Shaw, the welder who'd given him so much help in 1947, and found a reason to 'beat the shit out of him', as my dad recalled, even though Paul had already been weakened by his first stroke.

And in August, back in their small apartment, he took a belt to Cynthia.

The first time I beat you, I don't regret; there are times when there is absolutely nothing else a man can do. If I hadn't beaten you then, you would have despised me; as it was, you merely hated me. Plenty of people hate me, Cynthia, but no one that I know of despises me; I just couldn't live any other way.

The beatings, he told a friend, would not be termed cruelty by anyone aware of the whole story. At least, he said, the buckle had never left his hand.

What would you do, he asked Creed, *if your wife went around telling all your friends . . . of her suicide, treatment in a nuthouse, illegitimacy, incest, profligacy? You wouldn't beat her, you'd bloody well shoot her! And at the time I beat her, it was not known that she was pregnant; she was simply overdue and suspicious.*

Cynthia fled. She told no one where she was going, and Ben never found out where she'd gone or how she supported herself, even when she returned a few weeks later.

They tried again, with Ben determined to force his idea of domesticity onto the damaged marriage. He was working, he shouted, even if it didn't look like it when he was sitting in his underwear at the typewriter, earning $3.30 an hour, insisting Cynthia should do her share too instead of drinking a beer in front of the TV. Was it too much to ask that she cook something that didn't come from a can? 'Washing and garbage disposal are outside my province,' Ben snarled at her. He had certain expectations of what a wife should do.

In December, swollen with her unborn child, Cynthia left again. Two months later, in the final month of her pregnancy, she wrote from the Virginia Square Beauty Salon to Ben's sister, Jess, and reiterated that under no circumstances would she return to her husband this time. *To do so*, she said, *would be to sign my child's death warrant, and my own. It would be crass stupidity and grossly unfair on the child to return to Ben and expose a young life to his father's total lack of responsibility, sadism and out-and-out brutality.*

Jess was distraught. *What on earth has happened to you, Ben?*

Ben lashed back against Cynthia as best he could, trying to crush her – as if that would convince her to return – writing cruelly to tell her, *In normal terms you are unmarriageable. By that I mean that no normal man of anything like your age will ever marry you.*

Cynthia didn't come back.

When Ben realised she was gone for good he began revising their personal history, started telling people that when he'd married Cynthia she had already been pregnant, carrying someone else's child. He told this story even to close friends, as if the offence of her desperate flight was less of a blemish on his reputation if she'd entered the marriage pregnant with someone else's baby.

And there was a letter from Ben to a friend, written in early 1964, about their wedding night: *Cynthia fought madly, feverishly against administration of a contraceptive. During the next few weeks while Cynthia was back in Toronto, I fought feverishly (and silently) with the fear that she was pregnant before marriage; to a lesser extent, I still do.*

○

On 21 March 1964, at 3.07 in the morning, nine and a half months after Ben's marriage to Cynthia, Deirdre Scott Carlin was born in Arlington, Virginia.

And as soon as Ben saw Deirdre he knew she was his daughter. *Had there been any doubt,* he later told Cynthia's father, *I would have drenched the USA with blood from tests.*

But even as she was born, this beautiful child Ben had yearned for was slipping away. Cynthia refused to come home with the newborn, and six weeks later, on 5 May, Ben filed for divorce on grounds of desertion. He claimed to Cynthia's mother that *I CAN AND WILL DESTROY HER IN THE EVENT OF A HEARING,* just like that. But things didn't go the way he expected, and the court granted Cynthia custody of the child, with the provision that she lived within 30 miles of Washington. At first Ben visited every Sunday morning to see Deirdre, never for more than 30 minutes at a time, always with a duenna present, presumably paid for by Cynthia's mother. The arrangement lasted through the spring.

Then one day in late June Ben stopped by for his weekly visit, and they were gone. Sometime a few days earlier Cynthia had boarded a plane with Deirdre in a basket and flown off without a word of warning.

Deirdre was gone.

The next four years crushed Ben. Cynthia ignored his desperate letters and refused his calls, and it was only through her stepfather, Creed, that Ben eventually learned that she'd returned to Madeira, where she'd reportedly started drinking heavily, and that in July 1966 she'd run off to London and gone completely silent. One night in February 1968 he got two drunken phone calls, one after the other: Cynthia was distraught, Ben had to come to London *immediately*, by all means before 23 February, or . . . or *what?* She wouldn't say, but she gave him an address. Ben wrote to her there and she never replied.

There was another call in November, equally incoherent, with Cynthia claiming she'd remarried and was never coming home.

But that time Cynthia put Deirdre on the phone.

The four-year-old girl said *daddy*, just like that, the voice faint the way it was on a transatlantic call in the 1960s, travelling thousands of miles through a cable under the ocean. Ben felt his heart swell; he felt powerless and broken. It wasn't like when an engine died in the middle of a storm, or bandits threatened in the desert, or he was driving through rebel territory in Burma – all those things he'd known how to handle; now he was helpless. Standing with the phone in his hand in his basement apartment in the quietest part of the night, he felt some of the life getting sucked out of him; he began to feel like an old man.

Daddy. His daughter had called him *daddy.*

Soon afterward letters from Madeira spoke of a crisis, a critical situation, and in February Cynthia's father, Robert Henderson, who'd generally maintained a cool distance, urged that Ben fly to London immediately. There had been another suicide attempt on 27 January. Cynthia had turned on the gas in the kitchen. Ben had to come deal with matters for himself.

When Ben arrived in London on 12 February 1969, it was colder than usual, freezing, with rain turning to snow. Colonel Henderson had concocted a plan for Ben to meet Deirdre, helped by Eugenie Burdett, who ran a kindergarten in Knightsbridge and often looked after Deirdre for weeks at a time. Burdett was more a caretaker than a teacher, sometimes even buying clothes, filling in the gaps where Cynthia fell short.

On the afternoon of 15 February Ben arrived at Selfridges department store in Oxford Street, London. He knew the area well; years earlier Elinore had worked nearby for the US Air Force. He waited by an entrance, his heart beating fast, watching the crowds shuffle past through the grey slush. And then he saw her. The first time he'd seen her since she was three months old. His daughter, walking towards him with her grandfather, with her beautiful manners, her fine intelligence and independence. They spent two and a half hours together, Ben revelling in the child, perhaps unsure of how to act, trying to compress years of fatherhood into this fleeting, fantastic moment, absorbing her face, her voice, giving her a doll, taking her to the store's portrait studio for a series of small black-and-white photos he'd keep for the rest of his life.

'Apart from her beautiful manners she is all Carlin,' he told Creed with pride after the meeting. Deirdre was nothing less than 'heavenly'.

But something felt wrong. Even though Henderson had arranged the Selfridges meeting he was acting oddly cool, and Ben began to wonder why. After they parted, paranoia gripped him – it was all part of a plan, *they wanted the child to see me so that they could identify me in her mind with evil*. When he thought about it, it seemed the more attention Deirdre had paid to him at Selfridges the angrier Henderson had become, and according to Henderson himself, *Deirdre was sent straight to an (unmade) bed without food when they arrived home*. It was another plan, a way to steal Ben's daughter away from him, and Henderson's behaviour was all the confirmation he needed.

Evidence.

They were turning his daughter against him, had even introduced him as *Uncle Dick*, as if that wasn't obvious enough.

He heard Cynthia had given away the doll he'd given Deirdre.

Now that he'd seen Deirdre, he was certain Cynthia's family was trying to poison her feelings towards him, to end their relationship for good, and it was clear he had to get her back. He was afraid Cynthia's next suicide attempt would take Deirdre too.

He became desperate.

It was around this time that a 40-year-old widow with two sons, Evelyn Castaliogni, came into Ben's life and almost became part of a plot to retrieve Deirdre and bring her back to the States. I found Evelyn's name in one of the many legal documents spawned by Ben's battle to win custody. In it, Ben mentioned a proposed marriage; Evelyn had a nice house near good schools in Forest Heights, Maryland, and would make an excellent mother.

When I called Evelyn, who lives in retirement outside Washington, DC, it took her a moment to remember Ben. 'Carlson? Ben Carlson?' We went back and forth like that for a few minutes until I was apologising for dialling the wrong number and about to hang up.

But when I mentioned the jeep and the journey around the world it came back in a rush. Ben *Carlin*!

'I just totally put him out of my mind,' she said. 'It's so long ago.'

They'd met at a party in early 1969, Evelyn told me, when Ben was 56. Specific memories came back, one at a time.

'I was at a gathering with some people and he asked me if I'd like to go out with him to dinner,' she told me. 'I said okay. But he was a very strange person. Very, very strange.' She was especially concerned at how quickly he tried to force a relationship and move in with her after the first couple of dates. Evelyn's house had three bedrooms, and Ben was already doing the calculations: one for him and Evelyn, one for Deirdre and one for his office. 'He wanted to marry me! I had two boys and he had a daughter in England, and he said, "The boys can go down in the basement."'

And how was Ben going to bring Deirdre back to the States?

'I was supposed to go get his daughter from her mother in England!' said Evelyn, still sounding incredulous 45 years later. 'He wasn't going to be bothered with my two little boys, only his darling princess little girl. He was so determined! And I was very independent. I still am. I couldn't have someone tell me what I had to do with my children. *Go to England? Get my daughter?* You are the father! You need to do that, not me! It was crazy. It was insane.'

Once Evelyn realised Ben was serious about a rushed marriage and sending her off to fetch Deirdre, she ended the relationship. 'I told him I didn't want to have anything to do with him any more,' she said. Ben, dismayed at the rejection, later claimed without evidence or rationale that Cynthia's father had written 'poison letters' to Evelyn to sabotage the marriage he hoped for.

So he took the legal route, suing for access to his daughter. The result wasn't what he'd hoped for.

On 27 November 1969, the High Court of Justice decreed that Deirdre was to become a ward of the court, and granted Ben access to her in London for two hours on 28 November and two more hours the following day, the first time at a school and the second at Cynthia's flat.

It was a hollow victory. The decree further stated that once Cynthia left the jurisdiction of the court she was free to take Deirdre back to Madeira. And in Madeira Cynthia's mother, Scottie, had purchased a property for them, hired a nanny, made vague plans for Cynthia to get a job and, most importantly, arranged for Deirdre to enter St Margaret's School in England as soon as she was eight years old. In case the school's pedigree was unclear, Scottie stressed that St Margaret's was founded in the reign of Queen Victoria *for the daughters of the clergy*. In other words, Scottie was going to take care of things.

There's no evidence that Ben kept the appointments to see Deirdre in November. After five years, he knew he'd lost the fight.

He'd lost his daughter.

⌒

Ben returned to England once more in 1969.

My father was a visiting scholar at St John's College, working on *A History of Seafaring Based on Underwater Archaeology*, and we were living in a cottage outside Cambridge in the village of Trumpington.

In early December, just a few weeks before my brother Alan was born, my father got a call. 'Ben stopped by. We went to lunch at the Green Man pub and he ordered roast beef, and he stressed that he wanted a lot of fat on it. Even then I knew this was a bad thing. I knew or sensed Ben had a bad heart.

'I remember him telling me how he'd followed my underwater adventures, and I thought it was amazing that *I* had become an adventurer in the eyes of this man I'd nearly worshipped. In high school I'd asked him why in the world he was going to risk his life, and his answer was the same as that given by so many adventurers: you get the most back from life the more you put in it. He wanted to live life to the fullest.'

Before he left, Ben gave my father one of the copies of *Half-Safe* he hauled around the world, always hoping to sell another copy.

Cynthia

For George –

Occasionally on Sunday but never beyond Annapolis and
Cambridge

Ben Carlin

Cambridge, December '69

I don't remember it, but my dad says I met Ben that day. I was
two years old.

Ben returned home to Washington as the 60s turned into the
70s. He was unhappy with the fashion of long hair and side-
burns, the talk of love and peace. He wondered what the hell
the world was coming to, and where it held a place for him.

'I remember him coming over to the house, drinking a
bottle of wine with my parents, yakking away,' said Vermont
artist Ralph DeAnna, whose parents had known Ben and
Elinore in New York in the late 1940s, attended the first launch
of *Half-Safe* in 1948, and in the 60s lived near Ben in Washington. 'I got the sense he was a loner at that point. A lonely guy.
Things hadn't panned out for him. He had that one shot, but
he didn't have a lot of resources. He didn't know what else to do
with himself next.

'My mom said what he really wanted was to make money
from endorsements. *This was the razor I used on* Half-Safe*! This
was the radio I used!* That was his plan, but it never worked
out. He was ahead of his time. If he'd done something like that
today it would be a reality show.'

Ben visited the DeAnnas frequently, usually without an invitation. 'He used to scare the bejesus out of my little brother. He'd look down at him with his big grey beard and say, *What's the matter with you, ya little bugger?* Ben once came over to the house when my parents were out. I was a sophomore in high school. There was a bottle of wine on the kitchen table, and Ben opened it, finished it off and regaled us with his opinions of Shakespeare. He insisted the whole allure was the language. It had nothing to do with plot or psychology. It was just the language.

'Didn't he remarry? I remember him talking about his daughter. He had a daughter, didn't he?'

⌒

From the early 60s onward, the man who knew Ben best was Kelvin Minchin, a young doctor from New Zealand who was practising in Annapolis. The two men sounded the same to Americans, and someone insisted that they meet at a party one night in the summer of 1960. Over drinks they discovered they both had West Australian roots, they both had a passion for boats and adventure, and they were both mechanically minded. For the next 20 years Kelvin was Ben's closest friend, as well as his personal doctor.

'Kelvin, give me a couple pills for pain,' Ben used to say, not really caring about the cause of his ills, just wanting something to dull the symptoms born of decades of hard living.

Although in 2015 Kelvin had retired to New Zealand, after a long career in the United States, we both found ourselves in Western Australia at the same time, and he invited me to the flat he and his wife, Rosemary, had rented for a few days in Fremantle near Monument Hill War Memorial. When I arrived he was waiting for me outside, looking much younger than his 86 years, standing tall and lean in a black cable sweater and jeans, as if he'd just stepped off one of the many boats he's owned and restored over the years.

Like Ben, Kelvin wanted to see the world. He was born in New Zealand to Australian parents who moved to England when he was young, and at first all he could think about was moving back to the southern hemisphere. 'The only sensible thing was to build a boat and sail back to Australia,' he said. 'So I got a job, earned some money and built a 26-foot boat. When I was almost finished my parents sat up and took notice: this fellow may try this! So I got shipped off to America to get an education.' Kelvin got a job in a steam plant, worked the night shift, and between that and repairing cars under a streetlight at night was able to put himself through medical school and eventually become director of a nursing home near Washington, DC.

We sat on the terrace and talked for hours over coffee, and I understood immediately why Ben had bonded with him, had called him *an extremely decent, sensitive and sympathetic fellow.*

And Kelvin felt the same of Ben. 'He was very loyal once you became friends with him. He would die for you! But he did not suffer fools gladly. If he met you and you were skeptical of what he had done or what he could do, he would cut you off and that was the end of it. He may have had some sort of inferiority complex. Anybody who looked down on him, he couldn't handle that. I don't think he had any really close friends.'

Kelvin found in Ben a kindred spirit, sometimes as much a father figure as a friend. 'I think he thought I was a bit of a babe in the woods in certain areas.'

You mean, with women?

Kelvin laughed. 'Oh no. With boats and legal matters and that sort of thing.' Interestingly, like so many others, Kelvin told me Ben said almost nothing about women over their years of friendship. Never talked about Gertrude or Elinore, didn't say too much about Cynthia despite the turmoil, never spoke about other women who might be in his life. Boyé had said the same thing. It was partly a cultural and generational reticence, but partly because Ben had to hide any sign of weakness, and his relationships with women had all completely fallen apart.

In the early 60s, Kelvin told me, Ben had a scheme for what he was going to do next.

'He was a brilliant fellow, very clever with mechanical things. He decided that he was going to "dredge the hell out of the Chesapeake Bay",' Kelvin laughed. 'He thought he could build a portable dredge, reclaim lots of land, sell it and become wealthy. He designed a dredge that could be taken apart and reassembled, and he bought pumps, engines and hoses, and made a box with blades turning inside. The idea was that the blades would chew up the mud at the bottom of the bay and pumps would suck it up. He worked on the idea at Smitty's old marina in Annapolis where I had my 47-foot boat.' He thought back. 'I was there the day Kennedy was assassinated. So was Ben.'

Ben got a prototype running, but it never worked as well as he'd hoped, and he abandoned the idea.

Around that time Kelvin introduced Ben to Melbourne Smith, a Canadian with schemes of his own, who was making money by ferrying other people's boats up and down the East Coast and painting nautical paintings that wound up in bars in the Annapolis area.

'We'd go to bars occasionally and he was always looking for a fight,' recalled Melbourne, who now lives in West Palm Beach and made his name in the 1970s by recreating a fully functional Boston clipper. 'Somebody'd say something, anything, and Ben would say "What's that? Want to step outside and settle it?"'

Did he actually get into fights, in his fifties?

'Oh yeah! He did. And he was a bridge player. He joined groups around the way, people he didn't even know. And at one of them someone said something, and of course it was, "Want to step outside and settle it?" And one night three players decided they *did* want to settle it, and went outside and beat him up pretty bad.'

After a couple of years of driving a cab, editing articles and living a frugal life, Ben was in a position to buy property, ironically having been urged by Cynthia to become a homeowner. On 29 January 1964, he signed on a townhouse at 122 6th Street, NE, in Washington, DC, for $24,000, with the intention of turning it into a money-making venture. The previous owner had just obtained permission to convert the building from a single-family dwelling to a three-unit apartment building, and as soon as Ben moved in he began tearing the place apart to divide it up.

'I'd go down and see him every once in a while,' said Kelvin. 'We'd eat in the kitchen with plaster falling down around us, debris everywhere. One night he asked me to stay for dinner, and the pan on the stove was full of plaster, and he just dumped it out and cracked eggs into it.'

When he was done with renovations Ben had three large, one-bedroom apartments to rent out, one on each floor, for $150 per month each, while he lived in a small efficiency apartment he'd built in the basement.

'He had a million stories,' said a former tenant. 'He reminded me of Hemingway. He used to go out to get his paper in his boxer shorts. Everything was *bloody* this and *bloody* that. He was so gruff that nobody bothered the house – and Capitol Hill was a rough neighbourhood then.'

Half-Safe had brought a measure of fame, and now for the first time in his life Ben was finding financial security too. He continued a protracted battle with André Deutsch, convinced they owed him money for failing to properly promote his first book. Lawyers advised him to move on, but he wrote increasingly long and complicated letters, struggling to get lawyers interested in pursuing a case.

At the same time, he dusted off *Half-Safe*, which had languished for years in a marina.

'In '67 or '68 he brought the jeep to my house in Edgewater, Maryland,' said Kelvin. 'I had a place on the water where he could work on it, and he completely restored it over the course of a year or two.'

It wasn't because he had another adventure in mind. 'I think he was satisfied with what he'd done,' Kelvin said, after a pause. 'He'd gotten into the *Guinness Book*, and that was important to him. He never exhibited any desire to repeat his travels. He'd spent ten years of his life doing it.'

Interestingly, it wasn't until 1974 that Ben's full accomplishment was noted in the *Guinness Book of Records*, and even then Guinness got a detail wrong:

The only trans-Atlantic crossing by an amphibious vehicle was achieved by Ben and Elinore Carlin (Australia and U.S.A. respectively) in an amphibious jeep 'Half-Safe'. He completed the last leg of the Atlantic crossing (the English Channel) on 24 Aug. 1951 and his circumnavigation back to Montreal, Canada on 8 May 1958 covering 39,000 miles *62765 km* over land and 9,600 miles *15450 km* by sea and river.

Actually Ben arrived in Montreal on 13 May. The record, however, still stands.

Of everything that happened to Ben during their years of friendship, Kelvin stressed it was seeing Deirdre briefly in London in 1969 that most affected him. 'He saw me the day after he came back, and he was ecstatic. He was absolutely over the moon. He said, "Kelvin, I've just seen the most marvellous daughter anyone could ever have." He talked about her for days. He was really carried away with fact he *had* a child.'

But the joy had been fleeting, and by 1970 it was as if the events of the previous decade had exhausted him. Deirdre was gone, André Deutsch finally agreed to pay, the manuscript for the sequel to *Half-Safe* remained unpublished, and the jeep sat restored but motionless on Kelvin's property. Ben was too tired to keep fighting.

Things were slowing down.

Late in the year Ben took stock of his life. His Washington apartments were bringing in $5,400 per year, his editing another $11,000, and he'd managed to build a net worth of more than $60,000. It wasn't bad for a man who'd had absolutely nothing until his late forties. He resigned from his editorial job at *Science* and, for the first time in years, sat down at his typewriter to really write, to tell the rest of his story. It was time people knew his name again, knew the magnitude of what he'd once done.

He spent most of 1971 working on a rough manuscript that rehashed the Atlantic crossing before picking up in earnest with the continuation of the journey from London back to Montreal. His friends Kelvin and Melbourne tried to help him find a publisher and even paid a professional editor to take a crack at it. But it had been too long ago and the manuscript needed too much work. Nobody wanted it.

With no book deal, no job and no family, there was less and less holding Ben down now, less tying him to the United States, and he began to feel a nascent homing instinct pulling him back to the other side of the world, back to the place he'd once fled. When his sister, Jess, died in June 1972, Ben was shocked to find out that her house at 91 Blencowe Street in West Leederville, the home he'd grown up in, was to be kept available for his 'use and occupation' during his lifetime. The universe was putting the pieces into place for him.

On 20 September 1973, he sold his Washington townhouse to a long-time tenant for $70,000. Only after he was long gone did the buyer find out his basement apartment violated zoning regulations, and she spent the next six years in the District of Columbia Court of Appeals sorting out the mess Ben had left behind.

Half-Safe was next.

Ben had written to my dad on 4 November 1969 and said he planned to have the jeep fully restored by the spring; a fire of some kind had set him back a few months. 'When it is finished I shall spend $1,000 in advertisement around the world and then sit back to see what happens. It may bring anything from $5,000 to $100,000.'

It was strange that he would let her go, given the symbiotic relationship he'd shared with her for a quarter of a century, the longest relationship of his life. I wanted to romanticise his bond with the jeep. After all, he'd shaped her with his own hands, kept her running over continents and oceans by sheer intuition, lived in her, and in turn she'd brought him fame, however fleeting, and become the unmistakable symbol of his achievement. But he always denied having any emotional attachment to *Half-Safe*, and said he hoped to cash in on the jeep's fame after his second book came out, when he thought she'd command a premium.

In 1972 Ben's friend Dan Lundberg, a California oil analyst who'd made his reputation as a novelist, journalist, TV anchorman and publicist, agreed to read the manuscript. Ben waited anxiously for months before receiving a blistering six-page response that effectively killed his hopes.

Reprehensible. Unsatisfactory. Self-conscious. Turgid. Peculiarly stylized as only beginning journalists can wreak it. 'Jesus Christ, Ben, you are your own worst enemy,' said Lundberg, who went on to fame for predicting a 1979 petrol shortage.

If the book couldn't sell the jeep, Ben would have to do it himself. And he knew who'd take it off his hands: George Calimer, a drinking mate, industrial engineer, auto collector and one-time president of the Greater Baltimore Antique Car Club.

Calimer had run into Ben one night at a party – of course it was a party; everyone met Ben at a party – and knew the Australian adventurer by reputation. He wanted to hear about the journey, and about the jeep, but he knew about Ben's prickly reputation and approached him cautiously.

'My father circled Ben several times,' said his daughter Colleen, 'and Ben ignored him each time he passed.' Finally, Calimer decided the only way to get Ben's attention was to issue an absurd challenge: 'I'll bet you didn't roller-skate around the world!'

Ben warmed up to him immediately. *All right, mate, you want to hear about going around the world? I'll tell you about going around the world.*

Calimer's friends called him 'Ace', Colleen said, 'because he was a master mechanic, and he could tell what was wrong with a motor just by listening to it'. Just like Ben. The two men shared a mechanical lingua franca and became friends, and on an autumn day in 1973 Calimer and his son picked up *Half-Safe* at Minchin's property, where she'd sat for years. On the way back to Baltimore the engine nearly burned up.

But Ben couldn't completely let go. The contract he drafted gave Calimer only a half share in the jeep, serial No. GPA-1239, engine No. GPA-1239, originally manufactured in 1945 by the Ford Motor Company and rebuilt by Frederick Benjamin Carlin for the first and only amphibious journey around the world.

Conditions to be observed by the said George David Calimer:

1. The said vehicle will be housed unexposed to either the weather or vandals; it will be adequately insured against fire and thievery and vandalism.

2. The said vehicle will never enter water; if it be subsequently sold he will ensure that the subsequent owners do not permit the vehicle to enter water.
3. The said vehicle will not be driven on land except for exhibition or demonstration essential to its sale.

The contract stated that Ben could buy back Calimer's share in *Half-Safe* whenever he wanted for $4,000 plus any accumulated costs of insuring her.

Calimer wrote a cheque for $2,000 on 9 November and subsequently ignored every clause of the contract. He drove *Half-Safe* in vintage car rallies, took his family out on the Chesapeake Bay, sometimes left her parked by the kerb on suburban Beech Street where passersby would gawk. It was an odd and ignoble second act for the jeep, like Lindbergh's *Spirit of St. Louis* ending up giving joy rides at county fairs or Cousteau's *Calypso* being pressed into tourist service at a Caribbean resort. By the late 1970s *Half-Safe* was jammed into Calimer's garage behind his suburban home, covered in junk, thick dust and bird shit.

During the petrol shortage that spilled into 1974, Calimer thought it would be funny to drive *Half-Safe* to a petrol station and fill its tanks with hundreds of gallons of fuel just to watch people's reactions. 'We were worried he could get attacked, and told him the joke wasn't worth the risk,' his daughter Cathy Calimer Zumbrun told me. He decided against it.

A few months later a local reporter came to see *Half-Safe*. 'The yellow car-boat sits peacefully in Calimer's backyard,' he wrote. 'She looks peaceful, but puzzling. It still seems incredible that this vehicle had travelled around the world.'

The reporter lowered himself through the hatch over the passenger seat, surprised that the cabin still smelled sweetly of oil, gas and cotton webbing, as if it had just emerged from the sea. A scatter of tools, batteries and gauges cluttered the small compartments built into the interior. It was as if *Half-Safe* had been hurriedly abandoned, and in a way, she had. 'Once I started, I couldn't turn back,' Ben had said when the journey was done. 'The opportunities you fail to take gnaw at you. Now nothing will gnaw at me.'

The adventure had ended. But not the wanderlust.

'You can stand pain, but not an itch,' goes the saying, and Ben was starting to feel the old itch again. By the end of 1973 he'd done all he could in the United States. It was time to go home.

He couldn't go quietly.

'The day before he left,' said his friend Melbourne Smith, 'he came to my house and proposed to my wife that she come with him back to Australia –'

He was joking, right?

'He was serious! And he wanted his manuscript back too, but I didn't know where it was. Well, he took a whack at the back of my head, so I grabbed a shovel and chased him across the yard with it. When I cut him across the back with it the neighbours called the cops, and when the cops arrived they chased him off. But during the fight his watch had come off, the Rolex he'd taken around the world. I couldn't ever really stay mad at him, so I made sure he got it back.'

Melbourne paused.

'He was an odd man, but truly magnificent.'

A few weeks after my conversation with Melbourne I got an email from Linda Johnson, the daughter of Jerry Jowett, the

Calcutta friend from the 1950s who'd mysteriously vanished in the 1970s after returning home to England.

'I met Ben Carlin in Northampton, after my dad left,' said Linda. 'I would have been between four and seven years old, I guess.' That was the summer of 1967, when a cluster of stamps in Ben's passport shows he wandered for several months through England, France and the Azores for reasons unknown, maybe just because he'd become restless.

'He seemed very big to me. He liked Mum and wanted to take us to the USA and marry Mum. She declined.'

CHAPTER SIXTEEN
Homecoming

Ben Carlin touched down at Perth Airport on 4 January 1974.

It had been a long trip from Washington, DC, hopscotching westward from San Francisco to Hong Kong to the Philippines to Singapore. He made part of the trip on the Danish tramp steamer *Astrid Bakke*, which carried a dozen passengers along with cargo around the South Pacific. Ben would have felt at home on the ship, would have given advice about how to run her better, would have had a few drinks and told stories about his own adventures, about once sailing this same bloody sea in a jeep smaller than one of the ship's life rafts, you see. He would have been charming.

He was 61. In his passport photo he wears a dark suit and tie, his hair neatly combed back, the once-thick locks now thin at the temples. His neatly trimmed beard is fully grey and his left eyelid droops slightly.

'I remember the first time he appeared,' said Alison Carlin. 'It was a stinking hot January. No one in the family knew he was in Western Australia. Or that he was even coming back. We were having lunch out at Eric's mother's, and we were sitting on the back lawn, and he appeared through the side gate.'

'He was trying to re-establish himself in Western Australia,' added Lynne Carlin.

'Yes, and I think it must have been a rude shock to him when he came back, because he remembered Western Australia as a very different place. By the time he came back all his drinking mates, if they were still around, would have become members of the establishment, and very proper. Very *ooh la la*.'

For a while after his return to Australia Ben lived with Eric, Alison and their children, Jennifer and Michael.

'Ben showed up in Perth when I was in my teens,' Michael told me. 'As far as I knew, he didn't have any money. I think he was assembling aluminium windows in a factory. The assumption was, he wouldn't keep a job – he would have thought he knew better how to run the factory.'

A few others remember Ben making window frames in Perth around 1975, already in his early sixties, never too proud to do what it took to make a dollar.

'After a brief honeymoon period he wasn't welcome at our house. He clearly had a very high opinion of himself and appeared to have come from another era. He could be charming and funny but also quick to criticise. Women were either bitches or peaches. The adults around me would treat him with a certain deference. I suspect he was drunk most of the time, and I was scared of him.'

Once he'd worn out his welcome elsewhere, Ben bought a small two-bedroom flat in the suburb of Cottesloe, within a stone's throw of the ocean. He quickly established a pattern of appearing uninvited at the homes of friends and family, arriving in an old, cream-coloured jeep with a six-pack in hand that would always be gone by the end of his visit, along with whatever else was offered.

Ben had been in Western Australia for barely two years when he suffered his first stroke. It hit hard on 22 October 1975, and paralysed his left side. While in the hospital a second stroke hit and took the ability to write with his right hand. He spent the next year recovering, but it was slow going. Even though he was only in his sixties, he'd lived hard. He'd drunk heavily, he'd chain-smoked for decades, he'd been in the horrendous San Francisco accident, and there had been all the amphetamines during the hard years between Calcutta and New York, and sometimes afterward. 'He quite enjoyed them,' said Kelvin. Like my dad, he also remembered Ben's destructive appetite for fat. 'He would fry it and eat it! I said, "Ben, you're killing yourself."'

Around Christmas 1976 a third stroke hammered Ben's right side. He was 64 years old, and this time he knew there would be no complete recovery. Major Carlin, who had sought war, who had survived not one but *two* impossible ocean crossings, who had circled the world in a jeep, now laid up like a cripple, forced to depend on others! The goddamned unfairness of it.

For the first time he was aware of his mortality. He had loose ends to tie up, a legacy to secure.

He started almost back at the beginning, turning his attention first to his alma mater, Perth's Guildford Grammar

School. He'd done well during his post-adventure Washington years, had discovered an extraordinary aptitude for playing the stock market, and he now updated his will so that the majority of his estate would fund a scholarship program with the goal of recognising the 'proficiency in the study of the English Language and its expression with the avoidance of clichés'.

'The older I get,' he'd once said to Cynthia's father, 'the surer I get that the old British ideas on classical education were the best: teach the little bastards Latin and Greek and then kick them out to learn something.'

He called it the Charlotte Carlin Scholarship, after his mother, who'd died when he was four.

The name spoke volumes. He'd essentially cut all of his living family out of an inheritance, and more pointedly named the scholarship after the one woman in the world whose love he felt certain of, perhaps because he'd never really known her.

It was essentially a fuck-off to everyone else.

I was surprised he'd left even his daughter, Deirdre, out of the will. Kelvin thought that omission was practical rather than pointed; after all, Ben hadn't had contact with her for years and no longer knew how to reach her. On the other hand, in 1966 Ben snarled that he would never contribute to his daughter's support because, *The more often mother puts her hand in her pocket on Deirdre's account, the happier I am.*

With the scholarship plans complete, the old adventurer embarked on one last voyage on 23 July 1977.

'He managed to get himself on an airplane and struggled back to America,' said Kelvin. Ben spent most of the summer and fall on the East Coast with old friends, drinking whiskey, embracing his twilight, telling stories as best he could.

'We could barely understand him, but we had a marvellous time together.'

When I heard about the trip, I couldn't help thinking about Ben's leaving Australia for the first time nearly 40 years earlier, when he'd felt his luck was running out and had fled to China in 1939. It seemed he'd done the same thing a second time, making one last thrilling escape, one last run from trouble. But not out of fear. Ben Carlin was never really afraid. He was doing it because it always worked out wherever he landed, whatever his final destination, because he was Ben Carlin.

While in the States there was business to attend to. First, there was the matter of the sequel to *Half-Safe*, which Ben had struggled with for years. If Ben's first book was a raconteur's recollection of adventures told over pints in a pub, the final manuscript for his second, despite the years of revisions, recommendations and rewrites, was still an overlong late-night harangue by a man in love with the sound of his own story-telling, oblivious to his audience glazing over while he details transmission ratios and radio frequencies, and frequently veers away from the main narrative into tangential historical trivia.

Still, there was a compelling rawness and immediacy to the manuscript. In the hands of an editor like Diana Athill it could have been shaped into an extraordinary tale, but André Deutsch had long parted ways with Ben by the time he was trying to sell the sequel.

'We had nothing to do with it,' Athill told me, and she offered a simple opinion about why Ben had such trouble finding a new publisher: 'What I suspect is that Ben became increasingly pig-headed and could be counted on to fuck things up because of paranoia.'

No one else would touch it either.

But Ben *had* to get it published. On 11 December, with his own efforts exhausted, he drafted an agreement granting his friends Kelvin Minchin and George Calimer sole rights to publish the book, 'grantor being physically incapacitated'. The agreement granted a third of any proceeds from the book's publication to each of the grantees, with the balance being paid to Ben.

Next, Ben scrawled out a series of letters to his lawyer back in Perth, making minor changes to his will. He wanted the Western Australian Museum to have a sextant that he'd carried all the way around the world, but if the museum didn't want it then it could go to Guildford Grammar School. The museum didn't want it. For a neighbour who'd been kind to him, there was a pair of electronic wristwatches. Ben specified where everything could be found in his apartment, as if uncertain he'd ever make it home.

But he did. And although his mind was sharp when he returned to Perth on 6 January 1978, his once-strong body was ever more quickly betraying him. He reluctantly admitted himself to a nursing home. After two days he decided he couldn't stand it and returned to his Cottesloe flat.

His world was shrinking, becoming claustrophobic. He hobbled from room to room on crutches and struggled to make use of his hands. Meals on Wheels delivered lunches. Neighbours checked in on him daily and brought tea and cakes. Most of the time his only company was Puddy Cat, a Siamese he'd taught to use the toilet.

He went angrily into his final years, furious at his diminishing powers, especially during his hospital stays.

'When he could no longer speak,' said Alison, 'he used to write on this board, and one of the nurses came in one day when Eric was there. She pointed to the board and said, "Oh yes, Mr Carlin does this so he doesn't forget things." And Ben wrote, "Bloody bitch!"'

'We used to go see him in hospital,' continued Alison, 'because you do that sort of thing. He told us that we were vultures waiting for him to die.'

But Ben still had one more thing to do.

He'd never stopped thinking about his daughter, Deirdre, stolen away from him in the middle of the night as a baby in 1964. Everything else might be gone – the adventure, the fame, the women, even the jeep itself – but *she* was still out there somewhere, still his, and she was the closest thing to love that he could imagine, the child who had been denied him for 14 years, the missing piece that could have made him whole. She was the 'pit-a-pat of little feet' he'd dreamed he'd hear at the end of his adventures. She was the 'heavenly' child he'd bragged about in a letter years later, imagining what she might be, what she was doing, always a world away and beyond his grasp despite the years of raging letters, the late-night phone calls, the accusations, the pleas, the attempts to find her and to make himself complete.

Here, near the end, she was all he had left.

On 20 December 1978, Ben sat in front of his typewriter and began to type, slowly and with great difficulty. When he was finished he pulled the single sheet of paper from the platen, signed his name as carefully and neatly as he could, and sealed it in an envelope.

Now all he could do was wait for an answer.

From the balcony of his Cottesloe flat on Overton Gardens he could see the expanse of the Indian Ocean, the long curve of the western horizon. At night, after the sun dropped into the sea in a blaze, he could hear the roar and rush of the waves crashing on the beach, the sea beckoning, reminding him of who he was, who he had been, where he had gone.

He slept with a copy of *Half-Safe* under his bed.

When he needed to escape for a while, he turned to his two televisions stacked on top of each other, one with a working picture, one with working sound, and turned up the volume.

Sometimes he thought about the ghosts in his past, the friends and lovers long gone. Soon after writing to Deirdre he wrote to his old friend Richard Battey, who'd been with him the day he bought the jeep in Maryland in 1947, and asked for Elinore's address.

Battey refused the request: 'With Ellie's permission be advised she has two jobs, lives in the city with a country home on Long Island, owns one car, one dog, has an exciting love life and never felt better,' he wrote back. And then Battey opened the floodgates of pent-up anger:

If there ever was a man who had an absolute talent for losing friends and alienating people you must be the one. Is it possible you took the Dale Carnegie course in 'Winning Friends and Influencing People' and applied his teachings in reverse? You constantly downgrade women in general and your women acquaintances in particular. What is this trait in your character that seemingly compels you to derogate every woman you have ever lived with (even your own sister), and then if they reject you, as most have, become insanely vindictive?

In early 1979, on the other side of the world, a 14-year-old girl opened a letter with a Perth postmark.

Dear Deirdre, it began, *this is a strange way for us to meet after so many years.* It recounted the return to Australia, the strokes, the helplessness.

> I am pretty useless. I never go out, although I could. I plan to go to the States toward the end of next year. I shall go by way of Heathrow, but shall not leave the airport; the airline will look after me there. Either before I go or in the States I plan to get an electric-powered wheelchair; I could get one locally but they are probably much cheaper over there.
>
> Sweetheart, there is a great deal to tell you but I want to be sure that what I have to tell you reaches you; I SHALL NOT EMPLOY ANY TRICKS TO REACH YOU. Everything will be quite above board, and nobody can call me a liar. There is no way of your ever seeing me unless you come here or to the States. If your mother doubts my abilities or intentions she should write to me. I have two things connected with the registration of your birth that you should have and I have for you some photographs, the manuscript of a second book, and the names and addresses of two relatives. And I shall not die penniless.
>
> Your loving father

Below, Ben had added a note to Deirdre's mother:

> Dear Cynthia,
>
> You win. I give up because of the impossibility of getting around. Far from improving, I have slipped backward this

summer; with the coming of next winter I hope to improve to where I was. Fair go . . . I promise not to offend you in any way.

Deirdre Carlin put the letter back in the envelope. She went to see the headmistress of Tudor Hall School in Oxfordshire, England, the latest in a series of boarding schools she'd attended since being sent away from her mother's home in Madeira when she was six years old. She was advised not to respond.

Ben waited for weeks and then months for an answer. He grew weaker. By the beginning of 1980 he was unable to speak or walk. He typed out messages on a Canon Communicator, which looked like a bulky calculator and spat out his bitter words on a narrow tape.

Late in the year, he had no choice but to leave his cluttered Cottesloe flat one last time. He was driven to Craigwood Nursing Home in the Perth suburb of Como.

In one of his final letters, Ben pleaded with Kelvin to hurry up and get his book published. 'Get a move on or I die too soon.' The man who had traded in the currency of charisma, stamina and confidence was now bankrupt.

He had left even the sea behind. His world was closing in on itself.

Back in England, Deirdre held on to her father's letter. She mostly put it out of her mind. Sometimes she pulled it out and read it. And then in early 1981, when she was 17 years old, she made a decision.

Sitting in her room at Tudor Hall School, she began writing page after page in loopy handwriting, telling Ben about her life, her achievements at school, her feelings towards her absent mother. She wrote about wanting to know Ben. She too wanted closure and completion. She was ready. In February she put her letter, along with a photo, in the mail.

A few weeks later, on 7 March 1981, Ben Carlin died. He was 69 years old.

He never saw the letter.

On the way back to my rented cottage in Cottesloe one afternoon after a day in the archives at Guildford Grammar School, I realised I was driving past the entrance to the sprawling Karrakatta Cemetery, where Ben's ashes had been scattered to the winds three days after his death.

I pulled into a parking spot next to a sign that warned against leaving valuables in the car. Behind a computer in the modern reception area, just across from the cemetery's café, a young woman typed in Ben's name and pointed me to the Rose Gardens.

The rose bushes were bare, but a single Norfolk pine soared high into the clear blue sky above the triangular plot. In the garden around the tree hundreds of simple small stone markers memorialised the dead. No one had bought one for Ben, and he hadn't wanted one anyway: 'Funerals and all that goes with them are just about the height of human idiocy,' he'd once said.

Nevertheless, a small group of family and old friends had once gathered here to say goodbye, to tell stories, to pay their respects. This was the end of his journey and, in some ways, mine.

I stood by the garden, and for a while I simply looked up at the soaring pine tree. I thought about Ben's life, and what it meant, and why it meant so much to me.

It could have been so different. Ben could have returned home to the glow of fame; he could have embarked on subsequent adventures; he could have seen his second book turn into a blockbuster and his adventures come to life on the screen. Instead, when he arrived in New York in 1958 he was broke and alone, overwhelmed by loss, forgotten by the world. He spent the next two decades living in virtual obscurity and drinking himself towards death.

For years I'd wondered what happened. Now I was closer to an answer.

The easy one is that his journey took too long. By 1958 the world had moved on. Postwar infatuation with adventurers like Hillary and Heyerdahl had given way to fears of communism and nuclear proliferation. Khrushchev had initiated the Soviet space program and, just 90 miles from Key West, Castro's revolutionary army was testing Havana's defences.

There was more to it, of course. Ben had a hard time with people. He was alternately charming and loyal; belligerent and abusive. He was an intellect who was more comfortable with grease under his fingernails, a stubborn bastard who never pretended that he was travelling to prove a point or to spread a message of peace. There was no transcendent purpose to sustain him, not even the 'because it's there' explanation that sufficed for George Mallory. Travel was an escape from the ordinary. It kept him alive and fed a desire for attention that he never admitted to. It was all he knew. He couldn't rhapsodise on the deeper meaning of it all, because there wasn't one. It was simply who he was. Ben had said he was going to make the journey, and he did, and that was that. Life went on.

But still, he wanted people to know what he'd done. He wanted them to read his book. He wanted to be remembered.

'I understand Ben was quite pissed off that no one took any notice of his great adventure,' Michael Carlin told me. 'He was driven by desire for recognition.'

And on that front Ben Carlin had always been his own worst enemy, tending towards a self-sabotage that grew progressively worse the older he got. The poor reception of his first book and attendant fiasco with André Deutsch had been the first real blow. He'd never known how to promote himself or work the press. Then came the more personal wound of Elinore's mutiny halfway around the world in 1955, and the failure to get his second book published before he died.

But now, standing where his ashes had been scattered, I understood it was losing Deirdre that tormented him most. Her absence broke him and haunted his final decades. At the end of his circumnavigation he reached the finish line, but he never achieved his goal.

∼

In the days and weeks after his death, those who knew Ben were circumspect about his passing.

'Under the circumstances, it was probably for the best,' wrote Ben's friend George Calimer to Ian Bessell-Brown, a Guildford Grammar schoolmate who served as an executor of Ben's estate. 'I sincerely was fond of him despite his cantankerous disposition, which I learned a long time ago to ignore.'

'He had lots of good points, though [he was] a complex character and wouldn't win a prize in public relations,' wrote his neighbour Hilda Ranford in a letter to Deirdre. But, she added,

He was quite kind in a lot of ways, and I seemed to understand his unusual disposition and appreciate his very worthy character. He told me about you and the letter he had written and I did hope he would receive your answer each time I went to the box. He thought perhaps you had not had it delivered. He said you had hands and feet like his.

Towards the end, Ben had offered his nephew Eric Carlin a hundred dollars to hire a launch and dump him in the Indian Ocean after he died.

'He asked Eric to collect his body from the morgue and sew it up in canvas,' said Alison, 'and he had instructions about how thick the canvas had to be, and Eric was supposed to take it out to sea.' Eric declined. Of course by then, like almost everyone else, he'd had enough.

As Michael Carlin recalled, 'Ben's last words to my father, maybe to anyone, laboriously spelt out on an alphabet board after his stroke were: "You can fuck off. You won't get my money."'

Yet it would be too easy to dismiss everything Ben accomplished and focus on the disintegration of his later years. My father never let me forget the central point of his life. 'He did fulfill his dream, out of sheer determination,' he said to me. 'How many people have done that?'

⌒

One by one, Ben's ex-wives slipped away.

Gertrude Plath returned to her silence about Ben after his surprise appearance at her Nevada home in November 1957.

She settled in the small desert town of Sparks, earned a degree in education and taught German and Spanish for a few years. Mostly, she felt alone. 'I just do not have any relatives here in America,' she wrote to a friend in Germany in 1972, 'and only a few left in Germany who are, however, too far away to really care or to even write.'

Eventually she was married a third time, to a wealthy rancher from Wyoming. 'It was the last thing in the world I think my mother would ever have done,' said her daughter Betty. 'But the man was rich, and my mother used to say, "You don't marry for love, you marry for money." It didn't last.'

On a spring day in her 85th year Gertrude was found wandering in confusion along a snowy street after a massive stroke. She died on 17 May 1997.

'I don't think she was happy,' said Betty. 'I don't think she lived the life she felt she was entitled to. Sometimes you can't do what you want.'

⌒

Elinore Carlin kept Ben's last name for the rest of her life, but by the 1960s she'd put the man and the adventure far behind her. She embraced life in New York City. She had a small, fixed-rent apartment in Greenwich Village and a weekend house in Bridgehampton, a wealthy hamlet towards the far end of New York's Long Island. She played tennis, she did brunch, and she was successful in her career.

I visited Elinore's niece Carol Arone in a small coastal town in Maine on a rainy weekend in the early autumn of 2015, and she and her husband, Mark, invited me to pore through hundreds of letters and photos that Elinore had left behind, along with the journals that covered the London years and the travel into the Middle East. Elinore's journals, begun as a practical record of the journey, were literate, observant and deeply heartfelt. If she'd been born a few decades later she would have written her own books about the adventure, and they would have been beautiful.

Mark opened a bottle of Madeira, chosen because of the time Ben and Elinore had spent on the Portuguese island, and Carol reminisced over dinner. When she was a high school student in the late 60s, she told me, she used to visit her exotic Aunt Elinore in her West Village apartment, but Ben and the journey in *Half-Safe* were always strictly off limits.

'Elinore didn't like talking about the trip. She eventually felt like a fool, like she'd been used. I think she was embarrassed. She wanted to change the subject whenever Ben came up. She was alone after the divorce, and she became bitter.'

Elinore became successful in her own right. She was named director of placement for Paul, Weiss, Rifkind, Wharton & Garrison, a Manhattan law firm that has since grown to 900 lawyers. Until then, only lawyers at the firm had recruited other lawyers. It was equally unusual that Elinore was a woman.

'She wanted to be a professional woman in New York when women were pretty much pegged as secretaries,' Carol told me, 'and she worked hard to maintain that image too. She was attractive and worked hard to stay that way.'

In 1978, Elinore became director of placement at the then-new Cardozo School of Law, making $24,000 per year. The next year Betty Marshall, whose husband had met Elinore on board the *Oronsay* in 1956, visited her in New York.

'She did not dwell on her amazing past. She just said, "I was seasick all the time,"' remembered Betty. 'By this time Ben had had a stroke and had wondered if she might like to come over and perhaps resume their life, but she said she had answered, "I have a wonderful job and two lovers and wouldn't be interested."'

It was the very same thing Elinore had told Richard Battey.

As always, Elinore preferred serious conversation to what she perceived as the idle chatter of women. 'Elinore would show up at Christmas and wanted to be entertained,' said Carol. 'She wouldn't run into the kitchen and help with dinner. She wanted to have a drink with my dad.'

Elinore never remarried, but like Ben she ached for the impossible, and for years she threw herself into an excruciating affair with a married man that tore at her heart. She wrote desperate letters and poetry to him, and once went to France with him on a secret journey that she recorded on the pages of a small notebook, her giddiness mixed with the slow realisation it could never be more than an ephemeral moment.

'We saw her once when she came to DC,' said Ralph DeAnna, whose father had witnessed Elinore's wedding to Ben in 1948. 'She had a little yappy dog and looked like a rich old lady to me.'

The years of smoking finally caught up with her. With her health declining, she gave up her West Village apartment in 1995 and moved permanently to her weekend home in Bridgehampton, where she watched the sun set over the potato fields around her house every evening with Alex, her beloved white Highland terrier.

She died of emphysema on 22 January 1996. She was 78 years old.

'It felt like a nice death,' said Carol. 'She'd had a really hard life.'

⌒

After fleeing Ben in 1964, Cynthia Scott-Henderson travelled between Madeira and England for years until her health began failing in earnest. She wound up in London for good after her mother's death in the late 1970s, when there was no longer a financial safety net, no one to pay for a housekeeper, no one to cover the cost of travel.

She suffered from dilated cardiomyopathy; her heart had become enlarged and could no longer pump blood efficiently. She was short of breath and her legs swelled. In a photograph taken not long before her death, Cynthia looks 20 years older than her actual age – her face puffy, her features softened, her eyes defeated. She looks like a grandmother. Her body was failing and toxins were building up in her liver. By the time she was admitted to the Royal Brompton Hospital her eyes were turning yellow. When she could no longer get out of her hospital bed she developed bedsores. In her less-lucid moments she vented her anger at anyone in range, even her daughter, Deirdre, muttering, 'Go play in the traffic on the M1!'

Towards the end she clutched at straws, converting to Catholicism and commissioning a statue of Fatima that she couldn't afford. Alcohol was killing her, but she didn't want to hear that from the doctors. Instead, she ordered a crate of champagne delivered to the hospital to celebrate her own birthday on 9 July. It was stolen before she could open a bottle.

Cynthia was only 44 years old when she died at the hospital on 6 August 1986.

In 2006, I learned Deirdre was living in Perth, and I got her email address from Guildford Grammar School. I wrote to her, telling her about my interest in her father and about my family connection, about how my own father had helped Ben work on the jeep in a neighbour's driveway in 1947, about how my grandfather had helped Ben learn how to work a two-way radio, about how Ben had once called my grandmother a peach. I told her I might want to write something about Ben.

Deirdre responded immediately, but she was wary. Over the years she'd had a lot of people interested in her father's story, but nothing ever really seemed to come of it. The biggest excitement came in 1999 when Heath Ledger and his father, Kim, who managed him, floated the idea of a movie about Ben. Both Ledgers had grown up in Perth and gone to Guildford Grammar, and they were familiar with the story of *Half-Safe*. Heath's production company commissioned a treatment – a synopsis of a potential script used to pitch a film concept – but it had turned Ben's story into a slapstick comedy, the hope being to create a vehicle for someone like Jim Carrey, whose name was mentioned as a potential star. There's a scene in the treatment where Ben christens the jeep with a bottle of champagne before launching it on Weems Creek, and the bottle smashes a hole in the hull. Ben patches it with a wad of chewing gum and hands more sticks of gum to the gathered crowd, urging them to chew quickly. Elinore was transformed into a singer in a bar. Those missteps, among others, likely stalled development for a few years, and then Heath became famous and was pulled in other directions.

'When my son was around it was his idea to maybe follow this through one day,' Kim Ledger told me when I asked about Heath's interest in the story. 'Unfortunately, for obvious reasons that never occurred.'

Deirdre didn't want to get her hopes up again, but we corresponded sporadically for the next nine years. And then in 2015 I flew to Perth, and Deirdre agreed to meet me.

In August we sit outside at a corner coffee shop in Cottesloe in the sunshine of a warm late-August morning, surrounded by slim blonde women in yoga gear drinking tall macchiatos, a row of Range Rovers parked along the street. Deirdre stands apart from them with her heavy red lipstick ('it's my trademark') and short, spiked dark hair.

The hardest thing, she tells me, is how close she and Ben came to a reunion.

'He would have loved nothing more than for me to just turn up,' she says. 'There was no closure, even though he tried and tried and tried.'

But Deirdre needed some sense of finality. While Ben was alive no one would talk about him, least of all her mother, and she ached to know more about the shadowy adventurer who was her father. In the years immediately after his death she corresponded with friends and neighbours who'd known him in Australia. One of them told Deirdre that almost all of his manuscripts, photos and films had been donated to Guildford Grammar School and were safely stored in its archives.

Except, she added cryptically, for some 'personal letters'.

It turned out that shortly after Ben died, an old friend had slipped into his flat, sorted through his letters and boxed up the ones that were too personal to share with the public.

Deirdre knew she had to go to Australia, had to learn more about this extraordinary man, this adventurer she knew only through the second-hand stories and a book written long before she was born. She began planning a trip. It was postponed by her mother's death in 1986, but then there was nothing holding her back. She arrived in Perth on 1 March 1987.

The first thing she did was visit Ben's friend, a woman who had known Ben since they were children. 'She said, "I need to share something with you, but I'm not sure I'm doing the right thing. Come with me." And she walked me down to her shed.'

Inside was a large, grey box with a rope handle. Deirdre took it home, opened it and spent days poring through the letters, legal documents and logs inside, and suddenly she knew more about her father – his life and his relationships – than she could ever have imagined. She learned about the years of hardship in the jeep, the stormy relationships, and the devastating anguish her father had felt at losing her.

She kept putting off her return flight to London. Nearly 30 years later she's still in Western Australia, living in a Perth suburb, by chance just half a mile from the nursing home where Ben spent his final months.

During her first years in Australia, Deirdre worked with David Malcolm, a Guildford Grammar old boy who'd become Chief Justice of Western Australia, to polish the manuscript of *The Other Half of Half-Safe* and prepare it for publication by the Guildford Grammar School Foundation in February 1989.

It was another kind of closure. Sales were disappointing; the school sought a larger publisher but couldn't find one.

'Ben Carlin wrote engagingly enough in a breezy Australian action man vein,' an editor at one publishing house said in declining the manuscript. 'The result is workmanlike, but not something that is going to turn into a travel classic.'

The school sent a copy to Elinore in New York.

'I wonder if you could/would satisfy my curiosity as to how this came about,' Elinore replied. 'I was never consulted.'

My rented cottage in Cottesloe is tucked behind one of the few modest houses in the neighbourhood that hasn't yet been razed and replaced with a modern glass-and-concrete box. It's within walking distance of Ben's former flat on Overton Gardens, and I'm sure that building will be gone in a few years too.

Deirdre arrives with a small vase of flowers, the grey box and a brown leather briefcase in the back of her ute. I've seen the box before, strapped to the roof of *Half-Safe* in photos taken in the 1950s, a box Ben built himself of holoplast.

We sit on the floor and open the box to the sweet acid smell of decades-old letters and clippings, and the chemical scent of hundreds of negatives, some stored in glassine envelopes and others floating free. A navigational map of the North Pacific is pressed flat at the bottom, Ben's route marked in pencil, a series of Xs marking the slow arc across the ocean in tiny increments, the map perhaps folded for the last time just before Ben touched ground in Alaska in 1957.

I leaf through the letters, scanning the brittle pages. Shocking details of Ben's life and relationships jump out – bitterness, anger, violence and loss. I feel self-conscious about this glimpse into Ben's past in front of Deirdre, even though she's read it all years before.

The briefcase contains Ben's passports, his army log, a small silver medal from Guildford Grammar School awarded for first place in a 100-yard swim. And an envelope containing a small strip of photos. Deirdre pulls them out and her eyes tear up. They're the photos taken at Selfridges in London in 1969, black-and-white shots of a smiling girl, the last time she and her father saw each other.

The letters told a darker story than Deirdre had expected when she came to Australia, but they began a resolution for her. If Ben's life ended on a dark note, his death served as the catalyst that brought Deirdre to Australia and shaped *her* life.

'Not everyone is at peace,' Deirdre says, thinking of the turbulent times and lives that surrounded her father. 'I'm very grateful for what I've had in my life.'

A few days later, Deirdre and I meet the ever helpful and cheerful Guildford Grammar archivist Rosemary Waller in the cottage that houses the school's Jim Norwood Archive Centre, where I've spent days with thousands of meticulously filed and preserved records that Ben bequeathed to the school. Rosemary takes us to lunch in the school cafeteria, surrounded by a sea of boisterous and confident boys, and then leads us down a campus pathway to where *Half-Safe* is displayed in a small enclosure with glass walls and a red-tile roof. It looks sort of like a small pagoda. The Guild-ford Grammar School Foundation, a charitable trust that raises funds for the school, bought George Calimer's share of the jeep in 1983 as a way to honour Ben and his contribution to the school; his estate had ultimately totalled more than $150,000 thanks to a series of shrewd stock investments. *Half-Safe* was shipped to Fremantle the following year, making her final ocean crossing packed in a steel container on the deck of the M/V *Nagara*.

A plaque reads:

THE HALF SAFE
A 1942 FORD AMPHIBIOUS MILITARY JEEP
CONVERTED BY
BEN CARLIN
FOR HIS EPIC JOURNEY AROUND THE WORLD
1950–1957

More accurately, the journey ended in 1958; Ben would have raged at the error.

Rosemary swings open a pair of glass doors. Inside, *Half-Safe* looks the same as she did in colour photos from the late 50s, from her shocking yellow paint to the patch Paul Shaw welded on her port bow after an encounter with a breakwater in November 1947. There's a sadness about her situation, as if she's become a museum piece, an old lion locked in a cramped pen. Her axles rest on squat brick columns that keep her cracked tyres a few inches off the ground. All sense of motion is gone.

Deirdre, Rosemary and I pose with *Half-Safe* for a local newspaper. Then Rosemary asks Deirdre and me if we'd like to climb inside.

We grab the spare tyre strapped to the back of the jeep and haul ourselves onto the stern, swing open the rear hatch and hunch down to clamber in, stepping over the platform of the bunk and onto the bare metal of the front seats. The sweet perfume of oil lingers. There's a layer of dust and dead insects; nothing much has changed since Ben drove into Montreal in 1958. On a shelf above the radio a cardboard box holds spare radio tubes, and a few days later I'm astonished to notice the same box in the same place in photos taken decades earlier. Otherwise *Half-Safe* is empty. Even the seat cushions are gone.

It's Deirdre's first time inside the amphibious jeep that shaped her father's life. We sit next to each other in the front seats, Deirdre at the wheel, and I think about how 68 years earlier and half a world away, long before we were born, our fathers once occupied this same tight space, neither of them knowing where their lives would take them in the years to come, and how their paths would cross for the next two decades.

And what an influence Ben would play in my dad's life.

In 2012, Eric Powell interviewed my dad for *Discover* magazine about his life and career as an underwater archaeologist. 'Have you always been drawn to ships and the sea?' he asked.

My dad thought back to his childhood on the Chesapeake Bay just after the end of World War II. 'I grew up in Annapolis, Maryland, where my father taught English at the Naval Academy,' he said. 'My brother and I made a diving helmet out of a tin square that we cut out and put glass in as a faceplate. We would have died if we had ever tried it.'

I imagine them at the edge of Weems Creek, tempted to wade in with the makeshift helmet, the future archaeologist and his brother standing on the same muddy bank where *Half-Safe* first entered the water a few years later.

There was more.

'I was also inspired by a retired Australian army officer named Ben Carlin,' he said, 'who made an amphibious jeep that went all around the world. He put it together two doors down from us. I used to help him after I came home from school – you know, tightening nuts. He thought he'd make his fortune from it.'

Fortune proved even more elusive than lasting fame. Yet Ben persisted, and he endured, and he succeeded. He showed those who were still watching – from Norman Lindsay to a boy who would achieve success far beyond his childhood dreams – what can be accomplished when you refuse to listen to those who say impossible, when you push ever onward and eastward, out of the shadows, through the 'awful endlessness', enduring years of loss and anger and pain and suffering, beckoned by a call only you hear, driven by something only you understand.

Even if you understand it only incompletely.

Next to me Deirdre grips the wheel worn smooth by her father's hands and stares out the window, lost in her own thoughts, a distant expression on her face. For a moment the jeep is free. It sails effortlessly into the past, across oceans and deserts, over mountains and through jungle, bringing her home, bringing her closer to her father, gliding silently through time and space towards the true end of Ben Carlin's long journey around the world.

Acknowledgements

This book would not have been possible without Deirdre Carlin. I am so very grateful for her support, her gracious hospitality during my time in Perth, and her readiness to share the full scope of her parents' lives with me. I am forever indebted.

Alison Carlin, Lynne Carlin, Eric Carlin, Michael Carlin and Kelvin Minchin provided great insight into Ben's life before and after his years in *Half-Safe*.

Carol Arone and Mark Lutz welcomed me into their home and shared memories and boxes of Elinore's letters and journals, which were essential to the complete telling of this story.

Luceille Hanley explained why Barry Hanley joined Ben, and how the journey changed him.

Boyé Lafayette De Mente provided a first-hand copilot's perspective of the journey.

Betty Halvorsen shed invaluable light on Ben's years in China and his relationship with Gertrude.

Rosemary Waller runs the first-rate archive at Guildford Grammar School and was a gracious and accommodating host during my days at the school; I can imagine no better guardian for Ben's written legacy.

David Welch put me in the driver's seat of a Ford GPA, and David Doyle shared its history.

I'm grateful to my publisher Alison Urquhart at Penguin Random House Australia for believing in the story, and to my editor Brandon VanOver for making it better. Any remaining rough edges are mine alone. And thank you to Jesse Fink for making the essential introduction.

My brother Alan provided boundless enthusiasm and smart editorial suggestions, as did my parents, George and Ann, who have been life-long advocates of a writing life. I'm especially grateful to my father for his memories of Ben and Elinore.

Thank you to my sons Henry and Charles for their infinite patience while I spent nights and weekends working in the attic, and for the amphibious jeep drawings.

And most of all, thank you to my wife Jennifer for two years of patience, support and encouragement, and for being my most trusted reader.

I am deeply indebted to many others, including Brendan Abbott, Clare Allcard, Janice Arone, Diana Athill, José Henrique Azevedo, Beverly Barry, Evelyn Blatnik, Charles Booth, Keith Brealey, Ursula Brimble, Colleen Calimer, Marc Carlson, Tony Clark, Richard Coe, Valerie Collis, Sharon Cyrus, Anna Darrah, Ralph DeAnna, Michael Fink, Nancy Fink, John Funk, Dan Greenberg, Caroline Hagen Hall, Emma Hannah, Debbie Hansen, Leonie Hayes, Chad Hunt, Joel Jacobs, Linda Johnson, Richard Kaplan, Kim Ledger, Bill

Acknowledgements

Longyard, Diane Maxwell, Belle Moore, David Parks, Drew Patrick, Nigel Perrin, Michel Racine, Dick Reeve, Swaroop Singha Roy, Charles Samek, Helen Schreider, Moya Sharp, Ron Shaw, Mike Shellim, Tim Slessor, Melbourne Smith, Jérôme Stevens, Stephen Stuart, Aija Thomas, Martyn Tovey, Julian Treyer-Evans, Auke Visser, Will Wain, Colin Wardle, Barbara Way, Joan Williams, Neil Williamson, Tim Wright and Cathy Zumbrun. Thank you.

Gordon Bass lives outside New York City with his wife and two sons.